PRAISE FOR THE SERIES

"This book did everything right for me when it comes to what I'm looking for in a fantasy novel. More people need to read this book. Seriously." -SADIR S. SAMIR, AUTHOR OF *THE CREW*

"Excellently written...really ambitious in its craft." -JAMREADS.COM

"Different from typical fantasy novels in all the good ways." -ESCAPIST BOOK CO.

"Emotional and heartbreaking." -JAMES HARWOOD-JONES, GOODREADS REVIEW

"Who could ask for anything more?" -BELINDA RICHEE, GOODREADS REVIEW

"A complete, engrossing story...which packs real emotion and leaves you wanting to find out more." -NICK PROCTOR, GOODREADS REVIEW

"An amazing debut and I can't wait for the follow-up." -AMAZON REVIEW

THE CHILDREN OF THE BLACK MOON

Book Two of The Spellbinders and the Gunslingers

Joseph John Lee

Eclipseborn Publishing

For Annie

THE STORY SO FAR

<u>The Memories That Have Come to Pass</u>

In the year 1534 Anno Salvatoris, an Eclipse struck fear in the hearts of the Stone Tribe. During this Eclipse, an event carrying with it an ill omen, a baby girl was born to the Stone Chief Fannalhen and his wife Dennalhir. The girl was given the name Sennalhat, which in the Stone tongue meant "Child of Light."

Sennalhat, bearing the nickname "Sen," spent much of her childhood carousing with her close friends, Narva and Fann, as well as her older sister, Tez, and younger brother, Brin, unaware of the circumstances resultant from her birth. One day, however, during an adventure through the mountain ranges to the north of the Stone Tribe village, Sen inadvertently triggered a rockslide that horribly broke Fann's arm. Fann's mother, Koelhe, denounces Sen as a "Curseborn" and forbade her son from ever associating with Sen. Perplexed, Sen was given no clarification as to the meaning behind the label from her parents, and as the years go on, her friendship with Fann deteriorated into a rivalry of extreme animosity, often manifesting in Fann berating and bullying Brin. One such occasion led to Sen violently breaking Fann's nose.

Upon reaching eighteen years of age, Sen ventured into the mountain ranges of the Heart of the Land to undergo her Trial, a coming-of-age ceremony whereupon children of the Tribes passed into adulthood and were granted Boons associated with the Animal Deity under whose Sign they were born—either the Bear, the Wolf, or the Owl. Sen, however, still unaware of her being born during an Eclipse, was subjected to a strange non-Trial in which she was belittled by two entities acting as envoys of the Moon, revealing to her the nature of her birth and her status as an Eclipseborn, a being looked upon with disdain in Tribal society for the supposed calamity they were meant to bring. The Eclipseborn were meant to be shunned from society, banished from their Tribes, but due to her parents' intervention, Sen was permitted to remain within her village and Tribe, despite the implications that would inevitably arrive.

The two entities offered Sen a choice between life and death, elaborating no further on the offer. Sen chose neither and instead opted to reflect on the good fortune with which she was blessed to have been permitted to remain among her people. However, at seeing the horror upon the faces of those conducting her Trial, Sen realized that she would never be accepted among her people and admonished her parents for keeping her true nature secret to her. She ventured off on her own until finding herself at a tavern and taking up playing a card game with a stranger, a game based entirely on chance that Sen suddenly won with ease, a consequence of the new power of Luck that was just awakened within her.

The Events Now to Come

In the year 1556 Anno Salvatoris, Brin, accompanied by his family, underwent his Trial. Brin completed his Trial, bestowing upon him the Boon of Memory associated with the Owl, and turned to face his family, but realized Sen had disappeared. Sen was found drinking at a tavern by Fannalhen, who angrily led her back to the Stone Tribe village.

As the family returned to the village and Brin was granted his abilities, Sen once again wandered off to a tavern, where she met with Narva and lamented that she was an outcast for the accident of her birth, admitting her own jealousy at the adulation that Brin was receiving, none of which she was ever able to receive herself.

Meanwhile, as the festivities continued, Fannalhen's celebration at his son's success was interrupted by the Sun Chief Han'e, who came to plead with Fannalhen for the Stone Tribe's assistance in reclaiming the lands of the Sun Tribe. Fifteen years prior, an army of Invaders came from across the eastern sea and claimed for themselves all lands to the south of the Forest, which displaced the Sun and Arrow Tribes while also nearly wiping out the Haunted Tribe. The Sun and Arrow Tribes since relocated and were permitted to settle in the territories belonging to the Stone Tribe. For years, though, Han'e had been attempting to employ Fannalhen and the Stone Tribe to reclaim the Sun lands from the Invaders, but Fannalhen, once again, declined, much to Han'e's frustration.

The next day, Sen was admonished by Tez not only for her frequent drinking but also for her shirking of responsibilities pertaining to Brin. Sen made an unsteady peace with her brother and vowed to him stop drinking after he confessed that he no longer recognized her for the person she became.

Later that evening, Dennalhir encountered two haggard people collapsed at the entrance to the village. Convening with Fannalhen and the rest of the Tribal council, they learn that the two, named Shara and Ran, were once members of the Haunted Tribe who were now slaves of the Invaders, held in a prison camp in the Invaders' City to the south. Fannalhen and his council—which included Koelhe; Tawa, who was Narva's father; Rantalha, a stoic hunter; and Sharrabha, a huntress and liaison to the Keeper Tribe to the north—could not find common ground on which to agree regarding what to do with these runaways and decided to table the discussion for the morning.

However, a party of Invaders led by General Aritz a Mata arrived in the village in the middle of the night, having followed the runaways this far, and first questioned Sen as to their whereabouts over a game of cards, a request that Sen immediately rebuked. Aritz returned later with a greater and more furious intent, and when Fannalhen refused to give Shara and Ran up, Aritz shot him dead and instead stole away Brin and another villager, much to Sen's shock. Feeling she was to blame for her father's death and brother's capture, Sen resolved to go to the Invaders' City to the south and bring Brin back, despite her mother's objections. She left with Narva the next day, determined to prove her worth to the Tribe.

As the Stone Tribe's council, now led by Dennalhir, discussed what to do after Fannalhen's murder. Koelhe indicated her own intentions to claim leadership, pointing to Fannalhen and Dennalhir's supposed disregard and disrespect for Tribal customs after allowing their Eclipseborn daughter to remain in the village and therefore "dooming" the Tribe. Dennalhir banished Koelhe from the council.

Sen and Narva's journey south took them through the Forest, where they encountered the zealously territorial Wood Tribe. Upon meeting with the Tribe's Chieftain, Sen learned that the Invaders passed through the Forest with a bloody and violent disregard for the lives of the Wood Tribe, slaughtering them both times they passed through the Forest. At the same time, Sen began experiencing episodic visions of herself killing her father, the face of Aritz replaced with her own face. Narva attempted to quell her guilt as Sen confessed the degree of blame she placed upon herself for her father's murder and brother's kidnapping.

Sen and Narva reached the Invaders' City and, finding suitable disguises, set out to find the slave camp that was described to Sen by Ran before she left the village. To their surprise, they found a disoriented Brin wandering the streets of the City. They chased after him, but for some reason, Brin opted to return to the slave camp. Though confused at the decision, Sen freed her brother, deciding not to free the countless other Tribespeople who remained chained in the camp despite Narva's protests, and ran for the hills alongside Brin and Narva. Unbeknownst to them, however, a trap is deployed by an Invader soldier, and before they were able to get too far, Narva was shot dead by the Invaders while Sen and Brin were immediately captured and brought back to the City.

Meanwhile, Dennalhir and Tez began to grow suspicious of a possible coup by Koelhe. Tez inadvertently happened across a secret meeting with Koelhe and many of her co-conspirators, who also included Fann, Han'e—who was promised Koelhe's assistance in reclaiming the Sun Tribe territories— and Rantalha. Tez was dragged away by Rantalha, who explained that he could not abide by her parents' dismissal of Tribal customs in allowing her Eclipseborn sister to remain as part of the Tribe. Tez rushed back home to warn her mother, but before they were able to act, they were faced with Koelhe's attack. Though fighting hard against the odds, Dennalhir's loyalists were overrun, Dennalhir was captured, Koelhe installed herself as Chief, and Tez fled alongside Tawa and Sharrabha to recruit the assistance of the Lake Tribe to the west in order to reclaim the Stone Tribe.

Back in the City, Sen and Brin were paraded around the slave camp as a warning to the others not to attempt another escape. Sen and Brin were brought to an alleyway, where they faced an execution via a firing squad of four, but while Sen's innate Luck prevented any of the shots from hitting her, Brin was not so fortunate, and immediately died. While two of the Invader soldiers approach Sen to futilely attempt to shoot her, the other two soldiers turned on their fellows and shot them dead. The soldier who sprang the trap approached Sen and recognized the latent Eclipseborn power of Luck within her. The soldier dispelled an illusion, revealing herself as not only a Tribal woman named Kamataa, but also an Eclipseborn. Disregarding Brin's dead body entirely, Kamataa offered Sen an opportunity to learn from a fellow Eclipseborn.

The Future Yet to Come

In the year 1591 Anno Salvatoris, Lord Aritz a Mata returned to Ferranda for the first time in years, promising to give a lecture at the University. At the end of his lecture, he was admonished by a student who challenged him on the founding of Ferranda, questioning what happened to the Tribes who had once populated this land. Aritz disregarded the Tribes as little more than wicked spellbinders who could kill people with a single touch and worshipped animals as gods, and that he was glad to have banished them deep into the mountains after he claimed the land for the Acrarian Kingdom.

Upon returning to his Ferranda manor, Aritz found one of his pieces of memorabilia, an ornate flintlock pistol, missing from the trophy shelf within his chambers. In his search for the missing weapon, Aritz noticed a Tribal ornament placed on his desk, weighing down a handwritten letter pledging that the "Harvest" had never been forgotten. Aritz disregarded the letter but was drawn to the ornament, a pendant carved with a rune he recognized as being a Tribal symbol meaning "Memory." Touching the ornament, Aritz was forced to relive a moment at this estate in Acraria where he slaughtered the vast majority of his estate attendants and guards before brutally murdering his wife and children. Judging by comments made by those he killed, Aritz realized that this incident happened after his departure for Ferranda and that someone was framing him.

Before he could pursue that thread further, he heard the hammer of a pistol click behind him. The dissenting student from the lecture showed herself, promising that she was there to claim revenge against Aritz for her family. Aritz began to dismiss her claim, but the student immediately changed form, taking the shape of Aritz knew long ago. Someone who he knew to be dead.

CHAPTER ONE

FALL AND RISE

THE YEAR 1556 ANNO SALVATORIS
15 YEARS AFTER THE INVASION

At some point, the rain became torrential. She couldn't say precisely when.

Rainwater pooled beneath Sen's feet, a stream of red running into the puddles of dark mud. Her heart pounding and head swirling, she lurched forward, held up only by the bonds still fastening her to the wall. Panicked breaths of air heaved from her mouth in exasperated eruptions as pained tears continued to pour down her cheeks. Her hair, long since undone from its customary braid, fell in front of her face, drenched from the sudden downpour and clinging to her face.

She could only focus on the ground beneath her. Directly in front of her still stood this woman. This Tribeswoman in disguise. Kamataa, she had called herself. She claimed she was a fellow Eclipseborn. They should have been considered kin, and yet, she was the one holding a Deatharm, disguised as an Invader.

An Invader who had shot Brin dead.

Sen couldn't bear to look to her right. It wouldn't be true if she didn't look. She had already lost so much in the past few days.

And Brin's face, frozen in shock, was too much to look upon.

Her brother was motionlessly slumped forward, just as she was, crimson rivers flowing from his lips and the entry wounds on his torso. His tribal garments, not yet discarded from his brief time as one of the Invaders' slaves, were in tatters, stained in both grime and blood as the rain continued to pound down on him.

Hopelessly, Sen wished for a sudden, shocked breath to escape Brin's lips. Some sign of life to prove that she did not, once again, fail. But she knew better than to put faith in such blind hopes. Her father... her Narva... and now, her brother. They all were gone. *And it's all because of me*, she repeated in her mind. She didn't fire the Deatharm, true. *But I may as well have. This is the curse that follows me.*

The curse that so many in the Stone Tribe insisted she carried. The foul circumstances of her birth, of being branded Eclipseborn. Her entire life was built upon that burden, and though she had sought to escape it for so long, it was only a matter of time before her time would run out. Before her *Luck* would run out.

And yet. Despite that, despite losing the three men most dear and important to her in a matter of days, there she still stood. Alive, her own execution escaped, through no will or desire of her own.

And this woman before her? This other Eclipseborn? She had saved Sen's life, shooting dead two of the Invaders who were intent on killing her. *Only after she killed Brin, though.*

But there was something in this woman's eyes, a familial warmth that, if she had been hiding amongst the Invaders for who knows how long, she had to have kept hidden. Warmth was not something the Invaders could exhibit. They only knew slaughter and death, pain and destruction. In Kamataa's eyes and along the contours of her wrinkled, weathered face, there was a sincerity mixed with intensity, a ferocity mixed with contentment.

Sen could hardly describe it. Regardless of the contents of the old woman's eyes, she knew one thing for certain. She was on the other end of a Deatharm not ten minutes ago. Gods, there was no way in hell she would offer up her trust.

The sound of Kamataa's feet shifting in the mud bristled in Sen's ears, the woman's boots squishing in the combination of dirt and blood. Gently, she placed a bony hand on her counterpart's shoulder, sending a sensation through Sen that was somehow simultaneously warm and chilling. For all her efforts to look the old woman in the eye, Sen was blinded by her own tears, the mists of her own emotion impeding her vision just as much as the torrential rain. Her pilfered clothing, at one point dried by the sun, clung tightly to her body as the fabrics soaked through.

Kamataa, for her part, appeared unbothered. She continued to stare wordlessly at Sen, accompanied only by heady breaths and far-off commotion of a citizenry apparently appalled by a sudden rainstorm. "Have you given my offer a passing thought?" the old woman whispered to her as though anything other than her dead family could possibly pass through her mind.

"Have you gotten a chance to fuck off?" Sen croaked, her voice a grizzly rasp.

Kamataa grinned, holding out her hand in some sort of conciliatory gesture. "Many times, child, yes. But it's simply a chance I've never taken up. Now, hold still." The old woman fished in her jacket pocket and pulled out a small key, glistening already from the rainfall. Her face betraying nothing, she quietly undid the locks on each of the chains holding Sen to the wall, an indescribable weight releasing from her limbs.

In her split moment of freedom, Sen saw fit to take Kamataa by the throat and slam her against the wall. If not for the anxious adrenaline sending tremors up her arms, she probably could have held the woman with a tighter grip. But as it stood, Sen had to settle for a snarling growl, ragged breaths puffing from her nose with increasing ferocity.

Still, Kamataa's expression exuded nothing. Only the same satisfaction she had maintained the entire time.

"Give me one reason," Sen slowly spoke through gritted teeth, "why I shouldn't dash your brains against this wall."

Something clicked behind her.

From the corner of her eye, Sen could see Kamataa raise her hand, palm facing outward. "*That* would be one reason," she said with a smile, pointing a gesturing finger behind Sen, at her fellow compatriot bearing the long Deatharm. Sen had forgotten about him entirely. "Hold, Hollow. She won't do me any harm."

Regardless of whether Kamataa's partner heeded the dismissal—Sen was far too seething to pay any attention—the air remained no less tense. Every instinct in Sen's mind screamed at her to grip harder, despite her hand finding not the capacity to do so. "What makes you so damn sure I won't do anything?" she grumbled, dark eyes narrowed with bright fury.

"Because, child, then you become everything they claim you to be." Kamataa shifted effortlessly in Sen's grip, straightening her back against the wall. "The horrific Curseborn of the Stone Tribe, mercilessly crushing an old woman's skull against the walls of stone? Why, it'd be only too fitting. But, no. You don't want to be seen in such a way, do you, Sennalhat?"

Ears perking, Sen focused her attention even closer. "How do you know my name? Who the hell are you?"

"I told you. My name is Kamataa." Somehow, she maintained an air of innocence in her expression. "And did you think I'd be unaware of my own kin? Of my own flock? We must keep together, after all."

"You're no kin of mine," Sen warned. Before the woman's companion could say otherwise, she reached to Kamataa's thigh and drew the small Deatharm, which lay in its holster, holding it close to the crone's chest. "No one of my blood would *ever* side with the Invaders. The things they've done to our Land, to our *people*! And you would throw it all in with them...and for what!" Her thumb found the clip at the top of the weapon, the same one she saw the leader of the Invaders pull back just before he shot her father down. "Maybe you'd like this straight to the heart, just as my father did. And then maybe...then maybe you'd understand what it's like..." She trailed off, the memory too painful to reflect upon. The thunderclap still echoing in her head.

Softly, Kamataa began to chuckle despite the weapon still held to her chest. "Dear child—"

"I am *not* your child."

"—if only you knew how many times my heart has been ripped from my body." She shook her head, somewhat losing that semblance of innocence. Replaced with...regret, perhaps? Sadness? Sen couldn't quite make it out.

"Is that my cue to feel pity for you? I never did take direction well."

"I would wager it is more your cue to drop the gun before you lose your own head."

"You said it yourself, bitch. Who could be more fortunate than me?" The words tasted of ash on her tongue. She was already disgusted at herself for acknowledging them. But how could she deny them? *I am a lady of Luck*, she thought. *For all the misfortune it's brought.*

Kamataa grinned once more. "And already, you're learning." She looked past Sen's shoulder, to the direction of her companion. "Hollow. Release the boy."

That grabbed Sen's attention. Immediately, she turned her head back toward the second person, the man called "Hollow." In her lapse of concentration, Kamataa snatched the Deatharm—or "gun," as it was called—but Sen didn't care. She didn't even feel it pressed against her. From the sound of the rustling of leather, it seemed like the old woman returned it to the holster, for whatever reason.

Loosing her steel grip from Kamataa's weathered skin, Sen's eyes followed Hollow as he slowly made his way to Brin's unmoving corpse. She wanted nothing more than to see him drop dead for even looking at her brother. She wanted to see pain in his eyes rather than the emptiness synonymous with his name. But such wasn't her Luck, apparently. She couldn't wish things into reality. Her life would have been far easier had that been so.

The key turned in four respective latches as Brin's body fell in a heap, plopping unimpeded in the viscous mud. As though on instinct, Sen jumped after him, pushing Hollow out of the way, uncaring for the active weapon he still had in his hands. She rolled Brin onto his back, holding his head in her hands, brushing aside what mud and muck she could from his face. The tears came again, heavy and overbearing. *It should have been me*, she thought, her cloudy vision locked with her brother. *It never should have been you, Brin. You were the best of all of us. You brought out the best in me...which I guess was never much.*

There were a million and one things she wanted to say to him in these final moments, but not a one came to her lips. How proud she was of him, how much she would miss him, how unfair this world was to him. She was grateful enough that something, at last, had the prescience to pass from brain to mouth. "Keep Father and Narva company. I'll see you all soon." She wanted to melt into the mud as the rain continued to pound down. If ever there was a time to dissolve into nothing, now would be it. She knew she was never going to see her family again, her people. She staked everything on this one mission, and she lost. It was either to fall to nothing now and be a fallen remnant to the throes of time or return home a failure and be banished off to who-knows-where, only to suffer the same fate. At least now, she could get it over with.

"So, what are you waiting for?" she called out, still holding tightly to Brin. "Just get on with it." Faintly, she could hear the rustling in the mud behind her.

"I don't think you quite understand why you still breathe, Sennalhat." Kamataa's voice. It was already grating on her, like gravel churning through a braying goat. The woman approached and grabbed Sen by the arm. "Now, come, we must—"

"*Let go of me*," Sen nearly screamed, swatting the wrinkled hand away from her. There must have been some claw to the swipe—a faint line of red trailed down the back of Kamataa's hand. She felt no remorse for that. Call her an animal for blooding an elderly woman, but she was not moving from this spot. "I'm not going anywhere with you."

"Sennalhat." Kamataa's voice was commandeering, like a parent about to offer a stern lecture to their child. "Whether you realize it or not, we have saved you this night. The least you can do is—"

"You...killed...*Brin*." Sharply, she turned to face her so-called *rescuers*, all the malice in the world roaring in her eyes. "Tell me again why I should feel godsdamned *grateful*."

"You're still breathing," spoke a deep voice. Hollow. His eyes were sunken and near-soulless, his dark hair cropped short, almost to the scalp. "You still live."

"What a mercy," Sen said, rolling her eyes. "Pardon me for not having any gratitude for that."

With grandmotherly presence, Kamataa knelt beside her, now paying heed not to extend her hand toward her. "You play a greater role than you know, Senalhat." She raised a wispy white eyebrow, bearing a sage expression. "Though you may refuse to accept that, now. Your brother's passing is... unfortunate. But, with us, you may—"

"Gods above, woman. Look around you." Sen gestured broadly, first to the two dead Invaders pooling blood in the mud, then at Brin, then at the greater

City beyond. "What even *is* this? You're standing here, Deatharms at the ready, disguised like you're mounting some rescue mission only to say nuts to the rescue. And now you're trying to hand me a pile of your own shit and tell me it's a flower arrangement I should be grateful for. Spare me the horseshit and start making sense. Who *are* you? And don't just say 'Kamataa' because that means shit-all to me. You're Tribe, both of you. But what Tribe? Neither of you has any distinctive markings or adornments or—"

"I would think that'd mean precious little to you, Sennalhat," Kamataa interrupted. "You have gone your whole life without the markings of the Stone Tribe."

"Answer the damn question." Sen's patience was running thinner and thinner. "What Tribe are you?"

With a soft smile, Kamataa shook her head. "It doesn't matter. I do not belong to a Tribe. Not anymore. Those days have long since passed. No, I am of a collective far greater, of far more consequence than our petty squabbles and Tribal customs."

"Straight answer, you bag of bones."

"Heh." She was silent for an uncomfortable while, never breaking eye contact with Sen. Seemingly unperturbed by the storm swelling atop her, she exuded confidence and control. It was unsettling. "You still don't understand. You have your own part to play in this, as well."

"If only someone would be kind enough to tell me that part."

"If only someone would listen." Kamataa was past the point of respecting boundaries and reached out to grab Sen by the arm. With a flinch, Sen tried to pull back, but the old crone was deceptively strong. A faint and familiar glimmer shone beneath Kamataa's shirt, visible only for the encroaching darkness amidst the storm. "Trust me when I say I've ignored every opportunity to kill you. I would wager that there have been many who were stopped for reasons superseding their personal desires."

Sen frowned. In part because she was right. In part because she may have lost her chance at driving a stake through Koelhe's heart.

"Though our walks of life were different," Kamataa continued, "I, too, know that pain. Of course, I did not have the fortune of being born to the

Chief of my Tribe. But all of us present are *survivors*. Despite the world's intentions, we are still here *breathing*."

"You must realize how tone-deaf you must be to say that after you shot my brother dead."

"A mercy, truly." Kamataa's tone was blunt and to the point.

"Excuse me?" Sen's eyes grew wide, disbelieving. If not for the old woman's impossible strength, she'd have already pounced at her. But it was clear that Kamataa had reason for it beyond physical submission.

"You saw the state of the slaves in the camp, did you not?" A snarl, both disgusting and remorseful, creased the woman's lips. "Mindless, worn, and altogether *gone*, the lot of them. It would not have been long before he was broken just as they were."

That did little to quell Sen's anger. She gestured her free arm toward Brin's corpse, struggling to keep it steady from the tremors. "My brother seems altogether gone *now*."

"To be Eclipseborn is to know loss," Kamataa murmured plainly. "But to know loss is to know when best to let go. I have lived with our burden long enough to know this."

This time, Sen did break away, snatching her arm back from Kamataa's grip, the force nearly knocking her onto her backside and into the pool of Brin's muddied blood. "And you expect me to *accept* that? To just accept that killing Brin was a godsdamned *kindness*?!"

Unmoved, Kamataa gestured her arms out to her side in a near-shrug and nodded. "Should you live to my age, you'll come to understand what is a kindness and what is a punishment. You thought yourself fortunate for the status of your birth, but it blinded you to the harsh realities of what we as kin face."

"We are not—"

"We are. Trust me. We are few in number, but it means we look out for our own. Accept it or not, but that extends to you."

Sen had heard enough. In her life, she had faced the ire of her own Tribe, willfully driving her to a life borne only of misery. She had drawn disappointment from her family simply because she could no longer cope with the life forced on her by those who wished her dead. She was an outcast, a loner, and to many, a plague and disease upon her people.

And yet, *this* was the worst of it all. To be dangled acceptance—though it was guised behind a thin veil of deceit. "I choose not to accept it," she spoke assuredly, slowly rising to her feet. "I existed on my own before. I don't need anyone now. And *certainly* not you. I'm taking my brother and going home."

Kamataa was clearly unaffected by Sen's decision. In fact, it seemed she expected it. She rose to her own feet in kind, surprisingly nimbly for her age. Folding her hands at her waist, she looked at Sen with suddenly kind eyes. The speed at which she could change from stern to controlling to accepting was frankly unsettling. "Of course. That is your decision to make."

Sen didn't need to hear anything further. She knelt in the mud, shuffling her arms deep into the earth to get a hold of Brin.

Kamataa quickly cleared her throat. "But then again..." Her tone of voice changed sharply once more.

Distantly, the thunder roared and the wind howled. A chill rushed up Sen's spine.

"You traveled all this way to rescue your dear brother, and for what? Acceptance? Redemption? And now...two bodies are bloodied in your wake."

The rain grew ice-cold. Sen's skin prickled, her head a fog. She looked down at Brin's face, frozen in lifelessness, and all she could hear was the desperate pleas of a frightened and helpless boy facing down the shadow which threatened to engulf him. The boy's voice was joined by a man, loud and boisterous, a warrior bellowing his final challenge.

That sound, that nightmare—it had haunted her since the night both her father and brother were taken from her. She had first heard it—*felt* it—when she laid her father to rest, shocking her so profoundly that she was unable to recite any parting words to him. When she traveled through the treacherous darkness of the Forest, she *saw* it—a shadow bearing her face striking down a man and boy alike before very nearly consuming her.

It was Narva who saved her that time. But as two voices cried for peace and mercy, a third suddenly joined their ranks. So familiar and gentle, yet collective and combative. And clear as day, Sen could feel it caress her ear, as fleeting as a passing breeze, encompassing her in a passionate embrace. The voice became hot breath and whispered, *"Did you not love me?"*

Bang. A gasp of pain, and a collapse. The shadow crept ever forward.

Sen shuddered, hardly aware that she had long since removed her arms from beneath Brin and curled into a trembling ball, burying herself deeper into the mud and muck.

And standing high above her, proud and commanding, remained Kamataa. "They would only blame you if you returned empty-handed. If you returned simply on your own." All kindness had departed the woman's voice yet again. "There is a lesson in this, remember. Your brother's death should have taught you this. To know loss is to know when best to let go. Can you truly face your family, your *Tribe*, knowing that you failed?" She quieted, pacing two steps back and forward, gesturing her hands to dictate her own points to herself. "Hmm, but no. It is not *your* failure. It is the failure that your Tribe would impart on you. It was foolish to think that you would succeed, Sennalhat. Surely, you must know that. But your Tribe will be looking for any reason to expel you—not just from your Tribe, but from this earth—and returning with naught by the blood of two of the Tribe's sons will spell only pain for you. More pain that you feel now.

"It needn't be as that, however. I have said already, I no longer concern myself with the petty squabbles of our Land's Tribes. I exist as part of something greater. As do you, and as does Hollow over there. We have all lost, but we have lived far removed from the concerns of our previous lives that we have learned to live and cope with that loss. It has hardened us, made us stronger. And that would be your first lesson amongst us. To learn to let go."

Why would I let go? Sen thought. *Why* should *I let go?* She clenched her eyes shut, her fingers digging into the mud beneath her.

"I don't expect you to say yes immediately." Warmth returned to Kamataa's presence, and she knelt, her knee resting near Sen's face, her hand rummaging through the Stone woman's drenched hair. "But at least allow us to get you out of the rain."

Still shaking, Sen glanced her eyes up, not quite looking Kamataa in the face. The heavy rain peppered her eyes; she hardly registered the pain anymore. "W...w-where?" she asked feebly.

"Our barracks. Where *our* Tribe lives. Where *your* Tribe lives."

Indoors. That sounded nice. Where else could she go? She was days away from home, if she even managed to make it through the Forest alive this time. The Wood Tribe's Chieftain hardly had warm parting words for her the last they met; that was when she *wasn't* alone. Being inside, out of the rain—that was all she wanted to focus on right now. The screaming in her head had begun to quell. But there was one matter further which plagued her. "B-b...but Brin," she muttered. "What...what about...?"

A bony thumb caressed her shoulder, a strange comfort somehow found with it. She could feel Kamataa's kind smile above her. "We will ensure that your brother receives the burial deserving of him. Now, come. To your feet. We've spent too much time here already. We must return before suspicions arise."

Lifting her head off the dirt, Sen wiped residue from her face and chanced a final look at her brother. "Can I...say goodbye?"

Briskly, Kamataa shook her head. "There's no time. I'm sorry."

Sen dug her fingers into the mud, head lowered, and tearfully nodded to her departed brother. From the corner of her eye, she could see Kamataa shuffle forward and reach out toward the wall, where something glinted against the rain. She picked it up and held it out, and the weight of the world crushed Sen's shoulders once more.

Brin's pendant. The rune of Memory glistened with a different sheen than the rest of the ornament.

"Take it," Kamataa offered. "This way, he will always be with you."

Unable to hide her shock, Sen fell back, appalled at the thought. "Surely, you must know that that's taboo! I can't take another's pendant. That goes against all Tribal traditions!"

"So did you being allowed to remain in your Tribe—you are not particularly a follower of precedent, child." There was a hint of amusement in her tone. Nearly playfully, she tossed the pendant over.

After briefly fumbling with it in the air, Sen at last grasped it by the chain, letting it dangle in front of her. Despite accepting Kamataa's defiance as accurate, it still felt wrong to hold another's adornment. She held it only with the tips of her forefinger and thumb, as she would a newborn's fouled undergarments.

"No one's going to *banish* you for holding it, Sennalhat," Kamataa asserted, arms open wide. "It's your brother's memento. It's going to do very little buried in the ground. Keep it as a symbol of pride for his life." Obviously noticing Sen's lingering apprehension, she approached gently, again placing an affirming hand atop her shoulder. "You're among kin here. You're among your fellow Eclipseborn. You needn't worry."

Sen wanted to find belief in those words. But, she allowed herself to grip the pendant, her eyes wandered past Kamataa and could not break from the stains of blood adorning the alley walls.

Someone had told him of the commotion earlier in the evening. He was so engrossed in his work that he hardly registered it.

The lingering echo of multiple shots was enough to briefly break him from his trance. Strange that it took that many. There must have been many examples to be made.

Regardless, Aritz remained focused on his evening task. On his map.

He had spent much of his time since his return filling in the gaps on his map, past that range of trees that had for years acted as a natural deterrent to his people's needs. He knew the southern half of this island like the back of his hand. But the north? That was a frontier he greatly looked forward to exploring.

Already, he looked forward to returning.

A narrow pass was filled in to chart the route he had taken while retrieving the bodies he lost. Not the exact bodies, mind, but bodies, nonetheless. It was easy enough to put to paper. Those northernlands—or what little he saw of it—were mostly plain green fields. He had spent enough time learning that tongue his workers used to know word-of-mouth descriptions of the ranges beyond the trees and enough to know that his path took him roughly through the middle of that range. There were not many significant landmarks to denote. A couple trees here and there, a rolling dune or two, but nothing substantial.

Nothing until the village he visited and the mountain range beyond.

His cartographers had charted enough of the island's shape for him to know that the mountains extended northward all the way to the sea. It was a geographical marvel, the northern part of the island, truly. It naturally rose further and further above sea level, so creating seaports in that region would be impossible. Trade routes would have to be crafted through that forest at some point. Trees knocked down, roads constructed. It was all a matter of when and how.

The mountains particularly intrigued him. How deep did they go? What resources lay within them? Could it be settled? This city was beginning to grow cramped. It had been for a few years now. Here and his people's settlement to the east were the only areas with any strategic value. There had to be more to the north, to the mountains. If these heathens decided to sit themselves there, then they must have had a reason for it.

Meticulously, Aritz continued to fill in the ranges and plains when he heard a knock at his door. "Yes," he said plainly, the single syllable enough to burst the doors open on command.

Two servants walked in to hold the door, followed by a host of four soldiers, all self-assured and confident. They were a handful of the group who followed him to the north, heeding his every call. It was thanks in part to them their expedition was such a success. Aritz trusted them dearly.

Though, truthfully, he never bothered to remember any of their names.

Without a word between them, Aritz's trusted lieutenants filed in around the table, hands folded at the waist, awaiting orders and instructions.

The general waited for his attendants to close the door and listened for the welcoming patter of footsteps disappearing into the distance. He always preferred his attendants to remove themselves from earshot of his meetings. Not that he feared anything; he simply didn't deem it necessary for their ears to hear. "Gentlemen," Aritz spoke with a soft nod. "My thanks for your assistance on our northern voyage and my appreciation for arriving again on such short notice." *Of course, they know to arrive without a second thought, regardless of whether they are in the middle of a meal, middle of a shit, or middle of a woman.* "I trust the taverns have welcomed your return."

A dark-haired man with intense eyes nodded his head. "We *are* their best-paying clients," he said plainly. Aritz always liked this one. He had a glare that could shoot daggers and a hand that could wield them. And he hardly said anything.

Next to him, a wide-armed blondie with a scar along the length of his neck grinned. Placing a hand firmly on his firm-faced colleague, he said with a chuckle, "And how they love when we return from expedition. They treat us damn near like heroes."

Putting a hand to his chest, Aritz returned the grin. "You are all heroes to our Kingdom, as far as Their Majesties are concerned." *Only as far as they are concerned, I must stress.* "And I must insist that you remain heroes still."

Flanked all the way to the right, the pock-marked lieutenant stroked his chin. His complexion was pallid, his eyes sunken. He had survived some sort of wasting sickness years ago, and yet he ensured he was well enough to serve in this coterie. He actually had Aritz's respect for that. He didn't begrudge him his notions of heroism, that was for certain.

"What would you have us do, General?" asked the fourth lieutenant, who stood to the left of the pock-faced lad. He was a bruiser of a man long in need of a visible neck, a wall of muscle and probably not much else. But Aritz didn't need him for much else. Maybe laughs—a flintlock looked comically small in his enormous hand.

An air of satisfaction visible on his face, Aritz outstretched his arms over his map, gesturing broadly over the loose outline of the northern territories. They all hovered over the map, varying degrees of intrigue nestling in their brows. "This, gentlemen. I want *this*."

No-Neck scratched at his temple. "You want us to fill in the map for you, sir?"

"If you've a photographic memory of places you've not yet seen, then please, yes," Aritz said with amusement, derision grating in his tone.

No-Neck's face turned a shade of red darker.

"We're going back, then," Pock-Face said. "To fill in these blank spaces." He maintained a thoughtful look in his eyes as though he had a stroke of genius.

Aritz stood back a pace, staring intently at the blank reaches of the map. An empty swath leading to a larger settlement, but nothing besides. "Look at this map, gentlemen," he said. "Look at it and tell me what you see."

No-Neck, Pock-Face, and Blondie had blank expressions on their faces. They looked to one another, trying to surmise an adequate answer with their eyes, presumably. When one couldn't be found, Pock-Face looked back to Aritz with a frown and a shrug, shaking his head slightly as he murmured, "I apologize, sir, but we don't understand what you are asking."

"Is that right," Aritz muttered, unimpressed. He stepped back to the map, placing a firm palm on the unfilled regions. He traveled his hand through the northern territories, trying to illustrate his point more obviously. "In *here*, gentlemen. What do you see *here*?"

"Land," Blondie said quickly.

"Land," No-Neck repeated, trying to time his words to come off as having the same idea as Blondie rather than remain dumbly silent.

"Opportunity...?" Pock-Face said hesitantly, his tone offering no illusions of understanding behind the word.

If not for Pock-Face's half-handed suggestion, Aritz would have admonished them further, but the man was on the right track. "Opportunity, yes. But more than that, we are looking at—"

"Resources."

So shocked was he that Dark-Hair's speaking that Aritz actually stuttered a step. Affirmatively, he pointed at the intense-eyed soldier, gesturing positively at him. "Resources," he repeated. He tapped at the map again, shades of a grin curling his lip. "An untapped well, ripe for the harvesting."

Pock-Face started stroking his face inquisitively again. "Have we an idea of what resources lay in this region, though? I was under the impression that we were in great supplies now. It seems a risk."

"Our being here was borne of risk," Aritz reminded him. "Had we not deemed this worth the risk, Their Majesties would never have expanded the

Kingdom into what it has become already." That quieted Pock-Face, who resumed an assumption of thoughtfulness.

"I think he is right to be cautious, though," No-Neck offered, his brow scrunching. "We're only a few days removed from first venturing that far north, and we weren't exactly welcomed."

Aritz leaned further on the map, meeting No-Neck's eyes with his own. "Then we are fortunate not to seek neither welcomes nor hospitality." He stood back upright, folding his arms with a shake of the head. "Caution is never ill-advised; I grant you both that. And I would be remiss not to heed wise counsel." *Or the babbling of men whose jobs are only to shoot where I tell them to shoot.* "For well over a decade, we have been sufficient in our survival. We have performed well as a trading route stopover to and from the Far West. We offer lodging and earn a cut of the resources, and we have built a settlement worth of Their Majesties as a result. We have prospered off every inch of land we could adequately and strategically live upon in these reaches. In the name of Their Majesties and the Acrarian Kingdom, we control the seas, the ports, the comings and goings.

"But increasingly, our countrymen see the value in remaining in our settlement. With each trading ship that passes, a handful more decide to remain. And the more that people remain, the greater the need for space. We can build more and more in our city, true, but why limit ourselves to just this one space?"

He backed away from the map, hands clasped behind his back, chin jutting out as he soaked in a confident air, watching his men listening expectantly to his every word.

"If there is one thing I heeded from those first savages we met fifteen years ago," he continued, "it was to avoid that forest to the north. Had they only warned of wicked spirits or haunted passages, I'd have thought little of it. But they warned of a violent people instead. Wanting not to subject our people to blood so quickly, I listened to that advice. There was more than enough land to the south of the forest to lay claim to a new home for our people.

"Now, though, we know there is little to fear of that forest. The savages are violent and territorial, true. But, more important than that, they are *weak*. We have put them to rout twice now. We needn't fear the wrath of what sits hidden in the trees. Ours is a might far greater than theirs. And now that we know we can reach the north with hardly a scratch upon us, we can finally expand Their Majesties' reach.

"So, yes, I see opportunity in these far reaches. The opportunity for our people to expand, to grow, to settle. In that short span we spent up there, I saw bountiful resources. There is enough wood in that forest to build an entire nation's worth of homes. That village we stopped in clearly had a wealth of stone and grains upon which they've subsisted. And in that range of mountains beyond? Think of the natural ores we could harvest. The possibilities are endless. Our *opportunities* are boundless."

Aritz leaned back over the map, slapping a firm hand against the uncharted northern lands. He grinned as the act prompted a brief startle from Pock-Face.

"This is the defining moment of our history, gentlemen. *These* are the days when we will become more than merely a trading outpost, a stopover. *These* are the days when we will become a *nation*."

The four lieutenants nodded to themselves, satisfaction visible on each of their faces, hesitant though their eyes appeared.

Aritz fully expected them to file out without any further objection or affirmation. But Dark-Hair leaned forward on the map, pointing first at the forest, then at the blank regions. "That is well and good, sir, but we must take into account resistance."

That caught Aritz's attention. "Resistance?"

Dark-Hair nodded. "There were thousands dwelling in that village to the north. That is just in one filled-in space on the map. What about to the east and west? We are looking at perhaps thousands more. I have my doubts that they will simply give up willingly."

Acknowledging the point with a grin, Aritz leaned back on his heels, the pitter-patter of rain against his window relaxing him and seemingly him alone. "How many were we when traversing the forest?" he asked.

"Ten," Dark-Hair answered plainly, shrugging.

"Ten," Aritz repeated. "Against that number. And we survived with hardly a drop of our blood shed. We need not worry. It matters not their numbers.

Never have they faced the full might of our people. They will not stand a chance. Their options are simple: surrender or destruction."

Silence stilled the air. He anticipated Dark-Hair might voice a final objection, but he seemed pleased enough. "When do we begin, then?" he asked, the faintest of glimmers shining in his intense eyes.

Amused, Aritz chuckled and passed one more approving grin to his lieutenants. "The moment we have readied."

Onlookers hardly gave Sen a second look as she trudged through the rain and mud. For all they knew, one of the City guards was just helping her back home after a frightful encounter.

Hollow tended to Brin's body. Sen didn't get to see what exactly was done, but she had to trust it was better than being left to rot in a bloodied alleyway with two others.

Kamataa had resumed her disguise, restoring her younger appearance and red hair. That appearance instantly sent Sen seething once more, but she was hardly in a position to voice her anger. It was the longest day of her life—the longest handful of days, truthfully—and she just wanted to be out of the rain and to a bed.

With luck, she hoped her next sleep would be her last. But Luck stopped being on her side a while ago.

Wordlessly, Kamataa led Sen through the nighttime streets, discretely gripping her by the forearm to ensure she would not slip away. She wouldn't dream of stealing back into the night, though. Not now. Not anymore.

The rain had started to let up a bit, not that it really mattered. Sen's pilfered clothing was completely soaked through, fraying at the seams. She felt twice her weight in these waterlogged garments. And Kamataa wasn't in any rush to get back inside.

She was still trying to get a read on the old woman. Friend, foe, or something in between? She had killed Brin but spared Sen out of a wish for kinship or some such nonsense. It was too exhaustive a day to ponder on these things. She just wanted not to be staring death in the face any longer.

Though judging from Kamataa's age, it seemed like she was older than death itself.

Time passed, and Sen's vision and mind were roused in equally blurred fogs as Kamataa jerked her this way and that. Her ears flared with what sounded like the last calls at the nearby taverns, accompanied by resultant choruses of protest for another round or two. She thought back to her promise to Brin, her promise to herself, to quit her excessive drinking, to be a better sister and a better person.

What good was that promise now? Who did she need to prove herself to anymore? She must have been pondering that with enough pull to force her toward a tavern—a sharp jerk at the arm from Kamataa roused her back to her senses. What remained of them anyway.

Only one thing remained clear inside that fog. Sen knew that if any of her people were to see her now, cavorting with Invaders—disguised or otherwise—with two dead kin in her wake... Well, it wasn't worth thinking about. They only wanted to see her either as a foe or deep beneath the earth, regardless.

"Welcome home," Kamataa said eventually.

Sen blinked back to reality, the fog lifting, and she found four Invader soldiers staring back at her. She drew in a sharp breath, aware of Kamataa's tightening grip on her arm. Despite her every inclination to pull away, she froze, a chill running the length of her body, her heartbeat pulsing loudly in her ears. Only a slight tensing of her shoulders betrayed any indication of her nerves, but it was clearly enough for Kamataa to take notice.

"Calm, Sennalhat," she said softly. "I said that we were among kin."

They took a handful of steps forward and the doors closed behind them. Faintly, Sen recalled Kamataa calling this place a "barracks," which she gathered was where the City guards stayed. Eight beds lined the room, four to a side, each with a chest resting at the foot of the bed. All but one looked like they had been slept in.

To Sen, each of the four present looked equally ready to snap her neck at a moment's notice. All bore the typical appearances of any Invader she had met in the last few days—lighter complexion than she, a wide palette of hair colors ranging from auburn-brown to light-yellow, all sporting more or less the same scowling and shit-eating facial expressions.

But then, one by one, a glimmer shone from beneath their respective shirts, all reading the same rune: Illusion. Sen grimaced just as she had when Kamataa and Hollow dispelled their Illusions—it just felt dirty and wrong to see that ability used to blend with Invaders of all people.

Those feelings of disgust only marginally diminished when each fake-Invader restored their natural appearance as people of Tribe. Only marginally.

"Sennalhat," called Kamataa from behind, who had restored her natural appearance when she wasn't looking. "You may relax yourself. Untense your shoulders."

Sen did as requested, unaware of how tense her shoulders had been. A hushed silence fell over them, and she was unsure whether she should even say anything to these people, whether she should just up and walk away, or whether she should ignore them all and fall into that unoccupied bed.

"Introductions are in order," Kamataa continued, paying no heed to Sen's desires otherwise. As you can see plainly, Sennalhat, we are not so unlike one another. Each of us bears a common lineage. We all are borne of this land. We were just born under a sign none wish to acknowledge. We hold no allegiances but to each other, and we have no—"

"Yeah, yeah," Sen interrupted, waving her hand at the old crone with disinterest. "Just...just get on with it. Who the hell is who?" She was dimly aware of Kamataa's raised eyebrow—whether there was actual offense given, she didn't know nor care—but paid some degree of attention as the old woman stepped forward and pointed to each present.

First, all the way to the left was a young woman Sen's age, the shaved sides of her head and tuft of hair tied tightly back signaling that she was originally of the Lake Tribe.

"This is Zara," Kamataa said, and Zara nodded wordlessly, her eyes intense and wild. Naturally, Sen expected that from a Lake Tribeswoman—they weren't exactly a friendly people.

Continuing, Kamataa pointed to Zara's immediate left, another woman Sen's age, sporting the rows of tied locks emblematic of the Sun Tribe. "She is Sha'a, quite possibly one of the fiercest fighters I have encountered, kin or not."

"Good evening," Sha'a said softly, betraying none of that supposed killer instinct that Kamataa was apparently fond of.

Next to Sha'a stood another young woman wearing twin shoulder-length braids bound in leather. Sen had never actually *seen* a person of the Arrow Tribe before—she had only heard them. "This is Vanta," Kamataa continued. "A wonderful shot from any distance, with any weapon." Not surprising, given the bow was a way of life for the Arrow Tribe. Figures that the first in the Tribe in generations not to be born under the Sign of the Wolf was Eclipseborn instead.

"And, lastly," Kamataa started, and Sen was taken aback by the age of the fourth woman. She had to have been the same age as Kamataa—however old that was—but more than that, Sen's eye was caught by their common braid, the long interlocking strands indicative of the Stone Tribe. "This is Ziiahlan, my oldest and closest friend. Our people are not often afforded the luxury of friendship or close relations, but I am fortunate to have her."

Ziiahlan nodded to Sen, immediately noticing their shared background. "Please, call me Ziia," she said.

I won't call you anything if I can help it, Sen thought.

"Where's Hollow?" Zara sharply asked, not intent on exchanging further pleasantries, which was fine with Sen.

"He had something to take care of," Kamataa answered, stealing a brief glance at Sen from the corner of her eye, much to Sen's disgust. "But he should be back with us shortly." She paused briefly, then, without missing a second beat, asked, "Where's Cin?"

Vanta chuckled. "He had something to take care of but should be back with us shortly."

I guess this is what passes for humor, Sen wondered disdainfully.

A door opened behind her, her heart skipping a beat, but no one was alarmed. "And speak of the devil," Ziia said with a smirk.

By the time Sen turned to face the new arrival, they had already dispelled their Illusion. He was a sturdy-looking young man with sharp eyes and a sharper nose, skin darker than Sen was accustomed to. Her mind flashed back to the two visitors who changed her life forever. Involuntarily, she snarled at him, to which he either paid no mind or didn't care.

"Cin," Kamataa said. "This is Sennalhat."

Cin tossed her a passing glance, said, "Hi," and kept walking to his bed.

Finally, someone with as much enthusiasm for this as myself.

"Any news?" Sha'a asked Cin, almost eagerly.

With a shrug, Cin had a look of disinterest on his face. "Soon enough, I suppose. Only a matter of time."

"Excellent. I look forward to it."

"Where's Hollow?" Cin asked, echoing the previous question.

"He'll be back soon," Vanta and Ziia said almost simultaneously. They smirked at each other.

Sen shook her head in equal parts confusion and disbelief.

"Sennalhat," Kamataa said with a nudge. "I am sure you must have a wealth of questions by now, yes?"

Plainly, Sen looked the old woman in the eye. "No."

"Come now, Sennalhat, I must insist—"

"I must insist you don't speak my name," Sen growled.

There was a pregnant pause, a tense silence. And then Kamataa smiled and said, "Sennalhat." She raised her hand before Sen could snarl another objection. "We all are under this roof the victims of terrible circumstances beyond our control. Such is your plight, too, whether you wish it or not. Each among us here was borne under different circumstances, in different lands, beholden to different Tribes. But each of us shares the same fate: we are all Eclipseborn, and as such, we are all Tribeless. We belong to no one but ourselves because it has only been ourselves with whom we have not been neither banished nor rejected."

Kamataa paused and took a handful of elongated steps to the center of the barracks, eyeing each member of her Tribeless Tribe with a look of satisfaction. And, in turning back to Sen, she outstretched her arms by her side and smiled. "And so, we are our own Tribe. We are the Children of the Black Moon."

There was another silence, and Sen was suddenly aware that they were expecting a response from her. She scratched absently at her head, pacing her eyes from corner to corner, meeting eyes both exuberant and disinterested. Her own eyes fell into the latter category. "That's...great for you all. But I was never banished or rejected by my Tribe. I—"

Collectively, the gathering of Eclipseborn—the *Children of the Black Moon*—chuckled, and Kamataa raised her a disapproving yet amused grin. "Dear child," she admonished mournfully, "you know that is false. Banished? Perhaps not? But *rejected*? Come now." She shook her head as though she were scolding her.

Sen had no defense for that. And she likewise realized how tone-deaf it would have been to suggest that she still technically had a home to return to. She had it bad. But these people? If what Kamataa said was true...then they had it worse.

But despite that...

"More to the point," Sen said, circumventing the previous argument. "Regardless of your birth, you were all still people of this Land. You're all people born from the Tribes. And yet, here you are, standing on the side of the Invaders, living in housing given to their soldiers. How can you sit back so calmly while the Invaders displace our people and threaten to destroy our way of life?" She was growing more animated and upset with each passing word, the wounds of the past few days still fresh and raw.

Kamataa took a few steps over to her bed and rested on the edge, her hands outstretched behind her. "You say that as though it were a bad thing."

The words froze her. Sen blinked quickly, staring at the old woman with confusion, disbelieving what she had heard. "Excuse me?"

Undeterred, Kamataa smiled and shrugged. "So, the Tribes may be displaced or even erased. What's so wrong with that?"

CHAPTER TWO

A Stone Carved Anew

The rolling fields were a flooded slog as the rain continued to pour down. Each heavy step brought with it a heavy suction of mud that threatened to pull her boots clean off.

Tez's muscles ached terribly. Her legs felt as though they were carrying heavy boulders atop them, each subsequent step a laborious effort. If not for her spear to prop her up, she surely would have collapsed hours ago.

It had been some time since they stopped running. There was never anyone pursuing them, but in the dark of the storm, they weren't taking any chances. And though they were clear of any who would aim to hunt them down, there was something greater and worse they were all of them attempting to escape from.

Failure.

It seemed unfathomable earlier that day (or, by this time of night, the previous day) that an armed insurrection would topple the structure of their Tribe. That enough people would be so dissatisfied with her family's reign—or so swayed by treasonous words—that they would take up arms against their Chief. Or interim Chief. Whatever title her mother held. *Or, used to hold, I guess is the case now*, she thought.

It was too painful to look back. The only way back home was to the west, to a long prayer of a chance to reclaim what was rightfully theirs. To pry loose her home from those traitorous hands. Koelhe, her poisonous tongue releasing even more poisonous words. Fann, malice incarnate hiding behind a hardly-veiled malicious grin.

And Rantalha. Someone she thought was an ally or, at the least, a man of practical means. Now he was the most fearsome weapon her enemy had.

And she wouldn't rest until she saw each of them rotting in the ground, all having forfeited the right to rest beneath a proper stone cairn. They pissed on tradition. They wouldn't get to nuzzle back up to it when they were finished on this plane.

Tez couldn't say for sure how many trusted allies she had remaining. At the least, she had the handful who were trudging alongside her. To her right, Tawa, family to her in all but blood. He and her father were near enough as brothers. If there was anyone in this world she could surely trust with her life, it was him. He had already saved her once this night, preventing her from rushing back into a battle long since lost. Staring at his sullen face reminded her of his son, Narva, and the journey he set out on with her sister. Her heart only sank at the thought. *Sen...please be okay. Bring Brin back to us.*

Flanked to her left was Sharrabha, the huntress who staved off Fann and Rantalha long enough for her to retreat from the battle at the village with her life. Tez was not necessarily close with Sharrabha—the huntress had spent more time in the mountains with the Keepers in recent years than with her own Tribe—but she was a woman of loyalty whose actions spoke louder this night than any words could ever hope to do.

And now, as the three of them helmed a small coterie of retreating warriors, all battered and bittered by the night's defeat, they marched solemnly west with their tails between their legs, all in the hopes they could secure the help from a Tribe too entrenched in conflict with themselves to worry about the affairs of other Tribes. And yet, it was still a better option than anything else.

Tez sighed deeply and loudly, still not hazarding a glance back, if only to avoid the gazes of the hapless warriors she felt she failed.

Tawa seemed to take notice of the sigh and moved in closer to place a comforting hand on her shoulder, just like her father used to, a time that seemed half a lifetime ago.

"I still can't believe it," Tez muttered into the mud, her head trailing down. "No matter how many times I look back on it all tonight, it still doesn't feel real."

"Exiled by our own people," Tawa spat spitefully, his voice intoned with an aggression Tez was wholly unaccustomed to hearing from him. The comforting hand on her shoulder grew more tense. "Is this what the other Tribes felt when they fled north? Unsure what to do next, unsure where to *go* next?" He paused, his brow wrinkling in stern consideration. "No...maybe not. They were not betrayed by their own kin."

"They are entirely different horrors," Sharrabha mused wistfully, "but they are painful regardless. I'd like to say we could be cut from the same cloth as them, but..."

Firmly, Tez shook her head. "Our home wasn't ripped apart by Invaders. We were driven out from our friends, our family, people we grew up with. People we allowed into our lands, and people who have lived in our lands for generations. They weren't an unknown enemy. They were *our people*." Her free fist clenched with anger and frustration, the verbal admission as wounding as a spear to the chest. "And they turned on us just the same."

"One would think," Sharrabha murmured, brow furrowed, "that if any in that mob were to understand what it was like for someone to uproot your life entirely, it would be Han'e. And yet..."

Han'e. Tez grimaced at the thought of him, too. The Chief of the Sun Tribe, the first to be forced from their lands by the Invaders' arrival, only to be further massacred by the Wood Tribe while they passed through the Forest, just looking for a new place to call home until they were graciously allotted space in the Stone Tribe's territory by her father, Fannalhen. The Sun Tribe never were content in the colder climates north of the Forest, where they were also separated from the sea upon which much of their livelihood was, and on numerous occasions, Han'e approached Fannalhen for the Stone Tribe's assistance in taking back their lands.

And each time, her father rebuffed him, citing the well-being of the Stone Tribe above all else. It was Koelhe's pledge of support to the Sun Tribe's plight that swayed their Chief to back the coup attempt against her family. The promise of once again seeing their homeland, in return for raising a hand against the very family and Tribe that offered them a place when they had nowhere else to go.

"Han'e betrayed us just the same," Tez said, no hint of sympathy in her voice. "He should know what kind of person Koelhe is. She's spiteful and vengeful, would walk over a helpless child just to get what she wants. He's a fool for casting his lot in with hers."

Tawa massaged the bridge of his nose with his forefinger and thumb, wincing with apparent frustration. "How many times do you think you would be able to accept hearing 'no' when it comes to requesting help to retake your lands?" he asked.

"I would hope we won't have to hear it all," Tez said with a shrug.

"As would I," Tawa said, "but that he held faith at all despite over a decade of rejections is indicative enough of his patience. It just happened to be that his patience ran out—or at the least, that of his people. I am saddened, but...I cannot fault him. Koelhe has promised to do what Fannalhen would not. For someone in Han'e's position, that would be enough."

"Sounds to me that you're defending him for breaking faith, Tawa."

Briskly, Tawa shook his head. "I am neither defending nor condoning his actions. I just...understand." He sighed, brushing away a stream of running water from his brow.

Tez was hardly in the mood to understand. "But what comes next? It's only a matter of time before his deal with that witch comes back to haunt him. We all know who Koelhe is, and we all know what our village—what our *Tribe*—will devolve into with her in a position of leadership. We've seen the paranoia she created with my sister without having any authority whatsoever. Now just think what she'll do *with* that authority. I fear for anyone still in the village who remain loyal to my mother. Can you imagine what she'll do to them?" *Forget about them, even. What about Mother herself? Is she still alive?*

"She's spent her life not caring for the truth of the matter," Sharrabha said in agreement, her thumb fiddling with the plumes of the arrows resting in her quiver. "And when she's been proven wrong, she just continues and surrounds herself with those who will listen to her. All the more reason why we need to move faster toward our potential allies."

It was still surreal that it had come to this, that members of the Stone Tribe, the supposed bastion of the north, would crawl for the help of other Tribes, but that was the hand they were dealt. "Never would I have thought that *we* would be the ones seeking the help of the Arrow and Lake Tribes, as opposed to the other way around," Tez said, shaking her head. Perhaps it was her own pride talking, but it felt demeaning to be in such a position. "Why would they even be willing to help us in the first place?"

Shrugging her shoulders and raising her arms at her sides, Sharrabha merely asked, "Do they have reason not to?"

"Always struck me that they had larger issues to deal with. I always assumed my father pissed the Arrow Tribe off enough with his refusals to retake their land. I only recall their leadership coming just the once as opposed to Han'e coming through twice a year."

"They still owe our Tribe a debt of gratitude. Your father granted them the westernmost plains of our territory, after all."

"I think the Sun Tribe has proven that debts of gratitude don't hold much water these days. But let's say that the Arrow Tribe agrees to join with us. They're still a crippled unit of warriors—they were so dependent on the mobility provided to them by their horses that once the Invaders stripped them of that...I think much of their sense of livelihood disappeared along with that."

"Still no Tribe better with a bow than them, though. An army of Rantalhas, with or without their horses."

"I'm still fearful of just the one Rantalha, army or not." The ease at which the man had picked off members of his own Tribe earlier this evening, without giving it a second thought, was enough to send shivers down Tez's spine. She still half-expected him to emerge from behind one of the rolling dunes. She knew he could shoot each of them dead three times before they hit the ground. Wringing out rainwater from her braid, Tez squinted her eyes further westward. "And what about the Lake Tribe? Have they stopped fighting amongst themselves for long enough that they may be able to help?"

"Does it matter, one way or another?" Tawa posited, his face paint running down his face in steady rivers. "Of greatest importance is securing allies. This is larger than any one Tribe. It seems only a matter of time before the

Invaders return to the north. If that happens, the petty differences between Tribes will matter very little. This is more than just the Stone Tribe, or the Lake Tribe, or the Arrow Tribe. This is for the good of our Land."

"The good of our Land…" Tez muttered to herself. She stopped walking, allowing herself a moment's rest. She fell to her backside, her rear splashing in a pool of mud on impact. The others followed suit, relieved to at last be off their feet, despite the rain continuing to bear down on them.

"What is it, Tez?" Tawa asked, placing his spear tenderly on the ground next to him. It was still odd seeing the bookish man with any sort of weapon.

Tez frowned, her skin prickling in reaction to the biting wind coming in from the mountains. "You mention the importance of securing allies, of preparing ourselves for the inevitability of the Invaders' attack. We settled on the idea that we *had* allies on the virtue of granting the Sun and Arrow Tribes land after theirs were taken. But that was the extent to which my father helped them. He maintained Stone neutrality, just as his father did, and his father before him. That's how it's always been."

Sharrabha leaned in closer, squinting her eyes toward Tez against the rain. "Yes, but…"

Her eyes still fixed on Tawa, Tez continued. "By your logic—that the differences between Tribes don't matter when compared to the larger threat—it seems you think my father was wrong to maintain our Tribe's position."

Tawa grimaced, his shoulders tensing amidst the raging storm. It was immediately evident that he was deliberately averting his eyes from Tez. "I did not say that."

Tez clenched her fists, her fingernails carving indentations into her palms. She wanted to lash out, to admonish Tawa for only standing behind her father for posterity, not in any earnestness. But she couldn't bring herself to do so. It was Tawa. He had just risked his life for her and her family, and here she was debating whether he truly stood with the rightful leaders of the Tribe. She felt frustrated with herself.

Still, the words—unspoken though they were—stung. Tez turned her focus to Sharrabha, the huntress wringing the rainwater from her hair, listlessly kicking at a stone embedded in the mud. "And you, Sharrabha?" Tez asked.

"Was my father wrong? Would you have broken away like Koelhe, risen up like Han'e?"

The huntress shook her head with a prolonged breath. "I would never break faith as they had. But…" She turned away, wiping the rivers from her forehead as streaks of blue cascaded to the sodden earth. "It doesn't matter whether your father was wrong or right. There will be a time for that debate, but it is not now. If we are even afforded the opportunity for it at all."

"Doesn't matter…" Tez repeated, mumbling the words to herself. She knew plenty in the Tribe and out of the Tribe who disagreed enough with that statement to upheave the entire system her father had put in place. *At what point do we become dissenters just the same?* she thought.

Frustrating as it was, though, in the larger picture, Tez knew that her father's decisions truly did not matter. Not right now. She bit at her bottom lip, her shoulder throbbing from the grazed arrow she received from Rantalha, her arms howling from the prolonged duel with Fann, her heart aching for the sight of her mother being forcibly dragged into their home with a wounded leg. And her eyes flaring at the memory of Koelhe's sneering and vicious laugh as she led their Tribe onto a path of familial destruction.

She had to accept the larger picture. She knew that. It just wasn't easy.

Tez let the argument slide. She paced in place as deep pockets of mud threatened to pull her boots off. Gripping the shaft of her spear tightly, she stole one more glance toward home before returning her gaze to the west. "We're best served as a united north right now," she muttered, her voice only barely carrying over the storm.

Sharrabha approached her, still fiddling with the arrows in her quiver. "Or, at the least, a fractured union," she assured. A smile creased her lips—though one that did not quite reach her eyes—and she nodded to Tez, putting a hesitant hand on the younger's shoulder.

Tez allowed it as she dammed up the frustrated tears that threatened to flow. She eyed their small coterie, then passed glances to Sharrabha and Tawa both. "So, where to first, then?" she asked.

Tawa squinted through the stormy dark, as though anything could be discerned in that darkness, before saying, "We should make for the Lake

Tribe first. If we can convince them, we will have a much greater show of strength to exhibit to the Arrow Tribe."

"I didn't think martial prowess was high on the list of priorities for the Arrow Tribe," Tez said with a grunt.

"Ordinarily, you would be right. But fractured as the horsekin are, the idea of a stronger force is likely to be of much greater appeal to them. Especially where they do not have their horses."

Sharrabha nodded. "Where one hunter fails, a host succeeds." She looked up to the darkened skies as though in search of an answer within the storm clouds. "What the Arrow now lack in mobility, we can make up for it in sheer strength and numbers. They would respect and honor that."

With an acquiescing nod, Tez trudged through the mud with spear in hand, motioning their sullied band onward. "On to the Big Lake, then. And may we hope that the Lake Tribe hasn't started a new war with themselves." She forced a chuckle, which was joined by no one else. Listlessly smiling to herself, Tez thought of Sen. *She would have laughed at that bad joke*, she thought. A single tear escaped the dam she had erected for herself, but she was quick to bat it away. *Godsdamn it, Sen. Please be okay. Please bring Brin back home safely. And please don't condemn us for what we've done in your absence.*

"Another!" a host of voices called in unison, clinking their glassware together in raucous harmony.

Koelhe drank deep with satisfaction as victory songs echoed throughout the tavern. She had awaited this day for years upon years, and to see it finally come to fruition was immensely rewarding. Propping her feet up on the table, she felt akin to a god. With one stroke, she had toppled an institution of incompetence. With one move, she had begun an era of unity and accomplishment.

And to think, she did not even need a speck of Foresight to do it.

She surveyed the tavern, reveling in the sight of her allies and peers welcoming the fall of a horrid dynasty and the beginning of a brilliant one. She hadn't seen such a hearty smile upon the face of her son, Fann, in quite a long time. He had just as much to celebrate as she did. He had gotten to see that wretched Curseborn depart to her own inevitable death, bested the Curseborn's blasted sister in a duel, and watched the departed Chief's hellbound wife be driven to her knees by a boy barely old enough to exist in their society.

The good times were sure to roll.

Koelhe couldn't help but smile with the same degree of mirth as her son. They had both suffered so dearly under Fannalhen and Dennalhir's iron grip. Shunned so readily, thrashed so furiously. But no longer. To see Dennalhir indulge in the same taste of pain Koelhe had so voraciously supped upon for years, it was indeed a sight to behold.

And to have drawn the knife that felled her, oh, did that feel wonderful.

A number of allies rejoined her, having refilled their glasses with fresh drinks. Judging from the snippets of conversation she picked up, along with the frustrated and bemused expression on the barkeeper's face, Koelhe surmised that they didn't necessarily *pay* for their refills. *As far as I'm concerned,* she thought, *our Tribe's true heroes need not pay for a thing. This Tribe owes them—and me—everything.*

"To a new dawn!" one side of the table exclaimed.

"To stone carved anew!" answered the other side.

Koelhe raised her glass in response to both calls before snapping her fingers at the bartender, wordlessly pointing to her empty glass. She snarled when she noticed a slight hesitation on the bartender's part, which immediately prompted a swift retrieval of a new glass of fresh brew. Before she knew it, she was scarfing down half of a new glass. It certainly paid to be in charge.

"Koelhe!" slurred Barradhan, the ally to her immediate left. He was still splattered with blood along his forearms, yet to have washed away in the rain. He wore them as a badge of honor. "You need to tell us! How did you know to do that with the Haunted?" His gait was remarkably unsteady, his words equally so, but his eyes were intensely focused.

She couldn't help but chuckle to herself, resting one arm behind her head. It *was* a clever movement of pieces, after all. "Oh, come now, Barradhan. It was all too easy. Any among us could have tricked those fools as I did!"

They all cheered and raised their glasses to her claim.

"Truthfully, there wasn't much of a plan at all. Those two hopeless saps were all too eager, I assure you. I couldn't understand them worth a shit, but it was all too obvious that the woman wanted revenge for the Curseborn savaging her. I was all too willing to lend them a hand. They played just as important a part in tonight's proceedings as you all did." She smiled and raised her glass to them again, finishing its contents in a large gulp. Loudly, she cleared her throat and heaved the empty glass back in the bartender's direction, nearly missing her head. She only heard a startled yelp before the pouring of a new glass was audible, and a filled mug was back in her hand.

"They did still die, though," Barradhan said hesitantly, his drink sloshing violently in his hand. "Do you regret that at all?"

Koelhe scoffed. "Okay, maybe there was a bit of a plan—the older one had to die. Dennalhir was always too concerned with losing people. Same with her daughter. Some hypocritical 'valuing life' nonsense that they always spouted but never backed up. Hah!" She took a long swig and belched. "When Rantalha put that arrow in the Haunted woman's throat, oh, did I think we had it right then and there. I knew they would be caught off guard. Nothing else seems to matter when someone's dying next to them, apparently. It was the perfect opportunity for the boy to drive that blade through Dennalhir's neck." Another pause, another swig, another belch, another cheer. "Certainly was surprised at how quickly Tawa reacted to that, I will admit. The bitch still lives, but the result was the same." She placed her glass down forcefully, the remaining contents splashing over the table, and reclined further with both hands behind her head, all the satisfaction in the world settling into her head.

A set of fingers tapped on the table to her right. She turned to see the pensive and thoughtful face of Dolevhe. His sharp eyes met hers, and she was reminded how proficient an archer he had been that night. If not for Rantalha, he probably could have ended the evening as the greatest hero in their takeover. Not that he had the desire to be considered as such.

"Is something the matter, Dolevhe?" Koelhe asked, still comfortably reclining in her chair.

He raised a hand in dismissal but nonetheless asked, "So what is your plan with Dennalhir, anyway? I'm surprised you didn't put that knife in her throat as planned."

With a chuckle, Koelhe raised her eyebrow in a smirking acknowledgment. "Sometimes, I surprise myself, too." She spread her hands out wide, deferring any real explanation in the motion. "She's going to have a better use alive than dead. Tez did escape with her life, after all. Whatever she's planning next, it's will involve coming back for her dear old mother." A thought came to her, and a sinister smile along with it. "And I cannot wait to break Dennalhir one last time as I force her to watch her last child slaughtered before her." She laughed heartily, letting it echo through the walls of the tavern.

Others joined her, but long after the moment passed, Koelhe continued to chortle with great amusement as she was observed in silence. Her face grew radiantly red, her cheeks straining, a stream of mirthful tears flowing down her face as she tried to regain control. "Ah, mercy," she said, flicking away the droplets from her cheeks. She reached for her glass, still finding a veritable source of drink within, and raised it to her comrades. "Go! Drink! Merriment!"

Without further prompting, they dispersed to engage with the survivors of their victorious evening.

Koelhe watched them with further satisfaction, riding the most incredible high of her life. Each of them allowed her to accomplish her greatest dream, and she would not let anything rob her of this moment. She had every intention of allowing this celebration to extend deep into the night. She drank deep, and before she even had an opportunity to beckon the bartender for a refilled glass, there were already two sitting before her. *Now, this is service*, she thought.

A deep voice cleared its throat from behind. "May I join you?"

She turned to see Han'e standing reverently behind her, a new collage of cuts and bruises adorning the existing canvas on his exposed arm. "Chief Han'e," Koelhe said with a smile. She gestured to the seat next to her. "Please, sit."

The Chief of the Sun Tribe bowed his head in gratitude before settling into the creaking wooden frame of his seat. Immediately, Koelhe could notice a change in demeanor upon Han'e's face. He had always had a weathered, forlorn disposition, a distant glimmer in his eyes. Naturally, after the events of the past evening, he still looked weathered, and exhausted alongside it, but there was something else that glowed in his eyes. It almost looked like...hope.

Han'e smiled at her, though it did not extend fully to his eyes. "I believe congratulations are in order," he said, raising his glass. "Chief Koelhe."

It was the first time she had heard those words. *There's a wonderful ring to it*, she thought. She raised her own glass in kind. "Without your help, we may not have accomplished what we did tonight."

"Please," Han'e said dismissively. "Tol'e and I played but a small part. Two of us amongst a larger host. All credit should go to you."

He's right, of course, but I would never say that, Koelhe thought. "Chief Han'e, you fight with the might of ten, and Tol'e with the ferocity of a beast." Truthfully, the glimpses she was able to catch of Tol'e in combat frightened her. To say he savaged his opponents would be understating it. He struck with whatever was at his disposal, whatever he could remove from others, gave no quarter, and offered no mercy. *Clearly, some could bottle their frustration no longer. I'm glad he's on my side.*

"Your words do me a great kindness." Han'e drank deeply from his glass before pensively placing it back atop the table. That half-smile disappeared, no longer dispensing at the pleasantries. The hope once present in his eyes still glimmered, but it appeared more resolute, more focused. "I would hope it is not the only kindness offered me this evening."

Koelhe raised an eyebrow and couldn't help but chuckle at his words' implications. She took her feet off the table and leaned forward, her wild and unkempt braid falling in front of her shoulder. "So quick to talks of consummation, are we?" She placed a hand on his knee. "So much to celebrate, after all. After all, as two Chiefs, we are free to do whatever we—"

He did not hesitate to remove her hand from his knee. "That's...not what I meant."

With no small degree of shock, Koelhe raised her hands and reclined back, folding one leg over the other. "Hmph. What kindness are you after, then?"

Han'e's posture remained straight and rigid, his hands folded across his lap. "The very reason I agreed to join you. I would like to discuss our plans for reclaiming the south from the Invaders."

So quick to business, Koelhe thought disdainfully. Sighing, she rested her elbows on the chair's armrests, linking her fingers at chin height. In examining Han'e, she could not see any flexibility on the matter. She saw only a man at the end of his rope, leading a Tribe supposedly on its last legs, so quick to break faith when the opportunity presented itself. That gave her a lot of power with which to bargain. "Of course," she said. "I assume you do not expect to begin tonight. I think we have all of us earned a rest."

"I would not expect the Stone Tribe to begin immediately or in full force," Han'e answered. "But the warriors of the Sun Tribe have been ready for this day for fifteen years. We do not wish to wait any longer."

"Nor should you. Though, I must wonder. Just how many within your Tribe are ready to reclaim the south?"

With a scoff that hardly veiled the offense taken, Han'e said, "All of us are ready."

Koelhe shook her head. "That's not what I meant. In terms of numbers, how many of your people are serviceable on the battlefield to face down the Invaders?"

Han'e opened his mouth to respond, but then hesitated.

That pause told Koelhe everything she needed to know.

"Enough of us," Han'e finally said.

"How many is 'enough?'"

"Enough," he reiterated. "You said it yourself. I fought with the might of ten men, Tol'e with the ferocity of a beast. We are all of us of the same cloth. The Sun Tribe is unmatched on the battlefield."

"Unmatched, though thoroughly defeated not once, but twice."

Han'e snarled, clearly despising the reminder of his greatest failure—of first allowing the Invaders to displace his people after welcoming them into his home; and then, falling prey to the zealous Wood Tribe when he took the survivors of the Invasion into the Forest in search of a new home. "I won't repeat the same mistakes. *We* won't repeat the same mistakes."

Koelhe held out her hands in a calming gesture. "I understand your frustration. But your Tribe is spread too thin now. If you show your hand now, you *will* find yourself defeated for a third time, and I would be surprised if there's enough of you for a fourth."

A sharp breath escaped Han'e's nose with evident frustration, but he reluctantly nodded. He leaned back in his chair, slowly flexing his fingers in a show of resistant anger. "What do you...suggest?" he asked haltingly, as though the words were acid upon his tongue.

Putting a hand to her chin in mimicry of deep thinking, Koelhe sat in silence. When enough time had elapsed, she cleared her throat and took another swig of her drink. "Well, we can assume that Tez and Tawa and their ilk fled west. They may get to the Lake and Arrow Tribes before us, so surely, they're going to be trapped in whatever inane schemes that Tez has in her head right now. We may be out of luck there."

Han'e sat in wait as Koelhe remained silent, offering nothing further in terms of a plan. "Again...what are you suggesting?" He did not mask his impatience.

With a shrug, Koelhe started to say, "Unless you want to approach the Wood Tribe..."

"I'd sooner set the Forest ablaze." Han'e gripped the armrest tightly, the wood beginning to splinter within his grasp.

"As I thought," Koelhe conceded.

Leaning forward, Han'e growled softly. Within his eyes dwelt a fire that Koelhe had never witnessed within him. A desperate blaze holding on so quickly as to not become a dying ember. "I hope you do not take me for a fool."

If his intent was to threaten her, it was not working. "Not at all," she answered, her tone cold as ice.

Han'e remained unmoved. "The Sun Tribe does not take kindly to mockery."

"Nor does the Stone." Koelhe reclined further, away from Han'e's fiery glare, and propped her legs atop the table once more. "Please do not take my caution for mockery, Chief Han'e. I promised you the support of the Stone

Tribe, and the support of the Stone Tribe you shall have. I only humbly ask that you allow us rest after tonight's victory." She raised her glass.

There was a tremor in Han'e's hands, a despondent twitch reluctant to accept Koelhe's words. But for all his bravado, it was clear that Han'e was smart enough to know when to fight and when to hold back. His eyes screamed for a fight, but his lips said only, "Fine. We await the Stone Tribe's readiness."

A wide smile creased Koelhe's lips. "Very good. Then, tonight, join us. We revel in our victory!" Her eyes scanned the tavern, first to Han'e's averted eyes, then to all her comrades-in-arms. To her son, at long last with a smile affixed to his face. The days of glory had arrived.

And perhaps, tomorrow, we shall revel some more. She raised her glass to Han'e before downing its remaining contents and holding the empty mug up high for all to see. "Another!" she yelled.

CHAPTER THREE

SAME STORIES, DIFFERENT BOOKS

The Year 1556 Anno Salvatoris
15 Years After the Invasion

It had all been too much for Sen to take in at once. She sat on the edge of the nearby empty bed and buried her face in her hands.

She barely had time to process that not only were there other Eclipseborn out there like her, but that they were living amongst the Invaders. But to think that they were willing participants in the Invasion, that they saw nothing wrong with the eradication of her people...of *their* people...

I don't even know what to say. She pushed her hands through her hair, slightly wincing as her fingers got caught in the patches of soaked, tangled knots. Allowing herself to peer across the room, to take in these few at the edge of her world who looked so much like her, yet so different all the same, she couldn't help but shudder in place.

These...Children of the Black Moon. Sen couldn't help but feel she had traded one devil for another.

Her gaze focused on Kamataa, the old crone still thoroughly unaffected by her own casual admission. That weathered face still smiled as though nothing was out of the ordinary with her words. She remained relaxed, as though her hands were not still damp with Brin's blood.

All Sen could do was shake her head in disbelief. "You really...see nothing wrong with it?" she asked, dumbfounded. "I've seen what the Invaders do. Who they are. And you all are perfectly keen to just...go along with it?"

The other Children merely stood in silence. Not in embarrassment, though. If anything, they looked upon Sen with curiosity as though *she* was the one whose words were beyond comprehension.

Kamataa leaned forward, wisps of flowing white hair falling past her shoulders. She folded her hands together, still maintaining an indifferent and cooled demeanor. "Let me ask you this, Sennalhat," she said. "You have only been privy to the Acrarians' methods for no more than a few days, no?"

Sen's ears perked up. *The Acrarians,* she mused. *So that's what they call themselves.*

"Do you now think yourself an authority on who they are and what they do simply because you've had a run-in with them?"

"A *run-in*?" Sen asked incredulously. She jumped to her feet, fury in her eyes, the other Children offering no resistance to her sudden movements. "You would call my father's murder a *run-in*? What they did to the Wood Tribe a *run-in*?"

Kamataa shrugged. "You say that as though the Wood Tribe would never commit the same atrocities. Surely, you are aware of what they did to the Sun Tribe?"

Sen gritted her teeth and pointed an accusatory finger at the old Eclipse-born. "And if it weren't for the Invaders, the Sun Tribe would never have had to attempt to resettle in the Forest, to begin with! Don't act like the hands of the Wood Tribe are dirtier than the Invaders'!"

A round of soft chuckles murmured through the room.

Sen couldn't help but let her jaw drop. Her words could not reach any of them. They all looked at her as though she was beyond help, and she could not help but gaze upon them in the same manner.

She noted particular indifference upon the faces of Sha'a and Hollow, especially once she broached the subject of the animosity between the Sun and Wood Tribes. Whether they were touchy subjects for them both, she could hardly tell.

Pacing in place, Sen shook her head again, her mind spinning with so many questions that she didn't know where to start. All the queries vied for her attention that when she opened her mouth to allow one to escape, they found themselves stuck at the same juncture. The result was Sen standing dumbfounded with her mouth agape, unable to find the necessary words to question or explain any of this.

Kamataa seemed to notice this and slowly narrowed the gap between them, still maintaining the warm air of a kindly grandmother.

All a mask, of course. Beneath that, it's only as cold-blooded a murderer as the man who killed my father.

"You should not be so surprised, Sennalhat," Kamataa said, her arms wide open as though entreating an embrace. "We all shed our Tribal skins long ago. Our place is not among them. We could not be true to who and what we are among our Tribes because they did not allow for our existence. But *here...*" She paused to gesture to the outside of the barracks, to the lingering sounds and smells of the City. "Here, we are free to be faithful to ourselves. We need not hide ourselves any longer. The Acrarians do not cling to the past as the Tribes do; they look only to the future."

"'Free to be faithful to yourselves?'" Sen spat on the ground, the words acid on her tongue. "What a load of bullshit. You can't say that when you use Illusion to hide yourselves among the Invaders. You know they would kill or enslave you without a second thought were they given the opportunity. And for all your talk of rejecting your Tribes, you sure do like carrying your Tribal trinkets around." She pointed at the pendants adorning each of their necks, all marked with the rune of Illusion. "You're still clinging to what you've always been and where you've always belonged, so don't tell me you'd rather allow the Land to fall to the Invaders."

A deep, amused sigh passed Kamataa's lips. "Oh, Sennalhat," she whispered mournfully. "If only you realized."

When the old woman didn't continue, Sen narrowed her eyes and inched forward. "Realized what?"

Still, Kamataa only grinned. Her eyes lost a measure of their sharpness for a brief moment, instead appearing to focus on some distant nothingness, seemingly lost in a dream long since passed. With a deep breath, she closed her eyes, shaking her head back and forth in bemusement. "A long time ago," she began, "I lived among the Lake Tribe. I would like to think I was a person offering nothing but goodwill to the Tribe, just as I'm sure you feel you do, Sennalhat. Growing up, I never understood why I was looked upon as different. My parents, though they tolerated me enough, feared me for reasons unknown. The other children in the village tended to avoid me. Many tried to dissuade me from attempting the Trial when I came of age, though never explaining why. Of course, I ignored them all, and even when I passed what my Trial came to be, I was cast out. Despite doing everything required of me, they branded me a pariah and a curse, and I nearly died for it."

Sen grimaced, the tale feeling all too familiar to her. It was something she would not wish upon anyone.

Kamataa clearly noticed this and slowly nodded in recognition, a sly grin creasing her lips. "We are all of us the same. The same story with the same chapter, merely read from different books. So, you must realize this: a Land conquered by the Acrarians matters little to us, for we have no connection to it. Why would we see fit to defend a land that rejects us simply for being alive?"

I've still found a way, Sen wanted to say, but the words remained frozen on her tongue. She met the eyes of each of the present Children—not a glance, but a true, earnest examination of each of their expressions—and for the first time, saw that same conviction in their gazes that roared so fiercely in Kamataa's.

Hollow and Zara each balled their fists, a barely perceptible tremor of anger breaking their stoic faces.

Cin, though remaining silent and expressionless, eyed Sen with something akin to disappointment, something disbelieving of her virulent defense of the Tribes.

Sha'a and Vanta's respective body languages were each indicative of a desire to run headlong into battle. They both stood restless upon their feet, hands resting softly atop their weapons, as though discontent with waiting for their time on the battlefield.

Ziialhan filed in behind Kamataa, resting atop her elderly companion's shoulder an equally wrinkled and weathered hand. She passed Sen a knowing glance with those sharp eyes of hers.

And Kamataa, for her part, only continued to smile. A smile that lacked hesitance, that remained filled with fiery intent.

Each of them, their own tales, their own stories, only read in a different voice. The words weighed heavily on Sen. Her own chapters had to have contained similar lines, but did they tell the same stories as those in the room?

She sighed and buried her head in her hands. She did not want to admit any connection of kinship to this lot, to this troupe so viciously desiring the elimination of those she held dear and those she did not. But there was something that she knew bound them.

Fear. And suffering.

We've all suffered our lot. But I can't sympathize with them. I haven't suffered to the degree they have. For them to be pushed so far, they would turn against our own people... All Sen could do was stand her ground once more, look Kamataa square in the eyes, and merely ask, "Why?"

Kamataa raised an eyebrow, nudging Ziialhan's hand away from her shoulder. "Why what?" she asked.

Sen turned and narrowed her eyes, staring in the vague direction of the north, a land she did not expect to again visit. Her home, for whatever love she still held there, for whatever animosity still awaited there. Where the memories of those soft voices welcoming her with open arms were often drowned out by the loud voices wishing her little else but harm. "Why do they fear us?" she softly murmured. A shaky breath escaped her lips as she clenched her eyes shut, desperately trying to stave off tears. She heard a dismissive scoff.

When she turned, Cin was approaching, his arms folded calmly, his expression blank with indifference. "It's only human nature to reject those that are different." He did not quite glance directly at Sen—more into the middle distance—but it was clear that there were further thoughts ruminating in his mind. Thoughts that he did not appear willing to further share.

Kamataa nodded to Cin before returning her attention to Sen. "And who could be more different from them than we?" Holding her arms out at her side, gesturing to her fellow Children of the Black Moon, hers was a stance of defiance, not sadness. Her tone did not indicate a sense of regret at being different; instead, it appeared she embraced the hatred.

"But why?" Sen prodded further. "Why are we...different?"

"Surely, Sennalhat," Kamataa said with only a hint of arrogance, "you remember your sham of a Trial? When you finally discovered who you were? When you finally discovered *what* you were?"

Sen winced. "How could I forget? My life had been a lie until that day. And, just to find out that—"

"Yes, yes," Kamataa interrupted, holding her hand out to silence Sen. "Some of us here were not so fortunate as to even *have* a Trial, so please do not regale us with your tales of woe. I assure you, ours have been much grimmer. We are not all so fortunate as to be born the child of a Chief."

That immediately shut Sen up. Taken aback, she wanted to rebuff those words, but she knew that they were true. She remained quiet, waiting for the old woman to continue.

Kamataa pressed on, a sense of acknowledgment flaring in her eyes that seemed to recognize Sen had no further lines of questioning. "But yes, child. When the Keepers fell aghast at discovering your true nature, I'm sure they wanted to cast you from the peaks of the mountain, offer you as fodder for the gods to ravage, yes? Purge the abomination from this world?"

Not in so many words, Sen thought. *But the intent was probably there, all the same.* She nodded.

"Yes," Kamataa whispered. "Because *that* is what they see us as. Abominations. *Unnatural.*" She snarled at the word. "Our powers don't come from the Bear or the Wolf or the Owl. And that frightens them. Because the Moon Who Does Not Look *is* power. We are servants of the Black Moon Herself. We are not granted Her power because we *are* Her power. If we really wanted to, we could fell the Tribes' gods, but many of us simply wanted just to be allowed to live. But that could never be so. As long as fear remains in the hearts of men, those of us who are different will continue to be reviled as unnatural."

Sen thought back to her Trial, when those two voices haunted her with promises of the Moon's power. She still did not understand that day. She had long thought the Moon was forcing her to choose simply between living or dying. She had rejected the options and instead was granted the power of Luck for reasons beyond her comprehension. But if there really was more to it than that...

"Answer me this," she demanded, composure returning to her voice. "All this time, I've thought that the only thing the Eclipse could do for me was give me Luck. Like it was rewarding me for everything I endured because of being Eclipseborn. Please, I…" She drifted off, stammering over the request, willing herself to ask something of Brin's killer. "Just help me understand. All of this. The Black Moon, the Eclipseborn…there's never been anything to guide me."

"Would that there remained anything to guide us…" Kamataa muttered. There was something odd in her voice. It almost sounded…remorseful? After a moment, her focus seemed to return, and she looked to each of her companions, folding her hands behind her back. "The power of the Moon is more than just Luck. It could be there are many abilities that She grants that we are not yet aware of. Hers is a power that we do not fully comprehend. But we, in our capacity, are merely vessels for what She truly represents: the balance of Life and Death, the ebb and flow of light and darkness."

"I remember those…voices forcing me to choose," Sen said. "To choose whether to…to live or to die? Faced with that, I guess it should have been obvious, but…"

Kamataa laughed. "Oh, Sennalhat. If it were only that simple. No, that choice is far beyond such a petty decision. Life and Death…perhaps it's best to compare them to the Boons offered by the Animal Deities. It is not a matter of living or dying, but rather a decision of having the power to give life—" She held out an open palm. "—or take it away." And then, the other hand. "*That* is the true power of the Moon. When She is unhindered by the watchful eyes of the Signs, shining brightly in darkness, She can finally call to us. It is as natural as the flow of the tides, but it is feared because it is not understood."

Sen's mouth was agape, unsure what to make of Kamataa's words.

"You still do not understand, child." She did not offer the remark with any disdain. It was simply the tone of a grandmother offering a mysterious story to her grandchildren. "Allow me to perhaps introduce the Children more formally." She turned to face Vanta, whose hand still rested on her weapon. "Vanta was once a huntress of the Arrow Tribe. She, along with the remnants of her Tribe, resettled in the north with what few horses they had remaining. She was only just coming in to her powers of Death when she kept inadvertently killing her horses with just a touch. She only just escaped the Tribe with her life."

Her eyes nearly popping out of her head, Sen sharply turned to Vanta. "Killing things with just a touch? Is that possible?"

Vanta looked at Sen with confusion as though the answer to the question was an obvious one. "Yes," she said with a hint of annoyance.

Sen turned back to Kamataa. "But *how* is it possible?"

"Did I not explain?" the old woman said. "We hold in our grasp the power of Life and Death."

"I just didn't think it would be so...literal."

"And yet it is. From birth, these abilities are dormant within us, the Moon merely waiting for us to awake to them."

"From *birth*?" Sen said with shock. She turned back to Vanta. "How old were you when you left your Tribe?"

"I didn't *leave* my Tribe," Vanta spat. "They didn't leave me much choice. And I was thirteen."

"Thirteen..." Sen muttered, aghast. "So young...?" She stared sharply at Kamataa.

The old woman appeared exasperated. "We are not subject to those same customs. The Moon does not wish to wait for some Trial to arbitrarily declare us fit for Her power."

Listlessly, Sen trailed her finger in an arc, drawing a line connecting the other Children of the Black Moon. "Then, everyone else...?"

Zara stepped forward, her brow furrowed as she grimaced at what appeared to be a painful memory. "I was fifteen when I accidentally killed my cousin. We were having an argument, some dumb argument, when I slapped him across the face. He was dead before he hit the ground." She gritted her teeth. "My uncle walked in as I was hovering over the dead body. By Lake Tribe customs, I was to face a trial to the death against my uncle on the Big Lake. I didn't want to—I couldn't do that to another member of my family. But he never gave me the chance. He tried killing me in my sleep the night before the trial. He just crumpled into nothing when I pushed him off me." She shook her head in disgust and anger. "I had no choice but to run."

Before Sen could react, Sha'a also stepped forward, her eyes beset with fury. "I was only seven years old when the Acrarians came and overtook the Sun lands. My parents chose to abandon me when they fled, and I was taken here and put in the slave camps. I hated the Acrarians at first, like we all did. When I accidentally killed a guard just by tugging on his shirt to ask for water, they lined me up to face their guns. I was only twelve. But Kamataa saved me before they could fire. Now, where she goes, I go." A smirk managed to crease her lips. "I owe her a debt for taking me to the Sun Tribe to...deal with my parents, as well."

Sen let out another shaken breath. For everything she endured as a result of her birth...nothing could compare to what these three had to. "Are you all...?"

Kamataa shook her head, dismissing Sen's hesitant shock. "No, we do not all possess the Touch. Others, like Hollow, have the Draw."

"The Draw?" Sen asked, raising an eyebrow.

"Drawing in Life," Hollow said without emotion, his arms crossed over his chest. "When I was eleven, I fell from the trees in the Forest. The fall should have killed me." He shrugged. "It didn't. My bones healed just as quickly as they broke. The Elder didn't like that. Tried to shoot me full of arrows. He succeeded. I just kept running."

"So, you just...can't die?" Sen's eyes widened.

Hollow shrugged again. "I could. Just hard to."

Sen made a mental note not to find herself in a fight against Hollow. For all she knew, even if she had the prowess to match, it would be a fight that could never possibly end. She turned to Cin to ask him of his story, but something immediately irked her. Cin, Sha'a, Vanta, Hollow, Zara...they were all her age. They were all born during the last Eclipse. But Ziia and Kamataa...they were clearly older than she was. Much older. "You two," Sen said, pointing her forefingers at the elders. "If the Draw means that it's impossible to die..."

"Not impossible," Ziia said with a smile. "As Hollow said, it's just very hard to."

"You both were born during the last Eclipse before ours," Sen said haltingly. "You're both...over four hundred years old?"

Kamataa matched Ziia's smile. "And now, you realize. Ziia and I both, we have seen much. Reviled much. Been demonized much. And so, we are keen to see it all burn."

The breath had escaped Sen. She wanted to ask so much more, but no words could come to her. But at the very least, she understood. She understood how someone who had managed to live in exile for four centuries could be willing to pull it all out by the roots.

But what she couldn't help but wonder was why Kamataa and Ziia waited so long to uproot it all. She hoped to ask them, but her head was still spinning.

"You have more, I'm sure," Kamataa said, as though reading Sen's mind. "But you need rest first. Take that open bed—" She pointed to the vacant bed which Sen had sat upon earlier. "—and get the sleep you need. I will not force a decision upon you. We can discuss this further tomorrow. You deserve time to mourn your brother, as well."

Brin, Sen thought with a sharp gasp. *What I deserve is to drive a spear through your throat.* But if what Hollow said was true...killing Kamataa would be very difficult.

Instead, she focused her energy on Brin for the time being. Through all of the shocks of the evening, she had forgotten that she was still clutching Brin's pendant. The pit in her stomach gaped, and the hole in her heart throbbed. It hurt so much. She sucked in a shaking breath, choking back tears that had long since emptied.

"What's happened with Brin's body? You told Hollow to...take care of him."

Kamataa nodded. "And he did. There's a place of rest beyond this city."

"And...the two guards who you and Hollow killed? Are they also...in this place of rest?"

Kamataa looked to Hollow, who only shrugged. She matched the indifference. "They'll be found there soon enough. And from there, well, we begin again."

"Begin...again?" Sen asked cautiously, her eyes growing heavy.

With an amused scoff, Kamataa said plainly, "An escaped slave and a couple dead guards? That'll be enough to rile up the Acrarians." She walked softly over to Sen, the other Children of the Black Moon filing away in the background, off to resume their own duties. Kamataa placed a hand on Sen's shoulder, gentle at first until she reached a point of nearly forcing Sen down. "And you'll have your part to play in this as well, I promise you. But, for now, please just rest. We'll discuss more in the morning."

There were still a thousand questions running through Sen's mind. But her brain was in a fog, her eyes too exhausted.

And as soon as her head hit the pillow, she was asleep.

MEMORY

TRICKSTERS AND FIENDS

The cold mountain air greeted her like a dagger as she opened her eyes. What she had experienced was…frightening. Confusing. And yet invigorating. She felt herself imbued with something indescribable. It was as though a fire coursed through her veins, purging and cleansing every wound and ache within her.

But when Kamataa opened her eyes again, the flames within her may very well have been frozen to ice both by the biting gales present in the Heart and the equally icy glares presented to her by the Keepers. Even the mountain ranges expanding beyond her line of sight seemed to freeze before her, those unforgiving peaks and valleys stopping in indescribable shock. There was no commotion from the gathered Keepers, no rustling or ruminations from the nearby fauna. Only the judging whistles of the wind.

An Kehzan hastily smeared the mark away from Kamataa's forehead before stepping cautiously away from her. He was the greatest warrior the Heart and the Keepers had ever known and probably ever would know, a Bearsign unparalleled with the spear, even among Kamataa's peers in the Lake Tribe, a man of near equivalence to the Bear itself in both appearance and ferocity, a fighter imbued with the Boon of Fear who was so accustomed to instilling terror in the hearts and minds of those he met on the field of battle.

And yet, here he stood, a subtle tremor to his gait, backing away from a mere initiate into the throes of adulthood. At the slightest movement from Kamataa, he reached for his spear, holding it unsteady, the biting mountain winds jostling it in his shaking hands.

He was clearly afraid of Kamataa. "Back!" he warned, leveling the spear toward Kamataa, gesturing for the other Keepers present to file behind him. "Not another step!"

Kamataa held her palms out in an attempt not to convey a threat. "An Kehzan?" she asked hesitantly. "I don't understand. What is it?"

"I should have known by the solitary arrival to your Trial." An Kehzan appeared more confident in his stance, his fear seeming to be carried away on the traveling wisps of the wind. "No one would dare allow one such as you to attempt the Trial! Your impudence could have killed me!"

As An Kehzan inched closer, spear at the ready, Kamataa backed away. The reminder of her parents' absence only revitalized the pit that had long since disappeared from her stomach. She thought it odd that, even though they were among the few who encouraged her to attempt the Trial, they could not even be bothered to accompany their only daughter to it. It was so emblematic of their treatment of her: encouraging her to pursue her goals yet avoiding her all the same.

Bracing herself against the cold, huddling her arms for warmth, Kamataa slowly approached An Kehzan once more, facing the quivering spear again as it raised to her eye level. She was half his size, half his prowess, half his equal, and here she was, treated as nothing more than a rabid beast to be fought off before the evening meal. "An Kehzan," she said softly. "I do not know what I've done to trouble you. But I must assure you that I intend no harm to be done to you."

Slamming the spear on the rocky earth to resound an echo across the mountainous valley, An Kehzan snarled and appeared primed to charge her. "Do not think me so gullible! Your kind holds no tricks over me, Eclipse-born!"

Eclipseborn? Kamataa thought. She furrowed her brow, beset more by confusion than anything else. She had heard the term before, even read a few tomes on the matter despite the pursuit of knowledge not being her intended inclination—or not the inclination she was led to believe she was to pursue. She hardly saw the point in focusing only on the way of the spear or bow when the realms of knowledge and understanding were so fascinating, and the tapestry of Tribal history and culture was rich with interesting topics.

The term "Eclipseborn," though, was a strange one. There was nothing in any historical record to suggest anything malicious of those rare few born during lunar eclipses.

But superstitions often spoke different tales. And superstitions were often rooted in some degree of fact, ridiculous though they may have been.

Tricksters, warlords, murderers, fiends...all terms which had been associated with the Eclipseborn. But Kamataa did not feel any different than she had earlier in the day. She was hardly anything other than the same girl who knelt before An Kehzan a short time ago, submitting herself to her Trial.

What she felt, though, clearly mattered little. Even the winds of the Heart seemed to scream in her presence, whipping with greater ferocity than when she first arrived. Nature itself wanted her to leave.

She took the hint. She backed away slowly from An Kehzan and the other Keepers, cautious not to blindly trip over any protruding stones or find an inadvertent shortcut to the base of the mountains.

"Despite what you may think I am, An Kehzan," Kamataa called over the wind, "I promise you I am no fiend. I am simply a member of the Lake Tribe, wanting only to serve my Tribe and the people of our Land." She did not remove the great Keeper warrior from her line of sight, even as she crested down the mountain slope until she was little else but an echo of footsteps thundering over the valleys.

All the while, An Kehzan's booming voice roared through the ranges of the Heart. Some words were screamed in greater clarity than others, but as a messenger bird flew off beyond the reaches of the mountain, one phrase echoed in her mind over and over as she continued her descent, long after the words had ridden away on the southerly winds.

"You will serve our Land only when you lay beneath the earth!"

It was a lonely trek back to the eastern Lake village. The passage through the Stone village at the base of the mountains was largely without pomp or circumstance, many unsure whether she had succeeded or failed. She left no indication on her face to imply one outcome or the other and was met with hesitant greetings from all she passed, including the Chief of the Stone Tribe, who offered little else but an unsure nod.

Kamataa had much to think about as she carried along through the rolling and verdant green dunes of the north. The accusation and implication of being born under the Eclipse. What she would say to her family upon her return. What her family would say to *her*.

And the final words spoken to her by An Kehzan.

There was little else she could do but stare at her own hands, wondering if they were capable of such wickedness. If any of what she was capable of would be justification enough for the words sure to be levied upon her.

When the sun disappeared beyond the western horizon, illuminating the empty fields in shimmers of gold, Kamataa paused to rest in the valley of a dune.

Looking up to the sky, she could barely make out the outline of the moon, not yet shining to its brightest. She reached out a cautious hand, hoping to grasp it in her palm. "What is it that you've done to me?" she wondered aloud.

The moon failed to answer.

With a shaking breath, she rolled to her side and allowed the tears to finally fall. Home was still far, but for the first time, it felt to her unreachable.

The next day, she arrived at the entrance of the eastern village. When she awoke earlier in the morning, she ensured that the sides of her head were freshly shorn and the tuft of hair billowing behind her was tautly bound. If she was to be questioned on her belonging amongst her people, she would allow it to happen with a spear in her hand and her appearance proclaiming that she was, and always would be, a member of the Lake Tribe.

The village had come alive already, more so than usual. Against the backdrop of the glimmering waters of the Big Lake, the fishery markets were bustling, hawkers calling out bartered offers for the freshest catches. Several men and women, all adorning the same hairstyles as her with the sleeves of their elk-hide shirts rolled to the elbows, carried overflowing buckets of freshwater bass and sunfish parts back to their homes to prepare meals for the coming days. Others readied their boats and nets, held in fours, to replenish their stocks. It was a well-regulated operation honed over centuries of protecting the Big Lake.

When Kamataa took those first hesitant steps into the village, she had expected some manner of response. Growing up, she had watched countless celebrations come to pass as her peers completed their Trials and progressed into adulthood. Folk would wait at the mouth of the village for hours, eager to burst into an invigorating roar of applause and cheer as their kin shed the skin of childhood and emerged as a full-fledged member of the Lake Tribe. For years, she looked forward to her day. She looked forward to *this* day.

But there were none awaiting her return. All present merely went about their days as though nothing had happened. The few who paid her any mind just as quickly turned their heads back around and returned to their work, either gutting fish or honing their spearheads.

She felt like a ghost among her own people.

She may as well have been, given the number of folks who attempted to pass through her as they rushed home with bushels in hand. Some were strangers entirely, others were the families of those she considered friends.

Kamataa bit at her lip, frustration growing within her as the world around her continued but exhibited no interest in stopping for her. Her heart beat faster, sweat gathering on her skin, pulling her clothing firm against her, allowing the gentle lakeside breeze to nip at her as a result.

For as much as she wanted to scream, just for someone or something to acknowledge her, Kamataa could only find frustrated grunts to suffice. *I'd almost prefer to be run out entirely. The silence only makes it worse.*

She turned away from the market square, knowing she would find none to acknowledge her. There were only two people she could be sure would still allow her into their midst, to assure her that nothing would change for her, that all would remain as it was. And yet, those two people could not even be bothered to await her arrival, either.

Mother and Father...am I but a ghost to you both now, as well?

She shook her head, breathing in deep the smell of day-old fish heads, and walked home. The commotion of the square slowly died down as she pressed on. Too afraid to turn around, Kamataa could only assume they had all gathered along the main pathways to watch her. *Or to ready themselves to pounce on me.*

Doors shut in resounding thuds as she passed them by. Curious onlookers peered their heads out from their windows as though she were an oddity that needed to be seen firsthand. Sweat trickled down her forehead in steady streams, the nerves overcoming her as she gripped the shaft of her spear ever tighter, the wood splintering and wedging into her palm. Ahead, passersby cleared a path for her, sectioning off onto either side of the trail, forming a wall of frightened and concerned kin who, just a few days ago, were wishing her the best of luck. Now, they exuded nothing but fear and a sense of loathing.

The few who Kamataa gathered the confidence to look in the eyes shot daggers at her. Some were angry, others sad, and others seemed to wonder if the sky was due to fall upon them. Among these few were people she had considered friends, but everything had changed. She was a parade of one, on display for all to witness, not to celebrate, but to revile. As she drew closer to her home, she had to exert everything to keep her hands from shaking.

If they are going to look at me like an animal, then I'm will allow it with my head held high.

With every step, she heard An Kehzan's voice echoing once more in her head. His promise, his threat. And with each person she passed, she could not help but feel his words were to ring true. Eyeing several with brandished daggers or polished spears, she had to wonder just how many wished to see her beneath the earth.

At last, she reached her home, a modest hut of equivalent size to the others in the village, thatched together with straw, twine, wood, and hyacinth leaves. The hut reeked with the stench of old fish guts, and all she needed to do to determine the cause was examine the chunks adorning her roof and the stains of red trailing down her door. Frustrated tears welled in her eyes but did not fall.

She heard nothing but stark silence within, but when she opened the door, she found her parents seated in the middle of the room, propped on their knees with backs straightened in standard Lake Tribe posture, facing the door as though awaiting their arrival.

Kamataa wanted to run and embrace them, but upon looking at her parents' faces, she stopped herself. Amidst the sound of crackling and dying embers, their expressions appeared stiff and unnatural, a false bravery strewn along their faces that Kamataa could not help but feel unsettled by. All the same, Kamataa approached them gently, kneeling before them as one would approach a felled beast.

"Mother? Father?" she asked. "I'm...I'm home." She placed her spear in front of her, creating an artificial wall between her and her parents. A chill ran the length of her limbs that had nothing to do with the northern breeze that had run through the open door.

Stiffly, her father nodded. "Welcome home, daughter," he said. He was ordinarily a stern man, but this was something else. His dark eyes appeared sunken as though he had not slept in days. His hair was unkempt, allowed to fall past his shoulders in ragged strands. It was clear on his face that he was trying to betray nothing with his expression, but the scabbed splotches of red on his hands and knuckles spoke a different tale entirely.

The breath caught in Kamataa's throat at the sight, and she quickly averted her gaze to her mother, who looked no different than her father. She bore the same sunken expression, the same unkempt appearance, the same exposed indications of violence. Crimson stains were just barely visible on the sleeves of her shirt, the dim lighting doing enough to reveal a red stream traveling down the length of her hand.

Kamataa twitched to draw closer, but that stoic wall collapsed in her parents ever so slightly as they inched themselves backward.

"Mother, Father, *please*," Kamataa said with an outstretched hand, which was met with similar resistance. "It's *me*. You have nothing to fear. I'm the same as I always was."

Her mother vigorously shook her head. "We have been punished enough, Kamataa," she said softly, her voice breaking. "We do not need to suffer any more than we have."

"Suffer?" Kamataa said, aghast. Her eyes widened and she placed a wounded hand to her chest. "Is that what you think? That you've suffered because of me?"

"Enough that only *they* suffer, lest we all," a familiar voice called from the adjacent room.

Jerking her head off to the side, Kamataa reached blindly for her spear, not to hold at the ready, but merely to be prepared. Out from the adjoining room where her parents would sleep came the source of the voice, fashioned in rich pelts of finer make than was typically distributed to the people of the Tribe, rings crafted from lakebed minerals adorning each finger, a pendant inscribed with crisscrossing runic lines indicating Fear hanging loose from the neck, and malice blazing within sharp, bright eyes.

"Chief Azantt," Kamataa greeted with hesitation, her head bowing more as a reflex than a sign of respect. "What are you doing here? What have you done to my parents?" She was nearly to her feet, but something kept her grounded. Suddenly beset with further nervous sweats, she could see the glimmer of the Chief's pendant. He was already an imposing man, enormous in stature and a remarkably capable warrior besides, but when he channeled the Bear's ability to instill terror, it was almost impossible to move.

Now, her parents' expressions made more sense.

Chief Azantt tsked his tongue and looked down at Kamataa with a disdainful grin. He held out a gesturing hand to her parents. "I've done nothing that they have not deserved for hiding your true nature from us." He turned his menacing smile to them. "Is that not right, Taanta, Hetren?" He growled at them, not unlike a wild beast, and they nearly fell on their backs with fright. Azantt did not hold back his laughter.

"Stop!" Kamataa pleaded with a shaking breath. "Please, my Chief! They've done nothing wrong! *I've* done nothing wrong!"

Ignoring her pleas, Azantt stayed his laughter and walked calmly to Kamataa's mother before viciously smacking her across the face with the backside of his hand, knocking her to the ground in a heap.

"Mother!"

Azantt grabbed the felled woman by a clump of hair and snarled in her face, speaking just loud enough for Kamataa to hear. "Is it true, Hetren? Have you done nothing wrong? Did you truly *not* hide the existence of an Eclipseborn from us?"

Hetren spat out blood at the Chief's feet and looked fearfully up at him. "Please, Chief Azantt. She is my daughter."

"I would not allow a snow leopard into my home and call it my child. Why would I allow you to keep a similar beast in yours?"

"I am *no* beast!" Kamataa yelled, forcing herself to her feet, breaking free of the terror holding her at bay.

"No?" Azantt said, turning to her with a raised eyebrow. He dropped her mother to the ground and ambled back across the length of the room, towering over Kamataa in so doing. He was a giant standing atop an anthill, and Kamataa was the one ant biting at his toe. "I must admit that I had been perplexed at your parents' avoidance of you all these years. For ages, I had watched you roam this village, your parents never at your side, often twenty paces in back or in front, if anywhere at all. It was enough for me to wonder, 'Hmm, are they merely poor parents? Why do they fear their own daughter?' But now, it all makes sense. Not only was the answer to both questions, 'yes,' but now, having read the missive sent by An Kehzan, I have full awareness of the threat they pose to our people."

"I'm no *threat!*" Kamataa was suddenly gripping her spear. Faintly, she heard a murmuring chuckle from deep within the Chief's throat. The irony was not lost on her.

"Kamataa, please..." her father said in a soft voice, reaching out to her helplessly. "Put the spear down. This is what we've earned. Do not make this worse for us."

What they've *earned. Worse for* them. *But what about what* I've *earned?* Kamataa grimaced at her father's words. "I invoke my right of challenge," she growled at the Chief, ignoring her father's pleas. From the corner of her eye, she could see Taanta dip her head in disappointment.

Azantt tilted his head back and unleashed a burst of uproarious laughter. The room could have collapsed in on them for the raucousness of the noise. "You've certainly raised a resilient girl, Taanta," he said, wiping away an amused tear from his eye. "I'll give you that much."

Kamataa maintained eye contact with the Chief, fighting back the residual terror that still permeated her from his influence.

"Tell me, then, girl," Azantt demanded with a menacing calmness. "On what grounds do you invoke the right of challenge?"

Straightening her posture and gripping her spear tighter, Kamataa gritted her teeth and said, "On the grounds to remain in the village despite my being Eclipseborn. To assert that I am no different now than I was before I left for my Trial." She stopped to pass another glance at her parents, both of whom were beset by shock and terror that had little to do with the Chief's influence. "And to ensure that my parents will face no punishment for my birth."

Crossing his arms, Azantt's smile vanished, replaced instead with a scowl that needed no use of the Bear's power to instill fear. "You would ask us to spit upon everything our ancestors have told us of your filth."

"I would ask," she asserted, "that you recognize that nothing written of the Eclipseborn is based in any fact and that you would judge me on my own merits."

"You have not passed your Trial."

"I passed *a* Trial," Kamataa corrected. "And just as those who failed their Trials in earnest, I still possess the right to invoke challenge to assert my place in the Lake Tribe."

Azantt was quiet for a moment. A moment that stretched into several long, considering seconds. He narrowed his eyes, grinding his teeth. His fingers tapped impatiently along his arms as though he were loosening them in anticipation of having to wring her throat. But as those long seconds finally ceased, he sighed deeply, still meeting her gaze with antipathy, and said, "Fine."

Kamataa felt a grin on her face and managed to dissipate the Chief's invocation of terror entirely. Seconds later, she noticed the glimmer on Azantt's pendant fade to nothing, and in her periphery, she saw her parents regain their composure, though they still remained prone on the floor.

"At sundown, by boat on the Big Lake," Azantt said, lacking the usual formality he allowed for such instructions and doing little to veil his disgust. "First to five touches. You will face my champion there. Do not be a second late." And then he pushed past her with a brawny shoulder, nearly tearing the door off the frame of the house as he exited. He didn't even bother closing it.

It was a small victory, but a victory, nonetheless. But when that momentary presence of pride vanished, Kamataa felt the nervous tremors once again overtake her hands.

A weak voice called from behind her. "What have you done…"

Turning, Kamataa saw her mother looking up at her fearfully, her teeth stained red as crimson streams trickled down from her nose. Hurrying to her side, she tried to help her up but was met with resistance immediately. Her father shuffled over instead to help Hetren to her feet as the final spark of burning wood popped in response to a dying flame.

"Mother…" Kamataa said with clenched fists. "I *have* to do this. For me. For us."

"For you, maybe," Hetren murmured. Her voice was somewhat nasally; her nose appeared broken. "We should not have allowed you to take the Trial."

"You barely allowed me as it was!"

"Kamataa," her father said, holding his hand up for silence. He shook his head remorsefully. "This is not going to go the way you think. Even if you win your challenge, Azantt will not honor your request."

"He must," Kamataa asserted, barely able to keep her voice down. "We're the only Tribe that allows this to those who do not pass their Trial. If Azantt does not honor the right of challenge, then what does that say about us as a Tribe?"

Again, Taanta shook his head. "You're different from those who did not pass their Trials. It's not the same."

"I *am* the same." She rushed to grip the sleeves of her father's shirt, pulling him close to her despite all resistance. "I'm the same person who has been your daughter for eighteen years. And I'm not going to let a false superstition deny me my place in this Tribe for reasons beyond my godsdamned control!"

It was silent, save for the rough and ragged breaths that painfully escaped Hetren's nose. Parents and child alike regarded each other with hesitant aplomb. Kamataa's hands shook as she released her father from her clutches, and she watched in continued helpless silence as her parents again backed further away from her.

"You always knew," she whispered to them. Tears began to well, and she couldn't be sure if the tears were of anger or sadness. "You were always afraid of me. But you never said anything." She could hardly bear to continue looking at her parents. The tremors in her fists extended throughout her limbs, and for an extended while, the only sound in the room was her own sniveling as she pushed the tears again. "Why?" she finally asked. "Why did you not say anything?"

She heard nothing. When she looked back up, her parents only stood huddled in the corner, embracing each other for comfort, not even bothering to look back at her.

Kamataa turned away. She wasn't going to wait for an answer. She knew they had no answer to give. Biting her lower lip with disgust, she made for the door.

"If you fail," her mother's voice warned, "it will only be worse for you. Worse for *us*."

That stopped Kamataa in her tracks. She had been reaching for the door but backed away. Still not deigning to turn to face her parents, she only said, "Then I guess I better not fail." As she reached for the door again and opened it, she half-turned her head, still not catching sight of her parents, not that she had a desire to now. "For what it's worth, I *am* doing this for you both, as well. Whether you choose to accept that is up to you."

She exited the house with spear in hand onto an empty pathway, accompanied only by the fading sounds of her parents weeping.

At sunset, the Big Lake was an almost ethereal sight.

In the golden hour, the last remnants of sunlight glinting off the surface of the water were enough to forget the blood which had been spilled in its depths over the ages. Feuds were settled here, battles were won here, enemies were conquered here.

And on this day, Kamataa hoped to be fully accepted into the Tribe here.

With spear in hand, she ventured to the shoreline of the Big Lake alone. The last few hours were spent in solitude, in reflection. Hoping that what she was about to do would be worth it, even if none would appreciate it.

When she reached the shoreline, she found Chief Azantt standing in wait, his arms crossed in evident dissatisfaction. He was perhaps the only one upon whom the setting sun would not shine in gold. Instead, he was a creation of cloud and shadow, remaining only where the sun chose not to shimmer. As Kamataa drew closer, his scowl only deepened.

Beside him stood a tall and lean spearman with a pronounced scar traveling down his angular face from brow to chin, who she knew as Sehtohnn. Kamataa had only encountered him in passing a handful of times, hardly saying more than a few words to him over the years. Nevertheless, she held nothing against him—he seemed a nice enough fellow. A savvy warrior, he was a Bearsign imbued with Restoration, which made anyone difficult in a scrap. It made all the sense in the world, then, that he was appointed Azantt's primary enforcer and champion.

Rounding out the assembled group was a young woman with whom Kamataa wasn't familiar. She was examining the status of the boats along the shoreline, so Kamataa could only assume that she was the officiant, who would confirm touches and eventually victory and defeat.

She stopped in front of them, the world quiet save for the rippling of the water and birds cawing overhead. Acknowledging that her fate was to be determined upon this lake, she took one final glance at the rays of gold glowing on the water's surface, watching the glint of light trickle along the gentle currents, an inviting gesture of promise. It was said that the reason Lake challenges were settled upon the surface of the Big Lake was due to the way the sunlight plays with the surface water, almost as a divine indication of where best to settle disputes. Whatever the reasoning was, the middle of the Lake during sunset had long been the tradition, and she was hardly one to rebuff such tradition.

Feeling herself to be ready, Kamataa nodded to Azantt. "Chief," she said, veiling her disdain for him well enough, all things considered. There was still some decorum and formality to be displayed here, and she was not about to repeat the tone of earlier conversations in mixed company. "I am here to invoke my challenge."

Azantt regarded her in cold silence, still folding his arms with a deep scowl, before acknowledging her invocation with a simple grunt. "I'm sure that you understand the rules. The first to five touches is declared the victor." He gestured to Sehtohnn. "And, as I am certain you've gathered, Sehtohnn will act in my stead as champion." Next, he pointed behind him to the woman tending to the boats. "And Cleeoh will act as officiant."

The Chief's body language was notably uncaring and disinterested. Kamataa could tell that he was long set on the outcome of the evening, and thus couldn't even be bothered to explain the stakes of the challenge, as was the custom, and as she had seen several times before.

Azantt had half-turned and was ready to head for the boats when Kamataa called out, "Just as confirmation: if I win this challenge, I have your word that I will be allowed to remain in this Tribe with no consequences to my family, yes?"

Stopping dead in his tracks, the Chief craned his head back in her direction, the sunlight still doing little to deter him from being painted in shadows. His scowl still virulent, he narrowed his eyes at Kamataa before finally nodding. "On my word."

Kamataa was hesitant to press forward with her next question, but the stipulations and consequences had to be plainly stated. "And...if I lose?"

Her question was met only with silence. Azantt showed no inclination to speak further. He only sank back into his shadows, nudging his champion to follow.

Without missing a beat, Sehtohnn followed, though not before nodding respectfully to Kamataa. If she didn't know any better, she'd have thought a slight reassuring smile passed his lips.

Drawing a deep breath, Kamataa followed the group, sparing a glance back in the direction of her parents' hut. The sunlight no longer reached it.

Passing by Cleeoh, she boarded her boat and began to paddle out to the center depths, following her host of three in turn. The water was serene and calm, which was just about the only thing in this Tribe that did not run with tempers flared. It was only party to those tempers and the results thereof.

When they finally reached the center of the Big Lake, Kamataa and Sehtohnn positioned their boats in front of one another. Carefully, they both stood atop their vessels, Azantt and Cleeoh filing in on either side. The ripples of the water jostled the boats from side to side, nearly knocking both combatants off their feet. Half the difficulty of these conflicts was merely staying afoot without falling into the depths.

At last finding a balanced position, Kamataa held her blunted spear at the ready, the tip meeting that of Sehtohnn's, while they patiently awaited Cleeoh's all-clear. Heat radiated from the last vestiges of sunlight as beads of sweat trickled down the side of Kamataa's face, where the fading light hit the hardest. A large shadow was cast beyond her, overtaking the Chief, who sat patiently in wait.

Sehtohnn locked eyes with her, nodded once more in respect, and wordlessly mouthed, "Good luck."

Kamataa did not respond. She remained as focused as she could be, her heart beating louder and louder in her ears. Splashes of water began to soak her feet as the seconds dragged into minutes, the final chirps of daybirds fading into the distance. In her periphery, she could see Cleeoh slowly raise a hand, reaching skyward. Kamataa's fingers twitched along the shaft of her spear, her balance threatening to give way, and all the while, it seemed Sehtohnn's eyes were trying to pierce her with as great of ferocity as his spear would.

Deep breaths. In. Out. In. Out. In—

"Begin!" Cleeoh shouted.

Before she could react, Sehtohnn nicked her arm in a swift motion, a light tap that she only barely felt. Whether it was the adrenaline preventing her from feeling it in earnest, she was unsure.

"One to Sehtohnn!"

Shaking her head back to focus, Kamataa feinted to the left, back to the right, then went back to the left, catching the head of Sehtohnn's spear on a wide swing. She pushed in on his guard, straining for the effort, before finding herself in line with both his arm and leg. In a short arc, she swung up and down, hitting both appendages in quick succession, nearly knocking him off the boat entirely.

"Two to Kamataa!"

Noticing her opponent to still be off-balance, driven to a knee, Kamataa went back on the offensive, pressing again on Sehtohnn's guard, sending cascading splashes of water into the body of the boat. The lanky spearman had yet to regain his balance; seeing this window of opportunity, Kamataa jabbed quickly, finding a home in his ribs.

"Three to Kamataa!"

But she was careless. Just as soon as she had connected with Sehtohnn's ribs, Kamataa realized that she had overextended herself, and before she had time to make a note of her opponent's knowing grin, he had reached out, trapped her spear underneath his arm where she could not pull it free, and jabbed right back at her, hitting her square in the collarbone.

"Two to Sehtohnn!"

And then in the chest.

"Three to Sehtohnn!"

And the shoulder.

"Four to Sehtohnn!"

Desperately, Kamataa growled as she tugged hard on the shaft of her spear to draw it free, but her opponent was too strong, too crafty.

And she needed to be craftier. One more touch and it was over.

She dodged a jab aimed at her shoulder. Then a follow-up swing at her neck by ducking under it. The swing left Sehtohnn slightly off-balance, but she still could not pull her spear free. A backhanded return swing nearly had her in the head, but she barely avoided the touch.

Sehtohnn recentered himself, holding tight to Kamataa's spear with one arm while still deftly wielding his own in his other.

She knew she couldn't keep dodging him forever. She was defenseless. And after a dodge of successive jabs, she quickly realized that she did not have much more time to spare.

So, she got crafty.

She released the resistance on the end of her spear, sending Sehtohnn backward from the momentum, and just as he had stolen away her weapon, she got a hand on his. Gripping the center of the spear with two hands, she moved quickly and *snapped* the wooden shaft, removing the blunted blade and holding it as a makeshift half-spear. Quickly recognizing that her opponent was readjusting with her own spear, she hurriedly swung the half-spear at his leg, making rough contact before adjusting her grip and throwing it at his chest in a final desperation move.

It hit.

"Five to Kamataa!" Cleeoh shouted with her arm raised high. "Victory goes to Kamataa!"

A wave of relief washed over Kamataa as she allowed herself to collapse back into her boat amidst of torrent of splashing waves. She did it. *She did it.*

Silent laughter ruminated in her tired throat as she drifted along aimlessly on the currents of the Big Lake. Faintly, she could hear a boat paddling alongside her. She peered her head over to the side to see Sehtohnn looking down at her, nodding to her with a grin.

"Hell of a move," he said earnestly. "Risky as hell, but I must commend you for it. Well done."

Pushing herself out of the puddles within her vessel, Kamataa nodded appreciatively to Sehtohnn. "And hell of a fight on your part. Another minute and you'd have had me."

"Would that I could have gone another minute, then. Oh, and here." He handed her spear back to her, no worse for wear than when she was first relieved of it. "You do owe me a new one now, though."

Kamataa smiled and watched as he and Cleeoh paddled away, leaving her with the Chief. She peered over in his direction to see him silently gliding her away along the Lake's surface. That scowl had still not broken, though it was accompanied now by a state of what passed for surprise or shock.

"Chief Azantt," she said, still catching her breath. "Trusting that you are true to your word, I would—"

The words stopped in her throat, and a searing heat burned in her stomach. She looked down, and before she could realize, Azantt was pulling his spear from her gut, blood pouring from the wound in a violent river.

Distantly, she could hear cries of protest, fading further and further away as the words drew closer and closer. Her vision grew dim, the images before her becoming fuzzy and ill-defined. The Chief disappeared from view, rejoining the shadows where he made his home, and the last thing she felt was a forceful shove sending her to the depths.

Deeper she sank, trailing a stream of red until the darkness consumed her.

And then the warmth of light revived her.

Kamataa awoke along the shoreline beyond the reaches of the eastern village. The subtle nudge of nocturnal insects crawling on her skin drew her to attention.

Jerking her head upward, she sat up in a panic, hacking up lake water into the cold earth. She looked to the sky and found herself in nighttime darkness, the world still alive around her. Running her hands along her body, she tried desperately to convince herself it was all a bad dream. *But if it was a dream, why am I soaked?* she thought. *Why did I wake up alongside a lakebed?*

And, more importantly, why was there a gaping hole in the front of her shirt but no wound to accompany it?

Shocked, she shot to her feet, breathing in a heavy and deep panic. She ran her hand along her stomach and felt nothing there. No pain, no bleeding, and *no wound*.

"Impossible," she said hurriedly. "Impossible. I must be going crazy. I…No. Impossible."

But she remembered so distinctly the spear entering her, spilling her lifeblood into the depths of the Big Lake, joining countless warriors of ages past.

"I should be *dead*."

Dead by Azantt's hand. Despite her victory in the challenge. The Chief had no intention of holding to his word. And if he was so quick to betray his word to her…

"…No," she whispered. "Mother! Father!"

She ran as hard as she could back to the village.

The village was fast asleep by the time she returned, but her parents' house was recently awake.

Out of breath by the time she arrived, Kamataa stood in shock as the door was smashed to nothing, reduced to little more than splinters on the earth.

"Mother! Father!" she called out but received no response.

The interior of the house was deathly quiet as she entered. The air was still and stagnant, a pervasive aura overtaking the home. Nothing stirred within—not a flame nor a mouse, not even a whistle of the wind. Carefully taking step after step, Kamataa crept through her childhood home, fighting back the tears as the inevitable became reality the further she walked.

The floor grew more viscous and stickier as she drew closer to her parents' bedroom. The shakes returned as she witnessed the sight she had feared the most.

Splashes of crimson and black adorned the walls in a splattered pattern. Bloodied spear ends and smith hammers lay on the ground, the red upon them still fresh, yet to have dried.

And at the far end of the room, her father's head was caved in, her mother's face in shock as her entrails billowed out of her and onto the bedsheets.

Kamataa fell to her knees, wanting to scream but finding not the means to do so. The contents of her stomach rushed out of her as she retched on the floor, her own fluids joining those of her parents. She felt utterly frozen.

"I'm sorry," she sobbed into the bloodied floor. "I'm so sorry. It should have only been me."

And An Kehzan's words rang once more in her ears: *"You will serve our Land only when you lay beneath the earth!"*

Slowly, she pushed herself up to her knees, running her hands through the loose blood on the floor. The sobs began to break, the tears began to stop, and she allowed herself a long glance at her parents' savaged bodies.

"...No," she said, spreading the blood over her face. She reached for the smith's hammer. "Our Land is best served with me upon it."

She made her way out of the shattered remains of her home and into the night, hammer in hand, to complete her greatest service to her Tribe.

Azantt's hut loomed ahead, much more distinctly than the surrounding homes. In a sense, it was very emblematic of the Chief as a person: a dwelling of greater excess for a man of greater excess.

The darkness shone brightly as Kamataa approached the hut and kicked in the door, caring little for who heard. An immediate stirring roused the dwelling to life, and at the first indication of movement near her, Kamataa swung wildly, the hammer finding a home with a sickening crunch. She turned only briefly to see a woman slumped on the ground, very little remaining of what was once her face.

Following the trail of rummaging, Kamataa found her way to Azantt's bed chambers, which came complete with rich elk and wolf pelts on the floor and walls and a blanket made entirely of northern snow leopard, one of the rarest pelts in the Land. Beneath those sheets sat Azantt, startled to awareness.

"Kamataa?" he said with shock. "You should be *dead*."

"So should you," she snarled. And she pounced on the Chief, driving the hammer through his skull, leaving it wedged as it crushed bone and brain matter alike.

Azantt fell in a heap. It was far quicker than he deserved.

Kamataa stood over his body in silent regard. She thought she should have felt something. Anger, hatred, revenge.

But she felt nothing. That realization made her smile.

She exited the bedroom to find a young boy, probably five or six years younger than her, huddled over the dead woman's body. Probably his mother, now that she thought about it. *It never occurred to me that Azantt started a family*, she thought, shrugging it off.

The boy looked up at Kamataa, tears streaming from his eyes. "M…Momma…" he said, choking back fearful sobs. "Please, help m-m…my momma…"

Kamataa smiled at the boy and said, "No." And began to walk out of the hut.

"W-w-wait!" The boy tugged at her, but Kamataa pushed him off. He was resilient, though, and held tight to her arm. "M-m-my poppa, too! Please! He's the Chief!"

"And may he continue to serve the Land in so doing, when he lay far beneath the earth."

The boy released her arm, and she heard him collapse into a heap. "Please! Please! Why won't you help us?"

Kamataa laughed deeply to herself. "Haven't you heard? I'm the Eclipse-born. A trickster and fiend are all I am."

Without a further word, she left the hut. And then the village. The Tribe. Everything she ever knew. And she did not look back.

INTERLUDE

The Way to Dusty Death

The Year 1581 Anno Salvatoris
40 Years After the Settling

To his own surprise, Aritz's heart was pounding.

Few had ever displayed the gall to force him to stare down the barrel of a gun. Fewer still the courage to do so with his own weapon.

But as he sank deeper into the abyss of his oaken chair, nails scratching at the armrests, Aritz a Mata felt a sense of concern he had not experienced in a long time.

Because he knew the capabilities of the woman holding the gun to his face.

Beyond the sightline of the flintlock, she was smiling—but her eyes were overflowing with malice. Her sharp glare burrowed daggers into Aritz's chest, the flame within those dark pools matching the flames of her vibrant red hair.

She truly looked the same as she had twenty-five years ago. Of course, it was all a disguise, and Aritz knew that. But she was every bit the same woman who had fought beside him during the Settling. Every bit the same woman who had helped him topple those savage spellbinders in one fell swoop. Every bit the same woman who betrayed him when it was all done.

And yet.

He had found her dead.

But here she was, the gentle seaside breeze wafting her hair along as it passed through the opened window. Stray papers fluttered on the desk behind her, catching on the splinters loosed by Aritz's enraged fist. His chambers felt larger than ever, the door a beacon at the end of a long tunnel, and everything between him and there—his war map, his trophies, his desk, his assailant—were all impediments offering nothing but memories of bloodied triumph, all at once ensuring that any attempted escape would be little else but a quick way to a dusty death.

His assailant noted his wandering eyes and slowly backed away, pulled his flintlock up, pointed the barrel toward the ceiling. She seemed relaxed, leaning against the edge of his solid wood desk, that menacing grin still plastered across her face. And then, of all things she could have said, what she decided on was: "How nice to see you, Aritz."

Somehow, that only managed to unsettle him even further. The images flashed once more in his mind. Arnao and Luzia whimpering with fear into their mother's breast. Lucrecia staring at him with dead eyes, asking why he had done this. His beautiful wife's skull caved in, trailing rivers of blood, his children's limp bodies soon to follow.

White marble painted red.

An orchestra of shattered screams.

His shadow, his silent phantom, at the center of it all.

And here she stood before him, offering pleasantries while he was weighing his options of how best to wring her neck before she had a chance to raise the flintlock against him.

Instead, all Aritz could do was shake with fury, frozen in disbelief at the casual nature of the beast staring calmly at him.

"...Why?" he managed to growl. "Why have you done this? My wife, my children...they played no part in this." The fury in him began to rise, the blazes within him pushing him to his feet in the face of an unthreatened entity. "They did not deserve that. They did not deserve such brutality. And yet you subjected them to such atrocity." He balled his fists and gritted his teeth, feeling the imminent volume of his voice rising in his throat. "They were good, they were kind, and you *SLAUGHTERED THEM!*" His whole body quivering, he wanted to rush the woman, drive her to the ground, dash her skull into the floorboards until she was little else but a red pulp. But his legs remained stupidly frozen.

A deep growl rumbled in the back of his throat, threatening to rend the room asunder with its quakes. A fury of hot white flashed before his eyes, a devil rising inside him, promising him vengeance and retribution. But still, he could not find himself to move. His growl only grew louder until he bellowed at the top of his lungs, "*YOU GODDAMNED MONSTER!*"

The faint scurry of servants and cleaners hushed from outside his chambers. Long had it been since Aritz had instructed them—under penalty of death, or worse—that they were not to interrupt him and his matters under any circumstances unless explicitly bidden to do so. To this day, they obeyed him just as much as they feared him.

For decades, he was so accustomed to fear allowing him to do as he pleased. The threat of his temper, embellished as it was (by his own design), was enough to grant him whatever he desired, when he desired it. To him, it had been unthinkable that any remained who did not fear the name Aritz a Mata.

But he was wrong. The one person he had never found to fear him was here, and none were coming to save him.

She was undeterred by Aritz's fiery voice. She did not flinch at his bellow. She remained just as she was, staring just as much venom into his eyes as he was into hers.

Still holding tightly to the gun, she sauntered away, off to the side of the chamber where Aritz displayed his trophies. She bore the expression of a patron at one of the museums back home in Acraria, many of which had displays similar to the collection Aritz kept for himself.

Though it seemed the perfect opportunity, Aritz did not rush her while her guard was down. It was as though a presence kept him in place. The very one he had used in order to enforce his own will upon his subjects.

Fear. For once, *he* was frozen by fear.

The woman silently examined Aritz's collection, softly tsking as she shook her head with amusement. "And you would deign to call *me* a monster," she said.

As his nostrils flared, Aritz snarled at the remark. "What?" he barked.

She redirected her gaze back to him, angling the barrel of the flintlock to rest on her shoulder. Gesturing to the trophies, she scoffed. "For how much you object to the Tribes' existence, you certainly enjoy displaying reminders of their existence."

Aritz's fury quelled slightly as he narrowed his eyes at the woman. He couldn't help but feel amusement at the comment. He flashed a grin as a sudden gust of wind blew his graying hair into his face. Moving the strands from out of his eyes, he shook his head at her. "They are reminders not of their horrid existence, but of my triumph over them. My greatest triumph. All the more reason to keep them for myself."

"For yourself and no one else, it would seem."

"It would seem so, yes."

The woman chuckled. "I suppose when you keep a secret history to yourself, you can create whatever story you choose with it." She turned back to the shelves, muttering something inaudible to herself.

"The story matters little when the people care not for the truth."

"Truth is relative when you create your own truth."

Aritz grimaced. "*My* truth is *the* truth," he growled.

"A convenient lie for a convenient tale," the woman said. She ran a finger along the edges of the shelves, kicking up particles of dust that danced in the waning golden light billowing in through the window. "History, culture, accountability—of what use are these in the founding of a nation? The sins of an empire are always many and always stained in the blood of the lesser. The victors never see the atrocities they committed; they care only for the victory they perceive. A civilization falls just as quickly as another rises to take its place. Trampled underfoot lay the memories of times long gone. And scattered to the wind is a convenient little thing called the 'truth.' As long as they can keep their subjects stupid and ill-informed, any despot can cast aside what is real in favor of what they can attribute to themselves as victory and glory."

She paused, taking in a long, silent gaze at the gathered memorabilia before hawking and spitting all over one of the picture frames in disgust.

From where he was standing, Aritz could barely see that the frame contained the photograph of him and her, twenty-five years past.

"Of course," she said, "you're no victor. You're just a little monster who twisted the truth enough to fashion himself a god."

"Is that what you think?" Aritz asked, raising his eyebrows. Softly, he could not help but chuckle. "I twist nothing. My people needed a history behind which they could rally, one which stood for the dream that our land promises. For what you deem me a monster, I call survival. We were a people in need of new land, and your savage kin were selfishly trying to keep it for themselves."

"Pretty words," the woman said with a sneer. "I recall one of the Ferrandan stage actors speaking similarly recently. The one who plays the cattle wrangler who goes off to shoot and kill those 'savages?' I knew not that you were also a playwright, Aritz."

"*Pheh*," Aritz spat. "That matters not. *You* knew the cost when you joined with me. Civilizations are won with blood spilled, not entreaties for peace. A people do not celebrate a nation which won itself by flowery words; they care only for the life of a great evil to be emptied. A proud people honor not the word of the sophist, but they revere the exploits of their generals as they would their God. And *that* is what I am. I am their Founder, and if they revere me as their God, then I would gladly take up that title."

The longer he spoke, the wider the woman's grin became. Shaking her head with amusement, she clicked the hammer of the flintlock once more, pointing it back in Aritz's direction, and said plainly, "And you are the one who proved a god can be felled."

The floorboards creaked as Aritz paced in place, once again contemplating whether his life would be forfeit in a span of moments. Still, he managed to force a grin, that same grin he had exhibited time and again to those who had the better judgment to fear him. "And you think," he said, "that you could fell a god yourself?"

"I don't see why not," the woman said with a vicious sneer. "Need I remind you that felling a god was my idea, to begin with?"

"Your idea, my actions."

"Ah, yes. Your *actions*. As I'm sure that you'll attest that this wall of glory was all due to your *actions*."

Aritz raised an eyebrow. "If not mine, then whose?"

She smiled. Still as a statue yet menacing as a wild beast. Her simple act of baring her teeth carried with it a threat of something vile. It was the way it did not quite reach her eyes or how her eyes did not reflect the same emotion. While her smile called for peace, her eyes screamed for death.

Savior's breath, Aritz thought. *I didn't think it possible to be so unsettled by a smile.*

Turning back to the shelves, the woman playfully tinkered with the placement of the various trophies and photographs. "A good general knows when to send his subordinates to do his dirty work and when to take credit for their exploits." She touched the set of half-spears that rested on one shelf. "Besting a Tribal warrior in close-quarters combat with no such training. Aritz did it." In one quick motion, she knocked the spears off the shelf, the resounding clang and thud of steel and wood echoing through the hollow chamber.

Next, she played with the mysterious mask Aritz had kept mounted. "Discovered a keepsake of the Haunted Tribe, long-thought lost to the invasion? Aritz did it." She threw the mask to the ground, allowing it to shatter into several shards, which either shot into the air or slid across the floor. Two fragments of the adornment nearly found themselves in Aritz's foot.

She eyed the picture frame containing one of his most memorable kills. "Felled a giant beast. Aritz did it." The frame fell to the ground in a shriek of broken glass.

"The discovery of mysterious ores from the mountains? Aritz did it." Thrown to the ground.

"Ornate arrows found within the forest? Aritz did it." Thrown to the ground.

"A pelt skinned from the rare snow leopard? Aritz did it." Thrown to the ground.

One by one, she dismissed Aritz's accomplishments, violently throwing each trophy to the ground, many shattering upon impact, others damaging in other respects. But with each prize discarded, Aritz's fury only grew further and further. His voice caught in his throat, his anger so virulent that it had nearly silenced him. As much as he wanted to charge the woman and show her just what he was capable of, the threat of his flintlock aimed at him prevented him from doing so.

Soon enough, his trophy shelf was entirely empty, his prized possessions all strewn about the floor in broken pieces. The woman turned back to him, a clear sense of accomplishment adorning her wicked smile, and laughed in his face. Slowly, she made her way back to him, her approach frightening him back to the comfort of his seat, the shards of broken memorabilia crunching beneath her heavy boots.

With flintlock still in hand, she leaned in closely, drawing a deep breath in Aritz's face. "Ah, the smell of cowardice," she said longingly. "If I didn't know any better, I would say I now know the *true* Aritz a Mata. A sniveling opportunist hiding behind the exploits of better men." She raised a hand and touched her cold skin to his stubbled cheek.

Aritz winced at the touch. The very hand which had stolen away the life of his wife and children.

She sneered at his discomfort. "But I know you better than that, Aritz. I know you are much more than that. Are you a god? No. But you are a general, true. And in fact, I would go so far as to call you a 'great' general." Slowly, she turned and walked over to the war map, the final lasting memory of Aritz's campaigns against the natives.

Aritz gripped tightly the armrest of his chair once again, narrowing his eyes at the woman. Her words stung at him, the label of being a "great general" bringing with it a sense of acrid accusation.

Absently, the woman ran her finger along the outline of the island, back before Aritz named the land Ferranda. As she stared with solemnity at the overly-detailed south and the under-detailed north, she once again said, "A good general knows when to take credit for the exploits of his subordinates." She froze, ridded herself of her smile, replacing it instead with a deep scowl, and looked back at Aritz. "A *great* general knows when to deny the genocide of a native people and instead paint *them* as the villains."

Aritz's breath caught in his throat. "How little you know, woman," he growled, his voice barely carrying. "Did you not want this, yourself?"

The woman scoffed, narrowing her eyes. "It matters not what I want or wanted. What matters now is the truth." She gestured her free hand to the mess of shattered memories on the floor. "This...this is your lie. But your 'truth?' That lies right here." She prodded an angry finger at the war map and then slowly made her way back to him. "What you are *truly* responsible for, the only thing that you yourself can claim to have done? It is *that*.

"*You* are the one who led the pogrom of the Tribes and destroyed an entire culture.

"*You* are the one who performed atrocities and painted them as glory.

"*You* are the one who spread lies about the nature of the Tribes, branding them as little more than wicked spellbinders capable of killing with but a single touch."

She chuckled to herself as Aritz fidgeted in his seat, trying not to display any outward fear but failing miserably. The wind roared once more as a gust blew in the woman's face, allowing her red hair to flow in billows of bright flame. Cold sweat dripped down his forehead, the salt stinging his eyes.

And all the while, the woman displayed nothing but cruel amusement. "It would be naïve of me to say that none of my people were capable of wickedness. I am more than capable of it, myself." Her smile returned, and it was just as unsettling. "But I have heard plenty of you since the invasion ended, Aritz a Mata. I've had much to learn of you these past twenty-five years. I know what kind of a man you truly are. And just as you reduced my people to little else but cinders, I will topple your empire from within and bare to your people the lie you created."

She held the flintlock back to his face and clicked the hammer once more. "Let's talk."

CHAPTER FOUR

Bad Memories

The Year 1556 Anno Salvatoris
15 Years After the Invasion

Thunder roared against a plane of pure darkness. Carried upon the flashes of lightning were screams which themselves carried pleas for mercy and promises of retribution. In that void, shadows barely discernible began to take shape, stone building itself up only to topple, a process which repeated with each subsequent thunderclap.

Sen was the only living thing in that nothingness. She felt herself drifting aimlessly, nudged along by an unseen force. Little persisted within her mind other than the drive to approach the collapsing stones.

If not to build them up, then to knock them back down again.

Lightning flashed again and again, at last illuminating the blackened scene. She knew this place; she was uncomfortably familiar with it. Never again did she want to look upon these splashes of red again, but the force continued to send her along to it, and she did not find it in her to voice any objections.

Like a painting in abstract, shades of crimson began to extend across a blank canvas of reinforced stone. Small holes began to burrow out from within the red tinges, and out with them came indistinct voices, faint at first but growing in intensity. As the nondescript noises escaped from the openings in the blank wall, they carried with them glimmers of light, the sole illumination in this void beyond the flashes of lightning.

Sen felt herself stop before the light, the voices beckoning her in sharper clarity but overlapping one another as though multiple people were attempting to speak to her simultaneously.

Despite the overwhelming wall of noise, she felt numb, unaffected by the encircling voices. They were swarming her like hornets, threatening to sting her into submission at the slightest of provocations.

But she would not be threatened. Her will was her own.

And, in response, the voices settled, finding respective homes in the columns of light, which again took shape as crumbling stones. But these stones were no longer inanimate. The voices joined them in turn, finding homes against the falling pillars as though to reinforce them, to prevent them from collapsing once more.

As these glowing pillars began to take more defined shapes, Sen similarly felt a glimmer within her hand extending outward, reaching both in front of and behind her. At first, it appeared to take the form of a spear until the materials of the light became corporeal sensations within her grip. Metal touched upon wood, the sharp end became a wide opening, and the sudden weight nearly pulled her down to the ground.

Whispers in her ears still manifested as the stone pillars took on human form. Lightning continually flashed, illuminating the stonework faces as the first whom Sen could recognize was Brin. Her brother startled into movement, bound at the wrists by the chains hanging from her blank canvas. Sharp, pained breaths snarled from his mouth as he stared up at her, all the fear in the world glowing in his eyes.

The rest of the scene filled in, the loudest clap of thunder accompanying a blinding spark of lightning.

Sen stood in Invader regalia, adorned in the bright shades of blue she had seen worn by all of the patrollers within the City. Acrid stenches fought at her nostrils as she surveyed the scene, finding herself within that alleyway where Brin's life was ended. Where Kamataa showed her hand.

She locked glares with Brin, feeling nothing from the fear which still exuded from him in discernible waves. The whispers in her ears ceased. And there was nothing else but the cacophony of silence. No revelry off in the distance, no casual conversations carrying along the wind. There was only this moment, punctuated solely by the panicked breaths screeching from Brin's throat.

With the long Deatharm in her hand, Sen did not have to think hard as to why.

She narrowed her eyes at her brother, still feeling little in the way of remorse, and looked to the reforming stone pillar to Brin's left, expecting to find herself in a mirrored image, the same image of her reaching in one last desperate attempt for Brin's pendant to share a final Memory with her dear brother. If she focused hard enough, she could still feel the glint of the ornament settling into her hand.

But as the light and stone took their final shape, it was not her own shadow upon whom she looked. The frame was wider and bulkier, revealing a musculature that Sen could never dream of having. Often times when she was just a child, she had envisioned his as the form of the Bear turned human. She wondered if the chains along the wall were secure enough to hold him in place. But there was no ferocity in her father's face, no anger or wrath.

All that Fannalhen exhibited was a morose acceptance of what was to come.

And still, Sen felt nothing at all. Only a cold blackness within her, an acceptance of her own that this was the path she was destined to take, that she was the hand determined to dole out death. A predestined route with no divergence, no forks, the end of a road long since illuminated for her.

From the whispers which had buzzed in her ears like gnats emerged separate entities of light—though dimmer than those which comprised her father and brother—which found their home to either side of her. Always did she feel their looming presence, but in this instance, they did not act as a means of intimidation but rather a force of encouragement.

Closely, the form to her right leaned in, a gentle hand resting atop her shoulder. A pair of lips stopped beside her earlobe and whispered softly, "Do it. It's what you were always meant to do."

Sen would recognize Koelhe's grating voice anywhere. But in this plane, this void, it was comforting, reassuring. *Yes,* Sen thought. *It is what I was always meant to do. What I always have done.*

A flash of her father's usual fire burst about his face, a radiant glow shimmering over him, and he reached out as far as the chain links would allow him in a desperate plea. "Sennalhat, don't!" he yelled, his voice hoarse, as though the act of speaking was difficult. Sen hadn't noticed until now that streams of blood were trickling out from holes in her father's shoulder and chest.

A dismissive tsking rang in her left ear with equivalent reassurance as Koelhe's voice. "Sen, Sen, Sen," Fann's voice said.

Sen didn't turn to look upon him, but in her periphery, she could just barely make out his mangled arm and misaligned nose.

"My mother is right. You know that. It's not only what you were *meant* to do." He paused, seemingly to take the time to chuckle. "Why, the blood is still warm upon your hands, isn't it?" The words came in a sharp and sinister whisper.

"You consigned them to their deaths yourself, didn't you?" Koelhe said, speaking as a loving grandmother would to her grandchild. "Theirs, and countless others, isn't that right?"

Blankly, Sen nodded. "Yes," she said. "It's true."

"No!" her father screamed, his voice breaking as more blood spurted from his chest. "Sen, don't listen to them!" The words came out as a croak. "Fight it!"

The Deatharm twitched in Sen's hand. It yearned for blood to be spilled, and hers was the hand that would spill it.

"Do you hear it, Curseborn?" Koelhe crooned. "The pleas for bloodshed? The need to fulfill your duty?"

"Their deaths were promised by you," Fann whispered. "Only fitting that you are the one to pull the trigger."

Her finger itched. She could not find it in her to disagree. Sen slowly averted her eyes from her father, locking eyes once again with Brin, watching his lips move but with no words to say.

Tears streamed from her brother's eyes, intermingling with the blood which escaped his lips, the flow of red that stained his chest.

"Do it," Koelhe commanded.

Distantly, Sen could hear fleeting voices, familiar voices. The words couldn't have belonged to her brother—nothing escaped his lips in the form of speech.

And yet, from far away, the echo of Brin's voice said, Why? Why does she do this all the time?

"Do it," Koelhe repeated, unperturbed by what Sen had heard. She wondered if Koelhe even heard it to begin with.

Slight hesitation bit at Sen, the arm holding the Deatharm not obeying when she instructed it to aim the weapon. She stared at her brother, also unperplexed by the sounds carrying his voice, and slowly she forced her arm to rise.

A second voice sighed. I don't know, son. I...I can't explain it any longer.

"Father?" Sen whispered softly, catching Fannalhen's eye but not finding any words escaping his lips. The hesitation returned, and Sen looked back and forth between her father and brother, stung by their voices.

We just have to accept that this is who she is, the second voice continued.

There was a pregnant pause, bitter wind howling in the silence. And the first voice responded, No. I won't.

"DO IT!" Koelhe and Fann screamed together.

Sen snarled, raised the Deatharm, and pulled the trigger twice in quick succession, taking her brother and father both between the eyes. They slumped together, their faces frozen in shock as trails of blood streamed down the bridges of their noses, the pillars of stone and light which once comprised them once again crumbling to nothing.

Sen fell to her knees, head on the ground, and growled a muffled scream into the voided earth.

"Good, Sen, good," Koelhe snickered, grabbing her beneath the right arm to pull her back to her feet.

From her left side, Sen felt Fann also pulling her up.

"Now, you must do it again," he said in a reminding tone.

Sen looked up, and where the pillars of stone that had once been her father and brother were, now stood two others from her Tribe. She could not place their names, but she had surely passed them by on her walks through the village over the years, or perhaps during her forays into the tavern. She could not say for sure. Regardless, the braid and face paint gave them away as members of the Stone Tribe.

Their expressions bore little else but anger and hatred towards her. They did not struggle against their chains, nor did they make any attempt to charge at her. They only stared and seethed.

"I should have known you would betray us like this," the one on the left said.

"Koelhe was right," the other said. "We should have listened to her long ago."

"Back to the earth with you, Curseborn!"

"You never should have been born!"

Sen grimaced, her hand twitching once more to claim another life.

Next to her, Koelhe was chuckling mightily. "Do you hear them?" she asked. "They would deny you your purpose."

Sen balled a fist, shook her head back into focus, and raised the Deatharm. "No," she said. "They'll deny me nothing."

Two shots rang out again, and two stone pillars collapsed once more.

Fann clapped his hands with exaggeration, laughing all the while, the sound echoing throughout the void along with the fading sounds of Sen's shots. "Remarkable!" he exclaimed. "Oh, how I've longed to see this!"

The stone pillars reformed and took the shape of an elder couple, their braids falling to their shoulders and loosely held wisps. Sen had seen them both a handful of times in conference with her father, usually with poorly disguised anger coating their words.

The older gentleman spat at Sen first, saying, "I wanted to run you through the moment you returned from your Trial. You were an abomination!"

"And I wanted to run *your father* through!" screamed the older woman. "Because of you, I no longer have the chance. I'll just have to settle instead for your mother and sister!"

"Like hell!" Sen yelled as she fired two more shots with perfect accuracy, watching the old couple crumble to dust before their pillars fell in equal measure.

"Yes, yes!" Fann cheered with ecstasy. "All I've ever wanted to see, realized!"

One by one, different faces spat the same threats and insults at Sen. People she only tangentially recognized, people she had had direct conversations with. Those who reviled her from near and afar, nameless and close companions both. The faces all blended together, all met with the same stroke of death at the slightest of provocations. The stench of smoke filled Sen's nostrils, the raucous laughter of Fann and Koelhe filling her ears. To watch all of these faces fall to her hand, she reveled in it. It felt right.

Until the next faces to show were Rantalha and Sharrabha. Sen's breath caught in her throat, her hands trembling. The last few rounds, she had not even waited for her victims to speak, but now? To fell members of her father's council?

Koelhe seemed to sense Sen's hesitation. "Come now, Curseborn," she said invitingly. "You already shot dead your father and brother. Who are these two, compared to them?"

The Deatharm shook in her hands. Sen winced and grimaced, snarling her teeth.

"And so, you lack the conviction to do even this," Rantalha said coolly. Just as always, he betrayed no emotions on his face: no anger, no hatred, no regret. Just the same stoic expression and the same sharp glare. "You have run from much, Sennalhat. Are you going to run from the only thing you were ever meant to do, as well?"

"He's right, Sen," Sharrabha said, showing at the very least concern for Sen, but nothing besides. "The Keepers have feared you since that day four years ago, and their fears were justified." She looked down, the chain links on her wrists going slack as she offered no resistance. "You've run from it for too long. For once, *embrace it.*"

Rantalha scoffed, though Sen could not tell if it was directed toward herself or Sharrabha. "Don't think to tell us that you allowed your brother and father's deaths for nothing," he said.

Sen barely registered pulling the trigger until she heard the stones crumpling to the ground. The only sound in her ears was that of Koelhe and Fann's snickering.

She turned her head, gritted her teeth, and a single pillar of stone and light erected itself in her periphery. The face was turned down, in no rush to lock gazes with her. But it didn't take long for Sen to realize who it was. She shut her eyes, damming up the impending tears.

"Sen," Tawa murmured, his head still turned down. He was nearly hanging from the chain links, given how slack he allowed his body to become.

Slowly, Sen steeled herself to face Tawa, unable to stop the tears from flowing.

"Where is he, Sen?" Tawa said. "What have you done to him?"

Sen shook her head. "Tawa…"

"Where is he?" he repeated. "Where is my son?"

"Tawa…" Sen said. "Please…"

With greater quickness than Sen had ever seen from him, Tawa lifted his head, his eyes just about glowing red with fury in contrast to the yellow paint on his face. "WHAT HAVE YOU DONE TO MY BOY?" he bellowed.

The tears flowed in rivers. Sen had never seen such rage on Tawa's face, and she knew it was justified. She wanted to look away, drop the Deatharm, let all of this end. Let Tawa take the retribution upon her that he deserved. Let herself be consumed by the justice of a father's grief.

But something kept her from looking away.

Just as something kept her from dropping the Deatharm.

Her arms moved with a will of their own, locking the weapon into place. Sen tried to move, but her legs did not obey. Her finger itched for the trigger, and just as she heard Tawa's angry and mournful bellows, the roar of the Deatharm clashed with them in equal measure.

Tawa slumped down along with his accompanying pillar, and Sen realized she was frozen. The threatening laughter drew closer to her, embracing her, constricting her.

"Don't run from it," Koelhe commanded, all semblance of joviality gone from her voice.

"Remember, it's a matter of life and death," Fann said, "and *you* are death."

Why? Sen thought, the words not making it to her lips. *Is any of this real? Why are you making me do this?*

As though reading her thoughts, Koelhe snaked along beside Sen, gripping her shoulder with talon-like nails. "We are doing this to *help* you," she said. "Sometimes, to find your path, you just need a push in the right direction." A deep chuckle rumbled in her throat, quaking in Sen's skull. "And sometimes, that means reliving that which tried to set you along that road."

"We're only here to ensure you follow that road," Fann said. There was an unspoken *Or else* in his tone that sent chills up Sen's spine.

Another pillar began to take shape, and though Sen tried desperately to look away, a flare of pain jolted through her, preventing her from doing so. She knew who would be next, and she didn't want to relive it. She didn't want to watch him die once again.

"You've done it once," Fann reminded her. "Why can't you kill him again, then?"

Sen tried to close her eyes, but something kept them pried open. She tried to loose the Deatharm from her grip, but no luck. She tried to turn it on herself, but it only remained pointed straight ahead.

Straight at Narva. At *her* Narva.

He looked like a ghost, his face paint removed to reveal the pale and pallid expression underneath, eyes sunken, face starting to decompose as trails of blood trickled down his mouth, red streams continuing to spurt from the holes in his chest.

Narva's lips were moving, but no sound escaped them. He offered no resistance, asked for no assistance. He simply stared with dead eyes at Sen, accepting his fate.

Sen tried to fight it, to prevent this death at least. But what was there to prevent? It was already her fault that Narva was gone.

But despite his passing, the Deatharm would not lower. It remained with a fixed line of sight on him. Sen couldn't drop it, no matter how hard she tried.

"Stop fighting it," Koelhe warned.

"*Pull the trigger*," Fann commanded.

"Narva..." Sen whispered, though she doubted he could hear her. "Forgive me."

The shot rang out against her will, but Narva did not fall. He merely stood there, taking the shot to the head, but refusing to fall.

The Deatharm roared again, firing another shot at him.

Then another. And another. And another.

What seemed an infinite volley peppered Narva, blood erupting with each point of impact until he was little more than a pulped mass riddled with holes.

And all the while, Sen was forced to watch as she willingly played a part in it all. She was finally released from the force gripping her, allowing herself to fall into the solid void just as Narva's stone pillar collapsed into bloodied dust.

Sen let out a series of breaths in halted, sobbed gasps, her chest constricting with the effort. Her stone canvas was riddled with splashes of dark red, taking no defined shape or explanation. But the story of the piece was clear enough to her.

It was her power. It was her calling. The Luck to stay alive, but to leave others dead in her wake.

The sharp force drew her back to the feet in a sudden lurch, spelling the end to her brief respite. The Deatharm sprang back into her hands, her attention driven to stare straight ahead.

"You're almost done, Curseborn," Koelhe said in a melodic tone. "Just one more task to go, and then you're free."

Sen had the sensation of shaking her head in defiance, but she knew they couldn't be anything more than phantom shakes.

--you brought misfortune on the village you never should have been born you brought misfortune on the village you never should have been born you brought misfortune on the village—

The words rang in Sen's ears like whispers on the wind, repeated in a loop with no start and end. They repeated over and over as two final pillars of light formed in the shape of her mother and sister.

Or what passed for them. Their eyes were soulless, their expressions blank. And like puppets, they only repeated in unison the phrase:

"You brought misfortune on the village you never should have been born you brought misfortune on the village you never should have been born—"

To either side of her, Fann and Koelhe once again slithered in, guiding her stiffened arms to aim at her targets.

"You heard them," Koelhe said. "Now, show them the misfortune you truly bring."

Pressure built on her trigger finger, prompting her to pull. But Sen fought against it. Pain flared in her hands, an inferno threatening to reduce her to cinders.

"Follow the road, Curseborn," Fann said threateningly.

Sweat poured down Sen's forehead from the effort of fighting against the invisible force. "N-n-no," she said, struggling to get the words past her lips. "P-please…"

"You brought misfortune on the village you never should have—"

"Do it, Curseborn," Koelhe commanded.

"N-no!" Sen responded, resisting the compulsion.

"You brought misfortune on—"

"The road!"

"Do it!"

"—never should have been—"

"Stop!"

"—on the village you never—"

"—Curseborn!"

"No!"

"—should have been born—"

A shot rang out, and then there was silence. The grips on Sen faded, and she sank into the void below her, hearing no crumbling stone as the shadows engulfed her.

Light burst in her eyes once again, but this time, it was not resultant of flashes of lightning, nor with it the roar of thunder. Instead, when Sen opened her eyes, she was greeted by the rush of a cooling breeze, the sharp and pristine sights of a vast mountain range. The Heart? *she thought.* Why am I here?

She was surrounded by people, a constant din of commotion assaulting her ears. But they were no longer the haunting and violent urges pushed upon her by Koelhe and Fann. Rather, she found herself subjected to words of praise, of encouragement, of congratulations. She recognized the faces.

The Keepers. The very same Keepers who so long ago had reviled her for having attempted her Trial. The very same who admonished her parents for allowing her to come in the first place. But now, the wise Ko Zaran was staring down at her with a jovial smile, his long white locks of hair flowing carefree in the wind, the valleys and wrinkles on his face growing wider as the grin on his face grew larger.

Something felt off. This couldn't have been a memory. Sen tried to look around, but for all her efforts, her line of sight remained fixed on the old Keeper in front of her.

No, *she thought.* Not again. Why is this happening again?

She feared what that invisible force would command her to do again, but nothing happened. No roar of thunder, no trail of blood, no tragedy. All that occurred was the kind touch of one of the wisest men in the land, trailing his thumb across her forehead—two circles, one encircling the other, a punctuated dot in the middle of it all.

Immediately, she recognized the traced shape.

Memory? Why am I...?

The familiarity started to sink in. And so did the points of contention. Sen hadn't knelt before Ko Zaran for her Trial; it was Ne Shanne who conducted it for her. Likewise, the snow leopard pelt worn by Ko Zaran on this day was far more elaborate than she remembered it being on the day of her Trial.

No, she remembered him wearing this pelt on a different day. And when Ko Zaran removed his hand from her forehead, it became all the clearer.

"Young Brinnolhat," he said. "You wandered into the depths of our domain, our mountains, the Heart of the Land..."

The old man's speech carried on, but Sen felt too shocked to listen further. His voice felt too distant to fully comprehend. This is...this is Brin's Memory. The day of his Trial. *If she could have gasped, she would have, but instead, she was dragged along to relive a moment that was not hers.* How is this...?

"...Today, you presented yourself as a child. Now, rise, as a man."

Sen—no, Brin rose, feeling a tight squeeze of the shoulders from Ko Zaran's broad hands. Sen felt a pang of guilt and regret for being in this moment. It was a day that she should have been there for. Distantly, she heard the old Owlsign drone on, but all she could focus on was how she never saw Brin achieve his greatest accomplishment.

On the one hand, part of her felt relief at having the opportunity to see this moment through Brin's eyes. But on the other...

I swore I would make this up to him. That I would change for him. That I would make it all right for him. It's been only days since then, and now he's gone. How is any of that right?!

"...Yours is a new chapter in the lineage of our Tribes, of our Land."

Brin received his pendant from Ko Zaran and was immediately turned around, his line of sight focusing on all the gathered Keepers. And then on his family. On their family.

Though what right do I have to call it *our* family when I did not want to be in this picture?

It was evident Brin wondered the same thing, his gaze intently focused upon the gap between Tez and their mother. Where Sen had so briefly stood, before she decided to slink away.

"Today, we welcome another of our flock into the realm of adulthood. May I present Brinnolhat, son of Fannalhen and Dennalhir, an Owlsign of the Stone Tribe!"

The applause roared in Sen's mind, the rush of family quick to embrace Brin in celebration. It was such a happy and joyous scene, emotions overwhelming even as she observed it all from afar in days long past, a fly on a wall in a distant house. Words of adulation and praise shook Sen to her core.

In such stark clarity, it was painful to see her father's face again. The wounds were still fresh and deep. But what hurt even more was seeing the beaming smile on Fannalhen's face. A proud, exuberant smile. One that she did not remember ever seeing as being directed toward her.

"What is it, Brin?" she heard Dennalhir ask.

The vision narrowed as though Brin were attempting to gaze far beyond what his sense of sight would allow. "Um, where...where is...?"

Her parents and sister looked around just the same, frustration immediately evident on their faces.

"What in..." Dennalhir muttered. "Where is Sen? Tez, where did your sister go?"

Sen saw Tez roll her eyes with annoyance before softly murmuring, "Oh, you've got to be kidding."

What started as seeming like a gift, to be able to see this moment at last, now felt like a punishment to Sen. A remembrance of her worst moment. One that she would never have the opportunity to repent for.

The vision continued, and Brin's head trailed down, his eyes watering, blurring the uneven path beneath his feet, his balled fists shaking at his sides. It tore Sen to shreds.

"Why?" he barked. "Why does she do this all the time?"

Everyone seemed taken aback. Brin was never one to show anger; he had always been too timid to do so. But they all knew his anger was justified, just as Sen knew. There were no words to say in response, for they knew not how to answer to a furious Brin.

But it appeared their father was keen to try. "I don't know, son. I..." He paused, chewing at his lower lip, his eyes glowing equally in frustration, annoyance, and remorse. "I can't explain it any longer." Fannalhen crossed his arms and paced a few steps, his gaze seeming to follow the mountain path they had traveled earlier where they had passed Ko Seln's tavern, the aromas of which had so enticed and lured Sen away from more important matters. "But it's an easy guess where she is right now," Fannalhen continued, shaking his head. "We just have to accept that this is who she is."

"No!" Brin spat back, stomping his feet, knocking a stone loose beneath him before almost losing his balance as a result. Regaining himself, he stared back at his father and said, "Why do we have to accept that? That's horseshit!"

"Brinnolhat!" Dennalhir said with a gasp.

Fannalhen raised a hand before Dennalhir could speak further, his face understanding and grieving. "No, Denna, let's..." He sighed, his eyes closing tightly, before slowly looking back to Brin. "Go on, son."

The way Brin was stamping this way and that, it seemed to Sen that he didn't know how to adequately express his anger. Maybe he had done it by his lonesome when no one was around because he may have feared reprisal had he shown his temper. Sen couldn't say for certain. But nonetheless, her brother huffed and puffed, seeming to stutter on his own words, his vision still blurred with tears no matter how frequently he wiped his arm across his eyes.

Brin growled before the words finally escaped his lips. "She can't go a single day without wasting away with a drink in her hand, conning some new victim in cards.

Any time that anything requires her responsibility, she'd rather spend it at a tavern. Whatever person she is now, that's not my sister anymore. I don't know why she keeps doing this, but I'm not going to accept it!" He paused to take a handful of breaths but did not give any indication that he sought to compose himself.

Tez and their mother both took a hesitant step forward, but no further than that.

"For all we know," Brin continued, "Sen is probably just jealous that she doesn't get to be part of the Tribe."

"Brin," Fannalhen said sternly. "You know very well that—"

"What I know," Brin interrupted, "is that maybe she shouldn't be in the Tribe. Maybe that's for the best. If she couldn't be here today—for just one sober hour of her day—because of her own jealousies and insecurities, then why the hell is she even in the village to begin with?"

Everyone was silent. The Keepers had long since stopped their idle conversations. The family hardly knew what to say, but their expressions showed that, at the very least, they shared in Brin's anger.

And meanwhile, Sen felt trapped. Unable to say anything, unable to make amends. Only able to watch everything as it unfolded in witness to her greatest wrong.

As Brin turned his attention to Fannalhen, it was clear on the Stone Chief's face that he wanted to say something Sen hoped would be an admonishment for such words against her.

But her father hesitated, opened his mouth...and then closed it. In the absence of words, one thing was evident.

Fannalhen agreed.

Sen lurched forward, her face drenched in a cold sweat. Her chest heaved up and down, up and down, her heart beating a mile a minute. Deep within her, there was a powerful ache radiating throughout her body out from her chest.

As much as she tried to stop it, the tears wouldn't stop.

Through watery vision, she realized she was back in Kamataa's barrack, her sweat having completely seeped through the thin blanket she was given.

It was all...just a dream, she thought, relieved. She sighed, trying hard to quell her pounding heart.

To her left, she could see Kamataa sitting at the edge of her own bed, watching Sen with intent curiosity. Sen collected herself and wiped away a long stream of tears from her eyes. The Eclipseborn remained in her real appearance, her long wisps of white hair trailing down her shoulders, her face seeming to be more wrinkles than actual skin, a fact only exacerbated by her calm smile.

"It seems you were having quite the nightmare, child," the old woman said. She got up and slowly made her way over to Sen.

Her breath still heavy, Sen pushed herself up to a seated position and swung her legs over the side of the bed. "It...felt a lot more real than I would ever have liked it to."

Kamataa placed a gentle hand on her shoulder. "A recurring nightmare?"

Sen shook her head, one hand still planted on the bed. "Not...exactly," she said. She wiped away the beads of sweat which still trailed down her forehead. "I've...seen similar things in my waking hours. Since my father's murder, I mean. It...it just feels more real every time it happens."

The old woman sat beside her, taking her hand in hers. Her skin was cold to the touch. "It's a traumatic event. We all see the ghosts of our pasts when given no other option." She dipped her head.

Sen couldn't help but wonder if Kamataa had experienced the same, but she had to stop and remind herself once again just who she was speaking to. What this woman had done.

But in the absence of everyone else in her life, whether by passing or by distance, she had no one else to confide in. And the closest Sen would have to anyone who could understand her right now...was this murderer.

"There was...something else, too," Sen said hesitantly. She narrowed her eyes and stared blankly across the room, empty of all else but the two of them. Commotion murmured from outside the barracks, the City apparently coming back to life. She couldn't say precisely what time of day it was, but she had to assume by the faint trickle of light pouring through the front door that it was mid-morning.

"Yes?" Kamataa said, still gripping Sen's hand. "Go on."

Sen bit at her lip. "My...my brother," she said, the scorn still apparent in her voice. She was not going to allow Kamataa to forget what she had taken from her. "There was a second...something. Like I was reliving...his Trial. Through his eyes. It was a day that...I wasn't there for. But...I don't know how I saw it. It didn't make sense."

Softly, Kamataa chuckled. "Well, of course you saw that, child. You'd been gripping his pendant all night."

Her eyes widening, Sen at first did not comprehend the words. But she then turned her gaze to her other hand, still planted on the bed. She lifted her hand and found Brin's Memory pendant beneath it, glistening with her sweat from the strength of her grip.

"So, that all was just...part of the dream, too?" she asked.

Kamataa hummed with consideration, stroking a finger across her withered chin. "I suppose if you heard some things which seemed out of place in your dream, then that could be true. But if you saw two separate things—whatever post-trauma scene and your brother's Trial—then you actually just saw your brother's Memory. All you did was use his pendant."

Immediately, a flash of revulsion and shock washed over Sen. She jumped up from the bed, knocking the pendant away, ripping herself free of Kamataa's gentle grip. "Shit, shit," she said. "That's bad, that's really bad." She paced in place, running her fingers through her tangled hair, her heart beating faster once again.

"Sennalhat, calm yourself!" Kamataa said. She rose to her feet, extending both arms to Sen. "What are you in a panic about?"

Sen's eyes sparked with confusion. She shot a glance back at Kamataa. "What am I in—what are you talking about? You should know very well that it's a taboo to use another's pendant! I could be—"

Kamataa lowered her arms and rolled her eyes. Silently, she walked across the room to a chest by the end of her bed. It was identical to the ones at the other beds, including Sen's own. The old woman knelt and rummaged through the chest, humming idly to herself, before pulling loose a cache of pendants. All Tribal pendants, each adorning a different rune. Sen could spy the marks denoting Knowledge, Illusion, Fear, and Foresight, and she could only imagine what else lay in that chest.

"You see," Kamataa said, "I've collected my fair share of these over the years. And, as you can tell, I have been around for a long time, child. Whatever you think is going to happen to you for using your brother's pendant, unintentional as it may have been, I can assure you that it will not happen."

"But why are we taught that—"

At first, Sen wanted to ask about the taboo. But something more important hit her. "*Gods*," she gasped. "That *was* Brin's Memory. Then, that means..." She stopped in place, her hand covering her mouth, a deep pit forming in her stomach. That hollow, sinking feeling returned, a tremendous weight pushing down upon her.

Kamataa closed the chest and walked over, placing her hand back on Sen's shoulder. "You learned something that you wish you hadn't, didn't you, Sennalhat?"

Choking on a sobbed gasp, Sen pushed down a well of tears and stared back at her bed, to Brin's pendant. "He...he didn't want me in the Tribe. Neither of them did. Brin...and my father."

The old woman moved in front of her, holding her tightly by the shoulders, forcing her to look at the earnestness in her eyes. "And perhaps now, you understand what it is I have been trying to tell you." She smiled, and this time, it reached her eyes. "The Children of the Black Moon understand this pain. Walk with me, Sennalhat. Walk with *us*. I promise you there is so much more for you to learn."

Sen allowed herself to smile, and with a slight hesitation, she nodded. Nudging Kamataa's hands from her shoulders, she walked back to her bed and picked up Brin's pendant, eyeing it with curiosity.

"So, how do you work these things?"

CHAPTER FIVE

Alliances

The Year 1556 Anno Salvatoris
15 Years After the Invasion

Glimmers of morning light reflected in the distance, a blinding beacon indicating they had made it.

It had been a long, tiring night. Tez knew that if she laid down, her legs might not be so kind as to allow her back up. From the sunken faces of Tawa, Sharrabha, and all the rest, she could tell that the feeling was shared across the board. Tez ached in places she didn't quite know she had, the weight of everything of the past day bearing down hard upon her.

But she permitted herself and her companions to stop when their destination came into view. The sun was rising behind them. If they had not marched through the cold night air nonstop, it might have warmed her up. Instead, Tez felt she was going to overheat.

It was still worth it to see the eastern village of the Lake Tribe glowing at first light.

Tez planted her spear in the ground, leaning idly against it as Tawa filed in beside her. She eyed him from her periphery, her chest still heaving too much to offer any words of acknowledgment.

"It has been an age since I last saw it at sunrise," Tawa said haltingly, also still trying to find his breath.

Wiping a river of sweat from her brow, Tez raised an eyebrow at Tawa. "You made a habit of daybreak trips to the Lake of Bones once upon a time?" she said.

He smiled. "You joke, but your father and I would run through the night as boys to see the Big Lake at first light."

"As boys, really?" Tez crossed her arms. "I find it hard to believe that my grandparents would allow Father to run halfway across the north in pitch darkness. Never mind your own parents."

"I never said we were allowed."

That gave Tez pause. She stared with mouth agape at Tawa, disbelieving the mischievous smirk creasing his lips. *My father and Tawa,* rulebreakers? *There's no way he's not lying.* Her eyes only widened as Tawa chuckled at her shock.

"Unbelievable," she said. "And why am I only just hearing this now?"

Another chuckle murmured behind Tez, and she was surprised to see Sharrabha filing in on the other side of her, exchanging a knowing smile.

"You know that the moment your father told those stories, you and your sister would have gone off to follow in his footsteps," the huntress said.

"What can I say? He was a good role model," Tez said. "If only I knew the stick he kept up his ass was just for show." She turned back to Tawa. "So, who put who up to it: you or Father?"

Tawa laughed. "What do you think? It was always his idea—as the Chief's son, he felt he could do whatever he pleased. I was always saddled with the blame when we were caught."

"Saddled with the blame and suffered nothing else, I assume?"

He shrugged his shoulders, amusement still on his face, more than Tez had seen on his face in a long time. "My father eventually stopped yelling at me over it since *your* father would drag me along every other night regardless."

Tez furrowed her brow and shook her head. "While Sen or I would have had Wolfsigns trained on us from the first had we ever done something like that."

"There also wasn't an Invasion back then," Sharrabha said, nudging Tez's shoulder.

"Details, details," Tez responded, waving her hand in dismissal. She pointed a finger in the direction of the Big Lake. "These guys were probably fighting themselves over something dumb at the time."

Tawa cleared his throat, kicking at a loose rock in the ground. "Well, yes, but it *was* a particularly bad year for fishing that year."

Tez put her hands on her hips, looking back out to the western horizon, the clouds pink overhead, reflecting along the shimmering surface of the Big Lake. "You'd think with a view like this every morning, they'd be a more relaxed people."

"Horror defies beauty, sometimes," Sharrabha said, flexing her dominant shoulder and elbow. "Beautiful as a sight this is, they don't call it the Lake of Bones for nothing."

With a frown and nod, Tez yanked her spear out from the ground, the time for rest over. "They can call it whatever the hell they want, so long as mine aren't the bones going for a swim. Come on."

Down the grassy hills they descended, Tez leading her ragged host with Tawa and Sharrabha at either side of her. Now that she could be certain that none were following under the cover of darkness, she allowed a more deliberate pace after the stressful rush through the green dunes of the overnight flee. Her legs thanked her for it.

Fashioning her spear as a walking stick to support her weight, Tez wondered what she would expect of the Lake Tribe. She had been familiar with many of the Tribes due to the Stone Tribe's direct involvement in the relocation of the southern Tribes, but the Lake Tribe was a mystery to her, never having ever interacted with any from the western reaches. She didn't remember her father ever playing host to any from the Tribe, either, whether of the leadership or otherwise. Even those passing through the Stone village to embark on their Trial were an unknown to her, though she could hardly fault them for not wanting to stop to speak to strangers from another Tribe when a more important task was looming.

All Tez knew of the Lake Tribe was the conflicts. The many, many conflicts. The Long War, and everything else in between. They were a combative people, true, but such could be useful if she were to take back her home.

But there was something beneath all the martial prowess; she was sure of it. All she needed to do was figure out how to appeal to it in hopes of an alliance. An alliance that, so far as it had been planned, was only to the benefit of the Stone Tribe.

One step at a time, she thought. *The first is to ensure they greet us with words rather than spears.*

The sky was losing its pinkish hue by the time the western Lake village came into closer view. By contrast to the glimmer of the Big Lake, the village was, to Tez, rather disappointing. Not that it was unsightly by any stretch of the imagination. It was simply...little more than plain. Rows of identical homes of wood, straw, and what looked like freshwater weeds lined the perimeter, a market square situated in plain sight upon first entry. Ordinary passersby went about their business, betraying the image in Tez's head of every Lake Tribesperson being a musclebound warrior. The scents of fish and grains intermingled in the air, a strange combination about which Tez was unsure how to feel.

She was relieved at the normalcy of what she saw, especially after the pain and destruction she left behind at home. But she was still dismayed at the mundanity of a village settled upon one of the most stunning sights in the Land.

I'll take mundane. Rather that than being on the wrong end of a spear-running.

In fact, the disinterest—or the lack of any reaction at all to a host of outsiders brandishing spears and bows—surprised Tez. She expected something of a rise out of them, but quickly dismissed it in her head. *They aren't the Wood Tribe. They don't hate outsiders. Just each other.*

But as she led her fellow Stone folk through to the village square, in the direction of the fish market, she was delighted to hear no petty squabbles, threats on the life of another, or anything of the sort. Just people coexisting.

Clearly, I should have taken those sunrise runs out here.

That was beside the point. She needed to find the Lake Chief. The open market would hopefully provide her some answers.

Signaling her fellow warriors to hang back, Tez approached the first person she found in the market. He was an older gentleman, probably pushing seventy years, a lifetime of wear and tear visible on his exposed arms, scars running along forearms which still maintained an image of strength despite their age. A small tuft of white hair was tied loosely atop his head, though a bald spot was noticeable beneath the pushed-back locks, and the sides of his head were shorn, though it did not appear to have been recently done. Absently, the old man was perusing the selection of grains for sale, a half-filled wicker basket tucked between his arm and side.

Tez cleared her throat as she stepped beside him. "Um, excuse me," she said.

The man turned to her, a gentle smile on his face. "Well, good morning," he said jovially. "It's not often we welcome the Stone Tribe here."

She returned the smile. "What can I say? We're sheltered."

He laughed. "Or just comfortable where you are. I'm sure many here feel the same." The old man redirected his attention back to the grains. "Was there something you needed, Miss...?"

"Tez."

"Tez," he repeated. "The harvest is excellent this season, and the fish have been cooperative, as well. If you've come this far for the market, I'd have to recommend—"

With a soft chuckle, Tez raised her hands. "No, no, nothing like that, but thank you. I'm actually just trying to figure out where I can find the Chief."

"Is that right?" the man said, continuing his shopping. He was silent for a moment, trailing a finger along the rows of grains before finally choosing his selection. Stowing it in his basket, he turned over his shoulder, first looking at Tez, then to her Stone companions, and nodded. "If you'll be patient a few moments more, I'd be happy to take you to him."

Tez tapped her spear butt on the ground in acknowledgment. "That would be appreciated. Thank you."

Smiling again, the old man spent about five minutes further on his shopping, his pace noticeably quicker in making his decisions. Tez felt a pang of guilt at rushing the man, all for her own sake, but she was appreciative, nonetheless.

Gathering his catch, the man turned to Tez, his basket nearly overflowing with a mix of grains, fruits, and fish, and he gave her a quick wink. "Come now, let's be off."

Tez nudged her head toward her companions to follow. Out of earshot, she could hear the sound of Tawa saying something indistinct to many of the others, and afterward, only Sharrabha joined him. The rest dispersed into the market, probably with the directive to find some food for the day. *Probably for the best.*

The old man kept a steady pace along the main footpath. Tez found she had to quicken her own natural pace to keep up. With the identical rows of homes along this main drag, she had to assume it may be easy enough to lose the man once he retreated into one of them.

From up close, she was impressed at the make of these homes. They appeared to be of more intricate composition and construction than what she was used to back in the Stone village. On the whole, everything seemed more spacious, though she never wanted for space in her own home, being the daughter of a Chief. The same was not necessarily true of others in her village.

A few minutes passed, and they arrived at the Lake Chief's hut. It was a bit unassuming of a home; in closer proximity, it had some more ornate carvings along the façade above the door, but she would not be able to denote it from far away. There was space surrounding it where there could have fit some denoting markers, even some indentations along the frame of the hut where it appeared there may have once been such, but those had long since faded away.

The old man walked into the hut without announcement, which surprised Tez. Hesitating slightly to see if he was coming back out, Tez slowly trailed behind him, furrowing her brow at the strangeness of the situation.

When she walked inside, she saw the old man sitting in the center of the room expectantly, his basket from the market tucked away against the wall by the door.

Tez raised an eyebrow, a feeling of confusion seemingly matched by Tawa and Sharrabha at either end of her. She looked at the man, grunted, and with a tentative smile, said, "Take it you're the Chief, then."

He returned the smile with greater friendliness. "What gave it away?" he said with a chuckle. "My name is Tenazt. Welcome to the eastern Lake village, Tez of the Stone Tribe."

She nodded. "Thank you," she said. Directing to either side of her, she added, "These are my companions, Tawa and Sharrabha."

"You seem content to run with an older crowd, don't you?" Tenazt said.

"Not quite. They are close friends and advisors to my parents."

Tenazt leaned forward, curious. "Is that right, then?" he said. Gesturing to the seats before him, he rose to his feet to retrieve empty cups, filling them with what smelled like an herbal tea. "Please sit, all of you. I would hear what brings such a company to my village."

Tez sat, followed by Tawa and Sharrabha, and accepted the cup. The tea tasted just as good as it smelled. The aroma paired well with the modest interior of the Chief's hut. It was a wide, open space, little adorning the walls apart from weaponry and simple pieces of artwork. A small fire crackled in the corner, the pot of tea sitting atop it. Seating was available in the room in a circular pattern, all surrounding where Tenazt would sit, a stark contrast to what she was used to with her father sitting before everyone behind the fire. The hut appeared to have been deconstructed in some respect; there was a bed in the corner where Tez assumed Tenazt slept, but the way it jutted out, it seemed to have been once part of a separate room. Now there were additional furnishings either to sit or lay.

Taking a second sip of the tea, Tez nodded to the Lake Chief as he returned to his seat. "First, we would like to thank you for your hospitality, Chief Tenazt. The past night was long and exhausting for us all."

Tenazt drank slowly from his cup, seeming to take the time to enjoy the flavors of his tea. "I noticed you arrived today with a full host of Stone warriors. An interesting sight, to be sure."

"Yes, well, our village was just victim to a coup last night."

The Lake Chief raised his eyebrows, still sipping at his tea. "Oh my," he said. And nothing else.

Tez was taken aback by the brevity and bluntness of the reaction. *"Oh my?" That's it? Hmph.* She cleared her throat, trying to find the appropriate words. "Yes, well. With nowhere else to go, we came here. For help."

"Help, you say?" Another sip from his tea cup. *"Ours,* then?"

She took one look at Tawa, then one at Sharrabha. They only stared directly ahead at the Lake Chief. "Well, yes. You see..."

She explained the situation as best as she could with the details she had. Of Koelhe and Fann and their violent opposition to the Tribal leadership, of Han'e and the Sun Tribe's defection and betrayal of the Stone Tribe, of her mother's capture, knowing not what fate she had since suffered.

Tenazt leaned forward, raising his brow with evident interest, continuing to gingerly take sips from his cup while stroking his chin thoughtfully, his dark eyes focused entirely on Tez and her words.

"...and because of that," Tez concluded, "we need the help of the Lake Tribe to reclaim the Stone village. The Bearsigns of the Lake Tribe are unrivaled in their combat prowess. We need all the help we can get."

Firewood cracked and popped into sparks of embers off in the corner, punctuating a resultant silence. Tenazt closed his eyes, breathing in deep the lingering aroma of his tea, before finally putting his empty cup down in front of him. Slowly, his eyes reopened, his cheery smile diminishing, his expression bearing every resemblance to a leader amongst his people, his hands folded calmly in front of him.

And then he laughed. Uproariously, at that. His belly bounced in the act, all the enthusiasm and vigor in the old Chief's body centered squarely there.

Tez was speechless, unsure of what to do or how to react. She offered herself before a Tribe's Chief in a time of need, and she was met only with laughter. Looking to her companions, she didn't find much in the way of guidance. Tawa sat with his arms crossed, visibly annoyed. At the same time, Sharrabha leaned forward, thoughtfully resting her chin on a propped fist while watching Tenazt laugh away.

Her chest feeling tight, Tez raised a finger, doing her best to maintain a neutral composure despite wanting to snarl back at the laughter. "Chief Tenazt, please, I—"

Wiping away an amused tear, Tenazt finally ceased his laughing and stared back at Tez. "Oh, I haven't laughed like that in some time," he said. "Thank you, Tez of the Stone Tribe. I needed that dearly."

"I wouldn't call this a laughing matter," Sharrabha said, her chin still planted atop her fist. "People *died* last night. They—"

"And people will surely continue to die," Tenazt interrupted, brushing away the words with a hand. "Tell me, all of you. When our Tribe was at odds with one another, where was the Stone Tribe? Did the Stone Tribe come to our aid when there was conflict within our own ranks?"

Tawa scoffed. "Which time?" he quipped.

Tez turned and raised an eyebrow. *Certainly am not used to sass coming from Tawa*, she thought.

The Lake Chief laughed again, pointing a finger at Tawa. "I like this one," he said through chuckled breaths. "'Which time,' he says. Very good."

"Yes, well," Sharrabha said, pointing a finger of her own at Tenazt, "perhaps you should consider that it would be entirely unreasonable for our people to come to you whenever you found yourselves at conflict. If we had to constantly assist with infighting amongst the Lake people, we would never leave the Lake of Bones."

"Enough!" Tez shouted, holding her arms out at either side to silence her companions. "Enough. The longer we bicker, the more time the Invaders have to regroup, and the three of us know that they're not going to be content with remaining in the south." She turned her head back and forth to Tawa and Sharrabha, glaring at them in equal measure, watching them both grimace and bite at their lips with frustration.

His curiosity piqued once again, Tenazt leaned forward. "Hold there a moment," he said. "What's this about the Invaders now? It's been fifteen years, and they've never crossed the Forest border. That was just about the only good thing Han'e did against them, keeping them down there."

With a frown, Tez shook her head. "Not anymore. They crossed, and with little difficulty it seemed. They came to our village in search of runaway slaves but instead kidnapped my brother and killed my father. Never mind that they could very well come back, but it was because of them that that power vacuum led to Koelhe's coup, and—"

Again, Tenazt interrupted, but this time with a raised hand. "Stop there a moment, if you would," he said. "If they made it through the Forest, I shudder to think what they did to the Wood Tribe." He closed his eyes, shaking his head. "And another thing, I'd like to speak further about these 'runaway slaves,' but first, if you could also clarify on this: a power vacuum from your father's death? You're Chief Fannalhen's daughter, then."

"Uh, yes. Sorry, I should have led with that."

Tenazt bit at his lip, clenching his fists. "I am...sorry about your father. He was a great man, from all accounts."

Not all of them, Tez thought.

The Lake Chief opened his eyes, his expression somewhere between remorse and anger. "And your sister...she would be the *Eclipseborn*, wouldn't she?" He almost spat the title.

Tez furrowed her brow. "I fail to see how that's relevant."

"Is it not?" Tenazt asked. "You would have us ally with an Eclipseborn over this? Many would not be so keen about it."

"What the *hell*?" Tez exclaimed. "You'd really piss on this over my sister? Maybe stop and think for a moment that there are more important matters than—"

"Tez," Tawa said, outstretching his hand. "Ignore it. For one reason or another, the Lake Tribe is especially hateful toward the Eclipseborn. And there *are* more important matters now. Are there not, Tenazt?"

Embers sparked in the corner once more, echoing through the hollow hut. Individual conversations carried into the room from outside. A bird chirped against the door. And Tenazt sat in silence, breathing deeply as he stared at the three Stone folk before him, his eyes accusing, but lips quivering. But he at last relented and nodded.

The comment about Sen still irked at her, but reluctantly, Tez let the subject drop and refocused. Turning back to Tenazt, she raised her brow, trying to ensure that all semblance of annoyance and disgust towards a potential conflict with her sister was gone. "I take it you have another dilemma on your hands, Chief Tenazt?" she asked. She gestured her hands forward in offering. "If the Lake Tribe has looked for Stone assistance all this time, then let this be the time the Stone Tribe does."

Tenazt leaned back, crossing his arms. "This is about more than just reclaiming your village, isn't it?"

Sharply, Tez nodded. "Like I said before, I don't know if my mother is still alive, and if she is, what the hell Koelhe has done with her." A shudder ran through her at the thought, as much as she did not want to think of it. "But there's a larger picture. If we're going to face the Invaders again, we need a unified north now more than ever. That's going to involve taking back the Stone Tribe, and for that, the prowess of the Lake Tribe will be needed."

In silent consideration, Tenazt stroked his chin. This time, the silence was not broken by his boisterous laughter, but instead by a deep, unassured sigh. He rose to his feet, offering a gentle hand to his three guests to help them up.

Tez was surprised at the gesture, to be shown respect despite the tension, but she appreciated it.

"Follow me," Tenazt said, walking toward the door. "There's something you'll need to see."

A strange smell stung at Tez's nostrils as they approached their destination. It ran in stark contrast to the pleasant aromas of Tenazt's hut but did not quite equate to the pervasive scent of fish that wafted through the air from both the open market and the Big Lake.

Instead, it just smelled *stagnant*.

Tenazt led them inside another unassuming hut, sticking out from the rest on this street only by the fact that the door was framed red as opposed to the unaltered frames of the other dwellings. Tez noted two rows of beds lining the walls, some empty, some occupied. Some of the occupants were in poor physical states, either from wounds or illnesses. Regardless, those who were awake managed a smile or nod to their Chief as he walked by, appreciative of his arrival. He returned their greetings in kind.

Tez filed in beside Tenazt. "Why have you taken us to a healer's hut, Chief?" she whispered.

The Lake Chief held up a finger. "In due course," he responded. "Just a moment." He went on ahead again, pushing open a back door before waving Tez and her companions along.

With a grimace that she failed to hide, Tez was greeted with a sharp stench as she crossed the threshold. Tenazt awaited her, standing at the back of the room, while Tez surveyed the room. There was only one occupied bed, a man with eyes seemingly glued open, motionless besides, a member of the Lake

Tribe providing some manner of care to the man, their back turned to her. She couldn't quite tell what was being done to the man; healing was an art entirely foreign to her.

Tez looked at the unmoving man and then back to Tenazt. "Is he what you wanted to show us?" she asked.

Wordlessly, Tenazt nodded his head, his arms crossed as he leaned his back against the wall. He stared at the man and frowned, slightly gnawing at his lower lip with visible disapproval and frustration.

"Is he…?"

"He's not dead, if that's what you're about to ask," Tenazt said. He shook his head with a sigh. "I'm sorry, introductions are in order. The man in the bed is Barrah, one of our best Sneaks up until a few days ago. Working on him is Ket. They're a great Learned. We're damn lucky they decided to read up on Keeper medical history; they're probably the best healer you'll find anywhere, thanks to that."

Ket stopped what they were doing and turned, offering Tez a smile, forced though it seemed. In contrast to most of the Lake Tribe Tez had encountered, Ket kept their hair short, not long enough to tie back. Their shirt sleeves were rolled up to the elbow, a thicker material of shirt that Tez had mainly seen the men of the Tribe wear, though Ket's facial features were notably more feminine.

"Hi," Ket said brusquely. They were rubbing at the back of their hand, probably massaging out some cramp.

"Hi there," Tez responded, returning a smile, some genuineness to the act. She looked past Ket to get a closer look at Barrah.

The man couldn't have been much older than she was. His face looked frozen, his mouth agape in what seemed like shock, his eyes lazily opened, though focusing on nothing. Though at first, Tez thought he had passed, she could only barely see his chest moving up and down beneath his blanket.

Pointing a thumb at him, Tez looked back to Tenazt. "So, what happened to him? Battle injury, hunting accident, what?"

Tenazt only shook his head, frowning all the while, his gaze not breaking from the mindless man. "I wish I could explain it," he said.

"It was very sudden," Ket said. They crossed their arms, also not breaking sight from Barrah's motionless form. "Four nights ago, he was late for patrol duty. When the Chief sent someone for him, they found Barrah's sister cradling him, yelling for help."

Tawa stepped forward. "Did his sister see anything happen?" he asked.

Ket shook their head. "She had returned from a patrol of her own and found him collapsed on the ground, not saying anything, not doing anything other than breathing and staring up at the ceiling." They turned back to Barrah, placing a soft hand on his shoulder. "He still eats, drinks, pisses, and shits himself. We've just had to do it all for him."

"Did anything happen to him beforehand?" Tawa said. He looked back at the rows of the sick and injured in the other room. "A training accident or a knock to the head? Is there anything that those in the other room could say to explain it?"

"He's a Sneak," Tenazt said with a forced chuckle, still maintaining his distance at the other end of the room. "His job is typically to *avoid* getting knocks to the head. But no, nothing of the sort. He was with me the entire previous day, and I noticed nothing out of the ordinary." He nudged his head back toward the other room. "None of them would have seen anything. He's not exactly a 'field work' kind of patrolman, if you catch my meaning."

"It's also worth noting that his pendant is gone," Ket added, pointing to Barrah's neck, which Tez noticed was indeed missing the chain. Ket shook their head. "He's not exactly the type to misplace something, and I doubt it just fell off whenever what happened to him happened."

"So, you're saying it was stolen," Tez said flatly.

"It wouldn't be the first time among this Tribe," Ket said with a frown.

Tez heard Sharrabha grunt with interest behind her.

"Stealing your kin's pendant?" the Stone huntress said. She grabbed absently at her own pendant, gripping it tightly as though she was protecting against a thief in the shadows. "You're saying that's just another part of Lake history?"

With a shrug of their shoulders, Ket sighed, defeated. "Unfortunately. Why it's happened, I couldn't say. One would think that eventually, we would learn, but the western Tribe steals from the eastern, then the eastern Tribe steals something right back, and it just goes back and forth until someone ends up with a spear in their ass."

I like this one, Tez thought with a smirk.

"Then you think that someone from the western Lake Tribe stole Barrah's pendant," Sharrabha said.

Again, Ket shrugged, staring out at the empty beds across from them. They leaned against the wall and massaged the bridge of their nose with their thumb and forefinger. "If history repeats—and it usually does in this Tribe—then yes, probably."

"Why, though?" Tez asked, holding her hands out at her sides in confusion. "What's even the point of it?"

"If we ever figured out a reason, maybe we'd stop doing it," Ket answered, frustrated. "But, instead, we're here again."

Tez crossed her arms, shaking her head. She looked at Barrah again, seeing how helpless he appeared. "But that still doesn't explain why he's gone completely helpless. Someone had to have done something to him before they took off with his pendant, no?"

Ket scratched at their head and threw their hands up. "That's what I've been trying to figure out for the last four days. I really couldn't tell you."

The room was silent, all staring wordlessly at Barrah, whose ragged and short breaths provided the only noise.

Tez looked up from the man and back at the Lake Chief, who was scratching at an old scar on his forearm. "I understand the gravity of all this," she said. "But, why are you showing him to us? What does this have to do with us?"

The old man continued to frown at Barrah but finally broke sight and frowned instead at Tez. "You want the Lake Tribe's help, don't you?" he asked. "Call it a favor for a favor, then. You find Barrah's pendant and punish those responsible, then we'll help you retake your village."

With a raised eyebrow, Tez stared back at the Lake Chief with a frown of her own. She redirected her gaze from Ket to Tawa and Sharrabha to see if there was a joke that she had missed, but they all returned the same stoicism at the request.

Her mouth agape in stunned silence, Tez gestured her hands out to Tenazt in some vain attempt at communicating with her hands, to little effect. When the words finally came to her, they spoke only of shock. "You're telling me that you'll only help us if we help you with a godsdamned fetch job?"

Apparently not seeing the absurdity of the request, Tenazt merely nodded. "These are my terms. Barrah was one of my best, and look at the state of him now. I'll not see the western Tribe go unpunished for this."

"Do you even know it was the western Tribe who did it, though?" Tez said with arms outstretched, her face still disbelieving.

With indifference, Tenazt closed his eyes and shrugged his shoulders, his arms still crossed. "They're the best place to start."

"Unbelievable," Tez muttered beneath her breath, not loud enough for the Chief to hear.

"Why send *us*?" Sharrabha questioned, her face expressive with annoyance and anger at the request. "Can you really not send someone from your own Tribe to take care of this?"

Chuckling, Tenazt pointed a finger at the bed. "My guy for that is laying right there." And he said nothing more.

Tez flared her nostrils and was ready to say more, but she felt a tug at her arm pulling her back. Tawa.

"Come, Tez," he said. He sneered and gritted his teeth at the Lake Chief. "There is no talking our way out of this." He continued to pull Tez along with him.

Prying her arm free, Tez spared a final glance at Ket before shaking her head at Tenazt and walking out of the healer's hut. When she returned to the street, Tawa and Sharrabha behind her, she kicked at a rock, nearly hitting someone walking by. She absently waved a hand at them in apology and then breathed sharply out her nose with fuming frustration as she turned around to face her companions.

"What unbelievable horseshit," she growled. "How in the hell are we even going to sneak into the western Tribe and find a *pendant* of all things? Where the hell do we even start to look?" She turned her head to Sharrabha. If any of them had an idea how to begin at this task, it would be the huntress.

Instead, Sharrabha just shook her head. "I wouldn't know where to start. I'm not familiar with the Lake Tribe's lands. We'd have to wait for nightfall, but from there, who knows where—"

Tawa threw his arms up in frustration. Tez had never known Tawa to have anger or frustration or aggression anywhere in his body, but everything had changed since last night.

"For all we know," Tawa grunted, "this is just a trick to get rid of us on some pointless errand. They probably know exactly where his pendant is, too."

Placing her hands on her hips, Tez kicked at another stone. She couldn't find the words to adequately voice her anger, so she just walked away, off in the direction of the Big Lake.

The Lake of Bones didn't shimmer with the same beauty in the late-morning sunshine, but it was still beautiful. She sat at the edge of the water along a knoll of grass, a young couple, a boy and girl about Brin's age, seated a few yards away from her. She nodded to them in wordless acknowledgment.

Tez felt helpless and useless. She was left with so few options to help her Tribe, and the best option was already falling apart in front of her. Frustrated and angry, she pulled at some grass beneath her, listlessly watching the blades blow away from her hand and carry along the easterly wind across the surface of the lake.

Following the blades' path, she could see a line of boats breaking the horizon line, oars circling intensely through the water. Narrowing her eyes, she realized that there were multiple rows of vessels approaching.

"Hey, look," the young girl next to her said.

"Huh," the boy said, putting a hand above his squinting eyes in defense against the glimmering sun. "What's the western Tribe coming here for?"

Tez turned to them both with a raised brow and rose back to her feet, walking back toward Tawa and Sharrabha. *This may have just gotten easier.*

CHAPTER SIX

Hard Truths

The Year 1556 Anno Salvatoris
15 Years After the Invasion

Learning how to use Brin's Memory pendant was far easier than she thought it would be. It didn't make it any less difficult to watch, though.

At Kamataa's instruction, Sen spent a portion of the morning growing acclimated to using a pendant and, to her surprise, there were no bodily repercussions for breaking the long-standing taboo which warned against using the Boon of another Tribesperson.

Instead, the only pains at watching Brin's memories through his eyes were an aching in Sen's heart. Her brother's passage into adulthood was meant to be a joyous occasion. But within days, Brin lost his father, his home, and then his life.

Hard as it was, Sen brought herself in and out of the Memories stored in Brin's pendant, and the timing of it all meant that the only moments to relive were those of sadness and loss. His lonely return to the village after Sen's departure. Standing up to the Invaders when they arrived in the dead of night, only to find himself captured in turn. Being forced along a march away from freedom, through the blood-soaked roots of the Forest, bodies fresh with wounds and death.

Sen had to force herself to stop watching when the City loomed tall in the distance. She had seen enough for one sitting.

When she finished for the time being, the barrack had repopulated with some of the Children of the Black Moon. In her corner bed, Sen felt isolated and alone despite the company. All of her fellow Eclipseborn regarded her with either suspicion or indifference, and she could not bring herself to entirely feel a kinship to them.

Sha'a and Vanta barely even offered an acknowledgment of Sen's presence when they entered the room, instead traipsing to the opposite corner to rummage through the chest at the foot of one of their beds. They carried on with their own conversations, detailing some morning routine with which Sen was unfamiliar.

Zara and Ziia at least gave a brief greeting on their return, but they then immediately went about tidying the barrack, noting that it was their turn to do so. Not that the room needed much tidying, to begin with, as far as Sen was concerned. It was rather immaculate.

She hadn't seen Kamataa since earlier in the day, and Hollow not at all, but Sen found herself particularly curious about Cin. He had arrived between Sha'a and Vanta but did not acknowledge either of them, nor did he greet his other fellows upon their respective entrances. He only went to his bed, sitting at the edge of it, and pulled out a book from beneath his pillow and set about reading it.

In another time, he and Brin may have found common ground, Sen couldn't help but think.

From Sen's perspective, Cin seemed a loner. He had said all of a single word to her so far, and she hadn't had the opportunity to press him for information the way she had the other members of the Children of the Black Moon. Seeing as no one was interested in approaching her, Sen shrugged her shoulders and got up, crossing the plane toward Cin.

What do I even have to lose here? she thought.

Either Cin did not hear Sen's approach, or he didn't much care. He remained focused on whatever it was he was reading. Sen angled her head to try and read the spine, but it seemed to be in a foreign tongue. The Invaders' native language, she assumed.

"Cin," Sen said after standing beside him for about ten or fifteen seconds of silence.

"Sennalhat," he said, his eyes remaining glued to his book.

Sen scratched at the back of her neck, wondering what could be so interesting in that book that all else did not matter. "Can...we talk?" she asked with hesitation.

"We're talking now. What do you want?"

She was taken aback by how blunt he was. She couldn't tell whether the terseness was due to him being so engrossed in that book—which reminded her entirely of Brin—or if that's just how he was. She leaned toward the latter.

"I...just want to get to know you all," Sen said.

"Do you?" Cin finally looked up from his book, closing it sharply. "We both know you don't want to be here."

Sen's eyes widened. "I—"

"You don't have to pretend. You had privilege that these people don't. They killed your brother. Why would you even want to be here after all that?"

Sen still found herself dumbstruck. *I mean, he's right*, she thought. *It's not like they're forcing me to stay. And yet...where would I even go?*

"I'm just...trying to understand," she said.

"Understand what?"

"I don't know. All of *this*." Sen gestured to the other Children, who continued not to pay her any mind. "We're all born from this Land, but you all want to see our people up in flames. You all have...suffered, I know. By comparison to you, I really didn't. I'm coming to terms with my own discoveries still. But to wish for the destruction of your own home...I just can't fathom it. Please just help me understand."

Cin stared at her blankly, barely moving from his spot on the bed. His expression was cold, disregarding. But where Sen had seen in the eyes of the Eclipseborn flares of anger or despair, there was nothing in Cin's. Only a stark emptiness.

He was silent for a while longer, staring out across the barrack past where Ziia and Zara continued to clean. He cracked a knuckle and then looked back up to Sen. "Do you consider yourself Lucky, Sennalhat?" he asked.

The question surprised her. She raised an eyebrow and then sat beside him, uncaring whether he had any objections. "I mean, I suppose I was. My father was a Chief, so if it wasn't for him, I would have been—"

Cin shook his head. "That's not what I meant. The Moon granted you the power of Luck, did She not?"

"Well, yes. Can't say it's ever done me much good."

"Have you known to use it for anything?"

"Cards," Sen said. She blinked as Cin stared at her, stunned.

"You used the Moon's power...to win at cards," Cin said.

"To my credit, I wasn't fully aware that the Moon gave me anything."

Cin looked annoyed, but he didn't press the issue further. He turned forward again, narrowing his eyes at nothing in particular. "Regardless of what useless things you use your Luck for, you're not the only one. I'm different from everyone else here. I also wound up with Luck."

That caught Sen's attention. She craned her head at Cin with curiosity, humming to herself with interest. "Is that right?" she asked. "Were you also—"

"I'm not the son of a Chief, if that's your question," Cin said bluntly. "Truth be told, I haven't a clue why I would be considered a child of fortune."

"What do you mean?"

Cin regarded her for a long second, examining her with what seemed to be cold calculation. His dark eyes betrayed nothing, hidden beneath the loosed locks of hair that slightly obscured his vision. Something moved in his face. Not quite a grimace, not quite a twitch. Perhaps a remembrance of harder days. Sen couldn't say for certain.

Regardless, whatever flashed upon Cin's face, even for the briefest of moments, was enough for him to avert his gaze, to stare down at the ground with disdain. He closed his eyes and drew in a deep breath, silent but for his feet ever so slightly inching back and forth on the rough floor. Emotionless but for the fists clenched tightly at his knees.

He opened his eyes and hauntingly stared forward, releasing the tension in his hands with a long breath. As he did so, the other Children seemed finished with whatever they were doing, eyeing Cin and Sen both with interest before filing out of the barrack.

Sen thought it odd that they picked up as suddenly and quietly as they arrived. Only Ziia offered a passing glance, but little else. Watching the old crone leave, Sen turned back to Cin as though she would find any explanation, but his expression spelled nothing for her.

Cin scoffed. Suddenly, his eyes appeared tired. "I suppose I know this land better than most. Before the blood which taints the soil was spilled by the flesh and iron of the Acrarians. When we offered our own blood ourselves in search for answers that we would never find."

The words perplexed Sen. She put a hand to her chin thoughtfully.

"Before the Acrarians came and built on the blood of my ancestors a city from salt and smoke, I was just a boy. A boy with no one but himself. Not even a mother or father. I was four when their blood joined the earth, even if it was not their choice. I was five when their voices sang of my origins. I was six when a chorus from centuries past recited a promise spoken by a woman borne of the Moon, and I was seven when I sought that woman out. By the time I was eight, there was nothing left of my home, and less remaining of those who, for a brief period in my life, I considered to be my people."

He paused, his eyes seeming colder as he offered a stern glance at Sen. Slowly, he rose to his feet and walked to the chest at the foot of his bed, calmly parsing through it with measured concentration, removing and stacking items in a neat pile until he pulled out the object he seemed to have been looking for, apparently resting far at the bottom of the chest.

Cin returned to the bed holding the item, covered in a wool cloth, as he would a stack of fragile glassware. He sat back at the edge of the bed, still paying little mind to Sen and her curiosity at what it was he was holding. He held the object closer to his face, the cloth still covering it, and a flash of...something flared in his eyes.

Sadness? Anger? Frustration? It wasn't for Sen to say.

But when Cin finally removed the covering from the object, Sen immediately understood. It was a mask, painted in stripes of black and red, the contours of it matching perfectly the shape of a small child's face. For a small moment, Cin's hands shook, but his face remained as stoic as ever, offering nothing for Sen to read but that mysterious nothingness. The sharp angles of Cin's cheeks and chins quivered, his teeth gritting. A long sigh escaped his lips, something toeing the line between relief and frustration.

"This," he said, lifting the mask up, "is all I have left of the boy I was. It speaks more than I would care to, just as the voices of the lost force me to listen more than I would wish to."

Sen picked at a loose thread in Cin's blanket, her head turned downward, not wanting to match his gaze for fear of the reminder it would bring. The death mask, the voices of the lost, they meant nothing to her. But just as they spoke to Cin, despite his efforts to the contrary, they whispered to Sen in equal measure, painting the picture in her head of two faces she wished she had never encountered, two faces for whom her entire life changed forever.

"You were born to the Haunted Tribe," she said softly, not looking up.

Cin placed the mask on the bed, the empty eye holes seeming to stare menacingly at Sen. "A misnomer you all gave my people. But yes."

"Do you have another name you'd prefer your Tribe to be called?"

"What does it matter?" Cin said harshly. "They're not my Tribe anymore, and they're all but extinct besides."

"You can't change to whom you were born," Sen said. "They're still your people, regardless of whether you've left them behind."

Cin scoffed, gesturing his arm in a wide arc. "Look around you, Sennalhat. What people of mine are there to even leave behind? I did not abandon them, nor they me. They abandoned only themselves in a fruitless search for that which we cannot hope to comprehend."

"What do you mean?" Sen asked. "You mentioned a search for answers earlier, too."

The glare Sen received from Cin sent a chill down her spine. Not that there was anything malicious in the dark pools of his eyes, nor anything inherently fearsome in his expression. He did not have a frightening face—if anything, his face was just plain—but he instilled fear within her just the same.

His scowl deepened as he closed his eyes. "Calling them the 'Haunted' may have been a misnomer or even derisive. But it was a true name all the same."

Sen looked down at Cin's death mask, the scowling expression matching its wearer. "You mean the voices of the dead."

Cin didn't nod, but the slight grunt he offered was all the confirmation Sen needed.

"A curse upon the Tribe and all of its descendants. Not even I could run from it."

Sen sneered at the use of the word "curse." It was enough for a brief flare of anger to surge through her. "I thought curses were only of use to those too stupid or hateful to know otherwise."

"Our existence as Eclipseborn is not indicative of the existence of curses. But it doesn't mean that curses are not real." Cin did not return the sneer, but his words acted in much the same manner. He picked the mask back up, matching its glare with some measure of disdain. "The Haunted were a Tribe obsessed with death. With the stories that death told and what generations long since passed. My ancestors were so obsessed with the past that an eye was cast on neither the present nor the future. Moribund obsessions begat moribund tales, such to the point that our histories were not celebrations of the accomplishments of greater men but rather the blood which fell in their wake. Scholars were convinced of what bloodshed could instill upon us, and so, beneath our feet right now, beneath these floorboards built by hands stained by centuries of blood, there lie the lives of innumerable of my ancestors, spilled for reasons beyond what I can understand." He shook his head, not even sparing a glance at Sen.

She could feel the revulsion on her own face, but she doubted he would have any reaction to it.

"Ironic," Cin continued. "A tribe of killers, undone by the killer with the stronger weapon."

"I wouldn't label it irony," Sen said. "All of our Tribes have killed. It doesn't put us on equal levels of atrocities as the Invaders."

The mask shook in Cin's hands. "You presume too much, Sennalhat. The glimmer of a golden sunset against the southern waters is a false beauty. It's a mask, just as this." He dropped the mask to the ground, allowing it to clack against the hard floor unceremoniously. "The plains on which the Acrarians built this city weren't called the Red Fields for nothing. It was too ghastly even for them, if the haste at which they forced the Tribe to construct the city was any indication."

Sen shuddered.

"Who am I to say where this obsession with blood and death came from, and from whom it stemmed?" Cin stared at the toppled mask, the face resting on the ground. "All I know is that there was one group above all else whom my ancestors wished to see face-first upon the dirt, drained of all life."

"The Eclipseborn," Sen said. She grimaced.

Cin nodded slowly. "The histories reveled in tales of the destruction wrought by the Eclipseborn. If only we knew the truth of the matter. Histories written by the victors only ever tell one side, one tale, and our Land seems to conspire that our people, *our* people—" He patted a hand hard against his chest, gritting his teeth at Sen all the while. "—are written always as the villain. If there are any histories dictating otherwise, I've yet to find them.

"The only living histories remaining are those who lay dead beneath the ground."

"You don't mean—"

"I mean exactly that, Sennalhat. Maybe my curse is separate from that of the Tribe. To know the truth of it all, but with none to share it. Who would listen to the words of one doubly or triply cursed?"

Sen nearly jumped out of her seat to grab him by the shirtsleeves. "Cin, you could educate all of the Tribes! The truth of the Eclipseborn! You—"

"The 'truth' does not matter to those already gripped by hatred." Cin nudged his way out of Sen's grip, his long locks obscuring his eyes as he looked to the ground. "I was naïve enough to think I could change it all when I found the truth. But the word of an Eclipseborn matters for nothing. The word of one claiming to listen to the dead even less so."

"But, you—"

"But nothing, Sennalhat." Cin sounded defeated. "What more can one expect when you're told of your people's greatest atrocities when you're no more than a boy? To learn of a slaughter of your own kind so horrendous that the heavens cannot help but intervene?"

Feeling her heart skip a beat, Sen could not find the words necessary.

"Of course, why would you know any of this? Why would you know of the Pale Night of four hundred years past, when over a dozen Eclipseborn and their families were slaughtered simply for being alive? Simply because the Eclipseborn were written to be a group to hate, to fear, to revile, when all they wanted to do was coexist? A pogrom so atrocious that even the Moon herself was said to grow pale at the sight? A night so diabolical that the Moon ensured that the voices of her murdered champions would haunt their killers until their dying days, a curse that has endured to this day?"

They stared at each other and said nothing. What good could words even do?

Sen felt cold. Her heart pounded. Distantly, the thunderclaps roared in her mind, the coalescing of screams screeching in her ear. *Gods*, she thought. *Gods, gods, gods.*

Cin's fists clenched until his fingers became beet-red. "The voices of the lost care not whether you're a boy like I was. Just as the voices of those slaughtered Eclipseborn warned me to run as soon as I could. To find Kamataa and the Children of the Black Moon as soon as I could. Even at the age of six, I knew that the legacy of my Tribe was a legacy of monsters. Convince yourself all you want that the Acrarians are the greatest pox on this Land. I'll point you towards centuries of death and bloodshed instead."

"But..." Sen closed her eyes, the thunderclaps continuing to echo in her mind. "The actions of centuries ago are not justification for the deeds of today."

"That's where you're wrong, Sennalhat." Cin shook his head derisively. "The cycle of violence against the Eclipseborn still exists to this day. Did you really think that the small group of us were the only ones born during the last Eclipse?"

Sen opened her mouth but said nothing. There was a sinking feeling in her stomach. *Gods, how many others were killed?* she thought.

"Perhaps my Luck manifested in getting me out in enough time to survive the Acrarians' arrival. All I know is that I hear the screams of our brethren every night." He closed his eyes and grimaced. If Sen didn't know any better, she'd have sworn a tear was trickling from his eye. "I would see the Tribes ended for them."

There were no words that Sen could possibly say. *What could I even say to negate centuries of violence? Absolutely nothing.*

Cin stood, his gaze affixed to the door, fists still clenched. "There's a light you're still not allowing yourself to see. What more would it take?"

"I...I don't know," she whispered. But then she looked at Brin's pendant, still glinting brightly on her bed. She thought the pain she had experienced already was enough. She was afraid to find what else lay within.

Glancing over his shoulder, Cin seemed to understand as he followed Sen's line of sight. "Do it," he said. "Your hesitation gives you all the answer you need."

Sen nodded and slowly walked across the room. The pit in her stomach deepened, growing cavernous with each subsequent step. The glimmer of the pendant teased her with its knowledge, just as it threatened her. *Brin,* she thought. *You would have banished me if you could. Just like all the rest.*

She stood tall over the pendant, and yet she had never felt so small when she held it in her grip. *I loved you, little brother. But did you love me back?* She held the pendant close to her chest, and a light flared in her eyes.

Whispers of wind danced through the open window, and they carried with them the aromas of salt and opportunity. On mornings like these, with no noise save for the servants' footsteps downstairs and the ocean waves calmly splashing ashore, Aritz drew comfort in these simple moments, where he needn't think so much as where the last fifteen years had brought him, but rather where they would take him next.

With arms behind his back, fingers interlinked, Aritz a Mata watched the gulls glide in the distance above a boundless sea, off to wherever the stretches of the world end. At times he envied them.

The sun had been up for hours, but he was still in his morning robe, a long piece of blue silk fringed with a darker shade of blue, tied at the waist to hide his bare chest. The remnants of his breakfast remained on the table, his appetite minimal, as it was when he found himself in the midst of planning.

Much of the previous evening, after his soldiers departed, was spent filling in the gaps in the northernlands on the war map, recording in as much detail as his memory would grant him the terrain of the land, the rolling green dunes, the open fields, everything he could between the northern mouth of the forest and the village he encountered.

The fields are the easy part, he had thought to himself. *But that village—that shall be the key to everything.*

His auburn hair wafted in the entreating breeze as he turned back to the center of the room, back to the map. He had left his flintlock pistol on the table, the barrel running parallel to the southern reaches as though an indicator of the territory he had claimed for his people. *As it were. The north remains woefully underdeveloped and uncivilized. We will have to right that.*

That village continued to irk him. Aritz had been within the midst of those people for naught but an evening, but every detail of that village, from its primitive huts to its undeveloped infrastructure to its savage denizens, was ingrained in his mind. In one evening, he felt he had put as much detail on the map of this one village as he had the entire southern reaches.

The memory disgusted him just as much as the words he spoke, which still lingered acridly on his tongue. *I'll rid this beautiful land of them,* he thought. *Them and their putrid language. Foul.* He spat.

Right in the center of the village.

This is where we need to strike. We control here, we control the north. Everything else is just in the way.

And beyond the puddle of saliva, the mountains loomed. Aritz knew not what lay in those mountains. But he intended to find out.

He promised Their Highnesses this land, and he was going to give it all to them.

He tapped his knuckle on the map in two successive knocks and returned to the table where his breakfast remained. He picked at a clump of scrambled egg, rolling it between his finger and thumb, and deposited it in his mouth, bemused by the bland flavors. *There had better be better seasonings in the north, as well, else those savages will not be the only ones to lose their heads.*

The strips of peppered bacon were edible, at least.

As he gnawed on the strip of cured pork, a succession of three quick knocks rapped on the door. "Yes," he garbled, his teeth still working on the bacon. Much chewier than he would have preferred.

One of his soldiers, the pock-faced man who had joined him on his venture north. Aritz still couldn't remember his name for the life of him. He didn't much care.

"Sir," Pock-Face said, saluting in the Acrarian fashion.

"At ease," Aritz said, swallowing the remnants of food in his mouth. *Somehow, they failed at bacon. I'll be needing a new chef.* He looked at Pock-Face, his expression morose while barely hiding notions of anger. "What is it?"

"There've been troubles in the night, General," the soldier said, still not at ease. Not that he continued saluting. He merely looked terribly tense.

Aritz rolled his eyes, bemused, and picked up the glass of orange juice next to his plate. He sipped at it before feeling his face convulse at the strands of citrus filling his mouth. *I must inform my next cook that I'd prefer to have juice with my pulp.*

Spitting the juice back in the glass, he sneered and picked up a report of the previous day's news, previously folded in half at the edge of the table. He skimmed through it, finding little of interest before glancing back at Pock-Face. "There are troubles every night in this city, soldier," he said. "That's part of being a modern society."

"I am not speaking of a tavern brawl or lovers' quarrel, sir. Two of our men were found dead last night."

That grabbed Aritz's attention. He looked up from the report, eyebrows raised, and tossed the paper aside, the stack scattering across the floor as It missed the table. "Where?" he demanded bluntly.

"In...Execution Alley, sir," Pock-Face said. "A patrolman found them bloodied with their guns taken, one of the savages dead beside them."

Furrowing his brow, Aritz flashed the soldier a quizzical look. "Execution Alley?" he asked.

Pock-Face cleared his throat, looking sheepish. "Ah, apologies, sir. A name the lads have taken to calling the alleyway where we...you know."

"Hmph," Aritz grunted. "It's cute." He spoke the words with little humor. *I don't care what the lads call it, so long as they do their duty.* "Who killed our men?"

"I...don't know the details, sir. From what I have heard, two of the workers broke free and tried to escape but were quickly apprehended. They were to be executed in a show of consequence, but..."

Aritz crossed his arms, looking back to the war map. *There* was *an unusual number of shots that rang out. They couldn't have been* that *poor of marksmen.* An annoyed sigh traveled out through his nose as he shook his head. Pock-Face stared at him, apparently not inclined to continue his sentence. Aritz returned the glare in silence, watching as the soldier's discomfort became more evident.

A realization struck. "You said," Aritz began, "that there were *two* workers who attempted to leave?"

Quickly, Pock-Face nodded. "Yes, General."

Aritz held out his arms in a questioning motion. "Then, where is the other one?"

"Sir?"

"You said *one* was dead beside our men. Where is the second?"

The soldier shook his head. "I do not know, sir. I only was told a short while ago."

Aritz did not mask his frustration, nor did Pock-Face hide his uneasiness at the General's expression. He was not going to let his soldier forget who was in charge. "And are there any *leads* as to where this savage with a *gun* is?"

Pock-Face started to sweat. "Sir, we cannot say for certain that the worker fled with a—"

"Answer the damn question, soldier."

The soldier straightened stiffly as a board, probably to hide the sweat stains beneath his arms. "N-no, sir. There are not."

Aritz snarled. "And who was making the rounds last night?"

"I will find out as soon as is possible, General." Pock-Face flashed a salute, seemingly on instinct. As if he didn't know what else to do.

"See that you do," Aritz murmured. "Dismissed." The soldier turned to leave—and not soon enough, by the look of him—but Aritz cleared his throat, stopping him in his tracks. "One more thing, soldier. Find my cook."

Pock-Face nodded, relief settling in on his face. "Shall I instruct him to prepare a fresh plate, sir?"

"No. Hang him."

The soldier paused, flashing a quick smile as though taking the remark as a joke. The grin melted when he met Aritz's glare in earnest. "Ah, y-yes, sir." He saluted once more and scurried out of Aritz's chambers.

The general smirked at the departed soldier. *Either from the ramparts or "Execution Alley." Just do your damn job.* He sighed deeply, the wind whistling as it blew through the open window with greater intensity. Aritz ran a hand through his hair, pushing the windblown locks out of his line of sight. Leaning against the table, he knocked away the plate of subpar breakfast and stared ahead in muted anger. A heat rose within him, his ears near to steaming. *Two of my soldiers dead; I can deal with that. They're but replaceable numbers. But a savage with a gun? I can think of few things worse.*

The north-facing windows caught his eye. Rarely did Aritz ever look to the north; he had no need to see his flock fawn over him as he peered out the window, thinking he was passing them a glance. The far reaches of the southern horizon, where the ocean kissed the sky, held greater appeal to him. From there lay the promise of further discovery and opportunity.

But for the last fifteen years, the north had offered him only a finite opportunity. He was told that that forest was a hard border and that he would never progress further than that. For fifteen years, Aritz believed those words.

But no longer. He now knew the falsehood of those claims. He needn't have worried about surviving that forest anymore. Rather, the forest was to worry about surviving *him*.

That northern horizon had suddenly gained appeal to Aritz a Mata. And so he glanced out the window, overlooking the people of this city, of *his* city, going about their morning routines, unaware of the goings-on of the previous evening, unaware of the danger which may still have been lurking within their walls.

Aritz shook his head. *Not if I have anything to say on the matter.* He looked past the city limits, to the gently inclining pastures of green, following their trail until they met the pastel hues of the forest. Where the greens as pure as any of the works of the great Acrarian artisans and painters met with the ethereal swaths of oranges and reds, as though from a different world entirely. In many respects, this was a pure land. A pure land tainted by lesser creatures. To Aritz, it was his duty to cleanse it.

And if there was cause for alarm over even a lone savage loose within the walls of his city, then there was only one solution. A solution he would be proud to carry upon his shoulders.

Aritz gritted his teeth and returned to his war map, to the southern reaches comprising his city and neighboring settlements. He eyed his flintlock pistol, still lying parallel between the city and forest. A hard border between the past and the future, between the primitive and the industrial.

A turn of the pistol would change that. A path cut to the future. A swath cutting through the length of the forest, deep into the heart of that foul village and beyond.

And as Aritz looked at his northward-facing pistol, and the promise of what came with it, he smiled.

Distantly, protesting screams echoed from downstairs, followed by calls for some rope.

When the flare of light dimmed, Sen once again found herself in Brin's Memories, right where she had left off earlier in the day.

The City loomed in front of her—in front of Brin—as trails of dust were kicked up by the breeze.

Brin was flanked by a number of soldiers, the group headed by the man who had shot their father dead. They said nothing to Brin, and what words they spoke were incomprehensible to Sen's ears.

Watery blurs obscured the picture, evident that Brin was trying—and failing—to hold back his tears. He was pushed along every five to ten steps, and after the first few times, he stopped looking back.

They approached the gate to the City, the one that had been left wide open for them just the night previous. On guard stood four soldiers, all dressed in the standard arrangement of blues that Sen had seen so much already. Long Deatharms were held in one hand each, the butt end propped on the ground, the weapon held as one would a staff.

Brin seemed to crane his head around the frame of the stranger at the front of the pack, allowing Sen to get a good look at each soldier.

Truthfully, they all looked more or less the same to her. Three of them were men, each with the same pale complexion, the same cropped hair, the same expression of self-satisfaction. But the fourth soldier, a woman, perplexed her. While the three men stood to attention with the same rigidity and timing, this fourth soldier was behind by a fraction of a second, not holding the same posture as the others.

It was hardly a custom or tradition that the Stone Tribe practiced, to stand as almost mirror images of one another when a leader approached, so the idea was odd to Sen. But regardless, even to her untrained eye, even with the blurs caused by the tears welling in Brin's eyes, the delay and lackadaisicalness were just perceptible enough to her that she wondered whether the soldiers flanking Brin would bark something at her, but she heard no incomprehensible mutterings the closer they came to the City.

They arrived at the gate, and after a brief exchange that probably meant nothing, the lead stranger walked off, leaving Brin in the woman's care. Brin kept averting his eyes as she tried to get a look at him, but she was persistent. Her red locks aflame, she had a sinister and almost sadistic expression on her face. Brin wiped away the tears and looked more clearly at her for a brief moment before turning away again. Sen felt her heart catch in her chest at the sight.

Kamataa?

She'd never forget the face. Not after what she did to Brin. Not after what she did to Narva. Not after telling me it was all for my benefit.

Part of her wanted to withdraw from the Memory, but something continued to urge her onwards, just as Kamataa's Invader disguise did so to Brin.

Fluent in the Invader tongue, Kamataa softly blathered on and on to Brin, nudging him at times, pushing him along, seeming to be offering some profound soliloquy just for the sake of it. She had to have known that Brin could not understand her. And yet she droned on and on, shoving Brin toward the prison camp where Sen had freed him.

The last moment of hope that the boy would ever have.

Brin did not spare a glance at Kamataa, focused only on the pair in front of him, one a soldier, the other a man being dragged along just as Brin was.

Who is that? Sen wondered.

Mercifully, Kamataa quieted, other than exchanging a greeting with a guard at the final gate to the camp. The final gate to hell on earth.

When the rows of dispirited Tribespeople came into view, Brin immediately closed his eyes and turned away, but judging by the brief slivers of light which poked through his eyelids, he was still being forced along before being shoved down to the ground.

Brin was sat in the dirt next to an unfastened lock and chain. Kamataa gestured a hand toward Brin, directing his attention to the man beside him. The man's hair was undone, but the remnants of a braid hung over his shoulder, his hair splayed and frayed in a number of places.. And the faint traces of paint were still visible upon his face.

Wait, *Sen realized.* That man is from my Tribe.

Brin looked on silently toward his kinsmen, hearing the jingling of a chain and the creak of steel as the clamp was fastened over his ankle. The locking mechanism appeared looser than that of others nearby. Kamataa's face snuck in from his periphery, as she put her lips just before his ear.

"Black Moon," she whispered.

When Brin turned back to look at her, she was already several paces away, not sparing a look back. The gates were left ajar.

The whole sequence perplexed Sen. Why would she be whispering to Brin about the Eclipse? *she thought.* Did she think that *Brin* was the Eclipseborn from the Tribe?

"Brin," a voice next to Brin said.

Brin turned his head, not quite meeting the eyes of the Stone Tribesman. Listlessly, he shook his head. "I'm sorry," Brin said. "Dounhar."

Dounhar. The name is vaguely familiar. *She examined the man's face for as long as Brin's Memory would allow. His expression was sullen, understandable given the circumstances, but it also seemed naturally so, judging from the permanent bags dwelling beneath his eyes, the droopy contours of his cheeks, the weathered glint in his eyes barely holding on to their shine.*

He looked so familiar, and then a recollection outside of this Memory came back to her.

From the previous night, in this very camp. Hesitation on the part of Narva and Brin both. Looking back in the direction from where Brin was freed.

Narva's words back in the Forest. You *do* remember that we had another person taken from the village as well, right?

Another person. This man.

And he was right next to Brin the entire time, *Sen realized. Gods, I'm a fucking idiot. Temptation willed her to drop everything and steal away back into the camp where Dounhar was surely still chained. For all the good it would do.* Very little, at that.

Dounhar shook his head at Brin. "What did she say to you?" he said sternly.

Brin looked around at the sallow faces in the yard, his eyes closing periodically for long stretches of time before he finally looked back to Dounhar. "She said, 'Black Moon.'" His tone was disbelieving.

Immediately, Dounhar spat on the ground. "'Black Moon,' pah!" He sneered. "Your sister and your family. You've doomed us all."

Vigorously, Brin shook his head but said nothing.

"She was damned lucky your father lacked a single hardened bone in his body. There's no room for compassion when dealing with a beast like her. Your family knew the price of harboring a Curseborn like her, and look where it got them. The only thing your father ever did worth a damn was treat my brother with some dignity, and even then, your Curseborn sister mocked him relentlessly."

Brin softly grunted. "We all treated Grafhar with dignity. He's a good man. Just—"

Dounhar sneered and looked away.

Grafhar, Sen thought dejectedly. The mute Linguist from her Tribe. He had translated that evening when the two Haunted runaways, Shara and Ran, arrived in the village. And that was how she recognized Dounhar, from chance encounters alongside Grafhar. Her heart sank. I'm sorry, Grafhar, Dounhar. Nature's cruel joke hardly excused my own.

The two remained silent for a time, Brin staring blankly at the pile of dirt beneath him. Absently, he picked at clods of packed earth, balling them up between his fingers and then tossing them away like a piece of trash. "It wasn't my choice," he muttered.

Dounhar grunted, sounding perplexed. "What did you say?"

"I said it wasn't my choice."

"What wasn't?"

"My sister. It wasn't my decision to keep her around. You shouldn't be admonishing me for it. In case you forgot, I wasn't born for another four years after my mother decided to birth during an Eclipse."

"Brin, I'm aware of that," Dounhar said. "But your family—"

"My family's decision didn't exactly make things easier on me, either." He stared sharply at Dounhar.

The man's eyes widened, apparently shocked at the admission.

"Because of her, my life was hell. Even when I beat the shaking sickness, things didn't get better. They only got worse, whether through her own actions or those of others as a direct result of her. When they learned she'd fight back, they went after me instead. Why should I have suffered for my family's decisions?"

The words equally stunned Sen. She knew and acknowledged that those who wished to harm her decided to do so through Brin. She just didn't realize how vociferously he resented her for it. Her heart felt the weight of a boulder.

Dounhar shrugged his shoulders, a grimacing frown on his face. "Well. We're in the shit now. What your family did doesn't matter much here."

Brin scoffed. "Doesn't it?" He shook his head, disgust evident. "My sister was Curseborn. There's no use running from that anymore." Ever so slightly, his voice started to break. "Family or not, she was Curseborn. And I'm damn tired of paying the price for it."

Dounhar nodded and raised his hand as he would a toast.

There was silence, and Sen could hear her heart pounding like a hammer from outside the Memory. He had said it. Brin said it. Curseborn.

Of all the people to have called her that wretched title, Sen could not believe it was her own brother.

I've seen enough.

She forcibly withdrew from the Memory.

Cin had long since left when Sen returned to the barrack. Sen felt alone in this room as cold sweat trailed down her back, angry tears trailing down her cheeks.

Her hands trembling, she allowed the pendant to drop from her hands and onto the floor. She had no intention of picking it back up.

"Hard truths?" a voice called from her right.

As she wiped away tears, Sen turned her head to see Ziia standing in the doorway, hands thrown in her pockets. She was out of her Illusion, which made her stand out amongst this lot all the more. Her skin was perhaps more weathered than Kamataa's, her untied locks white as snow, falling past her shoulders in a heavy avalanche. Despite the cold her hair resembled, her face appeared genuine and warm, a concerned smile on her face that barely reached her eyes. Gently, she approached Sen, sitting beside her on the bed, placing a wrinkled hand on Sen's shoulders.

Sen stared at the floor, the pendant beckoning her further. She felt repulsed by it, by what lay inside it. The truth of everything that once tied Sen to her Tribe, now coming undone by the frayed knots that barely held her.

Heartache, anger, frustration, sadness. They all bunched together in Sen's heart, crushing her from the inside.

My sister was *Curseborn.* The words echoed over and over in her head. She felt betrayed. *If that was how Brin truly felt about me…then what good is it to honor his memory?*

Ziia's bony fingers massaged Sen's shoulder. "We share a closer kinship than merely the Moon, Sennalhat," she said. "Long ago, I found myself banished by the Stone Tribe. And by my own brother at that. I seethed for ages. He needed to be punished. To cast out his own blood in such a manner…it was despicable. And none stopped it."

Sen didn't turn toward the woman, but she did manage a glance out of the corner of her eye. "What did you do?" she asked, her voice barely carrying.

With a scoff and a chuckle, Ziia squeezed Sen's shoulder. "Nothing. He died on his own, and I'm still here, outliving all of the bastards." A long finger turned Sen's face by the cheek, forcing her to look at the old Stone woman. "This world is what *we* make of it. Not dictated by the whims and commands of those too stubborn and stupid to accept what is different. Words hold no power when we can instead *act.*" She nodded, withdrawing her hand away from Sen.

Considering the words, Sen trailed her line of sight back down and picked up the pendant, holding it tightly by the centerpiece as the chain swung slack against her wrist.

Words hold no power, she repeated to herself. Brin's words held nothing over her. None of their words did. Koelhe, Fann, Dounhar...Brin. And all the rest. She would show them all the power of her actions and see how their words held up.

She continued to grip Brin's pendant tighter and tighter. Any more, and she feared she would have ground it into dust.

Turning to Ziia, Sen felt a snarl in her teeth, a scrunch of her nose. "What do the Children plan to do?"

The old woman seemed pleased.

MEMORY

A Tribe

Fury. Rage. Hatred. Longing. For the past seven years, that was all Kamataa felt. This day was no different.

Every morning when she awoke, she felt the pain of Azantt's spear running her through, and every evening she felt the jolted impact of the hammer crushing the Chief's skull in a satisfying crunch.

Disdain. Emptiness. For the past seven years, Kamataa felt a combination of the two whenever she remembered her parents. A hollowness at their memory, and yet disdain for those who slaughtered them so mercilessly.

As she drifted off to sleep every night, she heard the pleas of *"Please! Please! Why won't you help us?"*

And every night, she remembered the expression of complete helplessness upon the face of that young boy and laughed.

After seven years, there was nothing left to feel but contempt. At those she once considered her people. At this wretched Land which discarded her as though she were little more than garbage. At being cursed still to live.

Seven years in solitude. They were not kind to her.

In the remote northwestern regions of the Forest, where the Wood Tribe rarely, if ever, treaded, Kamataa made her makeshift home. A transient home, but home, nonetheless.

As she opened her eyes to the start of a new day, a canvas of falling pastel leaves greeted her with a wet slap. Specks of mud and muck stuck to her face as she swatted away the leaves, a trail of dirt cutting a swath along her cheeks. She rubbed at it absently and felt it smear across her face, caring little for how it looked. At this point, her face was more mud than flesh.

With a grunt, Kamataa rose to her feet, wincing at the scar in her stomach that still tugged at her. She gritted her teeth, putting a hand to the long-since-healed wound. She closed her eyes, picturing Azantt's woman collapsing into a bloodied heap, her blood splashing in a viscous mess across the floors and walls. That made her feel better every morning.

She bent down to pick up the makeshift spear that slept beside her nightly. Her own spear was lost beneath the Big Lake, so this whittled mess that she had fashioned out of a tree branch had to do. To her surprise, it had held up well all these years.

Beside the spear was a simple sling that she put together from the threads of her clothing. It wasn't much, but it got the job done when needed.

Her hair fell in her face, obscuring the world from her sight. It had grown well past her waist and was painfully knotted and matted for it. She needed it to be. It kept her alert and focused.

Hardly anything remained of her clothing. What had stayed intact was woefully threadbare and repurposed to cover her extremities, supplemented by what she could salvage from mud, leaves, and twigs.

Kamataa was a lady of the Forest now. More so than any of those among the Wood Tribe, as far as she was concerned.

It was a new day. And yet, it was the same.

Kamataa traipsed through the mud as she did every morning. Her feet sank deeper and deeper with each step, the muck popping and slapping as she trudged further. For all the splendor she often heard of the depths of the Forest, this area may as well have been a pigpen for all the slop she had to bear.

For all she knew, that could have been the very reason why this area of the Forest was uninhabited. Sleeping and walking in pigshit would have been just as comfortable.

Every sloppy step carried with it a memory.

Slop. The Fear instilled in her parents.

Slop. Azantt's betrayal as the spear passed through her.

Slop. The bloodied remains of her parents, cowards that they were.

Slop. The bloodied remains of Azantt, treacherous bastard that he was.

Slop. A hammer finding a home among blood and bone, again and again.

Slop. Again.

Slop. Again.

Slop. AGAIN.

Kamataa gritted her teeth and hurled the spear. Within a second, there was a yelp, a *slop*, a thud. She chuckled to herself, licking her lips. The spear wobbled slightly before toppling, muddied water splashing upward as it met with the earth.

A rabbit was twitching its last, blood pouring out from its stomach where the spear had landed. Its breaths were ragged, clearly painful. Its grey fur was already staining in dark crimson.

Examining the dying animal, Kamataa picked up the spear in one hand and watched the rabbit weakly motion its tiny legs as though it were trying to run away. She grinned widely and swung the spear as hard as she could, meeting the trunk of a nearby tree with full impact.

The rabbit burst in an eruption of blood and bone fragments, its skull reduced to nothing. She wouldn't suffer a runaway meal.

Planting herself in the mud, she held the carcass—with blood still falling like a waterfall—and took a large bite, chomping viciously into the flesh, paying no mind to the mangy fur and loose bone. It was breakfast. She wasn't going to be picky.

Come lunchtime, she would do the same. Just as she would for dinner.

This was how it was every day for the past seven years. Perhaps she would find a second rabbit. Sometimes she could get her hands on a bird. Other days, she would have to subsist on the leaves themselves.

She cared not for her pride any longer. It left long ago. All she had left was her life.

Blood spurt across her face as she continued to gnaw at the rabbit carcass. She never took the time to savor the taste, not because of the flavor—which was typically awful, anyway—but to keep moving. Even though the Wood

Tribe had not found her these past years, she was never comfortable staying in one spot for too long. Even with how much she lost of herself, she still knew to retain that fear of the Wood Tribe.

A fatty bite worked her jaw for a bit, blood trailing out from her teeth and down her chin with the effort. She looked to the south while doing so. By midday, she was sure she could reach the western ridge of the Forest, perhaps knock loose a few bird nests for some eggs and an off-guard mother. Anything to survive the next—

A rustling drew her attention.

Immediately, Kamataa spat out the fatty meat and listened. Snarling, she remained in a crouched position, gripping her spear tightly even as the remains of the carcass continued to dangle from the shaft.

Another catch for later?

No. Voices.

They had finally found her.

Kamataa growled and drew her sling, bunching clumps of mud and leaves together along with bits of the rabbit carcass. The voices grew closer and more distinct. Five, six different voices. She couldn't understand any of them.

She'd give them little opportunity to understand her.

They were within striking distance. Kamataa swung the sling of mud and blood and let fly its contents. She missed.

Feared yelps rang as rabbit chunks and mud splashed out at them from the nearest tree trunk.

Kamataa grunted in frustration, watching the crowd freeze in place, trying to find the source of the strike. Good, they were afraid of her.

"I'm the Eclipseborn. A trickster and fiend are all I am." The words she had spoken to that hapless boy all those years ago rang in her ears. It was time to remind the world of what she was.

She laughed as she jumped out into the clearing, landing square in a patch of deep mud. Slowly, she turned to the group, still feeling the rabbit blood gush down her chin. She had no intention of removing it. It would speak just as loudly as her spear.

The group continued to stand cravenly in place, which perplexed Kamataa. *This* was the feared Wood Tribe? She expected them to kill her three ways before she even hit the ground. But these people...

She looked at them more closely. They were a mismatched group, all talking over one another with their hands raised, palms outward-facing, none in a tongue that she could comprehend. All they shared in common were their faces, but only in that they were equally stark white.

Fear. It had controlled those that Kamataa cared about. Now, it was *she* who controlled the fear. They all bunched together as she slowly approached, spear drawn, blood dripping, mud protesting as she set loose her feet from the ground.

She could only laugh as the memories of blood played once more in her head.

A man broke free from the huddle, staring at Kamataa with narrowed eyes. He would die braver than the others.

"Kamataa!" the man shouted, his arms outstretched as though they would guard the others. "Stop!"

Sure enough, Kamataa did stop, her own eyes narrowing back at the man. He was unkempt, though by comparison to her, he appeared well groomed. His hair flowed past his shoulders, a beard running long to the middle of his throat. The sleeves had ripped from his shirt, revealing slim yet veiny arms, more wiry than muscular. He looked so familiar.

"Kamataa," he said more calmly, taking two cautious steps forward. "Do you remember me? It's me...Ruhr."

Ruhr. The name flared in Kamataa's mind. She hadn't seen him since they were children. He up and disappeared when they were about ten or eleven years old, but she never knew why.

Why was he here, of all places?

Ruhr smiled gently, putting his arms down. His eyes indicated wanting to say so much more, but his lips did nothing of the sort.

Kamataa stared at him a moment more. And then jumped at him, spear aimed at his heart.

Ruhr sidestepped her and gripped the spear by the shaft, holding it against Kamataa's strength, or what little remained of it after all this time. He didn't look particularly fine-tuned in his years, either.

"Kamataa...please..." he said with strained effort, the words escaping through gritted teeth. "What...happened...to you...?"

Kamataa did not feel inclined to answer. She pushed back against him to no avail. So quickly was she already sapped of her strength. She slipped to her knees, burying herself in the mud.

Taking this as a sign of forfeit, Ruhr easily pried Kamataa's spear from her hands and threw it casually aside.

Flashing a smile, Kamataa jumped once more at him, tackling him to the mud, her nails baring at him like a hawk's talons, aiming for his throat.

With what seemed to be little effort, Ruhr gripped Kamataa by the wrists and pushed her off of him with his knees, flipping her entirely over.

Kamataa met the mud in a resounding thud, her skull and back simultaneously impacting the ground. At least the muck cushioned the landing.

Ruhr rose unsteadily to his feet, hands on knees, his breath catching raggedly. "Kamataa, please, that's enough!" he pleaded. "I know what you are. What happened to you."

She was ready to jump back to her feet and find her spear. But then she looked more closely at his eyes.

They were sincere. And they were frightened.

He put a hand to his chest. "It's a pain I know all too well. We're kin, you and I. More than the bounds of a Tribe can account for." He slowly approached and extended a hand to her. "I am also Eclipseborn. We all are." He gestured his other hand to the group.

Though hesitant, Kamataa grabbed Ruhr's hand and allowed him to pull her to her feet. Still wary, she took a closer look at the group he was traveling with. It had struck her odd how different they all appeared—different mannerisms, different styles of dress, unkempt and disorganized though they were—but now it all made sense.

Born to different Tribes. But born to the same curse.

She looked back to Ruhr. Words escaped her. She hadn't needed them for seven years. All she could manage was a series of breathy grunts.

Ruhr understood. "You may have fared better than most of us here, Kamataa," he said. "I was forced from childhood into this life of solitude. You at least made it to adulthood." He shook his head, staring at the mud. "All of us here have our stories that we would be happy to share. If you would be happy to add your own." He held out his hand again.

Kamataa looked at it quizzically, even fearfully. She did not reach for the hand this time.

Nodding, Ruhr flashed a soft smile, tucking loose strands of hair behind his ears. "I understand that you're frightened. All of us have been frightened. But we don't need to be frightened any longer." He looked back to his companions, fondness evident in the creases beside his eyes as he smiled. "We needn't be alone anymore. We're going to find the rest of our kin. The rest of the Eclipseborn. We've been traveling across the Land in hopes of finding more and more of our people. To create a Tribe of our *own*. A Tribe beyond a Tribe!"

The words were hard to believe. Kamataa continued to stare at Ruhr warily, even as the sincerity was unmistakable upon his exuberant face, his fists bunched together with excitement.

"It's only by luck that we came across you in such a dreary place," Ruhr continued. "It's enough to make me believe this is what the Moon wants. A Tribe in Her own image."

With clear caution, he put a hand on her shoulder. It was barely a touch at first, and Kamataa flinched at the initial contact, but slowly, he continued until the full weight of his hand was on her shoulder.

It felt...okay.

Ruhr nudged his head northward. "Come now," he said. "If you've been here all this while, you've suffered long enough. Let's find somewhere that the sun can reach you. What do you say?"

Kamataa still couldn't get the words to come to her, but she nodded regardless. A Tribe for the Eclipseborn...it seemed too good to be true. She didn't want to believe it. Part of her didn't want to go along with it.

But then she looked again at her surroundings, to the mud and decay that had been her home for seven years. If she were to fall victim to another betrayal, she would at least want the sun to beat down upon her for a final time in the doing.

No more words were exchanged. Ruhr merely waved a hand to his group, urging them onward. He stopped to pick up Kamataa's makeshift spear and tossed it to her. It was clear he didn't expect her to run him through while his guard was down.

As she caught it, she realized she had no intention of doing so. Somehow, that felt…good.

The menagerie followed Ruhr, Kamataa lagging behind, still wanting to maintain some distance between them. Having them all in front of her where she could keep an eye on them was also a plus.

One woman stayed behind with Kamataa, staring shyly at her. She kicked at a muddied rock and waved her hands in a circular motion. It appeared she was trying to formulate the words just as Kamataa was.

From the markings on her face, Kamataa could surmise the woman was originally of the Stone Tribe. She still maintained a braid, frayed though it was, and yellow paint was still faintly visible near her nose and within the creases of her forehead.

The woman extended a hand to Kamataa. "Nice…meet—you," she said haltingly, the Lake tongue clearly still foreign to her, though Kamataa was impressed at the effort, regardless. "My—name…Ziialhan."

Kamataa found herself smiling. Her hand tremored as she extended it to Ziialhan, but as their hands met, she felt calm. For the first time in a long while.

Grunting for the effort, words felt foreign to her tongue, as though they were a foul food she no longer had a taste for. But try still she did, and as she shook Ziialhan's hand, she managed to say with a heavy rasp, "Kamataa."

It was good to hear the sound of her own voice again.

CHAPTER SEVEN

CHALLENGE

By the time the western Lake Tribe's retinue had run aground, Tenazt was pushing past Tez with an entourage of his own.

An ache roared in Tez's shoulder as a succession of fighters and onlookers nudged her with varying degrees of intensity. She had just been getting over the residual aches of the previous evening's battle, too. She rubbed at her shoulder, rolling it and flexing her arm in the same act.

She saw Ket among the throng, an expression of consternation settling into their face. They turned and caught sight of Tez as well, behind the line zealous Lake warriors and curious passersby. They shoved their way through the crowd, stopping before Tez as a commotion ruminated from the shore where the approaching Tribe moored their vessels.

Tez exchanged a perplexed look with the Lake healer, nudging her head toward the approaching crowd.

Beside her, Tawa and Sharrabha grunted and crossed their arms, almost mirror images of one another.

A hush fell over the crowd as the light splashes of shallow water marked the arrival of the incoming host. Even from the fifty or sixty paces which separated them, Tez could hear the dull growl rumbling in Tenazt's throat.

At the head of the group of western Tribespeople was one of the tallest men Tez had ever seen, standing easily seven feet high, probably more. In contrast to most of the Lake folk she had encountered, Tez noticed that the man's hair was undone, framing the contours of his face with its soaked, wavy locks. A scowl seemed permanently affixed to his face, embittered wrinkles marring his forehead and brow. Dressed simply, his garb was comprised of little more than a sleeveless leather and hide top and wide-legged pants, his bared arms a tapestry of defined musculature.

Ket frowned and shook their head.

"Who is that?" Tez whispered to them, the tension not lost on her.

"Yhaan," Ket said plainly. "The Chief of the western Lake Tribe." They crossed their arms and scowled past the crowd. "The ruddy bastard."

Tez grunted in acknowledgment. *Huh*, she thought. *Two Chiefs, one Tribe. With these people, no wonder that can get a bit bloody.* That the Lake Tribe had two separate leaders—one for each end of the Big Lake—was something unknown to Tez, and it was safe to say it was not a fact well-known to most of her Tribe, either. *I wonder if Father even knew about that.*

Yhaan extended an arm at his side, his palm facing back, instructing his retinue to hold without even a word. He stopped a handful of paces in front of Tenazt, completely dwarfing the old man in the process. He narrowed his eyes, looking the eastern Chief up and down, his frown hardly budging an inch as the two men regarded each other in cold silence.

The residual waves from the lake gently crashed against the boats, gentle enough that it seemed the Lake of Bones was meekly whispering its objections to the matter, wanting not to add another resident to its murky depths.

The western Lake Chief folded his hands behind his back, holding his chin high, no longer staring at Tenazt and instead appearing to gaze out at verdant plains extending into the eastern horizon. His focus still laid upon whatever was more adequately capturing his interest, Yhaan grunted and said only, "Tenazt." He nodded.

Tez shoved her way through the onlookers, paying no heed to their annoyed objections, hearing her companions following closely behind her. She could see Tenazt more clearly. It was easy to tell how displeased he was at Yhaan's arrival. Far angrier than the man was just a short while previously.

"You have a lot of nerve to show your face here, Yhaan," Tenazt said, spitting on the ground with disgust. "I have to commend you for your gall, at least, to come all this way after what you did."

Yhaan scoffed, and a bemused grin finally broke the hold of his frown. "That's rich," he said. "Leave it to an easterner not to have the stones to own up to his thievery."

"*My* thievery?" Tenazt took an animated step forward, standing toe-to-toe with the western Chief.

Seems impossible that they could stand eye-to-eye, Tez thought.

Tenazt prodded an accusatory finger at Yhaan's chest. "You would *dare* to call *us* thieves? Find your own stones and own up to *your* transgressions, Yhaan. We'll suffer none of your accusations here."

Yhaan swatted away Tenazt's hand as he would a pesky gadfly. His scowl had once again replaced his grin. "You'll suffer the truth of your actions, Tenazt, in front of your people and mine. Would you have your kin view you as little more than a craven old man, hiding behind the backs of others when faced with *consequences*?"

"What lies are you speaking?" Tenazt bellowed, seeming to startle Yhaan's accompaniment but not the western Chief himself, so far as Tez could see. "There are no truths or consequences I need to face because it is *you* who are creating your own story. Explain yourself, Yhaan. By what right do you have to call me and mine 'thieves?!'"

"Why, the very fact," Yhaan said with a smirk, "that you and yours are thieves."

Tez buried her face in her hand, rubbing at the bridge of her nose. *Gods, give me strength*, she thought with exasperation. "Just someone explain what the fuck is going on," she muttered.

She thought she had said that in confidence with herself, but her voice carried far enough for it to be picked up by both Tenazt and Yhaan.

The two Chiefs turned sharply to her, eyeing her angrily.

Unperturbed, Tez merely brushed her hand off to the side. She held a neutral expression, raising at eyebrow to them both. *Go on, then. Some of us have an entire Tribe to reclaim. But no, take your time on this he-said-he-said horseshit.*

Yhaan chuckled at Tez before turning back to Tenazt. "Do you indulge in many visits from the Stone Tribe these days, Tenazt?" he asked. "Including them in your schemes?"

"For the love of..." Tenazt murmured.

Tez was thinking the very same.

"Enough beating around the bush, Yhaan," the eastern Chief growled, again prodding his counterpart with his finger. "Speak plainly so I may listen to your words and tell you how you are wrong."

Shaking his head, Yhaan paced off to the side, his hands unmoved from behind his back. Hardly a flare of anger or a spark of apprehension was visible on his face. He continued to appear calm, collected, in control.

Tez found it unsettling.

"You think I do not know about your appointed spy, Tenazt?" Yhaan said, a hint of malice tinging his words. "You would still assert that none among you are thieves when you deploy Barrah to pilfer from us without hesitation?"

The eastern Chief said nothing, though Tez was curious about the truth of the claim. Just a short while ago, Tenazt *had* requested she perform a task that he himself admitted to having Barrah regularly do.

"Nothing to say?" Yhaan said, his back turned to Tenazt. "No matter. Your silence speaks louder than your words would ever care to." His chest puffed as he visibly scoffed. "But if you would maintain your innocence, then how am I to explain the sudden mindlessness of several of my people?"

Wait, what? Tez's curiosity was piqued, and her attention was fully grasped.

The same could be said of Tenazt. The eastern Chief merely stared at Yhaan with what looked like wide-eyed surprise, his mouth agape as though words were scarce to come by.

Yhaan turned back to his opponent, watching with cold regard as Tenazt failed to say anything in his defense. "And again, you've nothing with which to defend yourself," he said plainly.

Adamantly, Tenazt shook his head. "What are you talking about?" he asked softly, the words barely veiling his disbelief at the accusation.

That actually made Yhaan laugh in what seemed to be genuine earnestness. He put his hands on his hips, shaking his head with an amused smile plastered across his face. "I must commend you, Tenazt, for your tenacity. To stand by your words, when all evidence points against them…to some, it must be considered admirable."

"*What evidence*?" Tenazt snarled. The old man gritted his teeth, his nose curling with evident anger.

A sharp finger shot out toward Tenazt, Yhaan's long arm nearly closing the gap between the two men all on its own. "All of them, all of *my people*, just as soon as their minds were lost, their pendants were stripped from them, not to be seen again!"

To Tez's ears, the collectedness of Yhaan's words had vanished. Now, his tone was hard, biting.

"You cannot expect me to believe," Yhaan continued, "that your man had nothing to do with that, do you? You should know just as well as I how treasonous it is across our Land to steal and make use of another's pendant for yourself. The Deities themselves would curse you at the first opportunity. But it is not something I would put past you, Tenazt. You hold regard for none but yourself. Why would you not have your spy spit in the face of the gods while you were at it, too?"

"Ridiculous," Tenazt growled. "If you're so convinced that Barrah did this to your people, then why don't we pay him a visit together?"

Yhaan raised an eyebrow, the lakeside breeze causing his soaked hair to flop and stick against his nose and forehead. He seemed to care little to remedy that. "What's your angle?" he asked.

This time, it was Tenazt's turn to chuckle. "My angle?" he said. "To show you that whoever or whatever stripped your people of mind and ornament did exactly the same to Barrah."

"Hmph," Yhaan said. "Then…"

"Yes," Tenazt asserted. "Exactly the same. If Barrah did this, why would he have ended up the same as your people? Of what gain would that be to me?"

"But, still, you admit," Yhaan growled, "that you would act in such a manner if it meant you had much to gain from it."

"When did I admit that?"

Tez looked back and forth to the two men, in equal measure perplexed and annoyed. *It's like watching Koelhe argue with herself,* she thought.

Yhaan grimaced and turned away his head from Tenazt with blatant disgust. "Enough," he said. "You can speak in circles all you want, deny all you want, deflect all you want. It changes nothing, Tenazt." Returning his hands behind his back, Yhaan slowly walked toward the Big Lake, looking only at the expanse of glistening water ahead. "It was a nice era of peace. While it lasted. But once again, Tenazt, you've seen fit to destroy it. As much as the Big Lake does not deserve it, this must be settled." He turned back to face the eastern Chief.

Tenazt said nothing, only narrowing his eyes in response.

"You wish to continue our old strife, then we will settle it in the old way." Yhaan pointed to the depths of the Lake of Bones. "I will see you on the surface of the water, tomorrow at sundown." Heeding no objections, Yhaan boarded his boat, his retinue in tow.

And just as quickly as they arrived, they paddled along the face of the Lake, the sound of splashing water the only voice accompanying the paralyzing silence.

One by one, the surrounding crowd dissipated until Tez was flanked only by Tawa, Sharrabha, and Ket. They all stared ahead at the departing western Tribe as they faded into specks shimmering on the Lake's surface.

Tenazt did not move for some time. Part of Tez wondered what was running through the old man's head. But part of her also couldn't shake the nagging feeling of how much of Yhaan's accusations were spoken in truth.

After a prolonged silence, the old Chief merely turned and walked away, his expression unreadable. He said nary a word as he traipsed along the village's main drag in the direction of the medical hut where Barrah had been tended to.

A grasp of the arm startled Tez. She turned away from watching Tenazt's departure to see Ket staring at her, determination apparent in their eyes. "Come by later," they said. And without further instruction, Ket set off after their Chief.

Tez could only continue to stand by the lake shore in stunned silence for the time being, looking to Tawa and Sharrabha for words she did not have.

It didn't appear they had the words, either.

After spending a length of time staring out at the Lake of Bones in solemn silence, Tez, Tawa, and Sharrabha took Ket up on their offer to come to the medical hut. A passing glance at the Big Lake filled Tez with conflicting feelings.

On the one hand, it was hard to deny that it was one of the most beautiful and serene sights she had ever seen.

But on the other, she shuddered to think of the horrors which adorned the lakebed, the bones of countless of the Tribe's ancestors laying the foundation on which the twin Lake villages were built.

"What do we do?" Tez murmured. She could feel the automatic frown as she said the words, and when she saw the looks of dejection upon Tawa and Sharrabha's faces, she knew that there was no easy answer to that question.

As they strolled along the main passageway, it was easy to be caught off guard by the glib demeanor of those walking the streets, some of whom Tez recognized as being in the crowd during Tenazt and Yhaan's conference.

"It's hard to believe," Sharrabha said, "how quickly they can all go back as though nothing happened."

Tawa shook his head in bemusement. "To them, it must just be expected. They go their whole lives hearing of dead men's wars that when a new one arises, it is just a part of life." He sighed. "It is...sad."

"Sad...and frustrating," Tez added. "We gambled on this, and look where it's gotten us."

"But still, we have a card to play," Tawa assured. "This...whatever it is. This challenge."

Tez frowned. She was still giving credence to Yhaan's accusations. Of what Tenazt may have been guilty of using Barrah for. "But on whom do we play this card?"

Sharrabha crossed her arms, gnawing at her lower lip. "You're unconvinced of Tenazt's innocence in all this, too, aren't you?"

"Is it worth it?" Tez wondered aloud. "All of this?"

"What would the alternative be, Tez?" Tawa asked. He gestured widely at their surroundings. "We are not exactly brimming with options. We gambled on there not being internal strife among the Lake Tribe, and clearly, that was foolish of us. But we are still here. We just happened to arrive on the more questionable side of the water."

"Hmph," Tez grunted. "If there's enough cause for grievances on this side of the Lake of Bones, though, then for all we know, Tenazt and Yhaan are shits both."

"And we have to decide whether to stay in the pile we're in, or wade to the other heap," Sharrabha agreed, though her expression indicated she was none too thrilled over the metaphor.

Tez threw her hands up and scoffed. "Well, might as well talk to the first heap, anyway."

They followed the path to the medical hut and found Tenazt and Ket in more or less the same positions as they had been earlier in the day. The Chief was pacing along the back wall, gritting his teeth and cracking his knuckles. Ket, for their part, continued to tend to the mindless Barrah, who responded only with a long continuous rasp of a breath, staring blankly at the ceiling above.

Tawa was first through the threshold and inclined his head toward the mindless Sneak. "Is he doing any better?" he asked.

Grimacing, Ket shook their head. "Same as he has been. Until we know what did this…" They threw up their hands in the absence of suitable words.

Tenazt continued to pace, paying no heed to any of his gathered company.

The more Tez watched wordlessly wander, the more it irked her. "Anything to say?" she said to the Chief, realizing quickly that she was nearly miming Yhaan. It hardly bothered her, given everything.

With a scoff, Tenazt stopped in place, putting a hand against the hard stone wall. He bunched a fist to his chest, scrunching his eyes shut. The air was still, save for the idle conversations of the injured and infirmed in the adjacent room.

On the silence went. Sharrabha sat down on an empty bed, Tawa leaning against the wall beside her. Ket hummed to themself as they held some combination of herbs, flowers, and liquid to Barrah's mouth, near to shoving it down his throat at one point. Tez stood in place, shifting her weight from one foot to the next.

And all the while, old Tenazt frowned at the wall in some wordless argument, barely moving a muscle, his focus appearing unhindered by any of the goings-on around him. To Tez's eyes, it looked like the Chief was visualizing the battle to come, or the argument to come, or the circular conversation to come. Whatever the case was, the miserable expression on Tenazt's face gave Tez the impression that the wall was winning.

At last, Tenazt opened his eyes back up, lowering his fist to his side. "I have been Chief of this Tribe for nearly five decades," he said, still facing the wall. "I have made mistakes. I have asked of others deeds which some would turn their noses from. But to call me a destroyer of peace, I do not accept that. We are still reeling from the effects of the Long War all those years ago. I would be a fool to rekindle that inferno."

He turned, not to face his visitors from the Stone Tribe, but to gaze upon Barrah. "Think what you may for what I employ Barrah. What Yhaan accuses me of, I deny it. Look at him." He gestured a shaking hand to the Sneak's prone form. "That I would be thought to wish this upon another is insulting. That Yhaan thinks me capable of that is even more so. He may as well be pointing his finger at the water's reflection. For some of his own to fall to the same fate is beyond suspicious."

Tez looked at Barrah with a frown, shaking her head once more at the poor sight. "You don't think Yhaan is responsible at all for this, do you?"

The Chief was quiet for a long moment, and then said, "No."

Unable to conceal a smirk, Tez could only laugh.

"Why even agree to Yhaan's challenge, then?" Sharrabha asked, her tone indignant. "You're trying to bleed him for what, exactly?"

The frown still creasing his face, Tenazt approached Barrah's bed and put a bony hand atop the man's forehead. "Atonement. Forgiveness. Retribution." He paused, shrugging his shoulders. "Tradition. I cannot deny a challenge. It's not our way. I have no choice but to meet Yhaan on the water with what strength still resides in my bones."

"And that solves...what, exactly?" Sharrabha continued to prod. "One of you dies, what happens next?"

"Our way is different than the Stone. Your traditions are rigid and firm. For us, we are fluid as though we were the Lake itself. A quarrel can end in the death of one, or both, or neither. Afterward, some choose to accept what has happened. Others wish to quarrel further. Those further quarrels sometimes lead to further wars. Such is the way of things."

Tez stared wide-eyed at Tenazt, her hands planted firmly on her hips. She looked down to the floor, doing her best to hide her bemused smirk, and said, "Gods, your people are fucking stupid."

"Tez!" Tawa said with an admonishing tone, just as her father once did.

Tenazt offered a gentle chuckle. "That's all right," he said. "It's not something I would expect your Tribe to understand. Our lives revolve around the battlefield. It's both our calling and our curse. The very calling and curse which brought you here in the first place, is it not?"

Tez said nothing.

Clicking his lips, Tenazt nodded tentatively. "It is an offer I would still honor, of course. Certain matters just take precedence at the moment. If you'll excuse me, then. I must prepare for tomorrow."

With a nod to Ket, Tenazt patted Barrah's unresponsive form on the shoulder and then made for the exit.

Tez held out an arm as the Chief attempted to walk around her.

"Stop," she said.

"Tez?" Sharrabha said, inclining her head.

Tenazt glanced at her from the side, not turning his head. "You must understand that there's no preventing this challenge from happening."

"I do," Tez said, also refusing to turn her head. "I volunteer in your stead."

"Tez, no," Tawa said through gritted teeth. "What are you doing?"

"This is *not* our fight," Sharrabha warned, matching Tawa's admonishing tone.

"Listen to them, Tez of the Stone Tribe," Tenazt said. "I can assure you that Yhaan is unlike anyone you've ever fought before." He tsked his tongue. "Have you ever crossed spears with a Frightener? The reason he remains so calm is that he knows he can instill enough Fear into a warrior to drive themselves to forfeit before he's even landed a single blow."

Ket stopped what they were doing to turn back to face Tez. "Did you see how unmarred his arms were? That's not by accident. I'd be shocked if a blow has ever reached him."

"Yhaan is more cunning than prowess, and yet, that is all he has ever needed," Tenazt continued. "But I can handle him. You needn't bloody your hands on my account."

"I'm not," Tez asserted.

"Oh?"

This time, Tez looked to the Lake Chief. "Your Tribe's prowess on the battlefield is indeed why we've come. And I won't deny that our hand was forced just to prove the Stone Tribe's commitment to a long-standing alliance with the Lake Tribe." She chuckled. "But this has little to do with that."

"Then tell me. For what reason would you champion for the eastern Lake Tribe?"

"It's because it'll be too much of a pain in the ass if you get sent to the bottom of the Lake of Bones and I have to start negotiating from the beginning again with Yhaan. We've been jerked around enough today, and time is of the essence. *That's* why I'm championing for you. Any more objections?"

Tez peered around the room, from Tawa to Sharrabha to Ket to Tenazt. Everyone seemed too stunned to say anything at all, much less object. "So, tomorrow at sunset, then?"

CHAPTER EIGHT

PURPOSE

A day ago, Sen could not have seen that this was where she would be standing.

Not after making it through the Forest, the City looming far along the southern horizon. Not after she and Narva risked life and limb to make it this far. So near was she to proving her detractors false.

But none of that mattered any longer, and she knew it. To her, it was a false hope for a fool's errand.

This day's revelations had stung so much already. Everything she had suffered over the last couple of days, everything she had lost—at this point, it was hard to fathom what it was even for.

"What do the Children plan to do?" she had asked Ziia. An evening ago, the words would have been poison on her tongue. Today, though...

It wasn't my *decision to keep her around.*

The warmth Ziia showed to Sen in that moment, in that admission of forsaking the Stone Tribe, it was something more genuine than Sen had ever felt. The old woman said nothing beyond the smile on her face as she inclined her head toward the door.

To Sen's surprise, that was enough.

Cin wandered back into the room, the stoic emotionless on his face seeming less a reflection of apathy as Sen had once thought. She knew better now that it was the mask he wore to replace the one he cast aside.

He nodded to Sen and Ziia both, making his way back to his bed.

"Cin, perfect timing," Ziia said warmly, the smile yet to fade from her lips.

"For what?" Cin said.

Something glinted in Ziia's eyes as she raised a hand toward Sen. "I believe we need to bring Sennalhat to Kamataa. Do you know where she is?"

Cin raised his eyebrows and slightly shrugged his shoulders. "The practice range, last I knew."

Ziia clapped her hands, the sound echoing through the barrack. "Sennalhat, shall we?"

Though she had the urge to return Ziia's excitement, Sen could only manage a blank stare. "You want me to go out *there*?" Sen asked, pointing a thumb behind her, the trajectory tunneling through the wall and out into the City streets. "I don't know if you've noticed, but I won't exactly blend in out there. I'm sure you all know not to wander around without any Illusion."

"In due time, Sennalhat," Ziia said, raising her hand as though to assure her. "Cin and I will accompany you. You won't know where to go, after all. Cin, a cloak, if you would."

Cin complied and dug through the chest at the foot of his bed, pulling out a long cloak composed of light fabric dyed in the same shades of blue that Sen had seen many of the guards wearing, this lot included. He tossed it unceremoniously toward Sen, hitting her square in the face.

Feeling the composition of the cloak, Sen couldn't help but frown. "Might be a bit warm for this, no?"

"Consider it year-round fashion," Ziia said. "The Acrarians don't care much for how much sweat they lose—the statement is all in the attire they wear."

That seems a bit ridiculous, but okay, Sen thought. "Fine," she said aloud, draping the cloak over her shoulders, lifting the hood atop her head. She tucked the fabric tightly around her, hoping the cuts and scrapes from the previous evening would be well hidden. She could already feel herself sweating a little, the warmth of the southern sun filtering in through the barrack even at this early stage of the morning.

Cin passed a glance at her and then made for the door, gesturing Sen and Ziia along with his hand. "Best not to keep her waiting," he said.

Taking him at his word, Sen followed, Ziia filing in beside her. The old woman seemed very spry and nimble for someone her age, to Sen's curiosity. *Granted, I've not met many other four-hundred-year-olds.*

The City struck her as completely different in the daylight. There was little of the frivolity and excesses that littered the streets the previous night. Few people were wandering around, and of those, fewer seemed to be entirely members of the patrolling guard, save for one or two people rushing off to who-knows-where, kicking up clouds of dust in their wake.

The dust clouds danced along with the wind, obscuring the path ahead as the rays from the sun passed through them. Sen had to shield her eyes as specks of dirt assaulted her, a sudden rush of dust headed her way all at once.

"*Heh,*" Ziia said, blocking her own face just the same. "You get used to it after a while."

When the dust settled, Sen peered her gaze skyward to see the smokestacks billowing deposits of black clouds upward, robbing the skies of a perfect blue scene. "You'd think if these people could do *that,* they could at least do something about the pathways, too."

"All things take time. I would know." Ziia smirked.

Cin continued to silently lead them through the empty streets until a clearing opened, just past the main drag. Two guards stood at the entrance, paying little heed to Cin's approach. Given the lack of ceremony to their arrival, Sen was hardly surprised that the guards couldn't even be fussed enough to care.

A loud bang startled Sen, nearly freezing her in place.

The familiar clap of thunder. She closed her eyes, the all-too-recognizable shadow laughing at her from behind her eyelids. Distantly, a spray of blood erupted and fell in a wide arc, two figures descending like a fallen tree. Spatters of blood continued to trail out from falling figures in a line, alternating faces and sizes in a set pattern, the laughter of her phantom shadow a shrill screech in her ears. The longer the laughter droned on, the more distinctly the grating noise turned to the sound of words. Of decipherable speech.

"Are you ready to kill them again?"

The voice was her own.

A sudden jolt shook Sen, her vision no longer flooded by the crimson eruptions illuminating the darkness. No, she was back where she was, back in the City, Cin and Ziia both staring at her with curiosity.

"Sennalhat," Ziia said, concern evident in her eyes. "Are you all right?"

Sen took a moment to allow her heartbeat to quell and then nodded hesitantly. "It's...it's nothing. I'm fine."

It was clear that Cin wanted to say something, but he only frowned before turning back to the clearing, dust kicking up with each step he took.

Ziia frowned at Cin as he walked away, folding her arms. "That boy..." she muttered, barely loud enough for Sen to hear. When she turned to face Sen again, however, it was as though a separate person entirely emerged, the jovial smile returning to her face just as easily as it had disappeared. She put a hand on Sen's shoulder as though to instill some reassurance back in her young kin. "You needn't say anything now," she said. "But just know that you can speak to any of us about anything that's troubling you."

A chill ran up Sen's spine. A flood of overlapping noise enveloped her ears.

You know you can talk to me.

What is it? Are you okay?

You know you can count on me to listen and help you make sense of it all.

It's just me, okay? You can tell me.

Her heart felt heavy, her body cold. The voice was clear as day, the memory of it all too painful.

"Narva," she whispered, hoping that merely voicing his name amidst the memory of his voice would be enough to bring him back. But she knew she didn't have the Luck for that. When she refocused, she saw Ziia inclining her head toward her, puzzled.

"Who?" she asked.

Sen stared sharply at Ziia, fighting back the tears as she felt her breath constrict in her lungs. She shoved her shoulder free of the old woman's friendly grip, heading off in Cin's direction. "Nothing," she said bluntly. *You all should know very well who. He's the one person whose memory I will* not *have sullied.* She stopped for half a step, half-turning to glance at Ziia. "Just take me to Kamataa."

Shaking her head back to focus, Sen grimaced as she listlessly followed in Cin's path. *Don't hate me for this, Narva. This...it's what I have to do. It's where I belong.*

Around a corner, Kamataa came into view, the fiery red locks of her Illusioned form dancing in the breeze. She was casually reloading her Deatharm, the smell of ignited smoke still lingering around her. Fifty yards beyond her stood a wavering object hung from a tree branch, something wrapped in burlap and slung up with a rope. Strands of hay appeared to be peeking out from the holes left by Kamataa's shot.

As Sen approached, Ziia sped past her, seeming to allow that awkward air between them to continue as she did not even spare Sen a glance. Frowning, Sen considered whether to offer conciliatory words but thought against it. *If we're to be kin, of a Tribe all our own...well, I can't say that I've been on kind terms with many from the Stone Tribe.*

Loudly, Ziia cleared her throat, grabbing Kamataa's attention. She folded her hands behind her back, her posture straight, far more formal than Sen remembered seeing in the barracks.

Kamataa turned around, flashing a smile as she saw Sen among the gathered. She rested her long Deatharm along a rack of similar weaponry and reached for a cloth to clean off her hands; black trails of residue had run along her hands and up to her wrists.

The old woman nodded to Ziia and Cin both and walked toward Sen, arms outstretched cheerfully. "Sennalhat," she said, dragging out the recitation. "Wonderful to see you out here. I trust that you encountered no trouble on your way here?"

Tugging at the hood of her cloak, Sen opened her mouth to speak but opted instead to merely shake her head. She bit at her lip, narrowing her eyes as specks of dust from the wind began peppering her face.

Kamataa's smile dimmed slightly, dropping her arms down to her side, an expectant gleam still glinting in her eyes. "I assume you've come to speak further on my offer?"

Hesitantly, Sen looked first to the ground, perhaps hoping that her feet may offer any guidance, before looking back to the Eclipseborn and nodding her head. "Yes," she said, still feeling a frown on her face. "I have."

With a sigh, Sen walked off to the side, looking off to the north, where the faint hue of the Forest's trees only barely cracked the horizon. "For all my life, past the Forest, the peaks of the Heart as my backdrop...that was home for me. I grew up within the cultural heart of our people, where all the cultures of our Land pass through at some point or another. When I was a kid, that was always so exciting for me." She paused, starting to chuckle to herself. "My parents...*heh*, they let me explore the mountains as much as I wanted. Get lost in the ranges, sometimes not returning until nightfall, sometimes alone, sometimes with friends—it didn't matter to me because it was fun. When those from other Tribes would pass through for their Trials, sometimes I'd tag along as a guide through the mountains, even if I wasn't supposed to. I never second-guessed why my parents let me do all of that when I was just a child."

Kamataa crossed her arms, nodding along to the story. She exhibited no joy, no amusement as she was wont to do. She merely...listened.

Sen furrowed her brow, flared her nostrils. "But then I got older. And then came the whispers. There were a few of them, at first. Really only after an accident that happened when I was ten and a friend got hurt. But those few whispers became many, and louder and louder they said, 'Curseborn.' First, it was a taunt, then it was an insult...and then it was a *threat*." Sen let out a long sigh, broken and ragged as she fought back angry tears. "And now, all those times my parents let me roam in the dark along unsafe trails, where a single missed step could have meant death...suddenly, it all makes sense."

From the corner of her eye, she could see Ziia kicking at stones on the ground. She could only wonder about their shared experience of being Eclipseborn among the Stone Tribe, even across the centuries.

Sen's bottom lip quivered, and she turned away from the northern sights in disgust. "My kin are not the Stone Tribe. They never were." She stopped to see how the words felt as they left her tongue. Nothing about them felt wrong. "My being Eclipseborn—something I could not control—brought misery to myself and those around me, even though it was never *because* of me. It was always because of those who were afraid of me, even though they had known me for my entire life. What good is a Tribe when it falls apart the moment someone is different?"

Turning fully to face her fellow Eclipseborn, Sen had to control herself against the angry tremors that threatened to overcome her. She could feel the heat rising in her face as she blinked away further tears of frustration of anger. Her breath shook as she took in each of their gazes, chief among them Kamataa, who only nodded with clear satisfaction and agreement. A laugh escaped Sen's lips. She couldn't help it. "It's all a lie," she said, her voice cracking. "The nature of the Tribe. To come together as one? *Heh*, no. They only come together to rid themselves of what they can't understand. Familial love? That never existed. My father was ashamed of my existence. My brother wished to have never been associated with me. So, what the hell was I even fighting for?" The laughter continued, overtaking her words.

Her three fellow Eclipseborn merely stood amidst the laughter, each of them seemingly bereft of words. Kamataa and Ziia only continued to incline their heads toward Sen, their gazes piercing Sen in equal measure, while Cin narrowed his eyes and crossed his arms, a deep frown set on his face.

"It's all a godsdamned lie!" Sen yelled, throwing her arms out to her sides. "All of it! And I want no part of it anymore. What's even the point, when the only person I truly had left, the only one who ever showed me consistent kindness and love, is—" She stopped herself, her chest pounding. She couldn't dam up the tears and they streamed heavily down her face. Clenching her eyes shut, Sen tried as hard as she could to push that final word to her lips, straining for the effort. "—dead," she finally said. She looked down, not wanting to look at Kamataa or any of them. One of Kamataa's own shots had struck Narva. The old woman clearly had no remorse for the act. No part of Sen could ever forget that.

And yet.

Sen laughed again. "All I have left is this. I have no home. No Tribe. Forget what remains of my family—I'm sure they'd love to forget what's left of me." She shook her head, wiped away the tears from her cheeks, and steeled herself enough to look back up at Kamataa. "*This*," she said, gesturing to Kamataa, Cin, and Ziia, "is the only home I have now. I'm in." *I'm sorry, Narva. Please forgive me.*

The resultant silence was long, stretching over several seconds as the wind began to kick up dust in gentle wisps.

And then, gleefully, Kamataa began to clap. "Welcome to the Children of the Black Moon," she said with a smile.

It was hard for Sen to know how to appropriately react. She equally felt a sinking sensation and an uplifting. To throw in with this group, the only people in the Land who would understand what it meant to be Eclipseborn, it was comforting, in a way. But at the same time...

She closed her eyes. *I can't turn back now. There's nowhere else to go.* With no words coming to her, she forced a smile and nodded.

Kamataa started to rummage through the pocket of her uniform jacket and pulled out a Tribal pendant. What rays of sunlight that broke through the layer of smoke in the air glinted off the surface of the trinket, casting a glow over its carved rune.

Squinting her eyes, Sen could make out the shape of three lines running parallel to one another, dancing in sequenced waves. The same mark which glowed whenever Kamataa dispelled her disguise.

An Illusion pendant.

"I had this ready for you," Kamataa said, "whenever you made up your mind. You can't keep cloaking yourself as you are now, Sennalhat. Someone may start to think you have something to hide." She flashed a smile and tossed the pendant over to Sen.

The trinket thudded against Sen's chest, bouncing into Sen's palm. She examined it with curiosity, feeling...*something* running through the item. An energy, a power. She inclined her head toward Kamataa, raising an eyebrow. "For someone who hates the practices of the Tribes so much, you sure do keep an impressive amount of their relics."

Cin audibly scoffed at the remark. "Our rejection of Tribal practices is the very reason we keep these in such a large amount."

Sen stared at him. *Is that why you keep your own Tribe's death mask? Is that part of your rejection, as well?* she thought about saying, but decided against it.

To Kamataa's right, Ziia withdrew her Illusion pendant from beneath her uniform, dispelling it just as quickly as she drew the power back in, briefly revealing the old and weathered face the Illusion hid. A second chain was visible along her neck, though what Boon it carried, Sen could not say.

"If we still maintained Tribal practices," the former Stone woman said, "we could never do what it is we hope to do."

Sen crossed her arms. "And what is that? What *is* the grand ploy of the Children of the Black Moon?"

Kamataa approached her, red hair bouncing along her youthful shoulders, the smile on her face invoking something more than welcoming the longer Sen stared at it. There was something sinister in the act, as well. The old Eclipseborn stretched out a hand and clasped Sen's in it, enclosing the gifted Illusion pendant and their shared grip. "Permit me to ask you this, Sennalhat," she said. "Why is it that the use of another's pendant is considered taboo? You have already seen we've suffered no retribution for using that which was not originally ours. In fact, why should anyone be relegated only to one Boon granted to them by the gods, hmm? It is clear among us that doing so causes no harm to the user, and our faculties are only the greater for it. If anything, it would make one even more useful to society. Just think: the knowledge of a Learned and the languages of a Linguist, together in one person? The power of a Strongarm and the shared mental cluster of a Packmind? That could make for a formidable army. But why are we told that it is 'wrong?' That it is 'taboo?'"

Throwing up her hands in deference, Sen shrugged her shoulders. "I don't know, but I assume you're going to tell me."

Kamataa nodded with a grin. "Therein lies the answer." She plucked the Illusion pendant from Sen's hands. "It is true that a person who would use the power of two pendants, three, four, however many at once—they would gain all of those inherent abilities with no harm done to their person. But what about those to whom the pendant originally belonged?" Her grin grew sinister once more. "You can think of the Tribes' relationship with the gods as...symbiotic. Mutually beneficial. We are born—or most of us are, I should say—under one of the star signs corresponding to either the Bear, the Wolf, or the Owl. And when one comes of age, they complete their corresponding Trial. You know this already. You're one of the few among us who attempted that damned farce."

Sen furrowed her brow, stroking her chin pensively.

"We grow up being told," Kamataa continued, "that it is the 'passage into adulthood,' a ceremony of lies the tune of which these fools happily dance to. But the truth is that just as we feed off of the gods for their power, they feed off of *us* in turn. Or, the Signbirthed ones, at the least." She began to pace back and forth, tossing the pendant up and down to herself. "The Trial is an assessment of how much power the gods can siphon from us, and the pendants, once carved with their runes, are the bridge to that power. You felt that power coursing through this pendant, Sennalhat, didn't you? The Owl's blessing, all in the palm of your hand." She stopped, staring intently at the Illusion pendant. "But it carries a great burden, this power. Once that bridge is created, the moment it leads to nowhere…the situation becomes dire."

Sen narrowed her eyes. *A bridge leading to nowhere…* She remembered the enslaved Tribespeople in the yard where she found Brin, those who looked entirely inattentive, lethargic. At the time, she thought they were merely bereft of hope, uncaring of the world around them after so many years of watching their home being stripped to nothing. But there was something else. They weren't wearing pendants.

"The Tribespeople here in the City…" Sen said. "Some of them looked entirely…mindless. You mean to say that…"

Pointing an acknowledging finger, Kamataa nodded. "Precisely, Sennalhat. When one is exposed to the Boon granted to them by their respective Deity, they grow…inseparable from it. It only grows worse the longer they are exposed to it. Think of it as a drug. The more you take it, the greater the dependency, and the longer you go without it, the greater the damage to your mind."

Sen shuddered. *You don't have to tell* me *that.* It had only been a few days since her last drink, but it felt like a lifetime. She had to wonder how much of the shakes she suffered through this were from her own withdrawal and how much was due to the moment at hand.

"And it's worse," Kamataa continued, "for those who've grown accustomed to their power for years or even decades. When that strong of a link is broken, the wearer effectively becomes brain dead the very moment the pendant is removed."

With a gasp, Sen's eyes widened.

"And *that*," Kamataa asserted with another pointed finger, "is how you destroy an entire system. *That* is our goal. As Eclipseborn, unborn to the Signs, untouchable by the Deities, *we* have the power, the *responsibility*, to break the taboo, expose the system for what it is, and destroy those who would benefit from it. And it's not just us as Eclipseborn who comprise the Children of the Black Moon. It is all of those who were rejected from the Tribes for not 'proving their worth' in their Trial, or, in truth, for not being suitable energy for the gods to consume. They're among us, too, patrolling this city, roaming the Land, standing among what remains of the Tribes."

Sen didn't quite know what to say. Cin and Ziia offered no guidance. They merely stood there, seeming to wait for her response, just as Kamataa was. The old crone stared at Sen expectantly.

Resting her hands on her hips, Sen took a deep breath. "And siding with the Invaders is all part of it, too? Even if you...*we*...succeed, we still find ourselves in hiding, just from a different set of eyes."

"The Acrarians are a means to an end, Sennalhat," Kamataa said matter-of-factly. "The road to change cannot help but be stained in blood sometimes. And you must remember—we hold no love for our former Tribes. Did you not just say the same yourself?"

Memories flickered in Sen's mind, but none of a serene scene. She heard only the chorus of *Curseborn* sung to her, a spiteful snarl to the tone, a sneering laugh. In her mind's eye was the image of Koelhe and Fann, their hateful smiles bearing down on her. She realized she had an opportunity to see them bloodied, just as they deserved. She wanted to seize that opportunity.

Kamataa ambled to Sen and handed her the Illusion pendant again. "I understand if you may be hesitant. You've had a lot to take in over the last day. If you wish to back out, I will still respect you for your decision. You are under no obligation, child, but trust that you will always have a place among us."

Sen looked once more at the Illusion pendant. There was so much that she could do with this pendant, with any others she could get her hands on. *It's a means to an end*, she thought. *A means to Fann and Koelhe's end.*

She glanced to Ziia and Cin, still wordlessly watching her, and for the first time, willingly looked into Kamataa's eyes. She knew she would not forgive the woman…but she felt she could understand her. Without further hesitation, Sen fastened the pendant around her neck and felt a slight current of power flowing through her, a different sensation from the tingling of Luck that would travel up her arms. This was more…discernible.

Kamataa nodded, clearly pleased. "The usage is quite simple. Just form an image in your mind of who or what you would like to be and let the pendant do the rest of the work."

Sen nodded and tried to remember one of the women she saw traipsing around the street the night before, linked arm in arm with a husband, romantic partner, brother, or whoever else it may have been. She wasn't going to judge.

The image became clearer in her mind. A woman in her late twenties, perhaps early thirties. A beauty mark beneath her left eye. Long locks of curled, brown hair frizzed slightly from the humid air, framing a face of pale skin. The outfit was much easier, given three dressed in Invader—Acrarian—regalia stood before her.

The picture complete, Sen breathed out and felt the surge of power from the pendant course through her body. A warmth overtook her, and when she opened her eyes again, she found a host of fellow Eclipseborn raising their brow in evident surprise.

Cin grunted, seemingly impressed. The nod of his head would have suggested so, at any rate.

Ziia's approval was more pronounced, a smile accompanied by muted applause. She filed in beside Kamataa, pointing at Sen and nudging her companion with her elbow.

Kamataa returned the gesture to Ziia and walked up to Sen to place a hand on her shoulder. "Perfect," she said simply. "You make for a fine Acrarian, child."

Looking down, Sen saw the vast shades of blue draped over her body, no longer feeling the cloak masking her face. *I'm not sure how I feel about making for a fine Acrarian,* she thought, *but I'll settle for a suitable disguise.*

She was grateful for the good disguise, at that, for a guard approached moments later. Sen recognized him as one of those who stood at inattention when she arrived at the training ground with Cin and Ziia.

The man conversed with Cin in the Acrarian tongue, and from what Sen could tell, the tone ranged invariably from excitement to optimism to gravity to indifference.

Cin kept his arms crossed, his brow furrowed, nodding along to whatever the guard was saying, offering a few choice words as a response when needed.

Eventually, the guard left, scurrying off with some expediency, nodding to the three women as he made his exit.

"What news?" Ziia asked.

Cin broke the slimmest of grins, a slight exuberance betraying his typically morose expression. "Aritz is ready to make his move."

"Meaning?"

He nudged his head toward the rack of weapons, his arms remaining crossed. "Better make sure the guns are good to go. He's sending the lot of us out."

Ziia flashed a smile toward Sen. "You've joined at just the right time, Sennalhat." She turned back to Cin. "When do we need to be ready?"

"The morning. Aritz is leading the front himself." He nodded to them before turning about-face and heading back in the direction of the barracks. "Going to rest. Tomorrow will be a long one."

Sen stood in slight disbelief. *I didn't think* this *would happen so soon.* She looked northward again, to the Forest, wondering what was happening beyond there. What was transpiring in her village, how her mother was handling the management of the Tribe.

Just as quickly, she shook her head. *No. I can't think about that. Not anymore. I have no Tribe but this one. The Eclipseborn. The Children of the Black Moon.*

"Sennalhat."

Sen looked over her shoulder to see Kamataa gesturing her over.

The old woman was standing beside the rack of long Deatharms. "I don't imagine you've used one of these yet, have you?" Kamataa asked.

Already feeling her heart pounding, Sen shook her head. She kept her eyes open, not daring to close them for far of the thunderclaps and all they brought with them.

Noting Sen's apprehension, Kamataa held out a hand in what passed for a calming motion. "Don't worry. The ones up front will likely do all the heavy lifting. All we need to do is hang back and let it all play out. Just point and shoot and act like you're contributing."

"I…" Sen breathed heavily, her cheeks puffing out as her heart continued to beat with a steady and rapid rhythm. "I don't know if I can do that much."

The old Eclipseborn grabbed a Deatharm from the rack and put it in Sen's hand. "Sure, you can. Just point the barrel at that hanging target over there—" She pointed to the bundle of hay she had shot earlier. "—aim down the sight, like you would have with a bow and arrow, and pull the trigger right here."

Lifting the weapon, Sen felt herself trembling again. *Keep your eyes open, stupid. It's okay. It's okay. It's okay.* The whole length of the Deatharm wavered in her hands, the weight unfamiliar and unwieldy to her, and she let it drop to the ground. *It's not okay.*

Kamataa put her hands on her hips, but she looked patient all the same. "I remember my first time with these. It was only, what, ten years ago, Ziia?"

Sen didn't look behind her, but she assumed Ziia was nodding.

"It's a nerve-wracking thing to hold in your hands. I certainly understand that, child." Kamataa helped Sen lift her arms back up and steadied the Deatharm in her hands. "Good, now just hold it like that. Stare down the sight right here. Something I've found useful: imagine the target as being someone you would really wish to see dead."

Scoffing, Sen glanced at Kamataa from her periphery. "Is that meant to be a joke?"

Kamataa shook her head, smiling. "Not at all." She seemed satisfied with the admission. "Every morning when I wake up, there is a man who I would wish death upon. Coming here allows me to imagine that desire come to life."

"The one that got away, then?" Sen asked. "You missed your opportunity, so you have to believe that he's a sack of hay?"

"Oh no," Kamataa said plainly. "I killed him a long time ago. I just wish to do it again."

Sen's eyes widened, unsure what to make of that.

"Surely there is someone," Kamataa said, "that you would love to use this upon."

Staring ahead at the hay target, Sen squinted her eyes, seeing nothing but the dangling lump of burlap swaying in the breeze. She drew a deep breath and, as much of a tempting of fate as it was, allowed herself to close her eyes.

The shadow laughed at her once again, the weight of the Deatharm crushing her arms. *No,* Sen thought. *I'm in control here.* Where the shadow had, at one time, shared her own face, this time, the shrill laughter took root in a different form. An expression of pure malice shone through the shadow's dark features, and suddenly, the image became clear: severe wrinkles peppered a miserable face with a permanent frown, streaks of grey marring a head of flowing braided locks.

"Your failure knows no bounds, Curseborn," Koelhe's shrieking voice said.

"Shut up and die," Sen said calmly. And pulled the trigger.

The thunderclap nearly paralyzed her again, but when she regained her focus, the shadow stopped moving, and the world grew still.

When she opened her eyes again, there was a fresh hole in the hay sack where her weapon had shot through. It wavered and swung back and forth from the impact.

"I'd say that's a kill shot," Kamataa said from beside Sen. "Helpful, no?"

Sen stared at the weapon, the smell of ignited smoke filling her nostrils, much to her distaste. She winced from the acrid stench but nodded regardless. "Helpful," she agreed.

She reloaded and aimed again at the target dummy. "But practice makes perfect," she said as she fired another kill shot.

MEMORY

The Homecoming

The Year 1216 Anno Salvatoris
325 Years Before the Invasion

The night air sang with the chirping of crickets. Moonlight shone brightly overhead, glistening in illuminative crescents on the face of the Lake, dancing along the ebb and flow of the sleeping water.

The village was at ease. Calm. Peaceful.

Utterly unaware of a hunter now on the prowl.

Kamataa's boots shimmered with evening dew, loose blades of grass trailing up her feet and ankles. She was a shadow in the night, donned in the darkest of shades. At her hip was a hunting knife, her hand resting on the hilt.

Should all go well, I won't have a need to use this, she thought.

The eastern Lake village looked the same as it always did, even after all these years. The faces may have changed and grown older, but the homes, the streets, the markets, they were all the same, nearly six decades later.

The same could be said for her.

Wiping away a bead of sweat from her forehead, she was consciously aware of the weathering of her skin, slow as it was. Slow as it was meant to be, thanks to the Moon's power flowing through her. She shook her head, knowing there were more important matters on which to focus.

She knelt beside the side of a hut and peered her gaze around the corner. If Ruhr's outline of the village was correct, then the homes she was to hit were just up the lane. Squinting, she could just make out the marker of one, a short red banner indicative of the aged fishmonger. An easy mark, an easy challenge.

Lifting a scarf up to cover her mouth and nose, Kamataa slinked away, moving in a swift crouch, her hand still resting atop the knife hilt just in case. There was no commotion within any of the huts she passed by, and what little noise she did hear consisted primarily of mighty snoring and infantile wailing.

The wailing was of particular irritation to her. As she approached the fishmonger's home, Kamataa glared further down the lane to the lavish hut, which still stood tall after all these years. She grunted behind the scarf veiling her.

Later, she reminded herself.

The drone of the crickets continued as she reached the fishmonger's hut. Pressing her ear to the door, Kamataa heard nothing from within beyond the rumble of heavy snoring. She pushed the door open, the frame cooperating with her as not even a creak of wood sounded.

The interior was unassuming, specks of dust noticeable even in the dim light upon the countertop, but rather clean besides. The lingering aroma from the day's catch still wafted in the air, a pleasant and familiar scent to Kamataa's nose.

Maintaining a light footing as she tiptoed around the counter, Kamataa peered her head into the fishmonger's bedroom, finding her mark entirely indisposed.

His blanket was half-thrown from his legs, revealing weathered, bony limbs with curls of heavy, white hair acting as covering. His chest rose and fell in a steady rhythm, his snoring unimpeded and uninterrupted by Kamataa's arrival. What hair he had remaining on his head stood wild, jutting out from his skull like a crown of pure snow. Frankly, he looked older than dirt.

Kamataa drew closer, taking her steps slowly, one at a time. The floor beneath her continued to cooperate, nothing in her way to act as an alert to the old man. As she reached his bedside, she saw up close just how frail the man looked.

His face was sunken, almost emaciated. His arms appeared spindly and weak, more bone than muscle. His ribs were visible in clear rows, almost as though he never ate any of the fish he peddled.

The shadows certainly did him favors, Kamataa thought.

All of that mattered little to her, though. What she came for dangled loosely around his neck. The carved runes told all that needed to be known of this man.

Strength. Even despite the fishmonger's advanced age, the Bear kept him fit and strong.

With a crack of her knuckles, Kamataa set to work. She knelt beside the fishmonger, holding her breath as she slowly reached toward the man's neck. She took a tentative grip of the chain of the pendant, lifted slowly...slowly...*slowly*...

The man snorted.

It startled Kamataa, freezing her in place.

But he continued to sleep, his snoring growing in intensity.

Beneath her veil, Kamataa could only grin, softly chuckling to herself. Inch by inch, the chain lifted from the fishmonger's neck. Past the neck, over the back of the head, the carved ornament hanging slack, barely touching the man's chest. Kamataa nudged the chain up along the back of the man's head, the feather pillow offering minimal resistance. Wisps of wild hair caught in the chain, a couple strays getting plucked along.

The man stirred in his sleep again, mumbling something to himself about a giant talking fish, though with the degree of familiarity he spoke of it, it could very well have been his wife he was talking about.

The chain cleared the back of his head, and Kamataa lifted the pendant free, holding it at eye level, tracing her finger along the Strength rune, the carving dully humming with an innate power. She grinned and stowed the trinket away in her pocket.

As soon as she did so, the man's breath caught. His eyes shot wide open, glowing with shock. Tremors gripped him as his entire body began to con-vulse, his fingers gripping air like talons, his back arching in a wide bow as an extreme spasm overtook him. His breath became little more than weak rasps, like a stone scraping across the head of a spear. Drool streamed from his agape mouth as his words became little more than mindless babble.

And then his back collapsed, greeting his bed with a resounding *thud*. His eyes were glossed over, his open mouth rumbling a weak, rough breath. But he was otherwise frozen.

"Well, that took quicker than I thought," Kamataa murmured. She leaned in close, her lips nearly caressing his ears. "Say hello to your giant talking fish for me."

With a chuckle, she turned back to the front of the fishery, finding no curious onlookers or passersby out on a midnight stroll, and exited the shop, closing the door as though nothing was out of the ordinary.

And nothing will seem out of place, she thought. *The village will awake to an old man shambling about to near death, and they will hardly bat an eye.* She inclined her head to her next destination, a taller hut with a rack of weapons in front, a collection of longbows hanging loosely from a drawstring. *But should the same happen to one so hearty and hale...so crumbles a sturdy foundation.*

Narrowing her eyes, she turned once again to the tall, looming presence of the garish hut toward the end of the lane. Part of her wanted to head there right now, even though it was not part of Ruhr's plan. When she closed her eyes, she could still feel the jolt of the impact running up her arm. The splatter of viscera and brain matter. The wailing. The unceasing wailing.

She shook her head. *One thing at a time*, she reminded herself. *One more stone to remove from the supports.*

Pushing aside the memory, Kamataa trudged through the soft dirt, clenching her fists at her sides. The world around her continued to sleep, but for some, those dreams would be eternal and final. She would see to that.

This time, she did not waste her time with the steady sneaking. She walked right up to the door, hand pressed to the hilt of her hunting knife, and pushed it open. A slight creak whined as the door thudded to a halt, ricocheting back to its resting position.

Kamataa couldn't remember who this next person was meant to be. Some hunter for the Chief or something of that sort. Maybe not the most important one, but enough for their fate to be noticeable. The same could be said of the hunter's hut—just a standard layout as far as a Lake Tribesperson was concerned. An open common area, a still-simmering pot of some fish stew brewing in the corner, a back room with a bed visible from the entrance.

Someone stirred in that bed.

"Uh, hello?" a voice said groggily. Shadows moved along the bed, a half-risen form eyeing Kamataa from a seated position. "Who is it?"

Kamataa said nothing, only slowly walking the length of the common area, her hand still ready to draw her knife.

"Get out of my home," the hunter said. "You have any idea what time it is?"

Picking up her pace, Kamataa broke into a half-run, jumped, and landed at the foot of the man's bed.

He was unperturbed. He didn't even bother to flinch or rise to his feet. "Woman, I don't know who the hell you are or what drug den you crawled out of, but you better get out—"

Steel scraped free of its scabbard, and Kamataa held out the knife in a reverse grip, silencing the man.

An expression of defiance flared in his expression. He wasn't a greenhorn; that much was for certain. He had the facial scars to prove it, a long line running from cheek to lip on one side, a part of his ear missing on the other. "You think that little knife can scare me?" he said.

Kamataa grinned. "I don't expect it to frighten you."

He grunted. "Hmph, some clever speech in the works about how you'll kill me before you scare me? Believe me, I've heard it, woman."

Jolting forward, Kamataa slashed at the chain of the pendant, cutting it loose from the hunter's neck. "Not exactly," she said, grasping at the falling ornament.

The hunter slapped at his own chest, trying—and failing—to catch his pendant. "The hell?" he muttered. He pushed himself up, snarling at Kamataa as he reached out to her.

But his movements were slow, as though a weight was pressing down hard upon him. From the look in his eyes, he knew it, too. He climbed to his feet, but his balance was unsteady. His brow raised and lowered, his eyes squinting—it seemed he was trying to make sense of the world around him. "Wha didj you..." he slurred, putting a hand to his head. "You...poishon...?"

Kamataa shook her head, smiling once more behind the veil. She looked at the pendant, the cut chain dangling loosely beyond her grip. The three waving lines carved into the ornament indicated the hunter's Boon was Illusion. *A valuable talent, indeed.*

She turned to leave but was interrupted by the man's nonsensical groans.

"Waaiii…" he mumbled. "You…cow'rdj…"

Looking back to her knife, Kamataa cut a thin line along her hand, letting the blood drip to the floor. "It's not poison, if that is what you insist upon," she said, throwing the words over her shoulder. She sheathed the blade and then held the pendant out by the chain, spinning it nonchalantly with a whistle before depositing it into her pocket alongside the fishmonger's Strength pendant. "Don't blame me—the fault rests upon your Wolf god. Howl at the Moon if you must, though. She'll actually listen."

A gargling groan fell from the hunter's mouth, and then he merely lay haplessly along the side of his bed, eyes and mouth agape in violent shock, the thin strands of breath the only indicator he still lived.

A pity, Kamataa thought. *Undue, but a pity just the same.*

Two down, and the village seemed none the wiser for it. Just as planned.

Kamataa returned to the main lane, breathing in the fresh nighttime air. She stared up to the sky, the Moon shining brightly upon her. Radiating life within her.

She squinted her eyes skyward, patting the pocket holding the pendants. With a shrug of her shoulders, she grinned. "I'd say things are going well; what about you?" she said to the Moon. Turning her head to her right, she once again eyed the tallest hut in the village. She was done here; she had gotten what she came for. "What harm would one more do, right?"

The Moon offered no objections.

"That's what I like to hear."

More wails for feeding or changing echoed through the empty streets as Kamataa made her way to her destination. They made her smile.

Another wail as another stone sinks to the bed of the Lake. One by one, they will all sink. Her fingers twitched with anticipation, her thumb tapping rhythmically along the knife's hilt. She hummed a tune, something she remembered her parents humming ages ago, one that, as a child, she thought was a happy and celebratory melody.

It was only as she approached adulthood that she realized it was an aria that acted often as accompaniment to the keening bell.

And once more, the bell will ring tonight from the depths of the Otherworld.

Kamataa stopped before the door, taking in the sight with interest. Not much had changed in the near-six decades since she was last here. The same gaudiness, the same flash of wealth, flaunted in the face of those who knew nothing but crumbling straw roofs and the stench of rotted freshwater fish. Additions had been made to the façade above the door: intricate carvings of the Bear, Wolf, and Owl, a flourish of flowery design acting as what appeared to be a signature.

And all the while, the lot on which her parents' hut was built was a pile of stacked wood and materials, as though they did not exist at all.

She pulled down her veil. There was no need to hide her face here.

How could that boy ever forget the face of the Curseborn?

Shoving the door open, Kamataa was hit by a wave of incense, a strange aroma that assaulted her senses. Her eyes watered, her face contorting. It was a pungent smell. It was enough to make her gag.

With a sneer, she scanned the room, still as lavish as ever with its leopard-skin rug, an oaken rack of pristine glassware, and a long table of expertly crafted wood, the quality of which she knew none in this village would ever hope to see. Two fire pits crackled as lingering embers glowed against the ashen coals, a pot of something delectable still simmering atop a cooking rack. Her stomach growled enough for her to forget about the smell of the incense.

The corner of a bedframe was visible beyond the threshold at the back of the room. Sleepy muttering echoed through the hut. Someone was apparently having quite the talkative dream.

Kamataa walked with purpose toward the threshold, taking a spoonful of the stew as she walked past it. She couldn't help but stop and take another bite. She didn't know what it was, but it was certainly something no one of humble means would ever have the pleasure to sample. The tang and spice assured her it was a southern flavor, and only a man with more wealth than he knows what to do with could convince a merchant to traverse the Forest merely to bring a meal.

She couldn't help but sneer at the thought.

The murmurs ceased, replaced instead with rasped, nasally snores. Her brow furrowed, Kamataa removed herself from the meal, passed through the threshold, and turned to the bed to see an old man and woman sound asleep, the woman resting peacefully within the man's arms.

Kamataa drew closer, narrowing her eyes at the old man. He had to have seen seventy years by this point, though he looked as healthy and fit as a man in his twenties. He still had a full head of white locks, tied back in the traditional Lake fashion. His face, though wrinkled, appeared unblemished and pristine, as if he had never fought a day in his life.

Please, please! Why won't you help us?! The voice of Azantt's screaming whelp roared in her ears.

It's no surprise, Kamataa thought, *that that sniveling brat would be so cowardly as to force others to fight his battles.*

She pulled up a chair and sat beside him. She never knew the kid's name. Never cared to know. All she knew was that she saw the image of his snotty face every day, looking upon her with fear and disdain at her choosing not to save his parents, who she had just slaughtered.

And now, here he was, clearly never wanting for anything, lacking for nothing, at peace with the world despite everything his father was.

Whether he became the same, it was not for Kamataa to say. Nor did she much care.

Azantt's son rolled in his sleep, the arm of the woman beside him—his wife, if Kamataa were to assume—still clinging tightly to him. The man had a serene smile on his face as his sleeping form turned to Kamataa. The chain of a pendant hung slack around his neck, the ornament just barely peering out from beneath his nightshirt.

And yet Kamataa only continued to sit and wait. For as long as it took.

The man's snoring halted after a time, shifting from a nasal snort to a calm murmur as a dream was clearly ending. Adjusting his head on his pillow, his eyes blinked once, twice, thrice, fluttering open and shut as he managed a stout yawn. He drowsily fluffed his pillow, burrowing the side of his face against it.

His eyes slowly opened.

A silent moment stretched to several moments.

Immediately, his eyes recognized her, and the rune on his pendant glowed beneath his shirt.

Kamataa flashed a smile.

The day was breaking along the eastern horizon, the sky emanating an orange glow that reflected off the Lake. From this height, it was gorgeous.

It had been ages since Kamataa rested along this grassy dune to watch the sunrise. She had seen plenty of beauty over the last five decades of wandering the Land, but nothing could trump the memories of one's childhood.

So long as you ignore the years of neglect and hateful words, she thought. But none of that was the fault of the Land's natural wonders. She could never be angry for that.

She had to get moving. She had spent enough time in this spot as it was.

She pulled the scarf back up over her nose and returned to traversing the dune. Something she always hated doing; this hill was forever a monster.

After some time, Kamataa reached the top of the hill, sweat trickling down her forehead and into her eyes as the morning sun brought with it the nascent late summer heat. The dark clothing didn't help matters, and she could feel every piece of apparel sticking tightly to her for her sweat.

Atop the dune, she found Ziia waiting, sitting impatiently, twiddling her thumbs as she stared accusingly at Kamataa. The years had been as kind to her as they had to Kamataa, her hair showing only a few traces of grey as it trailed down past her shoulders in full locks, framing her face, which exhibited fewer wrinkles than Kamataa's—enough to draw minor jealousy from Kamataa that her friend was aging more gracefully than she, slow as their aging was.

Somehow, Ziia seemed cold. She was tugging her cloak tightly against her chest, with a knit blanket draped over her shoulders.

Kamataa sat beside her.

A soft scoff escaped Ziia's lips. "We've been waiting for quite a while," she said. "I thought you weren't going to show."

Craning her head over her shoulder, Kamataa saw the smoke and steam of breakfast being made, the Eclipseborn camp peeking out past another hill.

She leaned back on her elbows, the glint of the Lake's reflection still holding much of her attention. "Apologies," she said. "It's hard not to get lost taking in this sight."

"It's a sight I've had no choice but to stare at while waiting for you."

Kamataa nodded with a grunt. She understood. Ziia had been a bit testy since…

She shook her head, wanting to redirect the conversation. "Did all go well for you?" she asked.

Ziia flashed her a glance, silent for a handful of seconds, before digging into a bag beside her and withdrawing four pendants. They clunk together on the space between them. "Just as Ruhr thought. They were easy marks." Her frown deepened.

Staring at a sight beyond the Lake, to the mountain peaks to the north, Kamataa couldn't help but sigh. "It's not right that he's not here to see this come to fruition."

Grimacing, Ziia snarled in the direction of the Heart. "That doesn't even begin to describe it. He should have been celebrated as a hero across the Land. Instead, the Keepers burnt all evidence of the truth to cinders just to silence him."

"We'll create our own truths, Ziia," Kamataa said with assurance. "One by one, the Tribes will awake to that truth, just as they will today. However long it takes, whatever we have to do. You and I have nothing but time, even if Ruhr or any of them—" She inclined her head to the camp. "—do not have the same luxury. We'll burn it all and watch it collapse if we have to."

"'Throw as many stones from the outside as you must, but know that to collapse, a stone need be stolen from inside.' Ruhr's words sing with you, too, don't they?" Ziia said.

Chuckling, Kamataa nodded. "Always."

They sat in companionable silence for a time while the aroma of breakfast tried to lure them from the beautiful sunrise.

"Time to eat, then," Ziia said, picking the pendants off the ground and returning them to her satchel. She offered Kamataa a hand as she rose to her feet. "All went well with you, too? I forgot to ask."

Kamataa took Ziia's hand and was pulled to her feet. She dug around in her pockets and pulled out three pendants. "That it did," she said.

Ziia grasped the pendants and put them in the bag, though her brow was furrowed. "I thought Ruhr only mentioned two marks for the eastern Tribe."

With a shrug, Kamataa pulled the scarf down from her nose and smiled. "There was another who I thought would be a good mark, that's all."

Her friend squinted her eyes, pointing a finger to a spot of her cheek that still felt warm and slick. "Is that blood?"

CHAPTER NINE

THE SURFACE

THE YEAR 1556 ANNO SALVATORIS
15 YEARS AFTER THE INVASION

"Tez, you really do not need to do this."

She had spent the better part of the past afternoon honing the edge of her spear, staring idly out at the shimmering waters of the Lake of Bones. Breathing, focusing, waiting.

And her concentration would then be broken by the same repetitious phrase.

You do not need to do this.

"But I do," Tez murmured, just as she had the time before, and the time before that.

Tawa and Sharrabha stood at either flank, Sharrabha casting a large shadow over Tez, her arms crossed, her expression that of a disapproving mother or worried aunt. The paint on her face was smudged in a broad blue smear from the number of times she wiped away a bead of anxious sweat or buried her face in her hands for the exasperation of it all.

For his part, Tawa paced back and forth, shaking his head furiously, just as he had done since Tez voiced her intent to volunteer yesterday morning. His braid had come undone, and he seemed to have no intention to remedy that, instead allowing his hair to flow past his shoulders in dark, frizzed waves.

The two had taken turns in insisting that she did not have to champion for Tenazt in the challenge to come. Whether they thought that one voice may strike true as one of reason, Tez could not say for certain, but it only instilled in her a desire to stand for this fight even more.

"Will you at least stop for a moment and think this through, Tez?" Tawa pled. He may as well have gotten on his knees with hands joined as though to beg, given his tone.

Tez closed her eyes, allowing an exasperated breath to trail out from her nose. "What do you think I've been doing for the past day, Tawa?" she said. "Nothing *but* thinking." She continued to scrape the whetstone along the blade of her spear in a smooth, methodical rhythm.

Shng. Shng. Shng.

Tawa grumbled beneath his breath, something Tez could not quite interpret, and massaged his thumb and forefinger along the bridge of his nose. "You must know that I am only going to tell you how reckless you are being until you finally quit this game you have decided to play."

Shng. Shng. Shng.

"Message received, Tawa," Tez said. "And it's not a game, but I'm not through playing."

The sun was falling low, the sky adopting an orange and pink hue. The waters reflected the rays in what appeared to be a sunburst, as though the Lake was fiery beneath those gentle currents.

"Sharrabha, please," Tawa pleaded to the Stone huntress. "Help me talk some sense into her. Time is falling short with the sun."

Sharrabha scoffed. Tez could see her shake her head bemusedly from the corner of her eye. "Yes, Tawa, just as I've been doing for the past day and a half. I think we're near to getting through to her."

I'm right here, you know, Tez thought.

Shng. Shng. Shng.

"Face it, Tawa. She's every bit the person Fanna was. Right down to how damned stubborn she is. Gods, the only time either of us has convinced her of anything was two nights ago when we stopped her from getting one of Rantalha's arrows between the eyes!"

Tez inclined her eyes toward Sharrabha, eyebrows raised, but said nothing, her focus remaining squarely on her spear.

"A stubborn bastard who raised stubborn daughters," Tawa murmured. He looked at Tez, breathing a long sigh through his nose. The faint shadow of a smile pursed his lips. "But Fanna's stubbornness did not always serve him well. You know that as well as I, Sharrabha, and you, Tez."

Shng. And then nothing.

Gnawing at her bottom lip, Tez dropped the whetstone and stared at the shoreline ahead, the white foam of the water swishing against the soft sand. Small critters skittered along the encroaching water, delving beneath the shallow depths in a small gulp. But just as quickly as they submerged, they breached and went back about the shore, no harm done at all.

There was a saying Tez heard from one of the Sun Tribespeople, years ago: "All who entreat the approaching water are inevitably submerged. The brave still find their way back to the surface." It had stuck with her all these years, to hear someone who had lost everything still broach the topic of hope, of finding a way back to the proverbial water's surface, no matter how murky and deep the reaches.

The stubborn dreamer is the hardy fool, and yet not worse off than the fool not stubborn enough to dream. Tez shook her head, squinting into the setting sun, unsure what she sought within that golden glow but confident she would find both the answer and the question.

"My father was stubborn enough never to quit and never to back down. It was to his benefit and his detriment," Tez said. "But he also knew the fights worth standing for. He knew who was right and who was wrong. He knew that sometimes, a spear speaks in louder volumes than words could ever hope." She paused, smacking her lips as she planted her spear vertically before her, the tip standing tall above her. A glare reflected off the polished sheen of the weapon. "He was my greatest teacher. And if following in his path makes me a stubborn bastard, then I'm not gonna argue. I'm just gonna fight."

Tentative unease was visible on Tawa's face, even if he appeared somewhat convinced of Tez's words. "Just remember, Tez. Yhaan is not like any you have faced before. Fear is the deterrent of even the savviest warrior. He *will* use his Boon to his advantage."

Shrugging with her hands, Tez flashed a grin. "And so will I. I think I can handle a nightmare or two. I already stood a battlefield against Rantalha and still have my life—this shouldn't be much different."

"Confidence is fleeting when faced with Fear. Your Endurance may make little difference in all of this."

Tez chuckled. "You really *are* trying your hardest to steer me away from this challenge, aren't you, Tawa?"

The Owlsign paused, his expression blank, but a sincere chuckle did manage to crack through. "I suppose it would be too much to dream that my words had any sway?"

With a nod, Tez rose to her feet and approached Tawa, patting him gently on the shoulder. "Too much to dream, indeed."

"And if you find a new home beneath the Lake of Bones?"

"Then I hope you tighten up your negotiation skills, my friend."

"May the gods help us all should that happen, then."

It was the first Tez had seen Tawa genuinely smile through this ordeal, but she was happy to see it.

A set of hands began to clap behind them, followed by the shuffled steps of an approaching group. "Some pretty words, Tez of the Stone Tribe. I do hope your spear speaks just as eloquently."

Tez raised an eyebrow as she turned to see Tenazt, the old man standing tall and proud before her, an expression of pure ease settled upon his wrinkled face. He allowed his white locks to fall down the length of his head, covering the shaved sides, a casual appearance for an entirely non-casual occasion.

Beside him stood Ket, and with the benefit of being outside the eastern Chief's field of vision, they appeared to be flashing him the look emblematic of Tez's feelings toward the situation. A deep frown framed Ket's face as they scrunched their nose, thumbs twiddling with annoyance.

"Chief Tenazt," Sharrabha said. "How kind of you to see Tez off." There was only a hint of sarcasm in her tone.

"I'd be remiss not to," Tenazt said. He walked over to Tez and nodded. "There is a part of me that wishes to condemn you for your recklessness in championing for me. But still, another part of me holds you in the deepest respect."

Tez stared at Tenazt with a bemused grin and tapped the butt of her spear on the ground twice. "As I've said already, this is purely in the Stone Tribe's interest. I'm not doing this for your respect. I just don't need you dying on me when I need your men the most."

Seemingly taken aback, Tenazt left his mouth agape before eventually nodding. "Of course. Regardless, that you would assist us in this matter is worthy of our respect, whether you wish to have it or not."

Pondering the words for a long moment, Tez merely grunted and walked to the shoreline, spear by her side as a walking stick. The Big Lake was beginning to glow in an ethereal orange as the sun started its final glimpse over the western horizon. "Were I given the choice..." she mumbled to herself, the wafting of the water's current enough to drown out her voice.

The choice is irrelevant, she thought. *We can't be picky, time is short, and I don't care a single whit about whatever the hell ignited this blood feud.*

Ket filed alongside her, pulling a looking glass from their trouser pocket. They stared along the face of the Lake, angling the tool this way and that, seemingly to fight past the eminent glare of the bright sun rays. Nodding to themself, Ket turned to Tez and nodded. "Yhaan and his second approach. Are you ready?"

"As I'll ever be," Tez muttered. She gripped more tightly to the shaft of her spear, the build unwavering. Closing her eyes, she pictured that the shaft was Fann's neck, Rantalha to one side of him, Koelhe to the other. *I'm doing this for them. To be able to go back and wring their necks, each of them.* If she held on to the spear any tighter, she knew she may have cracked it in half for her imagination. She turned her attention back to Ket, taking in their face for a handful of moments. She permitted herself a gentle grin, to which Ket reciprocated.

"For what it's worth," Ket said, "you have my thanks, as well." They glanced at Tenazt, who was speaking in a private conference with Sharrabha and Tawa. "He has his failings, but he is a good man who cares for this Tribe. On both ends of the Big Lake."

"Ket," Tez said, "you know I've said that—"

"I know, I know," they said, raising their hands at shoulder height, palms outward facing. "I know you're not doing this for thanks. You're doing this for your people. But word will spread about the stone who stood to fight atop the water. My people are pig-headed, but they respect strength, for all the good and bad it brings. Just know that you, Tez of the Stone Tribe, will be always a friend to the Lake Tribe."

"Would that I could cash in on that and forego this whole nonsense entirely," Tez said with a chuckle.

"The more of my people's histories I read, the more I say the same." Ket looked to the ground sheepishly, kicking at a pebble buried in the sand. When they looked back up, they offered a kind smile, walked up to Tez, and as they lightly grabbed the side of Tez's neck, standing on their toes, they softly and quickly brought their lips to Tez's cheek. "Thank you," Ket said.

Tez could feel her face growing red, but she did her best to conceal the fact. Brusquely, she nodded, offering Ket the same smile. She nudged her head toward the middle of the Lake of Bones. "Well, when *this* is over...hopefully that offer of 'friendship' among the Lake Tribe extends to you as well." She walked over toward Tenazt and the others before Ket could offer any sort of retort.

What in the hell *did I just say?* Spearwork was easier than wordcraft.

"It's time, then," Tez said to the Chief, massaging the back of her neck, feeling the fluttering sweat beneath her touch. "I *will* return." *As the stone that fought on the water, or whatever it was.*

She turned back to the shore where a skiff was moored in wait for her, the current splashing water into it from either direction. She took a handful of steps but quickly felt a tug at her arm.

Sharrabha was at the other end of the pull.

"You *are* granted a second, you know," the huntress said, raising her eyebrows.

"Don't trouble yourself, Sharrabha," Tez said, yanking her arm free and waving her hand with dismissal. "I volunteered for this, you needn't be a part of it, too."

"She should have said that you are required a second," Tawa chimed in.

"Not necessarily 'required,'" Tenazt corrected. "More that you make it much harder for yourself if you *don't* have one." The Chief pointed to the arrangement of the skiff, with one seat at the back with only one set of oars, and a long flat section intended for a person to stand upon. "Unless you want to steer the boat with one hand and wave your spear with the other?"

Tez sighed deeply. "Don't get yourself hurt on my account," she said to Sharrabha.

"You need not worry, Tez of the Stone Tribe, Tenazt assured. "The second is understood to be a non-combatant. It's a worse offense to harm one's second during a challenge than it is to forego the challenge entirely. Yhaan understands this. She will be safe."

"Besides," Sharrabha added, "Someone needs to ensure you don't get yourself killed. I have a good streak going with that, after all."

"One time is *not* a streak," Tez said, rolling her eyes.

Sharrabha patted her on the shoulder as she walked to the shoreline. "I'm preemptively calling it a streak, then." She turned and winked.

Tez walked alongside her, kicking at loose pebbles as the grass turned to lakeside sand. "Are you certain you'll be fine steering a boat while two people are trying to angrily stab each other?"

"Tezalhat," Sharrabha chuckled. "You've never steered through the Steel Rivers in the Heart while rain and sleet pelted you from every direction and jagged rocks sharper than any spear tip threatened to gut you at every turn. This is much easier." She smiled.

Well, I can't argue her logic there.

As the huntress settled into her seat, Tez caught another glance at Ket, their face glowing in the light of the setting sun. She nodded slowly to them, unaware of how long she paused until Sharrabha jabbed her in the back of the knee with the oar. "Hey! I need that leg," Tez grumbled as she climbed onto the boat, faintly hearing Ket's chuckle carrying along the breeze.

A few minutes passed, the water calmly splashing as Sharrabha rhythmically paddled forward. Tez closed her eyes to visualize the impending challenge. Even if her imagination led her astray enough that Yhaan stood twenty feet high, and she was little more than an ant.

I could at least chew through his ankles, given enough time.

The splashing ceased after a few minutes more, and with it left the forward momentum of the boat. Tez turned to find Sharrabha grinning at her.

"I couldn't help but notice your conference along the shoreline. It seems you have a separate reason to triumph this evening, don't you?"

Tez contorted her face with shock and bemusement, outstretching her hands as her mouth remained agape. "You're stopping the boat for *this*?"

With a teasing shrug, Sharrabha picked the oar back up and resumed paddling. "So quick to attract, though. Who was it, again, who wondered if love could bloom on the battlefield?"

"Maybe I can just speed this whole thing up and drown myself now," Tez said, staring far into the depths of the Lake of Bones, curious to know just how deep the lakebed lay.

"Now, now," Sharrabha chastised. "I've noticed you stealing glances. There's nothing wrong with it, is there?"

"*Must* we speak on this now, Sharrabha?" *Gods, this kind of teasing is reserved for Sen only.*

"Would you rather we speak on the challenge ahead?"

"A choice between the two, I choose neither. I'm going to just close my eyes and picture my victory instead."

"Suit yourself. I've always found the act of loosing the arrow more satisfying than merely picturing it flying."

"I'm about to send *you* flying if you don't quiet yourself." Tez said it quietly enough that it seemed that Sharrabha couldn't hear her over her paddling.

How long Tez closed her eyes and attempted to envision her triumph, she couldn't say. All she knew was, when she opened her eyes once more as the skiff waded to a stop, it was time.

The sun was a fiery backdrop, a beacon surrounded by a wave of reds and pinks as the day prepared to give way to the dark of night. The birds sang their final choruses, the whistles fading in a soft echo. Light splashes plopped around her as small fish breached for one reason or another, the sound akin to rainfall even though there was barely a cloud in the sky.

And silhouetted against the orange glow, a figure rose to its feet, higher and higher and higher to the point that Tez was curious if the boat was balanced enough not to tip over bowside down.

Yhaan calmly picked up his spear from the floor of the skiff, planting it at his side, his body language speaking only in unbridled stoicism as he watched Tez's approach. His second, who, as far as Tez could tell, was just a shadow given corporeal form, sat in silence, the oar placed across their lap expectantly.

Motioning Sharrabha to row off to the side so the sun would not be blinding her, Tez stood and drew her own spear, the lakefront breeze cooling her as sweat trickled down her face and arms. She let out a long breath and looked up at Yhaan's face, now fully aware that the man dwarfed her by nearly a foot and a half. Even at her height, she could see the consternation in the western Chief's eyes.

"I remember you," Yhaan said, his deep voice carrying even at the low volume at which he spoke. "You're that Stone woman who was in the village yesterday."

"And you're the tallest man I've ever seen in my life," Tez retorted. "So, if we're finished declaring the obvious…"

Yhaan grunted, his brow furrowing. "Say one thing for Tenazt, I did not think him so cowardly as to send another to fight his battles. Least of all, one from another Tribe."

"Say one thing for both of you, I think this is a waste of everyone's time," Tez said, rolling her eyes. "But cowardly, he's not. Just more advantageous for me to do this instead of him."

The western Chief actually seemed amused by the remark. "And what would the Stone Tribe stand to gain from my death?"

"Your death, specifically? Nothing. I just need Lake warriors to take back my home."

"…Who *are* you?" Yhaan no longer stood at ready, his spear held more casually than it was before. He no longer bore the appearance of a man prepared for battle. He was just a man confused.

Tez shook her head. "It doesn't matter. The Stone people are a Tribe that cannot stand to be fractured. Tenazt promised me his fighting strength in order to mend those cracks." She crouched, the boat swaying beneath her feet as she held her spear to a readied position. "So, I can't have him dying on me. It's nothing personal, Yhaan."

The sun poured on the left side of Yhaan's face, half his body illuminated in a golden glow. It was that side that seemed to smile. His half in shadow, however...

The Chief adopted his own fighting stance, the Lake bouncing beneath his skiff. "I must admit my surprise at meeting a Stone warrior in battle."

"Well, I'm surprised by it, too," Tez said. "But times are strange."

"Strange, indeed. Though my quarrel is not with you or your Tribe. I would grant you leave, should you request it."

Do you think I'd come out all this way just for you to say, "No, that's okay, we don't have to fight?"

Tez flashed a sneer. "And would your quarrel with Tenazt be settled were I to leave? We could just put a bow on it and call it done?"

The half of Yhaan that smiled suddenly lost all its warmth. "I think we both know the answer to that."

Tez's fingers twitched along her spear, her arms still aching from her fight with Fann. She drew in a sliver of Endurance, the pains in her muscles slightly alleviating. She took a deep breath, centering herself, their two skiffs slowly coming together in striking distance.

"Then I will not request it," she said, mustering up what gravel she could in her throat.

A deep chuckle rumbled in Yhaan's throat. Beneath his shirt, the rune on his pendant began to dimly illuminate. "Then *I* will not hold back. Steel yourself!"

Simultaneously, the opposing boats splashed into their own positions as foaming plumes of water crashed against Tez's ankles. She crouched to a striking position, her lead hand finding a home on the upper reaches of the spear shaft. Behind her, Sharrabha angled the skiff to the left, a sound of furious rowing filling her ears. Tez felt herself skirting along the surface of the water, the boat drifting horizontally.

She patiently awaited her opportunity to strike. Her spear twitched in her hands, eager to meet flesh and blood.

But something within her froze. She wanted to press and attack. Gods, she wanted to forego the nonsense of fighting in separate boats and clear the gap and introduce steel to blood. But for all her desires and intentions, Tez *could not move.*

Her heart pounded in her ears, her breathing growing more labored. A weight bore down on her, a presence, something altogether sinister and foreboding. Wincing, Tez let out a shuddering breath and snarled at her opponent.

Yhaan hadn't moved an inch. The western Chief remained in his fighting stance the entire time, but apart from his second following Tez's every movement, he showed complete disregard for his opponent's plan of attack. It wouldn't be outlandish to claim that he was *disinterested* in the proceedings of this fight.

And such a claim was reinforced by his abandoning his stance, instead withdrawing his spear to his side, standing as a mountain towering above Tez.

All the while, his pendant continued to glimmer. Only now, it brightened.

Shaking, Tez fell to her knees. She felt the panic in her eyes as they widened, near to bulging from her skull. Her spear fell to her side, only barely contained within the skiff, and she found herself on all fours, heaving into the wood below as nervous sweat cascaded down her face. Nausea rose in her throat, the movement of the boat combined with the overstimulated nerves within her threatening to empty her breakfast all over her feet.

"Tez! *Tez!*" she heard Sharrabha shout behind her. The huntress's voice seemed distant, muted. Tez may as well have been underwater.

It took everything in her for Tez to incline her head back up. She matched glares with Yhaan, but the very sight of the man sent further shivers down her spine. She bit back a scream as the world around her dimmed: the Lake of Bones and the curious fauna and Sharrabha and everything else, all fading away until nothing was left but her, Yhaan, and the aura cast behind him by the light of the setting sun.

With an amused expression upon his face, Yhaan chuckled deeply. He still made no move for his spear, keen to let it rest by his feet while Tez cowered. He crossed his arms, and the glow of his pendant shone brighter and brighter with the radiant shine of the sun itself. No longer did he appear a man; he was a presence, an energy, a force of nature itself. His features diluted in

Tez's line of sight, expanding into a formless yet corporeal *something* that Tez could not make out.

Whatever it was, it was slowly reaching out toward her with malicious tendrils, wavering in the air like puffs of black smoke. Inch by inch, the entity approached her, slithering along the gap between them, entwining and separating in a poetic harmony until, finally, Tez felt the waves touch her hand. It was a sensation comprising both everything and nothing. Sharp, cold pain followed an absence of feeling. The tendrils touched her with the tenderness of a lover's kiss, only to ensnare her in a hunter's trap as though steel teeth were about to chew through her wrist.

Tez snarled and growled, breathing hoarsely through gritted teeth as she swung a desperate fist at the darkness, only for her punch to pass right through it. The shadows dissipated and the sensation ceased, returning to their home across the narrow passageway that separated her from the entity that was once Yhaan.

"Dry your tears, Stone warrior. It ill suits you," declared a familiar voice. The sound was distorted beyond belief, but Tez could still recognize the voice as belonging to Yhaan. The Chief remained veiled in that formless nothingness, his presence marked only by the flashing glint of his pendant as he spoke.

Despite her best intentions, Tez could not find it within herself to dry her tears. Her arms would not stop shaking.

"I must say, you have done better than most," Yhaan's voice said. "But all must go as it goes. The steel of your spear will inevitably be bloodied, but it shall not be my life spilled upon it. So it is, and so it goes."

Shuddering, Tez struggled to turn her head toward her spear. Her hand shakily reached for it. The steel appeared inviting, an escape from all of this. "Y...Yes..." she gasped. "That...that's what...that..." She groaned, her forehead meeting the floor of the boat, her arm falling helplessly by her side. Rivers continued to stream down her cheeks as she couldn't control her sobbed breaths. A weak whimper escaped her lips, a splash of something dampening her face in a quick burst. Strands of loosened and soaked hair impaired her vision as a heavy and dense force pushed harshly against the side of her face, dazing her.

A fog filled her head, but at the same time, a fog *lifted*.

Tez looked around sluggishly, somehow now lying on her side. Something rocked her back and forth as splashes of what felt like water dampened her. The world was still a dimmed void of nothingness.

But the void that was Yhaan was *receding*. Not by a drastic margin. But noticeable enough.

"Stay your hand, second," Yhaan's voice commanded. "Interference will not be tolerated. Once more, and I cannot promise the Second's Protection will extend to you any longer." The distortion of his voice sent Tez searching for her spear again. She needed it. She needed the steel. It may as well have been a demon whispering in her ear.

A second noise—a second voice?—offered something in response, but it was far too muffled for Tez to comprehend it.

"Wh...who..." Tez said in a ragged breath. *S...se-cond? What...?*

The fog which throbbed from her right cheek fought against the mist emanating from Yhaan as Tez fought the impeding weight crushing her. She reached out, desperate to find her spear. Her eyes trailed upward, tears still flowing, whimpers still humming in her throat. The inhuman tendrils expanded and receded rhythmically, ever threatening to reach out once more to engulf her.

Her breath caught in her throat. Her heart was blasting a fiery beat in her chest, faster and faster. *Too* fast. Her thoughts felt heavy, her head light as a feather. Spells of heat and ice ran through her veins. She looked skyward for an answer, but the skies, too, were little more but a void.

"I am doing nothing that is not permitted by our ways," Yhaan said, his voice akin to a thunderclap. "Boons are not prohibited. Just as she could invoke that which the Bear granted her, so, too, can I."

The other voice retorted, but again, it was too muffled for Tez to comprehend. "Thi...ombat...ture!...What the he—T...ight it...ez!"

"Torture? No. *Strategy*. She will fight it, or she will die. From the look of her, she hasn't long left."

D-die? Yes, that...that...where's my spear? I need it. Where is it where is it where is it where—

"...ez! Get u...ubborn idio..."

St...stubborn? Tez's breath marginally steadied, despite her pounding heart. She reached out, arm still unsteady, trying to will her spear toward her, wherever it was. But that voice, that sharp, pervasive, distant voice...

"Sh...Sha-ra..."

A muffled response hummed in her ear, and Tez felt herself thrown to one side. Something hit her as she remained prostrate on the ground. A sharp edge stopped in front of her face, glinting in the darkness. Her spear.

Weakly, she managed to grip the shaft and push herself up to her knees, the surface below her wavering for the effort. She closed her eyes, damming the tears that continued to stream, and held the spear out with a concerted effort.

The shining glint within the formless entity began to blink once more. "You continue to impress me, Stone warrior," Yhaan said, his voice again sending a tremor down the length of Tez's body. "But you don't realize what will happen should you try to strike me, do you?"

Tez shook, the spear heavier than ever. "Nngh...n-n-no," she said, straining her throat for the effort.

The voice laughed. "I won't force you to find out. I assure you, it won't be pleasant."

With great force, Tez inched her foot forward, finding a way to grip her second hand along the shaft of the spear. "Sh-shut up..."

Yhaan is more cunning than prowess, and yet, that is all he has ever needed.

The tendrils began to spread once more, sharpening into a row of vicious quills. They curved inwards, facing Tez as though they were a wall of blades.

He knows he can instill enough Fear into a warrior to drive themselves to forfeit before he's even landed a single blow.

Tez took another hesitant step forward, the tendrils matching her glare.

"Your death is on your own hands," Yhaan said. "Final warning. *Drop your spear.*"

"...ez! Do it...!"

Shakily, Tez raised her spear high, her face straining, her body quivering. The tendrils slithered in place, eagerly, threateningly, like a hungry cat priming to pounce upon a meal. The glow behind the mass that was once Yhaan spread further outward into a shade of blood red.

Face it, Tawa. She's every bit the person Fanna was. Right down to how damned stubborn she is.

"DROP YOUR SPEAR!"

"SHUT YOUR GODSDAMNED MOUTH!"

The tendrils shot forward. Tez swung.

The brave still find their way back to the surface.

The strike was met with a sharp grunt, a hiss of pain, a spray of something warm along Tez's arms.

The shadows dissipated. Entirely. The tendrils faded slowly into a dense mist, falling and dancing away into the water and air as though they never existed at all. The formless mass in front of her shrunk and shrunk and shrunk until, once more, it took a corporeal shape, the shape of a man, the tallest man she had ever seen.

Yhaan had a notable grimace on his face. No longer was his pendant radiating light. It merely stood dormant—above a long trail of streaming red. The Chief put a hand tenderly to his chest and stomach, rubbing his fingers against his own blood, his eyes looking upon the viscous crimson with pointed curiosity.

"Well struck," he said to Tez, his voice no longer the haunting demonic warning it had once been. He did not seem at all worried about the gash—nor should he have, as Tez noticed it was not a deep cut—but at the same time, he was quite entranced with the sight. "It has been some time since I've seen my own blood. Quite commendable, indeed."

Growling through gritted teeth, Tez closed her eyes and breathed in deeply, feeling the surge of renewed energy as she drew in Endurance from her pendant. Her quivering arms stilled, the nausea receded, her heart quelled. She stared up at Yhaan, Fear no longer having any hold over her, instead replaced with anger flooding her vision.

"Pick up your fucking spear," she commanded. "And we'll do this properly."

Yhaan smirked, still rubbing his forefinger and middle finger against his thumb, letting the blood trail down his hand. Slowly, he nodded, crouching down to draw the spear at his feet, and as he returned to a standing position, he smeared the blood on his hand across his face, leaving a long crimson smudge traveling diagonally down from forehead to chin.

"No matter the outcome," he said, "today, you have earned my re—"

"I don't give a *shit!*" Tez thrusted her spear forward, aiming for Yhaan's heart or, more specifically, the pendant which had gripped her in the throes of Fear.

The western Chief turned the blow aside with a side-step and a two-handed push from his spear shaft. Their weapons meeting perpendicularly, Tez quickly raised her spear to meet the tip of Yhaan's, swung hard to knock it back, but again, her opponent reacted quickly enough to turn her away. Immediately, Tez pulled her spear back toward herself.

From behind, Tez could hear Sharrabha silently curse to herself as she paddled in a circle around Yhaan, the ripples of the lakebed rocking the boat to and fro. Adopting a wide stance, Tez stood completely balanced while waiting to be back within striking distance.

Yhaan's second pushed the skiff forward, the Chief not at all readying himself for a subsequent attack. He appeared studious, observant of Tez's movements, while giving the impression that he wanted not to give too much of himself away.

Tez had no objections to that. As her skiff drew just within a spear's reach, she feinted with a high strike aimed at Yhaan's neck. The Chief moved to block, but at the last moment, Tez ceased her momentum and instead altered course to offer a reverse lower strike with the shaft of the spear. Aiming for Yhaan's knees, Tez struck home, thwacking the side of the tall man's leg. Yhaan grunted, falling to that knee, the boat diving stern-first into the water to compensate for his weight suddenly falling upon it.

Seeming to be no longer content with waiting, Yhaan swung his spear horizontally in a wide sweep, trailing streams of water at the beginning of the swing. The move was overly telegraphed, and Tez blocked it with ease. Pulling back, Yhaan again prepared a swing, the same maneuver but from the opposite direction. Tez scoffed, furrowing her brow, and again turned away the strike, the sound of their steel echoing over the open hollows of the Lake of Bones.

Returning to a defensive position, Yhaan held the spear parallel to his body, no longer standing tall for the throbbing he surely felt in his knee. He was noticeably wincing as he tried to straighten that leg out.

The bigger they are... Tez thought. She did not hide her glare toward Yhaan's other knee. *See if you can block* this *one, big man.*

Spinning her spear into a reverse grip, Tez mimed the same maneuver that Yhaan attempted on her. Only this time, she struck in an upward arc, a crescent beam of water assaulting the Chief's abdomen. Yhaan paid no heed to the Tez's spear tip—it wouldn't have reached him, regardless—and instead held one arm in front of his face, blocking his eyes from the approaching wave.

Seeing her opportunity, Tez again cracked the spear against the side of his opposite leg. Just as the rush of water met Yhaan's face, he let out a gargled shout of pain, falling backward to the floor of his skiff. The sudden shift in weight nearly heaved his second into the air, but they were just barely able to hold their place in the back of the boat.

All cunning, no prowess, indeed.

She quickly turned over her shoulder to Sharrabha and nodded, not waiting for any nonverbal response. Distantly, she thought she could hear shouting from afar.

Yhaan slowly pushed himself back to his feet, standing horribly off-balance after the second strike to the knees. His forehead glistened with sweat and Lake water alike, a snarling breath escaping his nose as he gritted his teeth, noticeably biting off pangs of pain.

Sharrabha paddled furiously forward as Tez growled and roared a battle cry, channeling the Bear for more than merely its Endurance. "COME ON!"

Positioning herself along the rim of her skiff, ignoring all rocking and splashing beneath her, Tez unleashed a flurry of quick jabs, some managing to puncture shallow holes in Yhaan's flesh, others coming up short. As something splashed to her right, she swung in a wide, diagonal arc, not at Yhaan himself, but at the bow of his skiff. Unexpectant of the maneuver, Yhaan completely lost his balance, and again, his second was flung, this time off the boat entirely, meeting the Lake of Bones in an unceremonious splash.

From one knee, Yhaan held his spear awkwardly by the butt end and swung the weapon as he would an axe. Tez ducked beneath the blow, her balance maintained even as a sudden wave of water drenched her.

Another object splashed off to her side, and this time, Yhaan took notice. Seeming to look past Tez's approaching fury and flurry, the Chief squinted to the Lake shore and raised a hand. "Hold," he said."

"Like hell!" Tez responded, snarling as she swung a short strike that was mere inches from taking off Yhaan's ear, the Chief only barely able to duck beneath the blow.

Yhaan was slow to match her strikes, his reactions half a second slower than they needed to be, his maneuvers growing more sluggish as he struggled to keep up.

Steel rang against steel, screaming across the empty Lake in concert with Tez's roars and growls, each series of strikes punctuated by an additional splash between the two fighters.

The western Chief grimaced as he no longer offered any offensive counters, instead only watching Tez's jabs and slashes and blocking them to what little he seemed capable of.

"Giving up?" Tez said with satisfaction.

Yhaan rasped with short, heavy breaths as the crimson stain on his shirt grew wider and began to show along the waistline of his trousers. "We—need—to—"

Tez didn't care *what* they needed to do. She swung upwards, a move intended to open the Chief up from balls to brain, but she only managed to cut the threads of his shirt. Immediately, she swung back down, and in the next handful of moments, it was hard to tell what happened first.

Yhaan raised his spear horizontally above his head, apparently intending to either block or lessen the blow with the spear shaft.

Something sharp grazed Tez's shoulder, an uncomfortable flare suddenly coursing through the joint. It was enough to knock her blow off course and send the spear hurtling into the water below.

A soft *ting* of metal clanging against metal sent Yhaan's spear flying out of his hands, leaving him entirely defenseless.

Tez spun her spear out of the water, leveled it, aimed true for Yhaan's chest—

And something stopped her. A force tugging on her arms.

Sharply, she turned, finding Sharrabha holding firm to her forearms, a look of defiance and consternation upon her face.

"What in the hell are you—" Tez began to say.

Sharrabha pointed back to the shoreline. "Look back there," she said.

Complying, Tez squinted her eyes back to the shore, seeing a host of people waving their arms frantically. She raised her eyebrows with confusion.

Behind her, Yhaan groaned, continuing to breathe heavily through noticeable pain. "That's...that's what I was trying to...tell you," he said. "Messenger arrows. If...if they're interrupting this...it's important."

Yhaan's second returned to the boat, climbing awkwardly into the stern of the skiff. The Chief, not paying any mind to whether they were okay, held out his hand, to which his second obliged by placing a looking glass in his hand. Yhaan looked through the scope and gasped softly to himself.

With suspicion, Tez flashed a glance at Yhaan. "What is it?"

He tossed the looking glass over to her. "See for yourself."

Catching it with ease, Tez peered through the glass and saw familiar faces at the shore waving for them to return. Tenazt, Ket, Tawa, some of the Stone warriors who accompanied them...but also new faces entirely. A handful of outsiders were also waving their arms in equal measure. They were fashioned in mismatched cloths bearing a pastel of colors, their shoulders and heads armored in what seemed to be twigs and leaves, their faces painted in varying hues of orange and yellow like camouflage.

Dropping the looking glass to her side, Tez could hardly believe what she saw. "Is that...the Wood Tribe?" She turned back toward Yhaan. "Why the hell are *they* here?"

Yhaan sat back down, turning and nodding toward his second. "We're about to find out. Come."

With disbelief, Tez watched as Yhaan paddled away unceremoniously back toward the eastern Lake village. Even the fauna dwelling within the Lake of Bones seemed perplexed at the sudden departure.

"So...what about *this*?" Tez said, gesturing around her, holding up her spear. "Is this just...finished?"

Yhaan inclined his head back to Tez, shrugging with an unassuming grin. "As I said, if they're interrupting this, it must be important. And I'd not want to miss what brings the Wood Tribe of all people to our doors."

Dropping her spear, Tez couldn't help but just stand in shock at the proceedings. She looked at Sharrabha, who matched her disbelief.

"Well, that was a bit of an anticlimax," the huntress said.

Blinking with her mouth agape, Tez put her hands on her hips and contemplated throwing her spear in hopes of it finding a home in Yhaan's back. "So, if we waited an hour, we wouldn't have had to do any of this."

Sharrabha scoffed. "At least you managed to prove the lot of us wrong. Stubborn as your father, indeed."

Tez sat, head in her hands. She waved a hand dismissively. "Let's go...I guess."

A strange commotion roused Koelhe from her slumber. The weight of the previous night's frivolities still bore down upon her, even as the day began to disappear over the horizon.

As she rose to her feet, she was surprised to find herself in the central room of her hut. The flame still crackled, spitting out spurts of embers and popped firewood, the sparks landing but paces away from her. She shook her head, blinking her eyes back to attention, her head swirling with dizziness, each breath rattling her skull. *I was certain I was in bed when I last closed my eyes.*

With some effort, Koelhe managed to make her way to the door, her balance fighting her all the while. She groaned from the agony of each passing step and pressed a hand to her skull to instill some modicum of relief. It didn't work.

A cleared throat sounded from the other room when she made it to the door as though to attract her attention.

Instead, Koelhe brushed a hand over her shoulder. "Quiet, you," she said with dismissal.

A crowd had gathered in the central square, their collective voices sending a surge of pain through Koelhe's head. She delighted in seeing so many assembled at the sight of her greatest triumph. She intended to mark it as a symbol of liberty, a reminder to rise above oppression. How she would do that, she had hardly a clue. For now, though, all she wished was for the crowd to disperse so she could continue to recover. Felicitations were paramount to the toppling of failed leadership, but so was recovery from the task.

She drew a sharp whistle to call everyone to attention, and the crowd immediately fell to silence, their eyes turning to face her. "Now, now, everyone," Koelhe said, her hands raised as she did her utmost not to fall flat on her face. "If someone could explain to me the meaning of this racket, I would dearly appreciate it. I have many a matter to attend to." *And many a brother- and sister-in-arms to toast to.*

"Ah, Mother! I was *just* coming to collect you." Fann's voice echoed over the silenced crowd. People either dispersed or were pushed aside as Koelhe's son found his way through the gathering, a smile broad across his face. The grin cast shadows in the valleys and divots of his misshapen nose, matching the bruises beneath his eyes given to him by those bastards, Narva and Fann, but he did not seem intent on letting his appearance deter him from smiling to his heart's delight.

It did Koelhe's heart good to see him in such high spirits. *He has earned this just as much as I.* She reached out to him, clasping a hand firmly around his. "My sweet boy," she said. "Good news, I hope?"

Fann shrugged and flashed a slight frown. "News, at the very least. Follow me."

Koelhe raised her brow and fell in step with her son, despite the double- and triple-vision assaulting her. She passed through the parted crowd, using a number of them to maintain her shoddy balance, until she emerged into a clearing some twenty rows of people deep. As the smell of clean, unperturbed air returned to her, her nostrils no longer blemished by the stagnant air of an inebriated audience, she grunted with surprise at the sight of an outlander kneeling before her. The man's hands were bound, his head lowered, but even with his face obscured, Koelhe could still make out the band of twigs and branches fashioned against a backdrop of pastel, camouflaging colors.

She turned toward Fann, her lips pursed with interest. "To what pleasure do we owe a member of the Wood Tribe?"

Fann shook his head, soft consideration seeming to set into his gaze. "We found him carousing about the village paths. Our best Trackers could just *smell* the suspicion on him." He flashed his teeth.

A fire immediately burst in the Wood man's eyes. "I am *trying* to tell you. We are—"

"Shut up!" Fann halted the man's words with a swift kick to the mouth, blood and chipped teeth scattering everywhere. "You speak *only* when spoken to, understood?"

The visitor offered no protest but to spit bloodied shards of his teeth onto the ground beneath him.

Fann turned back to Koelhe, his smile returning. "What would you have me do, Mother?" He casually put a hand on his hip, his malformed arm hanging limply at his side.

Koelhe looked down at the grimacing man, a chuckle emerging from deep within her throat. "Perhaps it is the influence of our dear new comrade, Han'e," she said. "But I find myself distrusting of this man's intentions in our village, don't you, my son?"

No response was given save for an agreeable smirk.

Brushing a hand in the Wood Tribesman's direction, Koelhe turned back toward her hut. "Put him to the question, see what he knows. I'll not have my alliance with Han'e's people marred by misplaced faith in the Wood Tribe."

"But, of course, Mother. As you wish." Ever so softly, a giddy laugh burst from Fann's lips.

As Koelhe sauntered back home, her head still swirling, she faintly heard the mumbled and garbled protests of the Wood visitor, followed only by the smack of a hard fist meeting flesh and the dragging of feet to parts unknown.

The crowd fell to a hush. *Good,* she thought. *Now I may return to sleep.*

It was a strange return to the shore, to be sure. There was no celebration nor fanfare at Tez's return, nor admonishment for Yhaan's landing. Everyone merely nodded to each other with silent regard, words unclear, and departed for Tenazt's hut.

Tez trailed behind, flanked by Sharrabha and Tawa, not wanting to speak on what occurred on the Lake of Bones. She had no desire to describe what she felt, what she experienced, what she still felt a need to finish.

Neither Tawa nor Sharrabha appeared inclined to ask.

When the three arrived at Tenazt's hut, the eastern and western Chiefs alike were huddled around the firepit. Ket was tending to Yhaan's wounds, muttering to themself with raised eyebrows. Yhaan, whether or not he interpreted the murmurings, nodded in agreement, then inclined his head toward Tez when he noted his arrival.

Tez silently sauntered to the center of the room toward Ket and Yhaan, kicking up trails of dust as she shuffled her tired feet along. Despite the Endurance that she continued to draw in, her bones still ached from both the physical and mental strain of her encounter with the western Chief. She flashed a glance at him, his wincing face drained of color by a few shades, and part of her wished she had not left her spear at the door.

"Hard fought," Yhaan rasped to her, grimacing as his abdomen was stitched back together.

Tez lightly tapped Ket's shoulder, and once the healer finished the stitch they were working on, they glanced back up at Tez with a soft smile.

"You certainly got him good, Tez," Ket said. "I'm impressed."

"Never mind that," Tez said, not wanting to give Yhaan any further recognition. "The Wood folk who were here?"

Tenazt looked up from the central pyre, finishing his preparations. He stood, wiping soot and bark residue off his trousers, and whistled over to the side room. "You can enter now. We're ready for you."

A ragged, weathered face approached from the other room. Tez hadn't realized from the distance at which she saw the Wood Tribesperson initially, but waves of exhaustion were painted over their face just as much as the orange and yellow markings that covered their features in a vibrant canvas. Beneath their eyes were heavy, dark bags; along their arms and clothing were intermingled leavings of blood and dirt. Their hair was matted into tangled knots, twigs and leaves that Tez presumed were once a piece of armor scattered through that mess of locks.

They sat by the fire, holding their hands out to warm themself. Their palms were more blood than skin.

Tenazt sat beside them, placing a gentle hand on their shoulder. His brow furrowed in a deep crease, the crackles of flame and popping wood the only accompaniment. "The news does not bode well, does it?" he asked.

The Wood Tribesperson didn't turn, didn't nod or shake their head. They only stared ahead into the flames, squinting at the dancing pyre.

"The Invaders are coming," they said.

Nobody said anything. There was...almost a recognition of the inevitable. It seemed everyone expected the same. Why else would members of the Wood Tribe willfully leave the sanctity of the Forest, if not for a Trial?

Tez clenched her fists, bunching her nose. She couldn't help but flash another series of glares at Tenazt and Yhaan both. *If we didn't have to waste our time with this...*

Yhaan let out a deep growl, broken only by the wincing grunts resultant from the ongoing mending of his stomach. "How many? How bad?" he said softly, perhaps cognizant of Tez's own frustrations by the tone of his voice.

Again, the Woodsperson offered no physical indication beyond grimacing at the flames. "I don't know. Too many. I don't know if the rest of my Packmind still draws breath. Only that the Wood Tribe is not long for this Land. We sent as many of us into the north as we could, but..." They snarled.

"Then we have no more time to waste," Tez said, directing the words at Tenazt and Yhaan.

The two Chiefs looked to one another with both disdain and remorse. Neither offered any words to Tez, but it was clear that they recognized the truth of her words.

Turning to Tawa and Sharrabha, Tez frowned. So much still to do and so little time to do it. But it was work that needed to be done immediately.

"The Invaders know where the strength of the north lies," Tez said. "They've seen it, they've toppled it, and now surely, they're coming back to finish it. I have no more patience for whatever *this* is." She gestured pointedly to the two Chiefs, waving her finger back and forth at them. "We don't have time for this petty squabble over who stole what. Unless we want our people to burn to cinders, we need to have a unified north, no matter what."

She walked out the door into the village's main thoroughfare and inclined her gaze off to the northeast, where the peaks of the Heart still loomed tall over everything. Turning her head back inside, glaring upon those still basked in shadow, Tez allowed the waning light of the day's sun to glow over her as a beacon of hope, of defiance, of survival.

Raising a fist to chin height, she ground her teeth and said, "It's time to take back the Stone Tribe. Before it's too late."

Because if we don't have the north on one side, we won't have ourselves left on any side.

INTERLUDE

A Walking Shadow

The Year 1581 Anno Salvatoris
40 Years After the Settling

Despite it all, Aritz had to laugh.

Here he was, staring down the barrel of his own flintlock, the residual scent of gunpowder tickling his nostrils. It brought him back to earlier days, the days of the battlefield, when the aroma of powder and death were his nearest companions. For fifteen years, it was the closest scent with which he was familiar, and when he returned to the crisp, mountainous air of Acraria, he found himself immediately instilled with a desire to return to this land. This land marked by blood and death, arisen from wickedness and bathed in the light he helped to provide.

He didn't need to be afraid of this smell, of this sight. He had stared down far worse and survived. He had faced gods and lived to tell the tale.

He needn't fear a ghost with a gun.

Rising to his feet, a gust of wind roared in through the open window, knocking Aritz's hair loose, sending through the air stray papers from his desk. Not that damned letter, though. It still remained affixed to the desk, weighed down by that cursed pendant.

The woman kept her aim focused on his head, her arm unwavering, her trigger finger still, her expression as an unmoving stone. There was a fire in her eyes matching the blazes of her hair, but Aritz knew her to be fearless, too. Rarely had he ever seen her in the throes of terror.

That she wasn't now was a mistake.

Depositing his hands to his pockets, Aritz turned to the window and slowly sauntered in that direction. His assailant offered no resistance to the act, nor did any footsteps against the creaking wooden floors give any indication that she followed. He leaned his elbows on the windowsill, taking in the gentle salt air as it wafted along the breeze.

"So, you want to talk, then," Aritz said, his attention remaining on the vast ocean and the world beyond. "You wish for me to confess my sins, do you? To beg for mercy amidst the ruins of everything upon the floor? Is this meant to intimidate me?" He turned over his shoulder. "Because you must know that what you have done will accomplish little."

The woman offered nothing in the way of recompense. She still held the gun; her expression still betrayed nothing. If anything, she also bore a relaxed posture, her free hand finding its way to her trouser pocket. Almost as though she was disinterested in what Aritz claimed.

Aritz scoffed. "Of course, I'd hardly expect you to understand or disagree. Your people are victims of a failure to see the larger picture. You spill blood in my name and think it changes everything, but you were there *that* day, were you not? My reputation and standing suffered little in the eyes of the good people of this nation, in the eyes of Their Highnesses, ever since that day twenty-five years ago. Despite your understanding then, how unsurprising it is that you ultimately returned to what you truly are."

"And you," the woman responded. "How vain it would be to expect you to realize the taint of your legacy. That even when faced with the realities of your crimes, despite those who were there to *see* your crimes, you would still cry foul and label the truth as false."

He couldn't help but shake his head. "And how much blood stains your hand, I must ask? Are they not stained the same as mine?"

"The only stain upon mine is that which bleeds from your people. A necessary stain to expose you for what you are."

"And the stains of blood from your own people matter for naught?" He raised an eyebrow toward her.

The slightest of grimaces broke her face. Her lip twitched, her brow furrowed, but she said nothing beyond a small grunt.

Again, Aritz chuckled. Moving away from the window, he slowly walked toward the pile of debris on the ground, flashing an angry snarl at the now-empty shelves that once housed his trophies and memorabilia. Priceless collections, wonderful memories, now little else but shards upon the cold ground. He knelt and ran his hands through the mess, giving hardly a care to the sharp edges drawing blood along his hand, drops of red now littering the floor.

Still crouching, he looked up at the woman, the pistol's sights still set on him. He picked up a shard, a remnant from a painted pot he had collected from an abandoned hut near the large lake to the north. "You see, what you think you have done is much like the mess you've made of my chambers. They are as shards, but shards can be repaired, put together as pieces of a larger puzzle, reconfigured to return to their prior state. Nothing you've done here will last. In time, everything will be reborn anew, I will live on as I have, and you will be little more than the feeding end for worms and grubs beneath the ground."

A sly smile crept across the woman's lips, her eyes seeming to peer at the debris as Aritz sifted through it. "That you would liken the lives of your wife and children as nothing more than slivers of pottery to be rebuilt speaks to exactly the person you are. Exactly the person I am proving you to be, Aritz."

Aritz stopped combing through the broken pieces, his eyes closing as he clasped a glass shard from a broken picture frame in his hand. The glass carved through his palm like a dagger's edge, his blood streaming down his palm and into the sleeves of his shirt, staining the fine fabric underneath. He took a quivering breath, an angry breath. "Oh, no," he said, managing a sharp laugh. "Not them. It is for them that you will find yourself to be worm food soon enough. Due process has no home for you here."

"Not shall it for you, once the Royals' men have arrived for you. I'd not be surprised if they were but a handful of days away." That smile grew even more sinister, more sadistic. Like she enjoyed the bloodshed. "You know, what remains of my people, we have a name for you. A few of them, truly. Aritz the Bloody. The False Savior. The Blue Shadow. But the one that stuck with me the most was Lightscourge."

Aritz could feel the mirth rising in his throat and couldn't help but laugh. "I've been called many things, but 'Lightscourge' is certainly among the most ridiculous."

"Admittedly, the full literal translation is something along the lines of 'The Scourge of the Light Within that Gives Us Life,' but I'm sure you would agree that would be a mouthful. But, it is a true name, one that, at long last, your countrymen will be fortunate enough to see with their own eyes. To see the destroyer of not just our light, the light of the Tribes, but also of his own light, that of his family. If he was to turn his rage on his own wife and children...how can that be someone your precious King and Queen could ever hope to stand for? How can that be someone who could just as easily 'repair the shards,' as you claim? There are no shards with which to rebuild. There is only..." She walked over, a span of steps away from Aritz, and stomped hard on one of the shards, grinding it into the floor with her boot until hardly anything remained. "...dust. And when nothing remains of you and your legacy but dust, I will look forward to blowing it away to be carried off by the wind."

"And yet the wind will continue to carry me along," Aritz said.

"Off to a burial at sea, one would hope."

"Whereupon I'd still find my way to shore."

The woman sneered, grinding the final remnants of the trophy deep between the floorboards. "And behold my discovery that you fashion yourself a philosopher."

"Just as you would call yourself a hero," Aritz said, scrunching his nose. "We each of us adorn many masks that hide our true faces."

"Pot, meet kettle," she murmured.

They stood amidst one another's hostile silence, the distant crash of ocean waves and cawing of gulls acting in accordant punctuation. Aritz rotated his shoulder, feeling the crack of his bones relieving the built-up tension in his muscles. His assailant stood firm, the flintlock hanging loosely at waist height, her hand placed fiercely upon her hip as she stared bullets into him.

Aritz clicked his lips, turning back to the window, glancing at the unknown expanse far to the southern reaches. He sauntered over to the windowsill, his arms crossed behind his back, and craned his field of view as far to the east as his chambers would allow, back in the direction of Acraria.

"Hmph," he grunted. "You remind me of someone. Someone so beset by the desire to stand so tall above another, to hold another's life in his hand. Someone who, despite everything laid before him, could not see that the path he chose to walk was one built upon sinking sand. A shame. He was once a good man, an honorable man." He inclined his head over his shoulder. "At one time, I would have argued that *you* were a woman of honor, savage though you are."

She said nothing, barely moved at all from her place as remnants of memorabilia continued to crunch and crack beneath her weight.

Aritz flashed a smirk toward her. "You're little more than a child crushing ants on an anthill beneath your heel. Little do you know you're on a hill of your own, and there's always a larger boot. You have my word on that."

She pointed the gun back at him, evidently unmoved by his words. "One man's boot is another man's bullet. I'd say they kill ants just the same, wouldn't you?" The woman walked forward, arm still outstretched, the floorboards still crunching beneath her feet with every step from the residue still sticking to her heel.

She was near enough that she could easily shove Aritz from the window to the cold ground below. Or he to her. With enough acumen, one could traverse the walls of the manor safely to the rear garden, though Aritz had never the inclination nor desire to attempt to do so.

Still, something irked at him. "That you have not yet pulled the trigger proves that you're aware my murder will accomplish nothing," he said with confidence.

"Murder?" She hummed with disapproval. "Retribution is a more apt term. You could call me an angel of retribution, if you are so inclined." She flashed her teeth, though Aritz would be loath to call it a smile.

"I've no eagerness to deem you an angel of anything. The realm of angels, as dictated by the Savior's Scriptures, has no room for savages such as yourself."

"Sticks and stones, Aritz," she said. The barrel of the flintlock nudged to her left. Apparently, she wanted Aritz to move away from the window.

Chuckling, Aritz complied, walking along to the shelves of ponderous tomes topped with at least two layers of dust. He swiped two fingers along the carved oak, a smeared trail evidence of it. He held up the dust-covered digits, compacted grey trickling down to the floor in fleeting specks as he waved his hand toward her.

"You see," Aritz said, "for all we're concerned, *this* is what your people amount to now. Drifting dust, harmful to none save for those who suffer from an allergy. Hardly a thing to sneeze at." He clapped his hands together, specks of dust jumping to the back of his throat. He suppressed a cough, wanting not to belabor his point. "A bullet may spill my blood, but it will change nothing. What words you whisper into the wind will not change the fact that your people are nothing but the dust collecting atop the books I elect not to read."

Wiping the remnants of dust off on a nearby linen towel, Aritz returned his hands behind his back, maintaining unbroken eye contact with the woman across from him. "But let's entertain your point, shall we? Let's say that the people of Ferranda, *my* people, are removed from their cognitive faculties enough to believe your words." He raised his arms to his side, offering an indifferent shrug. "It's of little consequence, truly. Ferranda numbers only a few thousand. In the grand scheme of things, it matters little."

That got her attention. Barely perceptible, but just enough to break that indignant façade. Her brow twitched, her teeth gritted, the flintlock rose ever so slightly.

"How defensive you've grown over a nation that you argue does not matter," she said.

"I've merely grown to know the battles that are worth fighting," Aritz said. "And I know enough that if you were to spill my blood, if my brain was to be smattered across the fine bookcase behind me, it won't matter. My legacy will continue. You've seen to it that my bloodline will not, but my triumphs, my accomplishments, my *legacy* will survive through the centuries." He could feel his voice rising, but he did not care. "History will remember *me*, Aritz a Mata, the Founder of the greatest gem of the Acrarian Kingdom, a man who arose a nation from nothing, a man loved unconditionally by his people, a man who laid down everything in the name of his King and Queen. They would write me as a martyr to his nation, his time on this earth cut short by a lower creature! And *you*, you and your *people*—"

Calling them "people" was poison on his tongue.

"—will merely be a footnote to a greater story, and your revenge will be for absolutely nothing. You seek retribution? Seek it for yourself. The Savior will grant me leave enough to make you wish for it. He does not look kindly upon those who score in shadow the ones blessed in His light. If there was truly a Lightscourge, it would be *you!*" He pointed an angry, shaking finger at the woman.

She stared at him with disinterest, even going so far as to feign a yawn.

"And would your precious Savior not look upon you with disdain for the amount of blood you have spilled? Are we not all 'bathed in His light,' as you would say?"

Aritz let out a sharp scoff. "Your people rejected His light. So far as I'm concerned, my soul is cleansed."

"A riveting proclamation. Of course, we both know it not to be true. Do take heed not to hide behind petulant words, Aritz. Your Savior cares not for liars."

"The Savior cares not for filth such as you, either!" he barked.

Still, the woman appeared unbothered. She looked to the bookcase, walking past Aritz's frothing rage entirely, paying him absolutely no heed. A puff of dust erupted in the wake of a sharply blown breath as she examined the spines of the different tomes on display. Her forefinger loosely trailed along the row of books before she stopped on one, pointing at it expectantly.

"Ah, the complete works of Ofala of Glanna Hollow. He wrote a firsthand account of the Second Acrarian Civil War, did he not? The riveting prose of the heroic final charge of Sir Satarias, cutting down a platoon with a quarter the men and still claiming a necessary plot of land for the Northern Marches. Such wonderful theater!"

A deep growl rumbled in Aritz's throat. "What do you care of my people's histories?"

The woman chuckled. "Well, Ofala was largely discredited, was he not? And Sir Satarias had to be convinced not to abandon his post like the coward he was? Of course, no one cared in those days, at least in the Northern Marches. History shines brighter when time is allowed to pass."

"And what is your point, woman?"

"My *point*," she said, "is that I know nothing will change today. It may not change tomorrow, or next month, or next year. The scholars of our age will always look to you as a paragon of Acraria. The light shines brightly on who is deemed the heroes, history is written by the victorious hand, and drinks are toasted only to glory and success."

She paused, chuckling to herself as she parsed through more of Aritz's library, though what was so amusing, Aritz did not know, nor did he care to know.

You'll not find much to laugh about when the victorious hand writes of your folly, woman, he thought.

Before Aritz could blink, the flintlock was back at eye level, and he was once again staring down the barrel, threatened with the promise of a shot he was unsure the woman would even take.

"Of course," the assailant said, "I care little for what the scholars will say now. I'm the one on *this* side of the gun, and the minds of people are always wont to change, are they not? Besides..." She shoved the barrel into his forehead, shoving him in the direction of a nearby chair.

Aritz nearly fell over the armrest. He could already feel a dent forming in his forehead.

"I'm sure everything would turn over in a flash were they to know of the Harvests." She raised her eyebrows, the expression upon her face toeing the line between sinister and curious. Walking to Aritz's desk, she grabbed the chair which she had forced him into originally and dragged it along the floorboards, leaving a trail of deep white scratches in the otherwise pristine hardwood. She sat with relaxation in the chair, leaned back, and, resting the wielding arm on the armrest, pointed the flintlock at her target. "So, you see," she said, a smile on her face, "I have reason still to see you draw breath. Your greatest crime against my people. Your most heinous act. I was fortunate enough to escape them, but even I don't know the details. I'm sure your subjects would *love* to hear all about the Harvests." She clicked the hammer into place. "Speak."

Aritz squinted his eyes at her, whatever words she expected hardly necessary at the moment. He examined every inch of her face, trying to find some blemish, some error. But as pristine and unmarred as the woman's face was, he could not turn away the fatal flaw in her disguise.

You don't know the details? The whole thing was your idea!

Who is this woman?

CHAPTER TEN

MERCILESS

The Year 1556 Anno Salvatoris
15 Years After the Invasion

The Forest loomed tall before her, haunting her, taunting her, just as it had been for days.

The pastel portrait of the arboreal expanse had, at one time, instilled in Sen a sense of wonder and mystery, a ponderance of how something so beautiful from the outside could house such terror from within. But when last she passed through, the terror was not of the threat the Wood Tribe supposedly posed, but of the horror bestowed upon them.

And no longer did the exterior hold any grasp over Sen's curiosity. All that remained was the image of the stain of red marring the green pathways, her bellows to the skies, the fatal end of everything she once held dear.

She passed that very spot some time ago, by her estimation. It was hard to tell when trailing an army of countless...*Acrarians*.

Calling them by their true name still did not sit right upon Sen's tongue. *Acrarians*, she thought to herself. *But if I still call them Invaders...what am I for walking along their path?* Somewhere at the front of the pack, too, was the man who had killed her father. And countless armed men and women between him and her.

She thought on all of that often as she followed the march northward from the City. She had been fitted with a small Deatharm called a "pistol," after the larger "rifle" was a bit too unwieldy for her. A hunting knife had been strapped to the small of her back, which she found much more in her taste. The ends of her jacket fluttered in the wind behind her, the fit feeling odd and tight, so she had kept it unbuttoned, to which none seemed to take any objection. The Illusion she had cast as an Acrarian woman appeared bereft of flaws, too, so long as no one spoke to her. Ziia had the foresight to tell those around her that Sen was a mute, which, admittedly, Sen took no exception to.

Her fellow Eclipseborn flanked her at the back of the march, all Illusioned and all remaining as stone-faced as they could manage despite the rigors of the steady march. Kamataa and Ziia stood as a pair directly in front of Sen; to her left, Sha'a, Vanta, and Zara; and to her right, Hollow and Cin. As the Forest loomed closer and closer, Sen could not help but notice Hollow's grumbling become more persistent, his growls heavier, his breaths more a fury than a flurry.

Sen couldn't help but wonder how long Hollow had awaited this day, to march through the Forest with an army. And then how long the same could be said of the other Children and their feelings towards their respective Tribes.

But when the shadows of the Forest gripped her, Sen no longer allowed herself to ponder the topic. She couldn't afford distractions.

It didn't stop her from noticing the imposing grin stretching across Hollow's lips. It was unsettling.

Though the morning sun was shining brightly above just a short distance ago, within the Forest, the trappings of light held no sway. Flickers of sunshine made their way through the dense overhang of oranges and yellows, but just as it had been for her in those days prior, the thick shadows were disorienting enough to Sen that the passage of time felt altogether meaningless. They could have been marching for minutes or hours and she would have no idea of the difference.

However long they were marching, though, the Forest remained starkly quiet, save for the crunching of twigs underfoot and the skittering of arboreal fauna from the sight of the enormous host.

Sen looked from one Eclipseborn to the other, seeing the hair prickle on the back of Sha'a's neck, the focused glare in Cin's eyes, the grinding teeth in Hollow's mouth. Sen's hand twitched as it rested on the grip of her pistol, ready for the moment she would need to draw it. On Tribespeople.

Her heart pounded. She closed her eyes and remembered Kamataa's advice at the practice yard. *Just breathe, Sen,* she thought. *If they're all Koelhe or Fann...*

It still made her feel uneasy. That she didn't belong here. That her purpose was to fall along the hillside those few nights ago.

But if it's not here that I belong...then where?

On and on, the marching continued, the tense silence holding Sen firm in its grip. She had always heard from her father that when the onset of battle was looming, the waiting was the worst part. The ever-present threat of danger, the promise of death, the inbound baptism by blood. Each crack of wood underfoot was enough to make her jump, for the gooseflesh to trail up the length of her arm and neck. And yet, for however long she was forced to press on, there was nothing.

There was silence.

After seeing the state the Wood Tribe was in just a few short days ago, Sen knew they were in no condition to fight. She couldn't grasp how many of those injured and wounded comprised the Tribe's fighting fit, but if she were to estimate, the Tribe had to be at half-strength, if that at all.

But, still, she thought. *That remaining half of the Tribe will fight with a ferocity I've never seen before. I'm sure of that.* Calling the Wood Tribe "territorial" was a grave understatement. They were overzealous protectors of the Forest, such that they spilled the blood of a large number of the Sun Tribe who were only trying to escape the carnage set upon them by the Invaders—by the Acrarians. They would not stand long for the numbers marching through now.

But where are they?

Sweat dripped down the side of her forehead, trailing down into her eye. As she wiped at her eye, she looked up to the trees, trying to discern any movement at all within the dense shadows, listening for any fluttering through the treetops against the whispering wind. She knew where to look, but still, there was nothing.

Until, in her upward focus, she walked straight into Kamataa's backside. The old crone had stopped, a fist upraised, and then a forefinger. Slowly, she turned to face Sen, and then the others, a wide grin on her face. She inclined her focus toward Vanta, and when Sen turned to face the former Arrow Tribeswoman, she realized there was a glint beneath her shirt, the same rune that once adorned Narva's pendant.

She was listening.

And just as quickly as she started, Vanta opened her eyes, aimed her rifle, and fired.

Sen froze in place. Shadows gripped her, the wisping waves of the laughing darkness again rearing its ugly head. The thunderclaps echoed with the intermingling voices of her father and brother, the pleas for mercy, the howling cackles that matched her voice as the Deatharms roared into the sky. She felt a chill, a horrid, debilitating chill as her shadow turned to face her, rabid and snarling drool draping vicious fangs...

"No," she whispered. "Not anymore."

...and the face which stared upon her was that of Koelhe. No longer did the cackles come from Sen's own voice, but from the woman who made her life hell. Koelhe's form danced and contorted, shrieking with laughter all the while.

But Sen, for her part, broke free of the grasp. "Your time will come," she promised the phantom. "In due time."

The world snapped back. Plumes of smoke wafted from the nose of Vanta's rifle. The branches quivered and cracked. Leaves descended in a gentle wave. A series of successive thuds and crashes echoed from above, and a body fell to the earth unceremoniously, meeting the ground with a sickening crunch, blood erupting in a short burst from the force of the impact, staining the compacted leaves and motionless body of the Wood hunter in equal measure.

Sen snapped her head back and forth, seeing each of the Eclipseborn flashing the widest of smiles.

"Let's have some fun," Kamataa said giddily.

Hollow roared, aiming a pistol into the trees.

An eruptive sound of pistols and rifles screamed throughout the Forest.

Arrows rained down from parts unseen.

And Sen took cover.

Hiding initially behind the tallest Acrarian she could find, Sen took aim with her pistol, her hands wavering with unsteady intent. A flood of thoughts poured through her mind, not the least of which being whether she could truly kill another Tribesperson in cold blood.

It's only defense, she thought. *This is for the Children. If it's not here that I belong...then where?*

She closed one eye shut, continuing her attempts to locate a target in the dense overhang of pastel leaves painted crimson.

She heard a roaring shot. It was not hers.

The Acrarian in front of her fired, reloaded, fired, reloaded, with remarkable efficiency, given the number of steps it took to prepare the weapon. He barely paid her any mind as she continued to use him for cover.

Sen's finger itched, but no matter how hard she tried, she could not find it in her to pull the trigger. The pistol fell lackadaisically to her side, her heart still pounding, her ears ringing, the battle cries and roars of pain little more than a dull, muted murmur.

Blood splashed across her face as a pair of arrows took her covering man in the throat, the arrowheads jutting out from the back of his neck. The soldier collapsed in a heap, his rifle firing one last shot from the impact as it landed haplessly among the coniferous dirt.

Quickly, Sen smeared the blood from her face, likely doing little to remedy the situation, and spat out a wad that had made its way to her mouth. She felt a tingle run through her arm, the ever-present sensation of Luck, and a rush of wind passed by her on either side of her head, twin volleys of arrows finding a home in the bark of the tree some paces behind her.

Rolling to the side, Sen found cover behind a tall tree, a succession of arrows punctuating her arrival and thudding violently along the trunk. She chanced a glance around the bark and watched as yeomen fell to the trees, some by intent to attempt to face the Acrarians on the ground, others by virtue of catching a volley to the chest or the eye, leaving behind a falling rain of lifeblood as they met the unforgiving earth.

Several of the Acrarians seemed eager to meet the challenge, fending off the Wood ground attack, parrying the flutters of hunting knives and spears with the shafts of their rifles, swinging the weapons about as though they were spears of their own.

Sen couldn't help but notice that it was such a different manner of fighting. The Wood warriors were virulent, animated, fierce. All the qualities she would expect from a people fighting for what was left of their home, a home that, to them, was the sacred of sacred. They roared and screamed, ignoring all manners of pain, refusing to fall until their bodies simply would not permit them to go forward. To an extent, they seemed out of place on the ground, unsure of how best to fight. They were a people keen on a more guerrilla style of combat. They weren't expecting Listeners among the enemy.

But the Acrarians, bold and methodical, fought with none of the fight or flight instinct. They were a machine. Sen was in equal parts astonished and horrified. She had never seen such efficiency in the art of killing. The Acrarians move forward in a lined group, standing and firing, reloading, allowing the next line behind them to perform the same act. Their fallen numbers seemed to matter little to them. When one fell, the next in line stood to replace them, ready to fire, ready to march, ready to kill.

It was enough to remind Sen of that night when her father fell.

I guess it doesn't matter who *we come back with, does it?* That was what that stranger had said. The man who killed her father. The man at the head of the Acrarian army.

The mercilessness of their people knew no bounds. It extended not only to their pursuit of those two Haunted runaways who had changed everything in Sen's life. It was not just to the efficiency by which the Wood Tribe fell to their strikes.

It was also to the disregard for their fallen comrades.

They don't even mourn their dead as a tragedy, Sen thought. *They're just a number to be felled.*

But she knew she couldn't remain behind this tree for much longer. Despite everything, she knew.

If not here, then where?

Hurriedly, she slid back in formation, filing in beside the Illusioned Children. Cold sweat poured down her face and neck, her hands quivering as she raised her pistol just as a means by which she could blend in with the rest. The Deatharms continued to deafen the air with their incessant volleys; surely, none would notice that no smoke would plume from the barrel of her pistol.

A fog began to rise as more and more warm, bleeding bodies fell to the earth. At knee height, Sen felt that she was wading through fleeting life as it departed to the Otherworld. As much as she wanted to look upon the faces of each who fell, each for whom she played a passive role in forcing from this plane of life, doing so only unsettled her further.

Not merely for the loss of life in such volume.

But for the expression of pure *delight* that she witnessed upon the faces of her Eclipseborn kin.

Each of them wore a broad smile as they fired shot after shot into the trees, some laughing, others merely furrowing their brows as they pressed on with their attacks.

They weren't just taking part in the slaughter.

They *reveled* in it.

Perhaps to this point, Sen hadn't fully come to terms with how much they were looking forward to this moment. This had only been her fight—insofar as she felt she could call it that—for a handful of days. For them, it had been their whole lives. For Kamataa and Ziia, in particular, it had been *centuries*.

And that long wait was immediately evident upon the old crones' faces. Their eyes widened with glee and anticipation, each disregarding the standard rules of engagement for the rest of the Acrarian forces and ignoring the formed lines to fire their shots on their own. With each shot, another fell from the trees. With each shot, another cackle echoed in Sen's ears, overshadowing the otherwise muted carnage of the world around her.

For all the energy they seemed to have been exerting, none of the Eclipseborn had even broken a sweat. It was enough to cast Sen in a well of disbelief.

The main Acrarian force marched on, continuing their organized system of death, disregarding entirely the bloodstained soil on which they walked, evidently content with the splashes of red on their boots as though it was a badge of honor, a proof of victory.

As they pressed on, Kamataa raised a fist, signaling the rest of the Eclipse-born to stop. She went to one knee, ignoring entirely the present danger of a volley of arrows imminent to strike.

She turned to Sen, her gaze still wild with excitement. "Are you enjoying yourself yet, child?" she said, her breath heavy but tone exuberant.

Sen didn't know what to say. She fell to her knees, her weary legs thanking her for it. Part of her wanted to vomit from the nerves and death about her, but she managed to push the bile down and stare blankly at the old Eclipseborn. Thankfully, it seemed she was not expected to offer a response.

"Is this not getting a little boring, though?" Sha'a said, amusement in her voice. Despite her abandonment of her Tribe, Sen could see why she may be inclined to revel in the Wood Tribe's destruction, given her being born to the Sun Tribe. "Should we not...liven things up a bit?"

Kamataa offered a throaty chuckle and turned to Hollow. Sen noticed a fire within the former Wood Tribesman's eyes that she had never seen in another before. All emotion had left his eyes. All save for rage. All the pain inflicted upon him since he was a boy was ready to burst.

"What do you say, Hollow?" Kamataa asked. "Are you ready to let loose?"

A sharp breath snorted out from Hollow's nostrils. He didn't deign the question with a response. He held out his rifle in one hand, flintlock in the other, each pointed in the opposite direction, clicked back the hammers, and fired simultaneously.

The creak and crack of timber was the only thing Sen could hear, the roar of the shots so close to her ears sending a lingering screech through her ears. In her periphery, two large tree branches apparently had suffered their final blow, the force of the shots enough to tumble their mighty arms to the earth.

With their fall arrived a host of Wood hunters, each tumbling to the ground, wounded but alive. They were battered, broken, and yet resilience still lingered in their gazes. Slowly, they rose back to their feet, some clearly fighting back the pain of broken bones, deep gashes, running wounds. Sen holstered her pistol, reaching to her backside for the hunting knife sheathed there.

If I'm to spill Tribal blood, she thought, *then it will be by—*

She didn't get a chance to finish her thought. Hollow roared beside her, charging off to the right with his rifle wielded as though it were a club. He swung mightily at the rising group of Wood fighters, taking one in the head, caving his skull into a pulp of viscera and brain matter. The momentum knocked the dead man into his two adjacent comrades, toppling them like successive columns. Hollow approached the one mostly trying to push his brainless kin off of him, and rammed the butt end of his rifle into the man's face repeatedly. Splinters were made of his teeth, his nose was reduced to nothing, one eye burst from its socket from the blunt force, until finally—and mercifully—he finally ceased his breathing. The third fighter tried to take Hollow in the midst of his bloodlust, jumping at him with hunting knife drawn, but Hollow deftly dropped the rifle, drew his pistol, quickly fired at the man's knee, and blew it out entirely. As the man bellowed in agony, the bottom of his leg loosely dangling beneath his weight, Hollow ripped the knife from his hand, pressed two forceful stabs to his chest, and then carved viciously upward, cutting a path through the whole of his enemy's throat.

He tossed the knife aside, his face spattered with blood and gore. Crouching in a battle stance, his pistol still in one hand, he looked to the remaining gathering and bellowed at the top of his lungs, "WHO'S NEXT?!"

The Wood host roared to meet his challenge. As did the Eclipseborn.

Sen could hardly move as she watched the carnage unfold.

Sha'a parried the swing of a blade, her pistol drawn. She ducked under one swing, two swings, evaded a thrust, finding herself within her opponent's guard, and shot him point-blank in the gut. The fighter sunk to his knees, hands clasping at the blood coursing through the slits of his fingers. His face was near-frozen in shock, blood spurting from his mouth. He fell to the ground, reaching out to Sha'a helplessly as though wishing for the mercy of the kill, but Sha'a instead pressed his face into the dirt with her boot, walked over him entirely, and moved on to her next target.

Kamataa and Ziia teamed together on one poor fighter, the woman stripped of her weapons but still trying to do all she could to fell her assailants. The attempt was short-lived. Ziia threw her to the ground, sliced at her face with the tip of her hunting knife, and Kamataa rammed her rifle into the woman's throat over and over, crushing every bone in her throat. She choked her last pained breath, her eyes red, face purple as she lolled limply to the side.

Zara and Vanta were less violent in their approaches, but still just as merciless in their tactics. Evading flurries of arrows, they pressed into the Wood fighters' inner guards. In unison, they snatched quills from their foes' quivers and shoved them right through each of the yeomen's throats. It was quick but unsettling all the same.

Sen couldn't bring herself to move from her spot. If anything, all she could force herself to do was shudder. Even despite the tingles of Luck coursing through her arms, the Luck warning her of the imminent danger in which she found herself, she *could not move.*

This...can't be my fight, she thought. *But...I can't back out now. If it's not here, then...where do I go? Where do I...*

"Look out!"

A hand grasped her by the hip and spun her around, forcing her out of the way of a rapid volley of arrows. Just as quickly, the thunderclap of a succession of pistol shots rang in her ears, a score more of Wood fighters falling to the ground in short order.

Sen turned her focus away from the death and stared up, surprised to find Cin grasping her. A wave of revulsion came over her. She closed her eyes, and for a brief moment, Narva's face flashed in her vision. In another flash, his face was drenched in blood, his own blood.

With a sharp gasp, Sen pushed Cin off her, still bereft of the necessary words.

Cin held out his pistol to his right, firing without looking. Sen did not break eye contact with him, but from her periphery, she could tell another fighter had fallen.

"The hell are you doing?" Cin snarled.

Sen shivered, taking in all the death around her. "I..." she stammered before trailing off.

"Don't have time to babysit you. Either shoot something or leave." Just as quickly, Cin rushed off, joining Hollow as the former Woodsman continued roaring through his bloodlust, challenging any and all who would hear him.

Finally in control of her legs again, Sen took a tentative step forward, then another, and another. To her left, Sha'a continued her wicked slaughter, allowing her prey to bleed out rather than giving them the mercy of a clean kill. To her right, Hollow remained more beast than man. The other Eclipse-born maintained their own breed of bloodshed, each of them appearing to enjoy the killing. And ahead, the Acrarian forces pressed on, methodical and merciless, the last vestiges of the Wood defense falling to the ground unceremoniously from the trees as though a plague overtook them all.

Everything was muted around Sen. All she could hear was her own breath as she walked upon the bloodstained path. She turned to her left, off the beaten road, taking in the horrid sight of the Forest bathed in blood. She looked at her hands, still thankfully clean of the Tribal blood, but still, they shook. A sudden wave of nausea rose, and she fell to her knees. This time, she could not hold it back. She emptied her stomach in the compacted leaves, her chest heaving as she propped herself on all fours. She looked up to the skies, her eyes watering, bile-infused drool dripping from the corner of her mouth. Wiping away the lingering vomit from her mouth, Sen pushed herself fully onto her knees and let out a shaky breath.

"Fuck," she whispered. "What am I doing...?"

The ringing in her ears ceased enough for her to hear the endless volley of Deatharms echoing through the arboreal reaches of the Forest. Intermingled with those thunderclaps, she could still make out the exuberant laughter from the likes of Kamataa and the bloodthirsty bellowing from Hollow.

But standing out against the persistent din was a pained groan not forty paces away. A sharp, ragged breath rang out loud enough to carry over to Sen, and for the sake of her own curiosity, she cautiously waded along the mist and blood to the source of the noise.

The source of the noise came into view, just barely breaking the mist. A male figure lay prostrate on the ground, eyes facing toward the sky, blood trailing down from the corner of his mouth. His legs were horrendously bent, enough for Sen to feel another wave of nausea at the sight. Circles of blood were visible in two spots on the chest of the man's shirt, splatters of red adorning his long, white locks of hair. Beside his head, a crown of sticks and twigs lay upside down, not having fallen far despite the man's rapid descent from the treetops.

Immediately, Sen recognized the man. The Chieftain. She knelt beside him, saying nothing, wanting to reach out to calm him but finding not the strength to do so.

The Chieftain stared sharply at her. Coarse breaths escaped gritted teeth as he growled at her. The breaths grew shriller, more pained, as though her presence was further driving a knife through him.

"What do you want, Invader dog?" he snarled. "Come to watch a man die? Slaughtering my people not enough for you?" He shuddered, the act of speaking seemingly too much for him.

Sen gripped at her Illusion pendant. *If he's going to curse me...then let it truly be me he curses.* She breathed in deeply and allowed the Illusion to dispel, revealing her true face to him.

The Chieftain inclined his head forward, squinting his eyes. "What...*Sennalhat*?" he said incredulously.

Averting her eyes, Sen looked listlessly at the ground, flicking away a loose twig beneath her knee. "Hello again, Chieftain," she said with remorse.

"The hell...are you...doing? With these...Invaders?!"

"I wish...that I had an answer for you," she said.

He snarled at her. More fiercely than he had when she had still kept up her Illusion. "You...*traitor*. I should have...killed you when I had the chance." He clenched his eyes shut, pained tears escaping his eyes as a spasm ran through him.

Sen sighed. "It may have been better for all of us had you done so." She gnawed at her lower lip, planting her palms firmly in the bloodstained dirt. "There's no point denying the label. I...I shouldn't have..." She trailed off, looking off to her right, to the plumes of acrid smoke still wisping along what little breeze made its way through the Forest. "But it's too late. I can't go back. I...there's nowhere to go back *to*."

Settling back into the earth, the Chieftain stared fierce daggers into her. Again, he clenched his eyes shut, biting back another pang of pain. "I can't feel my arms...or my legs. If I could, I...*nggh*, shit." Opening his eyes again, he stared listlessly at the skies, paying no heed to Sen at all. "Why...? Why my people? Why would you...?" Another groan and another pang of pain. "My bow...where is my bow? I need...I need my bow. Damn it, I need..."

There was no helping the tears that flowed down Sen's cheeks. Her hands still trembling, she reached behind her for her hunting knife, drawing it out as it rasped against the interior of the sheath. The sound drew the Chieftain's attention to her. "Please..." she said. "I only hope that...that you can..." She trailed off, unable to keep her eyes on him. "I'm sorry."

His nostrils flaring, the Chieftain closed his eyes, blinking away tears of his own. He said nothing, only accepted the inevitable. There was no healing his body. There was no healing his people.

Sen couldn't change that. All she could do now was make it worse. But at the very least, in this moment, she could offer him something that the Acrarians refused. That the Children of the Black Moon resisted.

Mercy.

Slowly, Sen brought the tip of the knife to the Chieftain's throat, nodding to the old warrior as she pressed down. The initial wince of pain on the man's face gave her pause, but she forced herself to stay her hand. Dark red blood poured out from the entry point of the knife as the Chieftain choked and gargled on the cold steel. And as she pulled the knife out, more and more blood spouting from the wound, the mighty Chieftain lay dead.

Her entire body trembled, the act completely numbing her. Sen had never taken a life before. She didn't know what to feel. She felt no anger towards the man. She did not revel in his death. To some extent, she felt it more humane to spill his blood in such a manner, compared to everything that had transpired on this day.

She closed the Chieftain's eyes, granting him his final rest. "Find peace in the boundless Otherworld, great Chieftain," she whispered, hoping the rite would, in fact, bestow upon him the peace he deserved.

On shaking legs, she forced herself to her feet, sparing one final glance at the man. "I'm sorry," she said again. "I..."

But the next time you return to our Forest, I cannot promise that our encounter will be under as welcoming of circumstances. The Chieftain's words from her time in the Forest with Narva rang in her ears.

She sighed, wiping away a stream of tears.

The sound of the Acrarians' assault sounded further north, and so Sen made to follow, returning her Illusion to her Acrarian disguise.

As she returned to the clearing, she looked to the south, finding the Eclipseborn whittling down the last remnants of the Wood fighters. One final warrior remained, an unarmed woman holding out her hands in a plea for mercy.

Kamataa answered the plea with a gleeful laugh as she held her pistol at the woman's face and fired.

MEMORY

Renewal

"Would you mind passing the butter, child?"

"Yes, of course," Tua said, loose bits of leeks spilling out from the corner of his mouth. "Here you are, Nena—oh, shoot."

As Tua lifted the saucer, the handle snapped, the pool of melted butter splashing every which way, covering the table, spilling over everyone.

"Tua!" his father said.

"I'm sorry! It just broke!" He looked over. "Oh gods, I'm sorry, Nena, it's all over you."

"That's quite alright, child. You can blame eastern craftsmanship for it."

They all laughed.

"If you don't mind, I'm just going to step outside to the Lake to wash this stain out. I'll just be a moment."

Tua frowned. "I'm sorry, Nena," he muttered, eyes downcast.

She smiled at him and patted him gently on the shoulder. "It's no trouble," she said. "Just help your parents clean up the spill."

"Be careful out there," the boy said.

The winter sun had long since set, the nighttime chill bringing with it the promise of snow flurries from the mountains. The atmosphere was quiet but tense. Such as it had been over these past few decades. When the night broke, the day ended. Markets closed, doors shut, and choral silences rang.

There was a fear of the dark that had only grown worse over the last sixty years. Likewise, there was a mistrust of the daylight.

Regardless of cause, the effect was that gallivanting about the village was, to her, *easier*. Not more unsettling, not more fearful. There were none to get in her way, none to bother her, none to wish upon her good tidings or ill fortune, dependent on which side of the Lake she found herself.

But on this side, the western half, the shoreline spoke to her, still holding itself to be thawed despite the looming winter. She knelt on the sandy shore, stiff earth at half-frost crunching beneath her knees as she cupped her hands into the frigid water. The biting cold sent a shiver through her body as she sucked in a sharp breath and splashed her legs and torso. With due effort, she wiped down the trails of butter from her clothing and felt the same slick texture along the length of her pendant.

Peering over her shoulder for the unlikely event that someone was near, she removed the ornament from her neck, dunking it into the still waters of the Big Lake as a wave of energy left her body. The Moon shone brightly above her, reflecting on the water's waves like an illuminative mirror. She caught her own reflection, absently massaging at the unmasked wrinkles peppering her face now that her Illusion had been dispelled.

It had been some time since Kamataa had seen her own face. It was nice to be reminded of what it looked like.

"A beautiful night, isn't it, my Lady?" she said to the Moon's reflection. "Fret not, for the work continues, as always it does."

The Moon did not respond, only glimmered further on the surface of the Lake.

"Few we may now be, but with Your guidance, we may one day to you again return. With Your blessing." She bowed her head, looking at her withered hands as they continued to grasp the ice-cold pendant. *Whenever that guidance may come.*

Shrugging her shoulders, she braced herself for the frozen metal and winced as she placed the chain of the pendant back along her neck. The energy of Illusion surged through her once again, and her disguise returned: a woman in her fifties, the threat of grey not yet fully overtaking the hair that framed her taut, creased face. The wrinkles disappeared, and the exhaustion in her eyes dissipated. She certainly got used to looking well in her advanced age.

"Nena?" a voice called from behind.

Kamataa breathed deeply, practicing her smile to return some semblance of genuineness. *With Your blessing, my Lady. For You.*

She turned, catching Tua approaching from the direction of the hut. "Dear child, it is much too dangerous for you to be wandering out on your own at this hour," she chided.

Tua wrapped his arms around his torso, rubbing his arms vigorously in defense against the dark chill in the air. "The same could be said for you," he remarked with a furrowed brow. "It's too scary out here for someone as old as you."

Chuckling, Kamataa flashed him a kind grin. "Clever boy, how old do you think I am? It's rude to comment on a woman's age, you know."

"It's not rude to point out that you're old, Nena. Everyone knows you're ancient." Try as he might, the smile he had been holding back could not be stopped any longer.

If only you knew just how *ancient, boy.* She stood, wringing out the freezing water from her clothing, and shuffled over, huddling her arms around herself to retain and regain warmth. "Don't you worry about me, child. I've been around long enough to take care of myself. *You*, however, your parents must be worried about."

Tua shrugged, raising his eyebrows. "It was their idea. They were worried for how long you were taking."

"Then I must extend my thanks, but as you can see, dear child, I am fine. In fact, better than fine. I feel younger from the freezing water."

He looked at her suspiciously. "The Lake doesn't do that."

"And small boys don't question their elders. Come along, now; let us return to your parents."

Tua grunted with disapproval and folded his arms in a dismissive manner, but he followed along, regardless.

Kamataa stretched her arm around the boy's shoulders, pulling him in close. She looked down at him with a knowing smile, trying once again to force that exuberant grin back to the surface. It didn't take long for it to happen.

"How well you and your family have treated me all these years, Tua. I must emphasize that I do appreciate the concern you all show me as though I were your own family."

The boy looked perplexed but still maintained his smile. "You say that all the time, Nena, and I don't know why. You *are* family."

"Well," Kamataa said, "I would argue that it cannot be said enough." She tussled the top of his head, knocking loose the poorly-tied knot that ostensibly held his hair together. She peered over her shoulder, back to the Lake, narrowing her eyes across the darkened horizon that lay on the other side, finding nothing in that blackness. "The family of choice is sometimes just as important as the family of blood."

"Well, the family of blood would like you to come home."

She couldn't argue against that. Kamataa squeezed Tua's shoulder and led him back to the hut. One more look to the eastern horizon showed nothing but lingering darkness beyond the reflection of the Moon at Her fullest. *Whenever the guidance may come*, she thought.

The aroma of the fish and leek stew still lingered and wafted out from the entryway when they returned home. Tua's parents were waiting expectantly at the table, kind smiles strewn across their faces even if the gestures did not quite reach their eyes.

"We were beginning to wonder if something was amiss, Nena," Tua's father said. He rose to his feet, inclining his eyes with both suspicion and worry. He was a tall man, lanky more than bulky. His attire was more casual at this hour, the front of his shirt opened loosely, revealing the upper half of his chest.

"No, nothing amiss," Kamataa said. "I just...found the Moon to be very beautiful tonight. I couldn't help but admire it. My apologies for worrying you," she bowed her head respectfully. "Chief Noanat."

The Chief broke all semblance of worry and offered a laugh in its place. He walked calmly over, patting Kamataa on both shoulders, giving Tua's hair a further tussle as he walked by. "Ah, Nena. If we've told you once, we've told you a million times: no need for the formalities. You've raised the boy just as much as Yena and I have."

He gestured to his wife, Tua's mother, at the table. She smiled warmly towards Kamataa, her posture prim and proper as she sat patiently beside the table. Her hair was long and wavy, falling past her shoulders in a clear bucking of typical Lake Tribe fashion.

"You're *family*," Noanat asserted, smiling at Kamataa. "You need not call me Chief."

She patted a hand along the back of the Chief's hand. "Old habits die hard, I'm afraid," she said with a chuckle. "I hope you'll forgive this old woman for that."

In the corner, Yena tittered. She rose to her feet, joining the family conference. "It's been *nine years*, Nena," she said. "You came into our lives when we needed help after Tua's birth. It was as though the gods themselves sent you to us, and we're ever grateful for you in our lives." She turned toward the boy. "Isn't that right, Tua?"

The young boy stood with a silent grin upon his face, his hands folded behind his back. "Eh, she's okay."

Kamataa leaped into action and jumped at Tua, wrapping him in a fierce and playful embrace. "Just 'okay,' am I, huh? A perfect match for the 'okay' boy, then." She tickled him, much to the boy's fruitless and unenthusiastic protests.

The family laughed together again, a wholesome moment, the air filled with life and vigor. When the laughter subsided, everyone let out a collective sigh.

Noanat placed his hands on his hips, a smile broad on his face. "Well, shall we finish dinner? We've stowed away the shoddy eastern dinnerware—no chance of Tua shattering anything else." He winked at the boy.

Tua playfully stuck out his tongue, setting loose a damp rasp as he rushed back to the table, his parents quick to follow.

Kamataa felt a smirk crease her lips. She took in the sight with crossed arms, wanting to drink in the pleasantness of it all for just a moment. She passed a glance out the window, catching the shadows cast the night on the Lake, and then sat herself down, quietly smiling at each member of the family.

Family. A genuinely foreign concept. A term with which she had not been accompanied for a long time.

Idle conversations carried on deep into the night, complemented by the soft clattering of the dinnerware of a family at peace.

She still felt most at ease in the silence of the night. When all the world slept, Kamataa oft found herself at her most awake.

Standing against the backside of the hut, she looked up to the midnight heavens, watching the stars glint in the sky beside the ethereal glow of the Moon at Her fullest.

Kamataa looked forward to these nights. In the brightest lunar glows, she found herself to be at her greatest connection to her Lady. Once per month, she felt reinvigorated, like Life had been wholly renewed within her. With each passing cycle, she could not help but offer gratitude to the Moon.

And on these nights, she felt the need to pay special reverence, for just as she was at her strongest, so, too, was the Moon.

The irony was not lost on her, that she found herself at her most invigorated on the nights of the Full Moon, when the very reason for her communion was on the night of the Black Moon. She chuckled at the thought.

Crickets chirped in a rousing harmony as she continued to stare at the Full Moon. The chill in the air was growing more intense, but she didn't mind at all. She remembered to don a heavier overcoat this time, a reminder helped by not having to rush to prevent melted butter from staining her clothing.

"A beautiful night, isn't it?" a voice called from behind.

The sudden question hardly startled her. Very little surprised Kamataa these days, but she played the part regardless. She turned to the left, seeing Noanat approaching from the side of the hut.

He looked to the sky, a warm smile on his face combatting the frigid breeze in the air. "I see why you found yourself lost out here this evening. It's a mesmerizing sight, is it not?"

Kamataa caught herself absently nodding at the remark. "Seeing the Moon so full, it's...I suppose you could say it's calming. It puts me at ease with the world."

Noanat settled beside her, his arms crossed over his body in order to maintain warmth. His smile grew softer, a flash of concern glinting in what she could see of his eyes. "Have we done something to give you pause, Nena? If there is anything that we may do for you..."

Without hesitation, Kamataa shook her head with a grin, still keeping her eyes to the skies. "No, no. You need not worry, Chief Noanat."

"Nena," he chided playfully. "Again, you needn't call me—"

She raised a hand. "I know, I know. But I still must pay the proper respects and use the proper titles. Such is the way of things." She slunk down to the ground, sitting at the base of the hut, knees propped upward. Her grin grew more muted as she stared blankly across the Big Lake. The thought of those murky depths still sent tremors down the length of her spine, a searing burn through her stomach, no matter how many nights she took in this sight.

"What is it, Nena?" Noanat asked, sitting alongside her in much the same fashion.

Resting her head along the outside wall, she said, "Forgive me if my nerves get the best of me at times. This...whatever you wish to call it, between our two Tribes, sometimes, I cannot help but think that it is not a matter of 'if' something will set off our tensions into something worse, but rather 'when.' Who knows if it will be a minor inconvenience or a grave injustice? I oft spend nights pondering just that."

Noanat did not say anything. The frown on his face seemed to indicate that much the same worried his own mind.

"So much has happened in the last sixty years, and yet so little. The assassination of the eastern Tribe's Chief has left aftershocks that continue to this day, and yet, nothing has happened beyond the virulent mistrust from one side to the other. I fear it only gets worse with each passing year, each passing month, each passing day. I fear that even an honest mistake would be enough to stoke the anger of those merely looking for an excuse. Such that I am doubly careful not to misplace a thing for fear of what that would mean for the sentiment of the eastern Tribe. It is certainly enough to keep one up at night, irrational as the fear may be."

The Chief grunted as he stroked a thoughtful hand across the stubble upon his chin. "My father used to tell me of those days, when the eastern Chief was assassinated against a backdrop of strange thefts. Even back then, the separation of east and west was pronounced. So quick were they to point the finger at the other. But when that assassination happened...it was as though the world stopped. I don't believe anyone thought assassins lived among us, but it was enough for hatred to be replaced by fear, the idea of escalation the very deterrent *against* escalation."

Kamataa nodded. When she closed her eyes, she could sometimes still feel the thrush of blood spurting along her hand and face. The blood that could have threatened to flood the Tribe instead was dammed before it could flow freely, just as Noanat said. Fear was a strong deterrent indeed.

She let out a big sigh. "Never have I feared the thought of assassins, I suppose. My concern is only whether I may find myself in the wrong place at the wrong time." Narrowing her vision, she tried to look past the Moon's reflection on the water off to the east, with no answers to be found in the darkness. Looking back to the sky, back to the source of the reflection, she felt the calm once more. "But then I think back to my family. How we would spend evenings just like this, staring up to the Moon, looking for answers to questions we had not yet thought to ask. Even if the Moon did not respond, it was always enough to know that something was watching over us in the dark of the night. So now, whenever I have these fears, I feel at ease when I look to the stars and find the Moon staring back at me. It's...comforting, in a sense."

Offering a half-smile, Noanat lightly tapped Kamataa's shoulder. He looked up to the Moon and Her divine glow, evidently in search of that same contentment that she felt.

I promise that you will not understand Her the way I do, Kamataa thought. *She will not speak through you as She does through me.*

Suddenly, Noanat raised his brow and grunted with what appeared to be slight astonishment. He turned to Kamataa, nodding expectantly. "I think that's the first you've ever spoken of your family, Nena."

She thought on the claim a moment. It was entirely likely that she had not broached the subject once in the last nine years. "I suppose I haven't," Kamataa said.

"May I ask...what they were like?" the Chief asked earnestly. The glint in his eyes seemed genuine, that he was asking not to be nosy, but out of true interest.

Kamataa permitted a hesitant smile. "My parents died when I was...young. It's...not a memory I like to dwell on. I suppose I never truly had anyone apart from them. After their passing, I had to explore and survive on my own. Perhaps it was fate that I found a group of people who lived in the same circumstances as I. So quick were we to become companions, then friends, then family. We had something beyond the bounds of blood that failed to connect us, something that instilled within me a greater closeness than I ever felt with my parents, if I am honest with myself. The family of choice is sometimes just as important as the family of blood. But sometimes, still, those you choose are of greater import."

There was a flicker of hesitation in Noanat's eyes as he quietly listened to her. "What...happened to them?" he asked, though, by his tone, it was clear he knew the answer.

"The same that happens to us all when our time upon this plane has ended," she said. Years and years had passed since her kin had passed—all save for one—but the wounds were still fresh. "Little did I know I'd find myself in the same position as when my parents passed, but perhaps it was fate which guided me once more. To another life, as it were. Life does not always offer signal lights, but when they are offered, they cannot be ignored. I know not what lies beyond the path ahead, but I am...fortunate that it led me to this moment, here."

Noanat could not hide his smile. "And we are more than fortunate that you found your way into our lives. Nine years have passed in an instant, but I know I speak for Yena and Tua both that we would not trade it all for a second. The family of choice, was it?"

"Just so," Kamataa said softly.

They sat in companionable silence for a time, watching the stars shine and listening to the bubbling and splashing of the evening fauna within the Big

Lake. The wind offered a cold whisper, the promise of snow flurries from the mountains rich upon its breath.

The Chief shrugged and rotated his shoulders, his teeth clattering together. "It's getting late and it's getting cold. I better go back inside before Yena worries that I froze to death. The last thing she needs is to find me blithering like an idiot because I did not take caution." He laughed at the thought. "Don't stay out too much longer, Nena. Another busy day ahead of us tomorrow, eh?"

Kamataa nodded. "I'll only be a little bit longer. Worry not."

"Very good. Good night, Nena."

"Good night," she responded. "Noanat."

With a smile and a nod, Noanat shuffled back around the corner. The sound of his footsteps carried over the deafening silence; Kamataa could hear each step squish against the dew-soaked grass until he made it back to the stone-carved floors of the hut interior. If she listened closely enough, she could hear the ever-so-faint murmurs of a conversation between Noanat and Yena. She could not make out the words, but the tone was wholly positive.

Leaning against the outside wall, Kamataa outstretched her legs and folded her arms. Her eyes grew heavy, a long yawn escaping her mouth. She knew she should head in shortly. *Just a few more minutes*, she thought. *Either the time comes, or it passes another night.*

Exhaustion was setting in. She rubbed at an eye, wiping away the moisture as she let loose another yawn. Rising to her feet, she spared one final glance at the Full Moon, bowing to Her with a smile. "Until the next time, my Lady."

She turned toward the perimeter of the hut, stowing her hands in her pocket, fiddling with the ornament housed within. Huddling herself together, she fought against a biting midnight breeze and took a handful of steps.

Something flared in her periphery.

Turning to the east, Kamataa saw a dim glow far beyond the reflection of the Moon. Rushing to the shoreline, for what little good it would do, she put a hand to her brow, narrowing her vision to ensure that what she was seeing was, in fact, happening.

But faint as it was, she saw it. A flame danced and waved from the eastern shore, the benefit of the higher altitude allowing her to see off to the other side.

Nine years had she waited for this day. She had bided her time—*they* had bided their time—waiting for the perfect moment. The eastern Tribe was always the fierier one—she could easily attest to that—and if their time had come, then the western Tribe would surely follow.

"Sleep can wait then," Kamataa murmured with a smile. She looked down at her Illusion pendant, massaging the runes carved by someone she could not name with a knife to her throat. "I look forward to shedding this coat for good."

Returning to the hut, she chanced a final glare to the eastern shore, where the beacon flickered and danced for a handful of seconds more before being extinguished. "See you soon, Ziia."

Sitting at the edge of her bed, hands folded across her knees, Kamataa fiddled with the ornament that had laid within the pocket of her heavy cloak.

It was a reminder of her younger days, before everything in her life drowned in a river soaked with blood. Her father had crafted something similar for her, a pin of notable eastern make, the techniques identifiable by the molds set in the metal. Fathers of the eastern Lake Tribe would often try their hand at creating these pins for their daughters as a celebratory gesture—typically the passing of the Trial—but Kamataa received hers as a gift for her eleventh birthday. That should have been a giveaway that something was amiss with her.

Where her pin was, she couldn't say. Somewhere buried deep within the bed of the Lake of Bones, surely. The one she held was one she pilfered from the eastern village decades ago from some sniveling brat who demanded Kamataa offer her some spare coin.

She held the pin up to her eye line, smirking at the memory. *I kept my coin, she kept her life. A fair compromise.*

Hours passed since she had seen the beacon lit from across the Lake. Her eyes no longer felt heavy, the exhaustion nothing but a fleeting sensation that had long since passed. The excitement, the reinvigoration, the culmination of this entire farce of the last nine years was at last come. It was more than enough to keep her awake.

Nine years was plenty of time to prepare and learn the overnight idiosyncrasies of this family. The boy would wake to relieve himself outside no more than three times per night. The third time had passed half an hour ago, and already he was fast asleep again.

Yena, for her part, was a light sleeper, but something about laying beside her husband was enough to keep her in the throes of dreaming for the duration of her slumber.

And the Chief? It took Kamataa years to acclimate to the intensity of the man's snoring. There were some stretches where she went days without sleep simply because the sound was so disruptive. Even now, rest was difficult to come by, with some evenings feeling as though the earth beneath them was quaking.

But regardless, all the pieces were in place. It was time to move.

Quickly rising to her feet so she would not prolong the creaking of her bedframe, Kamataa shuffled across the length of the hut, keeping her footsteps as light and soundless as possible. She had practiced the task many a time, having not brought along a Stealth pendant for this task, but the stakes were not so high for this run.

She passed by Tua's bed, the boy spreadeagled on the mattress, a puddle of what she hoped was drool soaking his pillow. All the blankets had been kicked off the bed despite the early winter cold.

Her passage did little to disturb him from whatever dreams he was having.

The lingering aroma of burnt incense wafted from Noanat and Yena's bedroom. It was always a pleasant smell, one that Kamataa had no issue smelling at all hours of the night when the Chief's snoring kept her awake.

True to form, Noanat's throat rasped and grated as he breathed, the sound pounding in Kamataa's skull. Her ears protested mightily from the roar. She had never been this close to him while he slept, but it gave her a mountain of respect for Yena for being able to withstand such a foul sound at such a proximity.

Finding no need to mute her footsteps, Kamataa took full-bodied steps toward the Chief, staring down at him as he lay in a similar position to Tua, spreadeagled along his side of the bed, somehow not taking up the space reserved for Yena. If he was, she appeared to have no objections; she rested her head on his shoulder, a long arm wrapped around his ascending stomach, and delighted, sleepy murmurs escaped her lips as she maintained a contented smile.

The blanket was down to Noanat's waist, which made Kamataa's target all the easier. His pendant, bearing the mark of Courage, hung slack against his exposed chest, inching this way and that with the rising and falling of his abdomen.

Nine years had built toward this.

She didn't wait around. In a single motion, Kamataa grasped the medallion, lifted up, and managed to swing the chain around the back of the Chief's head.

The snoring persisted, but only for a moment. His breath caught in his throat, his body twitching until it lay still, and his tongue lolled out from the corner of his mouth, a stream of drool trickling out as a weak groan escaped his lips in a constant drone.

Kamataa stared at the pendant, largely disinterested, and shoved it into the pocket of her cloak. She looked down at Noanat with barely a shred of pity and said with a scoff, "Sweet dreams...Chief."

She departed the bedroom with head held high, caring not to mask her footsteps as she passed by a still-fast-asleep Tua. She stopped to spare one last glance at the boy, not for any sense of filial duty or expressions of regret.

Merely for a confession. "A family of choice as important as a family of blood," she whispered. "A shame that my chosen family perished ages ago." She stared dismissively at Tua's sleeping form, wondering what the boy would do when he heard his mother's desperate screams come the morning.

If anything, Kamataa would find herself a perfect vantage point to watch it all.

"Take care, kid," she said. "Try not to burn with the rest of them."

Kamataa made for the door, caring not enough to catch a parting glimpse of her home for nine years. Instead, as she walked out into the frigid night, she let slip from her pocket the pin that she had been fiddling with, the eastern ornament.

"Oops," she muttered. "Hopefully, nobody finds that and gets the wrong idea."

She snickered as she left the western Lake Tribe, dispelling the Illusion that had hidden her for nearly a decade, her eyes set on the welcoming hillside with the best seats in the house.

First light had arrived by the time Kamataa reached her destination. The frost-covered slope had made for a frustrating trek, but it was all the more worth it to see what remained of her family.

Ziia sat with crossed legs at the crest of the hill, a warm smile frozen on her face at Kamataa's arrival. She had aged gracefully, as she always did, much to Kamataa's chagrin. Ziia's hair was still only peppered with greys rather than the stark white which had gripped Kamataa's. Her face remained pristine, hardly a wrinkle to be seen, only accentuated by the hood of her cloak framing her in a way that only her face could be seen. She was otherwise a pile of heavy pelts and wools.

She rose as Kamataa approached, and the two embraced in a celebratory hug. Kamataa was loath to release her, partly for the warmth, but also partly for the reinvigoration and renewal inherent with the Full Moon's return.

For the first time in nine years, she felt *whole* again.

"It's good to see you, Ziia," she said, fighting back a chuckle.

"And you, Kama," Ziia responded, intertwining her gloved fingers in the waves of Kamataa's hair.

They separated and sat beside one another, staring downhill at the reflection of daybreak on the face of the Big Lake.

"Nine years in the making," Kamataa said. "Nine years of cozying up to a family I cared not a whit for." She stretched her arms, inclining her head toward the pink and orange clouds in the sky. "It feels good to be free again."

Ziia barked a sharp laugh. "It wasn't *all* bad, was it? Near to a decade with a roof over my head was quite nice, despite the constant doomsinging of the eastern Chief."

"A roof is nice, but I find myself more comforted in the open air. For better or worse, this is what I've known. It's much better than being assimilated with a trio who insists that you're *'family.'*" She sneered at the last word. "As though expecting me to forget my actual family."

Ziia placed a firm hand on Kamataa's shoulder. "And our family will be renewed. One day, whenever that may be."

"Whenever Her guidance may come," Kamataa recited. She reclined, propping herself up by the elbows, watching the world come back to life. She nudged her head toward Ziia, not breaking her line of sight from the twin villages. "So, how did *you* do it?"

Indifference settled into Ziia's posture as she reclined beside her companion. "Eh, strangled the Chief to death with his own pendant."

The bluntness was enough to make Kamataa choke with laughter. "Blessed Moon, Ziia!"

"What?" A smile was broad across her face. "Much less mess than the one you made sixty years ago."

Kamataa inclined her head in an acknowledging nod, grinning all the while. "Something I've learned since then is that you need to take a more nuanced approach." She reached into her pocket and withdrew Noanat's Courage pendant, dropping it in the space between them. "We can only do so much by killing one man, but...ah, perfect timing."

The twin villages seemed to awake at just the same time. Commotion rang loud enough that it echoed over the grassy valleys, the wind carrying their cries and protests to this vantage point. Little specks with spears in hand funneled out into the streets on either side, the Lake coming alive with the traffic of boats carrying torches and firing arrows with reckless abandon.

On the eastern horizon, the rising sun glinted in a grim crimson. As the sun shone on a Lake surface already painted red, it, too, appeared to bleed.

"The two Tribes were but a pin drop away from setting it all to burn," Kamataa said with a wide smile. "We ourselves can only do so much on our own, with one body at a time. But if we convince them to set about killing *each other...*"

Ziia seemed content with that. "And so, we play the long game."

Kamataa winked. "Long live the war."

CHAPTER ELEVEN

PROMISES

The Year 1556 Anno Salvatoris
15 Years After the Invasion

A stark hush fell over the gathered assembly in Tenazt's hut, the words of warning still drifting in heavy punctuation above the crackling of the center flame's embers.

Tez looked to the two Lake Chiefs, their respective gazes towards one another still mistrusting, but the understanding still evident upon their faces just the same.

There was precious little time to waste, but at the same time, there seemed to be precious little to come to mind in the way of words. All present remained in a static shock as what had seemed inevitable had at long last come to pass. A heavy burden, a fearful realization.

"We fight," Tez said, unsure if any possessed the strength to listen, nor did she care, "or we die."

Tenazt and Yhaan sat in the center of the room, the western Chief still grimacing at the blows given to him by Tez, and they both stared intently at Tez. An ocean of difference had separated them across the Lake of Bones, but in that moment, there was enough for them to work on to bridge the gulf.

"You there. Wood fighter," Tenazt said, pointing a finger to the escaped messenger. "What is your name?"

The Forest refugee had their face buried in their hands, their face sunken, eyes frozen with shock and worry. Camouflaging paint smeared across their face from the force at which they ran their skin along worried and sweat-dampened fingers, creating a canvas of mixed reds and oranges. "We are not given names in the Wood Tribe," they said, not raising their head an inch, still focused instead on the world between the slits between their fingers. "We are given only titles, descriptors by which we are referred."

Tenazt threw his arms out at his side, turning to his assembly with confusion and annoyance with a shaking head. He mouthed something to Yhaan that Tez interpreted as something to the effect of *What the fuck does that matter?* "Okay," he said. "What do I *call* you, then?"

A hesitant curl of the eyebrow preceded the Wood messenger looking at Tenazt with equal confusion as though reluctant to share their title. They passed a furrowed glare from the two Chiefs to Tez before finally saying, "Shadow."

Tenazt shrugged his shoulders to no one in particular. "Shadow," he repeated. "You came with a handful of your kinsmen to our people's territory. Have you an estimate at how many more wander the north with words of warning?"

Shadow shook their head, loose twigs jostling loose from their matted hair. "As many as we could spare, as quick as we could leave. All directions, all Tribes. To the Stone Tribe, the Sun Tribe. To the area we think the Arrow Tribe may be wandering. Here."

"Brave to send your own to hold favor with the Sun Tribe," Yhaan muttered, wincing through an apparent pang of pain as he gripped his stomach. "I was of the mind that many among that Tribe had the order to fight or kill on sight any of the Wood Tribe."

"With an uncertain future, I'd hardly think this the time to fight over the past. Though our own interruption here would seem to run counter to *your* people's beliefs, no?" Shadow raised an accusatory eyebrow at Tenazt and Yhaan both.

"Hold your tongue, Forest dweller," Tenazt said, pointing a finger at Shadow. "It is not *us* who are crawling to other Tribes while licking our wounds."

"Licking wounds is something you must be well accustomed to, no? Do they taste the same when they're self-inflicted?"

Tenazt shot to his feet, set to pounce on Shadow with agility that defied his advanced age. He towered over the Wood hunter, despite his counterpart's indifference. "Now see here, *Shadow*. We bleed all the same, do we not? The only difference is that *my* people are not so zealous as to bleed those who walk on our land."

Shadow slowly rose to their feet, eyes narrowed, paying no heed to the gathering gradually beginning to bury its collective face in its hands. "So long as you discount your own people from the count."

"At least we settle our own matters! *We* do not slaughter those doing nothing more than escaping those who stole their land! Not that *your* people seem to have an answer to the Invaders."

A flare of the nostrils, and Shadow rushed at Tenazt, hands outstretched and reaching for the old Chief's throat. Not to be outdone, Tenazt pushed the messenger's hands aside and found home with his own counter, gripping tightly to Shadow's throat, his teeth gritting as spittle foamed from his snarling mouth. The color of Shadow's face darkened beneath the smeared camouflage paint.

Tez rose to her feet, fists clenched, and surged across the room, ignoring the smoldering embers of the central pyre entirely as she landed a heavy right hook into Tenazt's jaw, knocking the old man off his feet.

Shadow fell to a knee, reaching a trembling hand to their throat as they massaged it through weak and wincing coughs.

Looking at both of them, Tez fumed, a quivering breath flaring from her nostrils.

"Tez!" Sharrabha called from behind.

Tez had forgotten that she and Tawa were still there, tucked in the corner of the room as a sound greater than silence fell over all. The Stone huntress didn't say anything else. Tez could feel the shock in her body language from behind.

"We don't...have...any...fucking...time for this."

She couldn't be bothered to check if any were rushing her from behind. It didn't matter to her. All that mattered to Tez was getting this shitshow back in order.

"The Wood Tribe is being slaughtered as we speak. My people fall under the useless thumb of a spiteful, egomaniacal madwoman. And you're quibbling over whose blood stains more of the earth." She looked at Tenazt, still rubbing the point of impact on his cheek, at Shadow, still regaining a clear airway, at Yhaan, still grimacing at the spear wounds she gave him. "We have no time left. We can join together and face the larger picture finding its way towards us, or we can die bickering amongst ourselves over trivial matters, at which point it won't matter *whose* godsdamned blood will stain more of the earth because the whole of our Land will be painted red. I've wasted enough of my time here. Tenazt," she said as she pointed a commanding finger at the eastern Lake Chief. "Your fighters are coming with me, whether you care to join them or not." She then turned sharply to Yhaan. "Yhaan, yours too. I fully intend to march on the Stone Tribe, put those turncoats' godsdamned heads on spears, and ready myself to hold fast against every last one of those godsdamned Invaders, because *that* is what is most important here, not whoever godsdamned stole what from whom or who godsdamned bleeds the godsdamned most!"

No one spoke. Tez towered over a stunned Tenazt, who still massaged his cheek and flexed his jaw. The knuckles of Tez's second and third fingers throbbed as she kept a clenched fist, the pulsating pain thumping in her ears.

A set of footsteps approached from behind, clacking along the open floor. A stern yet hesitant hand fell upon her shoulder, a tenuous grip. Tez flashed a sharp glance from the corner of her eye and saw Tawa standing at her side.

He displayed none of the shock incumbent upon Tenazt's face. Instead, his expression mirrored that of Tez, an anger held back, a nostril flared, frustration and fear melded together and at the risk of erupting. The combination remained on his face even as he softly walked up to Tenazt, offering a hand to the old Chief.

Tenazt, uncertainty apparent on his face, slowly took Tawa's hand. His eyes widened as he was hurled to his feet. The briefest of winces flashed in his eyes as though expecting further retributive bodily harm.

Tawa, instead, dusted him off and walked over to Yhaan, the work performed on him by Ket complete. Yhaan waved a hand dismissively before Tawa could offer it and sucked in a hissed breath as he pushed himself up to a standing position, his tall frame only barely fitting within the tight confines of Tenazt's hut.

"Now, then," Tawa said, extending his hands outward to both Chiefs. "Your people have followed a philosophy of 'might makes right' through the length of your history, and to your own detriment, I might add. We were asked of our inclinations to assist the Lake Tribe in their petty squabbles and why the Stone Tribe has never tampered in the affairs surrounding the Lake of Bones." He turned his hands inwards in a show of annoyance. "*This* is why. That when we are faced with a threat not of our Tribes but of our *people*, you all find comfort instead in bloodying each other.

"Do you truly believe that might makes right? That those of strength shall be the ones to lead?" Immediately, Tawa pointed a sharp finger toward Tez. "Because *she* is the one whom you should be following. Or need we unwrap Yhaan's bandaging as a further example of Tez's prowess?"

Yhaan turned his side, wrapping an arm across his bandages to prevent the threat.

With a sneer, Tawa shook his head at the two Chiefs. "Always are your people waiting for a skirmish, a battle, a war. Well, now we are faced with one larger than *any* of our squabbles. And I believe I speak for all of us present when I say I do not intend to watch for the outcome of an intertribal disagreement that will inevitably change nothing.

"Fight as you must when this has all ended. But for now, your spears and arrows are ours, promised as they were. Because when the Invaders fall upon us, it is in *her*—" Again, Tawa pointed to Tez. "—that I trust my life. The blood and strength of Fannalhen and Dennalhir run through her, and none better in oath and steel are those who share kinship with the *true* leaders of the Stone Tribe. It is her whom I protect, her whom I follow, and her whom will lead us to the survival of our people!"

Tez had never seen Tawa so animated, so angry, so resolute. *All the years with Father must have finally rubbed off on him.*

Yhaan and Tenazt both stood with folded arms, kicking absently at the ground below, hesitation on their faces.

The western Chief inclined his head, his eyes narrowed. "I was not made aware that you were Fannalhen's daughter," he said to Tez.

"Would it have made a difference?" Tez asked, still fuming. "Or would I have been made to play your games just the same?

Yhaan offered no answer, only stared blankly ahead, grimacing at his wounds. He grunted when it was clear no words would come to him.

A wordless grumble came from Tez's left. "Both of them are right, Yhaan. Admit it." Tenazt shuffled over and jerked Shadow up to their feet. He gave nothing in the way of an apology. Closing the gap between him and his counterpart, he looked up at Yhaan with animosity glowing in his eyes. "At the very least, *I* owe her my warriors. You are held to no promise or obligation, but...she speaks true."

The western Chief closed his eyes, drawing in a deep breath. "Tell me, Tez of the Stone Tribe," he said. "Your father. Is he...?" He trailed off.

Tez understood the implications. "Dead. At the hands of the Invaders."

Yhaan growled softly, running an open palm down the length of his face. "Then know that I grieve for your loss." The words sounded genuine. "I knew him many years ago before either of us became Chief of our respective Tribes. A chance meeting as I embarked upon my Trial. He seemed a good man. His loss is ours." He opened his eyes, turning to Tez. "I will join you in the hopes of crushing the devils."

Though she could feel her heart rising in her chest, Tez maintained as close a neutral expression as she could manage. "Thank you," she said, her tone stern yet hopeful.

"But," Yhaan added as he pointed a finger to Tenazt, "this is merely a temporary truce between us. When at last we have buried the Invaders, I shall meet you again upon the Lake. We will fight as intended, as men, with no champions."

Tenazt chuckled. "On my honor."

Oh, dear gods, Tez thought. *Well, this is as good as it will get, I'm sure.*

Sharrabha filed in beside Tawa, craning her head around her comrade to nod at Tez. The huntress appeared to have much to say to Tez, but within her eyes seemed to be an acceptance that it would have to be saved for later. She cleared her throat toward the Wood messenger, folding her arms behind her back. "Shadow," she said. "Have you an idea of when the Invaders will breach north of the Forest?"

Shadow was still wincing from the throttling they had received from Tenazt. They gritted their teeth, stretched the muscles in their neck as loose twigs fell unceremoniously from their hair. "I can't say. I would guess they are another day, at least, from making it the full length of the Forest, and that would be on a good day with no further distractions. My people numbers very few now, I am sure, but…" A despondent expression captured Shadow's gaze, fury and sadness at once gleaming within the dark pools of their eyes. "The Wood Tribe will defend the Forest to the last. My people…will die. But they will delay the Invaders just the same."

Everyone understood the stakes. Everyone understood the odds. And everyone understood the sacrifice.

"Then we'll be sure to make it count," Tez promised, cracking her knuckles.

Sharrabha nodded. "We'll plan for one day until they're through. With the might of the Wood Tribe, we'll expect two." She flashed an unreciprocated smile toward Shadow.

"It still does not leave us much time to tarry, does it?" Tawa pointed out. "Time has run its course while we have dallied here, and we have still not liaised with the Arrow Tribe. We will be cutting it close, Tez." He placed his hands on his hips and shook his head. "What do we do?"

Tez frowned, but from the corner of her eye, she could see the two Chiefs wordlessly conversing amongst themselves, nodding in silent agreement.

Tenazt raised his head proudly. "Your delay is our fault. Permit us to set it right."

Yhaan narrowed his eyes, letting loose a deep sigh from his nose. "Tenazt and I will journey north to find the Arrow Tribe and bring them to the Stone village. Should all go well, we will arrive just in time to assist you."

The sudden cooperation was enough for Tez to raise an eyebrow. "Is that right?" she said. "Are you certain you won't have an urge to—"

Tenazt shook his head and approached Tez, placing both of his hands on her shoulders. "Do not worry about us. We will do what needs to be done. And so shall you. Take our fighters. Go to your people. Take back your home. And when the Invaders come, save a few bodies for us." He winked.

Tez examined the old Chief, the glow of the center pyre basking him in an orange light. She could see on his face that he was resolute in seeing this through, just as she could tell from Yhaan. She fought back a grimace, instead allowing herself to force a tentative smile. "I've always wanted to see how the Arrow Tribe fights when they lack their horses. Make it happen, both of you."

With protest, Tenazt and Yhaan quickly shuffled out, nearly barreling over Ket, who stood outside the door.

Tez inclined her head toward her companions. "And we need to make our own things happen, don't we?"

Sharrabha and Tawa both offered a grin.

"You as well, Shadow," Tez said to the Wood messenger. "Be the ghost that haunts the Invaders to their graves."

Shadow chuckled but gave no other response. They walked toward the door. "I'll gather the others. Call when you are ready. My bow cries for vengeance." They left.

Tez smirked and caught a shadow still lurking in the threshold. "Ket," she called.

Ket filed in, smiling slightly as they caught sight of Tez. "Not many can strike a Chief and face no recourse."

"Not many have no reservations about punching a seventy-year-old man in the face, either, and still I stand." Tez looked out the door, to the waning evening light. Time was only growing shorter and shorter. "It's time, Ket. Gather everyone who can shoot a bow or swing a spear. It's time to go home."

Ket nodded. "And when are we departing?"

The implication of the "we" including Ket gave Tez a relieved smile. She turned to Tawa and Sharrabha, feeling hopeful and anxious and eager all at once. She was ready. She couldn't wait any longer. "As soon as we can," she said.

The aroma of incense and burnt firewood was a pleasant smell for Koelhe to awaken to. Even if it had only been but mere days, she didn't think she would ever grow tired of waking in this Chief's hut, in *her* hut.

Upturned and emptied bottles of rice liquor flanked her as her head, at last, felt rested, even as the hammers continued to pound away at it. Her mind was home to relaxed thoughts and loose feelings, and all this, despite knowing that when the liquor ran dry, the weight upon her head would come crashing down. But she had little intention of allowing the crash, regardless of what matters may next arise.

The crash would have been a signal that she had stopped reveling. And there was still much to celebrate, for she had accomplished everything she had sought.

The respect and adulation of the Tribe.

The power with which to lead the Stone Tribe to brighter days once again.

The dismissal of the godsdamned Curseborn and its family.

May the next interruption be slow to arrive, for I am still inclined to celebrate! She reached for one of the many liquor bottles about her but was upset to find that they were all emptied. "A pity," she murmured. "Fann? *Faaaaaann!*" No answer.

Koelhe hadn't seen her son for some time. Or perhaps it was quite recently. Time had already been coalescing and drifting apart seamlessly in the days since she took her rightful place as leader of the Tribe. It was all a blur. But she couldn't shake the feeling that it had been only a short time ago that she was speaking to Fann. *What was it? That noise...that crowd...*

The memory suddenly came clear to her. *Right...that wanderer in the village. Fann said he would see to it. How happy I am to see how protective he is of our Tribe, of our legacy. I won't need any council but him.* She fired a glance toward the back of the hut. "I would not be so vain as to remove my own kin from my council, after all." She laughed heartily until her breath caught in her throat.

The urge to find some fresh air was altogether too inviting to pass up. Koelhe rose unsteadily to her feet, nearly rendering herself as kindling for the fire, but catching her balance before she fell headfirst into the blaze. "Ho-ho, that would have been an untimely end indeed," she cackled. Still, she wavered back and forth, the medallion of her pendant smacking her in the chest a number of times before she maintained enough equilibrium to make it to the door.

"Surely, I'll find some more happy faces at the tavern," she muttered to the air. "Barradhan and Dolevhe, perhaps? Or Rantalha, if he ceases his being a stick in the mud. Another fine evening." She smiled.

So caught in her own thoughts was Koelhe that she didn't register that Chief Han'e stood waiting beneath the threshold. Her face planted itself in Han'e's thick chest with barely a flinch.

"*Mmh, Chief Han'e,*" Koelhe said, still muffled by Han'e's abdomen. She pushed herself off him, looking up at his sunken, tired eyes. "You caught me as I was heading for the tavern. Would you care to accompany me?"

"No, Koelhe, I would not care to," Han'e said bluntly. He grabbed her by the shoulders, pushing her back toward the center of the room. "We have matters to discuss that I would prefer to be held in private conference."

Koelhe smirked, a guttural chuckle escaping her throat. "Of course, Chief." She grasped at his hand to drag him toward the center pyre, but her grip was summarily spurned without struggle. She shrugged and sat beside the fire, regardless, nodding unsteadily as her head lolled back and forth. "Have you seen my son, by the by?" she asked.

Han'e remained standing, his arms crossed. "The lad with the crippled arm? Do you mean recently or just generally speaking?"

"Crippled?" Koelhe repeated, slurring the word. "No matter. It's no fault of his, and the Bear blesses him just as you are." She winked.

"Hmph. If you say he is."

Koelhe forced a laugh but found it not to be reciprocated. "Yes, well. He's been gone for quite some time, something about an outsider wandering within our walls. I only—*hic*—wanted to inquire if you've seen—*hic*—seen him. He and I have…many, many matters to discuss, of course."

Han'e seemed to look at the pile of emptied bottles strewn about the floor, his brow raised and expression unamused. "Far be it for me to interrupt your…important matters. But he is partly the reason I am here."

"Oh?" Koelhe said with a raised eyebrow. "You did see him, then?"

Han'e shook his head. "I did not see him, but…" He grunted, something brewing in his eyes that Koelhe could not quite determine. Anger? Annoyance? "Koelhe, were you aware that the wanderer your son saw to was of the Wood Tribe?"

"But, of course! It was by my request that he questioned him. Far be it for me to be trusting of the Wood Tribe after the great help we have received from the Sun Tribe." The smile upon her face widened. "If you want, I could set them aside for you. As a favor, of course. It must get your blood boiling, I'm sure."

"Given the man is already dead by your son's hand, the offer is irrelevant. It would appear that Fann was rather forceful in his questioning. He went a bit too far merely extracting that the man was Wood Tribe, as though the fact that they cover themselves in leaves and twigs was not enough of an indication." He frowned.

"Why, Han'e, I thought you might show delight at a dead Woodsman, given everything they put your people through. Shall I remind Fann to save the next one for you?"

Undeterred, Han'e shook his head. "It fails to add up. From what I am hearing, the man was much too old to have been embarking on his Trial. Elsewise, the Wood Tribe do not leave the Forest."

"Then what are you saying?" Koelhe asked, head tilted with curiosity.

"If members of the Wood Tribe are venturing this far beyond the vale of the Forest, it could only mean one thing: a warning."

"A warning," Koelhe said with little humor. "A warning of what?"

"Who else? The same threat that has lurked above our heads for the last fifteen years."

Koelhe laughed, pushing herself to her feet against the unsteady shape of an emptied bottle. "The Invaders are coming, then," she said mockingly. "Just as they have come with your every warning in the years since."

His eyes flared open. "Use your head, Koelhe. Tell me the last you saw of a Wood Tribesperson wandering outside their Forest. Tell me it does not strike you as suspicious."

"I never thought I'd see you on the side of the Wood Tribe, Han'e," Koelhe said with a smirk. "It ill suits you after all these years. And yet, the same Han'e I've always known still remains." She stumbled over, trailing her first and second fingers up the length of his chest like a spider. "Still the same paranoid and vengeful man as ever."

He slapped Koelhe's hand away, his gaze indignant. "Woman, need I remind you that I lost my home to those Invaders? A home that *you* promised to help reclaim. I have had my people readied for days, waiting on the readiness of yours!"

Koelhe threw her hands up in deference, a smile still wide across her face. "Sometimes, words must be said in order to forge alliances."

Han'e balled his fists. At the sight of it, Koelhe could not help but suck in a breath. She was unsure if she could withstand a single blow from that fist.

"These are not merely *words*, Koelhe," Han'e growled. "I have wanted to return to my land for fifteen years. *You* promised that the Sun would rise again in the south. And now, you expect me to honor *my* promise to you?"

"*You've* already held up your end of the deal, Han'e. I have everything I sought. What more do I need of you?"

It was silent save for the mountain winds howling to the tune of a sharp whistle. Han'e's heavy breaths rasped from his nostrils, flared and furious. He ground his teeth, his fingers clenching and flexing in a rhythmic threat.

"And what more do I need of *you*?" Han'e said quietly, turning on his heel toward the door. As he reached the threshold, he stopped, his rasped breath becoming a bearlike growl. "I respected Fannalhen. I disagreed with him. But I respected him. I will not dishonor his memory any more than I have already. I would call for you to do so, as well, but I know that would fall upon deaf ears." He walked into the waning daylight.

Koelhe chuckled to herself, her hands planted firmly on her hips. "Ah, Han'e," she murmured. "Perhaps in another lifetime."

She took two steps toward the door but stopped and turned to look at the back room. A hiss of pain whistled in her ear. "Fine, fine, I'll come see you," she said derisively.

Her gait swaying from one side to the other, Koelhe made her way to the back room, where three beds stood disheveled and disarrayed. Along the wall beside the bed with yellow paint stained on the pillow, that mighty bear of a woman sat with dead, hateful eyes.

"Yes, dear Denna. What do you need?" Koelhe sneered.

Dennalhir snarled her teeth at Koelhe, beads of heavy sweat cascading down her forehead, her hands tied behind her back. A bandage was wrapped tightly around her thigh where the Haunted boy had misplaced Koelhe's knife. *It was meant to go into your heart.* Still, there were certainly advantages to keeping Dennalhir alive. Mockery, for one. She enjoyed being on this side of it.

"I could call you a fool, Koelhe," Dennalhir said. "But I've also been calling you that for a long time."

"Eye of the beholder and all that, wouldn't you say?" Koelhe responded.

Dennalhir scoffed. "You've made a mistake, you know. Han'e is a tremendous ally to have. And a fearsome enemy."

Koelhe rolled her eyes. "Ah, Denna. Don't tell me you believe his hogwash. After all these years, you think *this* is the time that Han'e speaks correctly? Only after *I* claim my place as Chief?"

"I wouldn't think to presume anything, Koelhe. Of course, you could very well see for yourself. Or did you grow tired of your Foresight constantly proving you wrong?"

Looking down at her Foresight pendant, Koelhe shook her head with a sneer. "What a waste of my time, Denna. You and I are both smart enough to know that Han'e's warnings have never had merit."

"Then what's the harm in looking, Koelhe?"

Koelhe knelt beside Dennalhir, staring the warrior in the eye. "You truly want me to humor you, don't you? I really must decide what to do with you."

"If you're going to keep me alive, then I may as well provide you council so that you do not entirely destroy our Tribe."

"Ah, just as I counseled you, Denna? And why should I listen to you?"

"You haven't done it in twenty years, but it's never a bad time to start."

Koelhe grunted dismissively. "Fine, then. Just to humor you, my dear Denna. And then you'll see." She gripped her Foresight pendant. For the first time in years—decades, even—Koelhe felt the echo of things yet to come surging through her, flashing before her. Her eyes widened, and her jaw dropped at the horrors.

CHAPTER TWELVE

THE ASHES OF MEMORY

THE YEAR 1556 ANNO SALVATORIS
15 YEARS AFTER THE INVASION

The day was won, and yet Sen felt lost.

The dirt beneath her feet was soaked in blood. The stench of death drifted through the dense arboreal surroundings, unable to escape into the open air. Bodies littered the traveled path, overwhelmingly those of the Wood Tribe.

As darkness fell over the Forest, the Acrarian army put down their arms and made camp, beacons of flame flanking them as they attempted to rest away the rigors and trials of the day's battles.

Sen stood at the perimeter of the encampment, stunned at the casualness by which the Acrarians sought respite. That any outsider—not just an invading army, but any Tribe apart from the Wood—would be so content as to rest in the Forest and blatantly announce their location was enough to instill tremendous anxiety in her. And yet, she knew that, at this point, the Wood Tribe was likely more concerned with their own survival than that of their home.

The other Eclipseborn had faded into the midst of the army once camp had been settled. Sen hadn't said a word to any of them since the fighting had ceased for the day. She leaned up against a tall tree, arms crossed as her eyes trailed listlessly across the celebrations held among the surviving fighters.

The soldiers indulged in revelry and song, a rousing melody that Sen could only assume translated to some proclamation of victory. Drinks flowed aplenty, and for the first time in days, Sen felt the longing for the haze that only alcohol could provide her. That she had made it this long since that morning with Brin—what felt like half a lifetime ago—seemed to her an accomplishment all on its own.

But when she closed her eyes, the shakes returned, the memory of the Chieftain cursing her in spite of his pain, in spite of *her*, sending chills up her spine. She looked at her hands, still stained red no matter how furiously she attempted to cleanse them.

Kamataa made it seem so easy, she thought. *The Tribes don't care for us. They would wish us dead at the first opportunity. So...why do I...?* At one point, she knew the means by which she could suppress those thoughts. She simply did not know how lost she would become were she to indulge in that vice once again.

She chewed at her lip, hiding her face in her blood-marked hand, caring little that her face would be stained just the same. *You...traitor. I should have...killed you when I had the chance.* The Chieftain's words repeated in her head. They made Sen sick to her stomach.

Not because of the justified anger in his voice, the desperation in his eyes as he feebly and futilely searched for his weapons, despite his body no longer working.

It was because Sen felt the words to be the truth.

Her hand found the leather holster that held her flintlock pistol. The one she did not once shoot during the day's travails. It felt cold to the touch despite the dense heat of the Forest. And yet, the fire within the weapon was all too inviting.

The celebrations carried on, but there was nothing within Sen that could match their excitement. A ragged, broken breath pushed out from her throat as she choked back a sob. She stared ahead at the gathering of foreign soldiers carousing about with drinks in hand, the flames of the day's victory offering her everything that Kamataa promised. And when she turned back, she instead saw a vast, dark emptiness, devoid of the hope of acceptance that she sought among the Children of the Black Moon.

It was in that darkness that Sen felt the most at home.

Into the murky depths she ventured, bloodied dirt squishing underfoot. She couldn't see more than two feet in front of her, tree roots tangling upwards with threats to trip her. She didn't care. The further away from the Children and the Acrarians she could be, the better.

Sen walked far enough off the beaten path where she could barely hear the voices echoing off the trees, where the campfires were little more than faint glints of light. That was enough.

She leaned against the body of a tree and slid her body down it, planting herself at its base, head exhausted as it propped against the bark. Her hands shook as she withdrew the flintlock from its holster. It remained dormant at her side, her finger resting far from the trigger.

"I don't know what I expected," she whispered to the darkness. "This march north...I knew what it would mean...but I still didn't expect this." She propped her knees up, rested her free arm atop them, and buried her face in the fold of her arm. "Fuck." The tears came.

The shots from the pistols and rifles screamed in her head. Death cries echoed as warriors and hunters fell from the trees, blood raining down from the branches. Laughter, bellows, grunts, curses, laughter.

Sen's heart raced. Her eyes shot up, finding nothing within the blank void before her. The trees painted nothing but a backdrop of darkness. Wisps of shadow played in that nothingness, the laughter surrounding it, yet staying far from her. Further wisps filed in behind the laughter, marching in coordinated lines, the shape of rifles resting atop what passed for shoulders. Their weapons roared in the darkness, met by screams from points unseen. Men, women, children, all of them succumbing to the shadows' wrath.

Her fingers wrapped more tightly around her pistol. Unsteadily, she aimed it at the wisps, her aim erratic, a tremor completely overtaking her hand. The rows of soldiers saw her challenge and responded in kind, sending a volley toward Sen, followed by another, and another.

Sen threw herself to the ground, her head buried in the dirt. "Shit shit shit shit," she muttered, her pistol still held close to her head.

The shots did not cease. When one row of soldier fired, the next row would line up and act accordingly. Barely a second passed between shots. It was terrifying.

A cold shudder ran up Sen's body. "Why? Why did I do this? Fuck. Gods-dammit." She pushed herself back up to her knees, the volley of rifle shots ceasing. The shadows stood in place, as though awaiting further instruction.

She looked upon the shadowy forms with shock, finding nothing of their victims in the void beyond. Past the endless row of soldiers, she thought she could see the shape of familiar figures. Figures she had often seen take the form of shadows. And often accompanied by her own shrieking phantom.

"I took the easy way out," she said to those familiar shadows. "I finally found a welcoming comfort, a place I thought I belonged. And if giving up everything I ever knew what the price I had to pay…I thought it would have been worth it."

The soldier wisps continued to stare blankly ahead at her, weapons drawn.

Her own weapon continued to shake in her hand. Slowly, she began to lift it.

"Fuck, I was wrong, and I'm sorry. My place isn't here. If anywhere, I should be among those bleeding to the end because if it's not among our own people that I am welcomed, and the only arms which open to me are soaked with blood…then it's among the dead and dying that I should call home."

The shadows beyond the soldiers wavered but did not falter.

Tears still running down her cheeks, Sen looked at those forms. "At least that way, unwelcomed as I'll be…I'll still see you both again. Father…Brin…"

The faces were finally clear, reminiscent of their final moments. Blood trailing down their lips, eyes rife with pain. But against the backdrop of darkness, the disapproving expressions of Fannalhen and Brin were clear as day.

Despite that, a smile still passed Sen's lips, even as she tearfully continued to raise the pistol. The barrel kissed the side of her temple.

The shrill laughter from the leading shadow returned.

Sen clicked the hammer, placed the barrel firmly to the side of her head.

Louder and louder the laughter grew, eschewing malice for pure enjoyment and giddiness.

Short, sharp breaths escaped Sen's nose as the pistol shook in her hand. She gripped the dirt beneath her, clenching it in her fist, dirt and twigs and leaves getting caught beneath her fingernails. Her eyes clenched shut, her teeth gritting. Her breath became a shriller wheeze. The rivers cascaded down her cheeks. Her finger danced around the trigger, unable to bend, unable to find it. The laughter rose in cadence. A cavernous pit formed in her stomach. Nausea rose. Her finger met the trigger. The river became a waterfall. Half-second breaths became labored. She growled. She screamed.

A loud bang erupted. Sen fell on all fours.

There was laughter.

Sen opened her eyes. Still she remained in the arboreal darkness. But the pistol was gone from her hand, fallen to the ground beside her.

The amused wisp danced between the soldier forms, slinking between the formation like a snake. A loud bang punctuated its laughter as one of the soldiers disappeared into the void. And another. And another. The laughter was almost childlike in its enjoyment.

The voice belonged to Kamataa.

Sen clenched her eyes shut once more, bringing both fists down like a hammer onto the cold ground, mud and leaves bursting upward as she brought them down again and again. "Fuck," she growled. "Fuck, fuck, *fuck!*" She whimpered, planting her forehead in the ground as her chest heaved with sobs. "I can't...I can't..."

"Sennalhat?" A voice called.

The laughing shadow and her soldiers vanished, along with Brin and Fannalhen.

Meekly, Sen rose to her knees, reaching for the flintlock pistol. She uncocked the hammer, returning it to the holster, and swiped the streams from her eyes with the sleeve of her uniform.

A torchlight approached, and beside it, someone walked. Sen recognized the Illusioned disguise.

"Ziia?" she croaked, her voice still raw.

The old Eclipseborn turned over her shoulder and, once ensuring that none followed her, dispelled her Illusion, her pendant flashing in a bright glint beneath her uniform top. Her long white braid fell over her shoulder, the torchlight casting shadows among the deep-set wrinkles upon her face. She rose her eyebrows at Sen, a gentle smile creasing her lips, and she sat beside her young compatriot, softly placing a hand on Sen's shoulder.

Sen winced at the touch, feeling only the anger which flowed through the woman. A sense of swimming within her, she turned her downcast eyes toward Ziia.

"I was beginning to grow worried, Sennalhat," Ziia said, inclining her head toward Sen. "The Wood Tribe may now be fewer, but the dangers are still many."

"We don't need to worry," Sen whispered, holding her own hands down to prevent the tremors. "No one else is here. There are only…ghosts."

Ziia stared deep into the darkness. It did not seem to stare back into her. She grunted with curiosity. "Ghosts, is it? Has Cin gotten to you too, then?"

Sen shook her head. "No. Just…" She frowned, averting her eyes. *My own ghosts. My own lost people.*

The torchlight flickered and swayed as a very soft breeze whispered through the dense trees. Revelry and celebration continue to echo from far away, now accompanied by rhythmic thumping and a discordant melody. Someone had brought some instrument with them but apparently knew not how to play it.

"What troubles you, Sennalhat?" Ziia asked, trying to position herself within Sen's field of view. She planted the torch in the ground between them, the flame close enough to the earth to give Sen pause, but not enough to break Ziia's apparent indifference.

The words were slow to come to her. Sen gritted her teeth, looking up to the obscured skies where the stars could only struggle to glimmer. "I…I've never seen anything like this before."

"Why, Sennalhat, you're familiar with blood and death, are you not?"

Sen's eyes shot up, trying to find a hint of remorse or sadness in the old woman's face. The words' implications were plain. *You were just witness to your father, brother, and closest friend all dying before you within days of each other. Are you not desensitized to it yet?* They were phrased so bluntly, so matter-of-factly, and the tone was matched by Ziia's unchanging expression.

She had to take a deep breath, quell the anger at the woman's dismissive tone. Her fingers flexed and clenched, hot and cold. A tremor ran the length of her spine as she forced herself to lock gazes with Ziia.

"No," Sen said, half a growl, really. "That's not it. It's…the intensity of it all. I've…seen fights. I've *been* in fights. But they were just skirmishes, scuffles. Something to air out and then share a drink over afterwards. But this…I've never seen all-out war. Unbridled bloodshed. The mercilessness of it all. It was all just…too much, I guess."

Ziia flashed another smile, her voice rife with levity. She put her hands on her hips with amusement. "Ah, Sennalhat, is that all? It was your first battle, was it not? I promise you, it shall get easier as time goes on." She tapped Sen's shoulders again, twice in quick succession.

Sen tried to back away from the touch, but had nowhere to slink away to. Her brow furrowed as she felt her breath constricting, her heart beating faster. The casual acceptance of such slaughter, the assurance that it would only get easier…

This does little to put me at ease, Sen thought. "Does it?" Sen asked, hesitation in her voice. "Do you really not feel…anything?"

A considering pause, and then Ziia softly chuckled. Expectation glowered in the shadows cast over her eyes as she looked at Sen. "You killed your first today, didn't you?"

The chill returned. The Chieftain's cursing words echoed in Sen's ears again, the gushing of blood as she drove her knife through his throat. *He was suffering,* she thought. *I had to do it. I had to.*

"It was mercy," Sen said, her voice little more than a rasp.

"Mercy?" Ziia barked, still amused. "Heh, you're young still, aren't you? Relative to your fellow kin. You needn't offer a show of mercy to those who would refuse to do so in kind." She shook her head. "Did you believe that your life would pass without taking another's life? Were you not expected to show competence enough to spear someone if the need arose? Do you think that none among your family have shed the blood of another, have taken the life of another? We are creatures unfit for grants of mercy, Sennalhat. The hand to show mercy is removed just as quickly as the head of the merciful."

Sen clenched her eyes shut. Images stained red flashed before her. Her father. Narva. Brin. Rejections of mercy three times over. "A merciful hand is not a weak hand," she said softly. "If we do not have it in us to extend mercy, then we're not better than…" She trailed off, the thunderclaps of the

Acrarian weapons piercing in her memory. A hail of shots raining down, death greeting all with but a simple touch, the trees above weeping blood as the march continued, each felled foe less a fellow human and more just a number. Childlike laughter preceding a monstrous bang. Kamataa's teeth shining brightly against marks of erupted crimson. "…beasts," Sen said, finishing her thought.

"'Beasts' is a relative term, Sennalhat," Ziia said in an admonishing tone.

Sen opened her eyes. If she could strike daggers into Ziia's chest with but a gaze, she would have. "Was she always like this?"

"Who?"

"Kamataa." She held her gaze.

Ziia laughed again. Genuine surprise was visible on her old face. "Is that an earnest question, Sennalhat?

Sen said nothing, didn't move at all.

The old Eclipseborn rolled her eyes and shook her head, the grin on her face nothing more than disapproving. "Live for centuries and you will see everything stripped from you, child. Kamataa has been betrayed, beaten, bloodied. She has seen family punished, friends and companions succumb to the flow of time. She has watched Tribespeople be discarded as though they were nothing, branded as failures unfit for society, and even when she offered them a place, it was only inevitable that they would be gone from this world.

"She has awaited this day for centuries, Sennalhat, as have I. Nearly four hundred years is a long time to seethe, to stew, to fume. We as Eclipseborn are derisively called cursed, as I am sure you are well aware. In a sense, we are, though not for the reasons you would think. The gift of Life—sacred in its own right, but to us, it is only a reminder of everything that has passed while still we live on, awaiting the day when we can change it all. Ask your forebears if mercy is all that separates us from beasts and tell me what you hear. Their silence shall be your answer."

Sen narrowed her eyes, shaking her head. "That's not it, though. Or it's not all, anyway." She bit at her lip, her nostrils loosing a heavy breath. "You just enjoy the killing, don't you?"

A long, uncomfortable silence passed between them.

It was made all the more unsettling by the slow grin that stretched across Ziia's lips, the torchlight casting a dark red glow over her face.

"Await a day for centuries and you will revel just the same to see it arrive," she said. "You should know this already. The downfall of a people, of a way of life, that is our purpose as Children of the Black Moon. Your fellow kin have not waited as long as we, but they have had cause to anticipate these coming days just the same. From the frontlines in this Forest to the expanses of the Heart, the Children have been ready for *this* moment. Civilizations rise and fall just as the tides change across the flow of time. The Acrarian homeland is much the same. What is reduced to ash and cinder is reborn as something greater. The choice is only ours to determine whether we wish to be the ash or the flame."

Sen leaned back, her arms folded. Images flashed before her, faces strewn across the ground in shock and horror. The faces of her family, her friends, even her closest adversaries. All of them consumed by the fire.

"It's a bit shortsighted, don't you think?" Sen said, allowing the corner of her mouth to flash the barest of smiles. "Destroying an entire culture, an entire way of life, all for revenge, I mean. It's all talk of 'higher causes' or 'the price of progress,' isn't it? But sooner or later, the wheels keep turning, another 'greater cause' rises up, and then it does whatever it needs to do. And then what becomes of what you—of what *we*—do today? The flame eventually becomes ash, as well, and after that, all we are is nothing but a memory."

Shrugging, Ziia could only scoff. "I hardly had you pegged as a philosopher, Sennalhat," she said with annoyance. "But say you're right. If or when that happens as you suggest, what does it matter?" She held her arms out at her sides, welcoming any objections and receiving none. "By that time, we will be long gone, but our purposes will have long since been served, just as the Moon had decreed to us." She looked up past the roof of trees where the night sky was hardly visible. Somewhere in the vast expanse, the Moon was glowing above them.

Slowly, Ziia returned her attention to Sen, the grin gradually fading, the amusement vanishing as the glow of the torchlight danced against the shadows of her face.

"I must wonder, Sennalhat," she said, "whether your heart is as into this fight as you had previously indicated."

Though her heart raced, Sen gave no indication. She straightened her posture, hands folded in her lap. She opened her mouth, knowing the words to say...but they did not come to her.

It could be my heart was never in this fight, she thought. *That it was a mask only to hide the hurt from my father and brother. That the kinship I wished to feel ended the moment Tribal blood was spilled. And may the Deities curse me for it.*

But she said none of it.

Ziia grunted, taking the torch from the ground as she turned back toward the encampment. "I'll leave you to think on it, then," she said, all warmth gone from her voice. "Do return to camp, though, Sennalhat. The dangers are still present in the Forest. It always *has* been overrun with...*beasts.*" She spat the final word.

Sen watched Ziia restore her Illusion, the glint of her pendant flashing once more, as she began to walk back to the Acrarian camp. "What will happen, though?" she called, stopping the old Eclipseborn in her tracks. "When the Acrarians realize just who we are, who the Children of the Black Moon truly are?"

She could just barely make out a low chuckle as Ziia slowly turned. "Kamataa and I have been among the Acrarians for over a decade, Sennalhat. The others for long enough, as well. You needn't worry about such things."

"I'd think it would be a bit foolish not to consider the possibility, though. You've seen what they do to the Tribes. I don't see why we would be any different. Just what would they grant us first: slavery or death?"

Ziia scoffed. "The Acrarians are not so callous and dense as to relegate their own loyal soldiers to such squalor, despite what you may think. Now, goodnight, Sennalhat. Return to camp soon." She walked away, the torchlight fading into the distance.

The dirt and leaves were comfortable enough for Sen to wish to stay for a while longer. She exhaled a long breath as Ziia's illuminated form disappeared deeper into the woods. "Either she's a fool, or she doesn't mind wallowing in her own ashes," she said to herself.

Looking back to the south, or what she assumed was the south, Sen could think only of the trail of blood left in the Acrarians' wake and the pit of despair constructed to sate the Acrarians' hatred. "It's one or the other, and I don't know which is worse."

The pistol felt heavy at her waist. A presence seemed to loom behind her. With a tear in her eye, she ignored both and rose back to her feet, slowly making her way back to the encampment. "But I'm sure I'll find out soon."

The commotion was too damn loud for Aritz to get some sleep.

There was plenty of cause to celebrate, of course. He granted his soldiers that much. They had struck at the heart of these forest dwellers and suffered hardly a scratch.

That he himself had felled a number of the savages, it was a rush unlike anything he had felt in the last fifteen years. The Settling was such a long time ago that he had forgotten what it felt like.

But the time for revelry had passed. Tomorrow, they would continue their march, eliminate those remaining among the trees, and set their sights on that gorgeous mountain range—and the beasts in between.

But now is the time for some bloody sleep, you bastards! he wanted to say, bellow it at the top of his lungs. *Soon. Soon, this stench and blight from beneath the Savior's eye will be removed by my hand. And then I shall be able to get some goddamn sleep.*

He tossed and turned, snarling his teeth as he pressed his pillow to his ears, trying to drown out whatever disharmonious cacophony was erupting from outside his tent. He had purposefully instructed his squires to pitch his tent far from the rest in order to remove himself from this rabble, but apparently it did little good.

And whoever insisted upon that lute is about to learn how to play it with the inside of his arse.

Suggestive whistles rang out in a chorus of greater harmony than the stringed instrument, piercing Aritz's ears. He turned in his bed once more, and again, but still the unnecessary noise broke through. A harsh twang of the lute—as though all the strings snapped at once—was enough for Aritz to wince. In a rage, he heaved his pillow across the tent, pushing himself up to a seated position, his cleaned fists clenched and ready to be dirtied once more.

A figure stood at the entrance to his tent. A woman, face obscured, a glow emanating from her chest that extended to her entire form until she was bathed in ethereal light.

It froze Aritz in place. He couldn't move. His hands shook, his body heavy as though a weight bore down upon him.

His breath caught in his throat. "A...an Envoy?" he stammered. Envoys were the agents of the Savior, appearing only to those deserving of great salvation...or grave damnation. Aritz wanted to prostrate himself before the Envoy, pay her the proper respect she deserved, but his body simply would not cooperate with him. "M-m-my lady," he said. "Pray forgive my...indecency. I...would bow if I could but I..."

The Envoy strode up to him, something resembling a smile visible upon her concealed face. Her glow was obscenely bright, nearly blinding.

Aritz felt her breath, hot against his ear and the side of his neck.

"You have done well thus far, Aritz a Mata," she whispered, barely discernible over the irritating din outside. "The wicked are slain by your own hand, yet still many remain."

"My lady..." Aritz said, his own voice little more than a whisper. "I promise you, under the light of the Savior, I shall smite these beasts from this land."

The Envoy was silent a while, her light waving around her like a dense mist. It was only when her lips nearly met Aritz's ear that he could surmise that she had more to offer. "He shall be overjoyed to hear of it. And perhaps I may be offer you a great boon for your bravery and devotion to His name. An easy means by which to defeat these tribes."

"I will do whatever you ask, my lady." If Aritz didn't know any better, he could have sworn the Envoy began to chuckle.

"Are you aware, Aritz a Mata, that the three beasts that these tribes worship as gods in fact walk the earth?"

MEMORY

PEACE IN OUR TIME

Slow, methodical footsteps thumped on the battered ground with the intensity of a war drum. For a century, this field had been hallowed ground, consecrated with the blood and bones of countless of the Lake Tribe's finest warriors. No matter how many fell, more arose, some seeming not to accept death and continuing to fight long after they fell.

Such were the tales of this Long War. Kamataa had heard them aplenty over the past hundred years. She was hoping there would be more stories to come, but all things must come to pass eventually.

And this war has run its course, she thought.

She stood tall among the second row of eastern Lake Tribe negotiators, warriors, and other well-wishers, all lined in rows of seven or eight that ran approximately twenty rows further back. To her right stood the eastern Chief's twin boys, Yheron and Qonrha, twenty-three years of muscle upon them both and zero years of scars. To her right, the Chief's trusted Learned, Naamak, a man of prominent stature yet low cunning, his face a sea of smug yet undue satisfaction. Negotiations started and ended with him, and he was loath to allow any to forget it.

Starting, of course, meaning his insistence that this war must end, and ending with his agreement to the western Tribe's terms of which he had no part in negotiating.

If only you truly knew, you sad, sad man.

Kamataa had spent months listening to Naamak's drivel of how he would bring to a close this Long War. In those months, the daily skirmishes had been reduced to weekly, the sudden disappearance of Tribal pendants and resultant mindlessness had become a thing of the past, and the sun no longer accentuated the rotting carcasses of those slain in nighttime duels with as frequent of regularity.

"This is the result of the desire for peace!" Naamak had often said. "Those phantoms who plague our people's minds and steal their pendants will know that this Tribe is stronger *together!*"

That the belief remained that the stolen pendants—by "phantoms," no less—followed the mindlessness, instead of the other way around, was music to Kamataa's ears. As was the Tribe's inability over the past century to decide whether these "phantoms" were indeed malicious and mind-altering spirits with kleptomaniacal tendencies or if there were greater and stupider evils lurking within both sides of the Tribe.

It was Ziia's idea to allow both rumors to fester.

It had been a productive century. A long century. But it was one in which Kamataa felt herself well-prepared for what was next to come.

In the approaching crowd comprised of western Lake Tribe counterparts, Kamataa spied Ziia in a similar position to her own, flanked by the useless western negotiator and the children of the Tribe's Chief. She had to commend Ziia for her ambition in the last few years especially; she had essentially become the power behind the western Lake Tribe with no eyes cast upon her, leaving breadcrumb trails to different realizations, provoking the "right" people into battle only to ensure their own fall, and seating an easily manip-ulated fool to the position of Chief.

She always did *find the more useful pendants*, Kamataa thought.

For her own part, Kamataa found greater utility in playing a number of roles over the last century: warrior, counselor, stepmother, martyr, orator. Now she was but a scribe, tasked with putting to writ the words and doc-trines stipulated either by Naamak or by the eastern Chief, Ruwexi. Not that she ever performed the duties as needed. She wrote only what she deemed necessary. Pen, spear, might, power. In her last decade as scribe, she found great pleasure in twisting the words just enough that they would incite fights as opposed to peace, and Ziia knew just how to receive and twist those same words.

When an intelligible society is domineered by steel, the written word has all the more power, Kamataa would often think. *All the greater when faced with a largely illiterate society that cannot disprove a thing.*

When the western host completed the forward march, Ruwexi, who had been directly in front of Kamataa, approached the center point as a means of greeting. He was a tall man, lean and sallow, his face torn to tatters not for the battles in which he took no part, but for the stresses of a war he had no power in quelling, despite his own feelings to the contrary. He stood with a prim and straight posture, exuding a self-satisfaction rivaled only by Naamak, who was humming a rather unmelodious tune to himself, much to Kamataa's annoyance.

The western Chief, by contrast, was rather sickly in appearance, dark circles beneath his eyes punctuating a hollowed and paled expression. His cheekbones stuck out more prominently than most, almost as though the skin upon his face was withering away. He approached with back hunched, grey-spackled hair barely tied back in the traditional Lake fashion, his breath heaving a shrill wheeze with each passing step. Kamataa had seen very little of the man prior to this day, and despite his bearing the appearance of an old man, he was actually, to Kamataa's surprise, no more than forty years of age. If it wasn't the Long War that had done that to him, it was indeed whatever sickness claimed him.

The two Chiefs faced one another in what could only be described as an exercise in humorous opposites. Were this day to have occurred five years prior, there was no doubt in Kamataa's mind that these "peace talks" would have been little more than a farce by which Ruwexi could crush the western Chief without a second thought. A single punch to the weak man's battered chest would be enough to do him in, by her own estimation. But nowadays, abled fighters had grown sparse, the age of wisdom returning, and with those inclinations for higher thought returned a desire for sustained peace. Neither Chief would be so callous as to jeopardize that on this day, not after the prior long months of negotiation.

Ruwexi cleared his throat for all to hear; his counterpart could muster only a hacked cough.

"Chief Tenrir," Ruwexi said plainly.

Tenrir inclined his watery eyes up as he seemed to fight back another wave of coughs. "Chief Ruwexi," he answered, his voice a weak and cracked mess.

Ruwexi held out an arm and placed it around the weaker man's shoulder, guiding him to the negotiating table, which stood off to the side on the slight hill overlooking the Big Lake. The two men approached the table at their own pace, Tenrir trailing behind Ruwexi as he heaved exhausted breaths up the length of the hill. When they sat, a thin stack of scribed papers was ready for them, fluttering in the gentle breeze but held in place by a crude paperweight fashioned from a nearby rock, flanked to the right by a ceremonial knife used for commitment to the terms of the treaty.

Kamataa rustled her hand into her trouser pocket, finding the Sound pendant that she had nestled away in there. Outwardly, she had to maintain the persona of an accomplished Illusionist, but the other members of this Tribe need not have known the extent to which she accessed other Boons.

Ruwexi cleared his throat once more, loud enough to echo over the hills. He drew the top page from beneath the paperweight, holding it up with a relaxed hand as he leaned back in his seat. "'Beneath the sight of gods and men, we gather among ourselves this day to draw to an end this long conflict which has embittered upon we two halves of the great Lake Tribe extenuating animosities resultant in mistrust, hatred, and bloodshed...'"

The eastern Chief read from the sheet verbatim the words that Kamataa had put to pen. Drawing in Sound from her pendant, she could hear every hesitation, every gruff scoff at the florid nature of the script, every pause to correctly pronounce an unfamiliar word. It was her own intent to write in an elongated and overtly complicated tone. To her impression, the Lake Tribe had always been so focused on individual might that the comprehension of literary complexities was too much to grasp, and so they would often default to and agree with whatever words made it from pen to paper without further examining or understanding their meaning.

Naamak, though, to his credit, was trying his utmost to listen closely, though Ruwexi's voice did not quite carry far enough to be audible to the rest of those gathered. "Can anyone hear him?" he asked in a panic to those around him. "I wish to hear my words recited loudly and proudly! We are witnesses to history, all of us! My words helped bring to a close our Long War!" His smile was wide, excitable, and largely unwarranted.

Many of those around him merely murmured to themselves, some rolling their eyes at Naamak's insistence to listen closely, some showing clear disdain for the man taking sole credit for the closure of the bloodiest chapter in the Lake Tribe's book. All of that seemed lost on Naamak, regardless, as he continued to flash his grin at his neighbors.

Kamataa shook her head dismissively, stifling a personal chuckle. *How laughable that you'd think I would allow your words to landmark this day, Naamak,* she thought.

"'...and on this day, committing ourselves to a renewed partnership and brotherhood built upon a foundation of peace, understanding, and the hope for an everlasting tomorrow,'" Ruwexi continued.

From off to the side, Kamataa could see him squinting at some of the smaller script. She had taken to writing her words smaller as the treaty grew larger, primarily in a stroke of pettiness and to quell the monotony of drafting the document.

"'To us, to arms need no longer be a call to action to protect for ourselves the lives of whom we cherish from a foe we despise, and instead it shall be a call to unity, to ford the division between us, separated not by the body of water from which we derive our name, but from the mistrust instilled in us by the force of our own nature. For it is today, by the grace of our great Deities for whom we owe our thanks, we put to writ and blood our everlasting commitment to the peace and prosperity of our Tribes, no longer separated by east and west, but unified in heart and spirit.'"

Ruwexi put the agreement down upon the table, grasping at a nearby cup of water to sate the dry tongue he surely had at this juncture. He read the entirety of the document with barely a pause, wordy as it was. Kamataa could not argue against his need to rehydrate, especially in the present heat and sunshine.

After the Chief finished gulping down his water, he turned over in the direction of the eastern Tribe, nodding at what appeared to be Kamataa. Naamak, however, took that for his own acknowledgment and laughed haughtily to himself, bowing deeply to his Chief. Ruwexi wasn't even looking as he did so.

The Chief's twin boys groaned simultaneously as the self-professed negotiator took his proverbial victory lap.

"We are almost done, Tenrir," Ruwexi said to his counterpart, who was looking increasingly worse for wear as the recitation carried on. "It seems each of us must recite our respective sections." He cleared his throat. "'And so it is known that I, Ruwexi, Chief of the eastern Lake Tribe, do hereby pledge in perpetuity my commitment to the closure of this Long War, to the reunification of the Lake Tribe, and to the restoration of brotherhood among our people, in the hope for peace and an unsetting sun above us all.'" He drew the ceremonial knife and cut a swath across his thumb, imprinting the pooling red into the fibers of the treaty, and passed it across the table to the western Chief.

Tenrir repeated Ruwexi's words as written, replacing his name and title where appropriate, and slowly cut the equivalent mark across his own thumb, his gait unsteady as the blood pooled. He meekly left a crimson thumbprint in the relevant section denoting his name.

The treaty sealed, Ruwexi put his hands together in a resounding clap and held the document high. He rose to his feet, crossing the threshold in a first act of peace by helping Tenrir to his weakened feet, motioning one from the western side to assist in kind. As one of Tenrir's faithful took charge of the weakened man, Ruwexi descended the hill to the former no-man's-land between the two sides of the Lake Tribe and tilted his head backward as though to bellow to the heavens. When his voice escaped his throat, he may as well have been summoning the strength of the gods.

"*IT IS SEALED!*" he screamed, his voice echoing over the rows of people, likely past the northern reaches of the Big Lake and with all possibility finding its way to the green steppes south of the forest that the Arrow Tribe called home. "*OUR TREATY IS SEALED IN BLOOD. OUR LONG WAR HAS ENDED. WE...HAVE...PEACE!*"

The crowd erupted in a chorus of raucous cheers and jubilant proclamations. Boots and spear butts alike thumped in the ground with enough intensity that the resultant quakes caused ripples and waves on the body of the Big Lake. Kamataa turned with her arms crossed, taking in each of the surrounding faces, a smile cautiously creasing her lips.

The twins silently jostled each other, words unnecessary to exemplify the joy and relief they assuredly felt at that moment. The ear-to-ear smiles they shared with one another were proof enough of that, the already-undone locks of hair even more so.

Naamak, predictably, ran to each of those in the row behind him and threw them each into his arms with unbridled glee. "I did it! I did it!" he proclaimed. "By the gods, I cannot believe I did it! We, at last, have peace in our time!" Tears were streaming from his face. Everyone caught in his embrace was forcefully attempting to push him off them, with little to no avail.

Kamataa couldn't help but chuckle to herself. The celebration, the reverie, the relief at the momentous conclusion of such a prolonged and bloody conflict...any would be moved to such tears and laughter. For her part, though, Kamataa maintained that same assured smile, but one that did not quite reach her eyes.

Had I the choice or ability, she thought, *you all would be dead beneath the ground. But it is not within my power to do so.*

Despite the wish, she sustained her smile, nodding to those who looked her way, avoiding Naamak's exuberant embrace, acquiescing to the twins' requests to shake hands. But she offered no words of encouragement of her own. Everything she had to say, she said within the heart of that treaty.

And I did not mean a word of it.

"Chief! Ah, Chief Ruwexi!" Naamak pushed past Kamataa—despite her being nowhere near him to begin with—and walked toward the approaching Chief with arms outstretched. "My dear Chief, I feel as though I could cry! We must celebrate this evening! I must insist upon it!" He threw his arms around the unwilling Ruwexi.

The Chief masked his aversion well enough but could not stop the advance as he was ensnared in the embrace with a grip quite unassuming and surprising for someone of Naamak's spindly stature.

"*Ahem*, y-yes, that's wonderful, Naamak. Thank you," Ruwexi said. "Release me now, if you'd please."

"Oh, of course, of course!" Naamak did as requested, backing way three paces, but still maintaining that childlike exuberance of which he was undeserving. "To hear my words from your mouth, oh! It was magical! That I could contribute to peace so!"

"I was unaware you could hear my recitation, Naamak. I spoke to Chief Tenrir in little more than a conversational volume."

"Well, truthfully, I was disappointed that I could *not* hear, to speak plainly..." Naamak trailed off, mumbling something inaudible to himself. "But! I imagine they were as poetry from your lips! All these months! At last, the work of all these months has come to a close! Drinks are on me this evening! I implore you to permit me to—"

"Sounds perfect," Ruwexi interrupted. "You shall be responsible for each drink poured this evening as both Tribes join as one. I trust you are well equipped to handle such volume?"

In an instant, Naamak's smile vanished, his once flowery tone and animated mannerisms reduced to nothing more than sputtering nonsense and twitching hands.

"Excellent. What you cannot manage today, you shall continue in subsequent days until complete. Good day, Naamak." Ruwexi shouldered past Naamak rather forcefully, nearly knocking the man off his feet as he continued to contemplate how much he was to be in debt and for how long.

It was enough to put a genuine smile on Kamataa's face. *The first successful negotiation he's ever managed. A solution that works well for us all.*

Ruwexi passed Kamataa by, not even sparing her a glance, and went directly to his twin boys. "My sons," he said. "I am proud of you both. Brighter days are ahead of us now. When this Tribe becomes yours, you shall preside over the first era of peace in generations."

Qonrha spoke first, shoving his brother out of the way. "It's an honor to serve, Father! I cannot wait for what is to come!"

Yheron pushed back as though fighting his twin off to be the center of attention in his father's eyes. "Myself as well, Father! I will gladly help lead our Tribe to prosperity!"

"*We* will do it, Brother," Qonrha asserted, pushing him on the shoulder with not quite a shove but greater than a nudge, at any rate.

It shall be the first time either of you has lifted a finger, Kamataa thought, more closely examining their pristine skin, devoid of any and all scars, their faces still youthful and hopeful.

"I must insist, *Brother*," Yheron barked, "that *I* will help lead. It can only be one of us, after all."

"Boys, that's enough," Ruwexi commanded. "This is not a day for arguments; this is not a day for fights. We are at *peace*, at last. By the efforts of many, chiefly the Deities themselves, we have *peace*. Let us enjoy it this day. Please."

The efforts of many? *Bold words from another who did nothing but bask in his own sense of self-importance.*

The Chief raised his mighty hand to the gathered eastern crowd. "*MY FRIENDS!*" he bellowed, gesturing off to the western Tribe. "*NO LONGER ARE WE SEPARATED BY EAST AND WEST. FOR NOW, WE ARE ONE! GO FORTH AND MEET YOUR FELLOW KIN FOR THE FIRST TIME!*"

He walked away without even giving Kamataa a passing glance, off to the throng across the former no-man's-land, his echoing laughter grating her ears the longer she was forced to listen to it. A near-stampede of people pushed past her as she continued to eye Ruwexi in silent regard, shaking her head and absently biting at her lip. The Chief was shaking hands, greeting folks with an overt and perhaps exaggerated friendliness that, to Kamataa's eyes, was evident to anyone with a functional mind as being less than genuine.

One word that she consistently picked up from Ruwexi's loud voice, having ceased the use of her Sound pendant, was "drink," often followed by a gesture toward a still-catatonic Naamak, who seemed to shudder more and more with each subsequent non-introduction.

As more and more people pushed past her to meet their western counterparts, Kamataa, at last, decided to join the herd and sally forth. Her arms remained crossed, her smile forced. Her eyes were set upon one person only, and she was relieved to see Ziia looking for her just the same.

Ziia had effectively brushed off Ruwexi's greeting, ignoring the man's offer for a handshake entirely, which Kamataa quite respected. When the two of them met in the middle, near to the center of no-man's-land, they opted to ham up the fake-introductory handshake, exaggerating the motion as two children would do when practicing the gesture for the first time.

"I hear talk that celebratory drinks shall be covered this evening," Ziia said with a grin.

Despite the panicked visage of Naamak still playing over and over in her head, Kamataa could only manage a half-smile. "Yes, one man was so kind as to front the ensuing cost for the entire Tribe. I am certain it won't be a problem for such an important negotiator. Did you know the peace talks were all thanks to him?"

Ziia chuckled softly, looking off to the Lake, past the throng of people passing them by, and then back to her companion. "It's good to see you, Kama. Would that we had been able to more often."

"Not so long as it was a century ago, but frustrating, nonetheless. I agree. But seeing as all *this* has ended, it would seem the avoidance is now unnecessary."

"You sound disappointed," Ziia said. She grabbed firmly to Kamataa's shoulders, tilting her head curiously, a knowing smirk on her face. "All these months later, and you're still frustrated, aren't you?"

Kamataa winced, flaring her nostrils at the thought. She looked away, averting eye contact, masking a snarl at each person who walked by, excitedly meeting their neighbor as though they had no desire to kill the same person just this morning.

"Let's take a walk, Ziia," she said softly. "Away from this crowd."

Ziia nodded, and the two walked over to the southern shore of the Lake, the sunlight glinting marvelously on the water's surface as it always did. It was a touch more peaceful here, despite the overwhelming din still echoing over the hills. Birdsong offered a melodious respite from the overbearing crowd.

"A fun ride while it lasted, at least?" Ziia said as the silence stretched between them.

Kamataa sighed, staring out at the ripples of the water. The flare in her stomach returned, the jolt in her arm. She winced and grimaced, putting a hand to her gut as she snarled the memory away.

With clear hesitation, Ziia put a hand on Kamataa's shoulder but quickly withdrew when Kamataa pulled her shoulder away.

"It's been over two hundred years," Kamataa said, gravel in her voice as the pain rose in her chest. "Since that day. When I realized the bounds of cruelty that our kind will forever be subject to. What those who surround us will be subject to." She clenched her eyes shut, taking a deep breath to quell the flare. "I think about that moment every day when I awaken, every evening when I retire to bed. And in those moments, there is nothing I would want more than to see this Tribe—what I once believed was my own—burn to nothing until not even the memory of it remains."

Averted eyes were the only response she received from Ziia, her friend's gaze seeming to be focused entirely on the gentle ripples of the Lake.

Kamataa picked at a pebble near her feet and flicked it listlessly toward the water before her. "When we...started this war...I thought it was at last time. A people hotblooded enough to set the fires of war upon themselves with only the slightest of provocations. It was pitiful how easy it had been to stoke those flames: a casual theft here, a mindless husk there. When the flames reduced themselves to embers, it was all too enticing to set them ablaze again, to watch these fools rip each other asunder. I thought we could have done it again and again until there was nothing left to burn. Until..."

Ziia sighed, a hint of regret audible. "Until I found us a pendant of Foresight."

"And then we discovered that the calls for peace would soon overtake the calls for blood," Kamataa said, frustration in her voice. Behind her, the celebrations of peace rang in the same place that had so frequently been the site of spilled blood. "One hundred years. We spent one hundred years stoking these flames, and in the end, what was it all for? The Lake Tribe still thrives. It still lives. And now, it *celebrates*. And what have we to show for it?"

"A century's worth of stolen pendants and weaponry, for starters," Ziia said, the glint in her eye showing some modicum of hope. "For when the next time arrives, we will be more than ready. When the *next generation of Eclipseborn* arrives, we will be more than ready."

"The next generation, *pheh*," Kamataa sneered. "The Moon has not graced us with another generation. Are we the last ones? Has She become so irate with our failures that She does not see fit to replenish our ranks?"

"Have faith, Kama. The time will come."

"And how long will that be from now, Ziia?" Kamataa snapped. "What does that Foresight pendant tell you?"

Ziia opened her mouth but seemed hesitant to answer. "I...nothing yet, truthfully."

Kamataa threw her hands up. "You see—"

"I said, nothing *yet*. I am merely...cautious with it. Futureseers are rare enough as it is. What I've studied on Foresight is enough to warrant restraint when looking far ahead."

"Restraint? Why is that?"

"Those who wish to tempt fate and see what has yet to transpire put themselves at the risk of witnessing their own demise. Now, I've taken the liberty of seeing quite far ahead, but even that was a journey I was loath to take. The damage to one's mind can be quite...irreparable, should they run into a vision of their own passing."

With a grunt, Kamataa picked up a nearby stone and flicked it over the surface of the water. She felt a sinking feeling in her stomach. "When you say you saw far ahead..."

Ziia sighed, shaking her head. "At least another generation. This Tribe still exists. And we remain as the only Eclipseborn."

All urges within her pressed Kamataa to the point of screaming, but she withheld her desire to bellow to the horizon. "Then what are we still doing here? What more can we do?"

"Kama...for now, we wait. The next generation is committed to these peace talks. Anything we attempt to do...unfortunately, it is for naught."

Kamataa craned her head skyward, sighing heavily. "Blessed Moon above," she muttered. "Truly, we ended up among the worst generation in the era of peace. Two Chiefs, one existing solely for the stroking of his own ego, the other so frail it impresses me he even manages to stay on his feet. Heirs apparent who wouldn't know what to do with a spear if they were each stuck upon one. Self-grateful bastards so entranced in the mythos they've created about themselves that they are unaware of their meaningless contributions."

"And we are privy to each and every one of them," Ziia said. "Each wrapped around our fingers."

"That's easy for you to say, Ziia. I drafted the entire peacetime treaty and received little more than half a glance during the review period. I'm but a ghost here, nothing more."

Ziia chuckled. "Then let's do what ghosts do, Kama. Have we ceased being the 'phantoms' who cause these people such fright and stress? This era of peace will only last for a generation, remember."

"But, I thought you said—"

"All I said was that our success would be limited to this generation. What's the span of a generation to people such as us, after all?"

A meek chuckle managed to escape Kamataa's lips. "And so the waiting game begins?"

"I will say, though, that it will be worth the wait. No conflict between east and west as such, but we are just a generation removed from witnessing the twins take up arms against one another. That much I *do* know." Ziia winked.

Kamataa's chuckle developed a harder edge, honing sharper until it emerged as a full-fledged laugh. "Peace in our time, indeed. A shame that none specified the length of time."

"The beat goes on, Kama," Ziia said with a warm smile. She grasped at her friend's hand, squeezing it tightly, the water trailing along peacefully beside them. "We have the luxury of all the time in the world."

Kamataa reciprocated the squeeze before looking to the northeast, where the mountain ranges loomed tall in the distance. "Have you ever thought of your own former Tribe? What you could do to the Stone Tribe?"

Ziia shook her head. "If there's anything that this conflict has taught me, it would be that the destruction of the Tribes is a task far beyond what you or I am capable of, and the Stone Tribe is not as easily manipulated as the Lake. Those who trespassed against me are long since passed, but the edifice of their memory still remains. One day, I'll set it to rights. *We* will set it to rights. The Stone Tribe, the Lake, all the rest of them. There will come a time when something greater than ourselves will rise, and on that day...we will, at last, find our way." She held up the Foresight pendant, letting the chain dangle from her fingers. "Until then...this shall light our path."

It wasn't much, but it was enough. Kamataa found a modicum of solace in that. "To peace in our time, then."

They turned back to the still-rowdy celebratory din, the calls for drinks ringing loudly into the air. Faintly, Kamataa could hear a familiar voice desperately pleading for no more. It was enough to make her smile as she rose back to her feet.

"And to the flames of war in another."

CHAPTER THIRTEEN

Cross to Bear

The day's march begot further bloodshed but none of the controlled chaos of the preceding days. Sen did not even attempt to hide her apathy and listlessness to the proceedings. All of it was, to her, naught more than backing noise, the roar of rifles a death knell for a once-proud people.

The Wood Tribe came not in the droves at which they fell during the previous battles; rather, they approached with caution, as though with the full knowledge and acceptance of their imminent death, but wishing to take with them at least one Acrarian soldier.

I don't fault them for that, Sen had thought as she watched a hunter grappling on the ground with an Acrarian, a knife filling the space between them, the steel finding the pulsating home within the Invader's chest, only for the Wood hunter's brain matter to erupt from the back of his head mere moments later.

Sen had not seen any of the Children of the Black Moon on this day. It seemed to be mutual avoidance; after her discussion with Ziia the previous night, she had no desire to seek out her fellow Eclipseborn. Likewise, none saw fit to find her. *Perhaps it's better that way.*

Her head pounded, her arms heavy at her side. The merciless efficiency of the Acrarian war machine had numbed her. The rows to her front aimed and fired in a ruthless choreography, still paying no heed to the comrades who fell at their sides or the adversaries who bled from the trees. She couldn't help but wonder if they, too, had grown desensitized to the bloodshed or if it merely was the natural state of the Acrarian people to view the "other" as nothing more than prey to be belittled and slaughtered.

Yet, still, Sen wondered the same of her own people in their treatment of her and the other Eclipseborn. To Ziia's words from the night previous. *Was she right?* she thought throughout the day, in spite of the arrows and bullets and other projectiles flying about her. The Luck within her would not allow any shot to reach her. At some point, the Luck felt counter to its purpose. She wished one of those shots would find its way to her.

But as the day progressed, the minutes went by with encounters with the Wood resistance growing scarcer. And as those minutes stretched to hours, Sen realized that the opportunities for a true-aimed arrow to find her were growing slimmer and slimmer.

The Wood are gone, she thought, keeping in step with the engaged soldiers before her. *They either bleed on their sacred earth, or they've abandoned their Forest for help from the northern Tribes.*

A pattering of rain found its way past the dense overhang of pastel leaves and branches. The rhythmic tapping overhead accompanied the stark silence of the march, punctuated only with the soft suction of muddied footsteps. Commotion had been reduced to nothing, not even the roar of a rifle to be heard among the gathered soldiers.

Impossible as it was for Sen to believe, the Forest was conquered. A tear found its way down her cheek. She shook her head, her lower lip quivering, her hands trembling.

The thought of her mother and Tez being on the receiving end of these deadly volleys sent tremors through the length of her body.

Her pace slowed, her eyes clenching closed. *Mother...Tez...gods, I'm a fool.*

She stopped her march entirely, the Acrarian soldiers who trailed behind her paying her no mind at all as they pushed past her. *Let them pass,* she thought. *What difference does any of it make?*

A dense gathering of trees flanked the current clearing, calling to her with the promise of respite. Sen was loath to refuse such an offer and wandered into the pass, propping herself up along the body of a tall tree as she caught her breath. Droplets of rain continued to trickle down in intermittent bursts, dampening her hair and forehead as she drew in the pungent smell of storms and death.

The sound of marching feet disappeared into the distance. *Good,* she thought. *At last, some quiet.*

Sen looked to her hip, observing the holstered pistol at her waist. It felt insurmountably heavy as she drew it, holding it out, her gaze caught along the length of its barrel. The echo of thunderclaps past rang in her ears, so much of it consuming her in such a short time.

And no matter how hard she tried, she could not remove the image of her father falling to the ground, a mighty bear defeated, blood following him like rain.

And he was felled with a weapon just like this.

"And how many more will fall in the coming days?" Sen wondered aloud. She looked to the north, back to where the Acrarian soldiers marched. "It could be tonight, it could be tomorrow morning. But sooner or later, that army is going to make it to the Stone village...and there's nothing that my people will be able to do about it."

Her people. The words lingered on her tongue, considering their meaning.

For days, Kamataa, Ziia, and the others were doing their utmost to reinforce the idea that Sen's "people" were those like her, her kin among the Children of the Black Moon. But Ziia's words still rang in her ears.

I must wonder, Sennalhat, whether your heart is as into this fight as you had previously indicated.

Sen looked to her hands, still trembling. She could still feel the spurts of blood erupting from the Chieftain's throat as she pulled her knife out from it. The angered expression of betrayal upon his face. The fatal acceptance that what came for the Wood Tribe—just as with the Sun, Arrow, and Haunted Tribes—was rapidly making its way north. To the final bastion of Tribal sovereignty and liberty.

As the faces of those lives lost among the Wood Tribe flashed in her mind's eye, Sen felt the tears welling, streaming listlessly down her cheeks just as the mournful leaves descended from the ruined branches overhead, no longer painted in vibrant colors pronouncing nature's beauty, but bathed in swaths of blood.

The shock-frozen faces stared intently at her against the dark backdrop behind her eyelids, heads all lolled to the side with mouths agape, blood streaming from their eyes. Sen knew none of them by name, fewer by appearance. And yet, when those lifeless forms found their vigor once again, their appearances changed, all of them whispering her name, their voices ravaged by gravel and malice, condemning her first as "Curseborn," and then as "Traitor."

Where once the faces before her were those of a nameless host of Wood Tribespeople, they turned to the faces of those whom she had known her entire life. Those of her people: the Stone Tribe. Like a mask, the dead Wood fighters shed their prior faces, and in their place appeared the faces of her father and Brin. Narva, and Tawa beside him. Her mother and Tez, wild defiance and fury flaring in their eyes. She saw the faces of those with whom she shared no strong bond: Sharrabha and Rantalha and Grafhar and countless others who she could probably have named at one point or another in her life. Even the visages of Koelhe and Fann appeared, menace strewn proudly and broadly across their faces per usual.

Each of them cursed her in a haunting chorus. Everyone, from the usual suspects of Koelhe and Fann to even her still-living mother and sister.

You've killed us, Sennalhat, rang the chant, ominous and monotonous, equal parts a declaration and a threat. You have killed us and betrayed us.

The voices had Sen entirely in their grip, the weight of the words bearing down so forcefully that she found herself curled deep into a rut in the mud. The stern faces, too many to count, continued to repeat their condemnations, increasing in volume to a near inhuman level as though the hells below opened.

"I...I couldn't..." Sen stammered, trying to look at all of the sunken, sallow faces. "I can't save any of you. I've...I've betrayed all of you—the memories of everyone we've lost. I'm no better than any of these Invaders. I...I..."

She trailed off, her body frozen to the mud. She looked to her father and Brin, their chanting faces angrier than ever. "You both have every right to hate me as you did," she said, tears still running down her face, her breath ragged and frantic. "And I'm sorry that I've done nothing to remedy that. I couldn't stop them, Father. I couldn't save you, Brin."

Their voices continued to drone.

"Narva," Sen pleaded to her friend's reanimated visage, blood still fresh on his lips as he continued the group's chants. "I would give anything to feel you again—but I feel *nothing*. Just a void you left that I've tried to fill in the worst possible way." She wanted to crawl to him, to touch his face and his hands one more time, but Narva stayed further and further away. "Please, Narva. I'm sorry. I'm so, so sorry. I miss you so much."

Narva's voice did not cease the condemnations.

Sen felt the sensation of her arms outstretching, as though appealing to the large audience before her, this mob of those she would have once done anything for, now quick to condemn her just as she consigned to condemn them in turn.

"All of you," she said, her voice breaking. "I'm sorry. I couldn't stop them. I can't save you all. I...I failed you all."

The ominous chants faded to a whisper, a murmur, until finally, they ceased.

The air was still and stagnant, heat rising within her.

You *have* betrayed us, Sen, a singular voice said. It sounded like Tez.

But you *can* save us, another voice said. Her mother.

Slowly, Sen looked up, managing to force her eyes open. The faces were gone, the world around her nothing more than the bloodstained leaves and soil she had rolled herself in. She was still holding the pistol in her hand, the mouth of the barrel inviting as it had been.

And, yet. The promise. The idea that she could still save her people.

"How?" Sen whispered, finding no answer in the wisps of wind which scurried past her. "How *can* I save you all?" The pistol shook in her hand as she held it out, aimed at nowhere in particular in the space ahead of her. "Soon, they'll all be in the Stone territory. Soon, *I'll* have to be there, as well. But what am I to do? I'll be either in the path of a bullet or the one pulling the trigger." She collapsed onto all fours, groaning and grunting as her hands hit the ground. "*Gods, what do I do?*"

A weight slinked its way out of her coat pocket, clinking unceremoniously atop the mud underneath her stomach. Investigating the sound, Sen pushed herself back to her knees, finding the source of the sound to be Brin's Memory pendant. She tried to force a smile but could barely muster a quiver of her lips.

"Was it quick for you, at least, Brin?" she said to the pendant, picking it off the ground, running her thumb along the carved rune. "As far as deaths go? The long march to slaughter that our people are soon to face? At least for you, you were quick to see Father again. Me? Well, I don't know what Luck has in store for me? Not anymore."

She gripped the pendant tighter in her hand, clenching her eyes to dam up the approaching streams. "The darkest days are approaching for our people. Perhaps all the Luck is yours, little brother, that you will not be forced to endure them."

The surge from the pendant coursed up her arm as she leaned back, her back resting against a tall tree. *There is no solace in any of this, little brother,* she thought, *but please, let me be by your side at the end one more time.*

A bright light blinded her, removing the sensation of the Forest bearing down upon her. The Owl's power coursed through her arms from the point of touch of the pendant until it traveled all the way up her neck and into her head. Slowly, the light dissipated before her until it at last formed the image of where she had last left off with Brin's Memories: in the slave pit, just as Kamataa left him with Dounhar, the man of Sen's Tribe who she neglected to save along with her brother.

Just as Brin had condemned her for her being Eclipseborn, just as all the others had. Solemnly, Brin sat in silence, paying no heed to Dounhar, who muttered something incomprehensible to himself. He focused on nothing more than the dirt in front of him and the clamp fastened loosely around his ankle. In a slow arc, his vision panned across the length of the camp, his eyes homing in on all the mindless husks who had once been proud members of the Tribes of the Land.

And to think, I believed their forlorn faces were just from their enslavement. The godsdamned Acrarians tore their minds completely asunder when they stole their pendants. Bastards.

Brin focused for quite a while on the sallow faces in the crowd, all listless with eyes glossed over, doing little more than breathing and existing, the disruption of their connection to the Deities removing them of all their cognitive faculties. It was hard enough to experience just a few days ago. It was worse now with the knowledge that Sen had gained.

It's no wonder Brin tried to get himself out of there. It wouldn't have been long before he'd have ended up like the rest of them. It almost seems worse than death.

Yet, despite the inevitable, Brin seemed completely fixated on the gathered Tribespeople, as though pondering how long it would take for him to reach that state. His vision narrowed, his breath quickening, but no tears formed in his eyes, no words from his lips.

If Sen were to guess, she would assume that her brother was in shock from it all—numb from the days of misery immediately following his capture and now at a loss for words at the state of those he could consider his own people, herded like livestock, though treated with less humanity.

Sen had to assume that the more Brin stared at those soulless eyes before him, the more it instilled in him a desire to escape. She couldn't know for sure just how long he had been chained in that camp between when Kamataa brought him in and when he encountered Sen and Narva in the streets of the City—though what drove him to immediately return to the camp was beyond Sen's understanding still—but she knew her brother. She knew that, for all his strong qualities, he was, at times, a coward prone to running away. Part of that, she understood, was because of her and the hatred which spilled over her and onto him. But if there was one fate Brin was to run from, to find a way to escape, she was glad he had found a way to escape this one, though it was a short-lived freedom.

Despite that, though, Brin gave no indication of escaping. He offered no illusion of breaking free from his chains, only to find his disguised sister in the streets by chance.

No, he just sat *there, picking at pebbles beneath his feet, tapping his thumb along the chain linking his ankle, paying no particular heed to those around him yet still looking upon those who had been there long before him.*

Sen focused her mind just as Ziia had instructed and willed the Memory to progress onward at twice the speed. All she wanted to do was be with Brin at his last moments again; she didn't need the added fluff of his sitting by his lonesome.

Eventually, he would leave this spot. She knew that.

But the more time went on, the more Sen grew annoyed. Nothing was happening. No one moved, least of all Brin. She may as well have been watching a still image, a painting or carving. Instead, Sen just impatiently awaited the moment she was reunited with him.

But it never came. Brin didn't go...anywhere.

This isn't right. He had to have tried to leave by now.

The field of view shifted toward the entrance to the camp, the sound of Brin listlessly clicking his tongue the only accompaniment in these drab environs. Beyond the fence, a shadow blurred past, somewhat meek and small in stature, running beyond the entrance to the camp and into the adjacent alleyway. To Sen's eyes, it could have been some kid wandering where they were not meant to be.

But faint voices followed the shadow. Exasperated but commanding whispers. Brin's head craned downwards. The voices came nearer. Voices all too familiar. Not in the Acrarian tongue, but her own.

"Come on. We don't need to see this."

"Don't we, though? This is what the Invaders want to do to us. Animalize us, break us...and then just leave us to rot."

The voices were too faint to pick up anything further.

But then footsteps approached. Brin looked up—and there was Sen and Narva, disguised in the Acrarian garb they had found on the street.

"Sen?" Brin said. "What...what are you doing here?"

Immediately, Sen pulled herself out of the Memory, returning to the arboreal grave of the Wood Tribe.

"...What?" she muttered, a chill running up the length of her arms as she stared in shock at the pendant. "That...that wasn't how it happened. I...he..."

She shook her head, her brow furrowing, mouth agape. "There's...no, this can't be right. Someone must have...changed it? Is that possible...?" Her hand went to her mouth, covering it to hide the shock from the curious fauna that may have seen her. "No...even if it was possible...it couldn't have been changed. There was no time for it to be changed. I had his pendant right from the moment he was killed. But...what...that means..."

Brin never left the camp. He never found Sen and Narva in a disoriented state, never led them back to where he was chained.

Sen's mind flickered back to the shadow that ran along outside the camp gate. Meek and small in appearance...something that always fit Brin's description.

Her skin prickled as she reached for the chain around her neck, pulling it loose from beneath her shirt. She caressed her thumb along the carving of the Illusion symbol. Her eyes widened with shock.

"Illusion," she muttered. "Brin never left the camp. It was...Illusion."

She rose to her feet, her eyes facing north. To where the army continued to march. To where the northern mouth of the Forest was looming.

"A trick. A lie." Sen clenched her fist, drawing the flintlock pistol at the ready. "And if there was someone who had cause to trick me with an Illusion..."

She ran, tucking Brin's pendant away in her trouser pocket, the medallion thumping against her thigh as she scurried back to the clearing to find the advancing Acrarian army.

Shit, shit, shit! Her mind raced. *There's not much time left. I can't stop them. Mother...Tez...Tawa...they're coming. They're coming for slaughter, and for what?*

For Kamataa's revenge.

Please hold on. I'm coming.

CHAPTER FOURTEEN

Best Interests

The mountains stood tall before her like a crown atop a regal earth. A cold and biting wind flew down from peaks glowing in an orange mist against the setting sun.

Though it had been just a handful of days since she had last seen her home, it had felt ages to Tez. The pyre smoke funneling out from the rows of huts looked the same to her as it always had, but the air still carried with it a different aura entirely.

Never before had her home, the village in which she had spent her entire life, felt altogether unwelcoming. And yet, here she stood, at the head of a contingent of both Stone and Lake warriors, unsure of what the reception would be to her return home.

She was never meant to be an outsider among her people. She didn't know what it was like, despite the troubles with her sister.

She stopped, holding a fist up. Chattering and whistles behind her were signal enough to command her newfound forces to stop.

Tez closed her eyes, drawing in a deep breath, the crisp air filling her lungs. She gripped the shaft of her spear tightly, the wood near to splintering in her hand. A pit opened in her stomach, threatening to swallow anything and everything within it. She let out a long exhale, the tail end breaking into a meek shudder.

A hand clasped her shoulder. "Are you ready?" Tawa said, gravel in his voice and anger in his tone. From her periphery, Tez could make out the cold scowl settling into his brow. He stood with spear at the ready, drawing the same deep breaths as Tez.

Tez frowned, bit at her lip. "Can any of us actually be 'ready' for this, Tawa?" She narrowed her eyes, listened for the village sounds she had grown so accustomed to, of children being called home for supper and warmth, of laughter ringing out upon return from the taverns, of crackling flames and evening critters. The thought of putting spear to it again filled her with dread, for as much as her anger carried her to this point.

"No," Tawa said. "But remember that it is not the whole of the village we need fight. We know who leads this folly."

"And I'm ready to put an arrow through the eye of at least one of them." Sharrabha pushed past a row of Lake and Stone spear fighters, breaking standard formation. Wolfsigns were typically instructed to keep rank behind the Bearsign warriors as means of cover. Tez would not fault her the break.

"So long as you leave some for the rest of us," Tez said, managing a grin. She gritted her teeth as she redirected her focus back to the village. It was a long walk to the village center, plenty of time for the Koelhe's fighters to spring a trap or ring an alert.

That's what I'm hoping for, she thought.

"We make our way for the Chief's hut. Whoever occupies the hut occupies the title of Chief of the Stone Tribe. And I'll rip Koelhe out of there in pieces if I need to." Tez turned her head to Tawa. "Any objections?"

Tawa tapped the butt of his spear rhythmically upon the ground. "I find that to be a wonderful idea. I would be happy to take a piece for myself." His grin was sinister, quite unlike him, but this new side of Tawa was such a welcomed find for Tez.

Sharrabha fished through her quiver, her arrows tapping together. "We stand with you, Tez," she said, placing an arrow between bow and hand. "With you and your family, always. Let none of these bastards stand in the way."

"And leave none among them the strength to stand," Tez said in response. She nudged her head at Sharrabha, politely commanding her to return to formation. "I'll see you when the battle is done."

"I shall see you when the battle is *won*," Sharrabha assured, returning to her position with the other Wolfsign yeomen.

Tez could already hear her giving orders to Stone and Lake alike, the tone ferocious even if the words were at times indecipherable.

"Let's be off, Tawa," she said, tapping her spear on the ground. The row behind her mimicked the action, followed by the next row until all spear fighters announced their arrival to the field.

Tawa nodded, offering no words but displaying his respectful and reverent smile all the same, despite everything. He filed in among the leading row, even though those surrounding him were much more able fighters.

The mind of a scholar, but the heart of a warrior, Tez thought, her own heart heavy and hopeful all the same. She turned to face the village, the spear trembling in her hand ever so slightly. Pointing the tip of the weapon toward the village, roughly half a mile away, she shouted, "On!"

She proceeded slowly at first, but then motioned to an excitable walk, double her normal pace. Whether it was the anxiety of the battle to come or the anticipation of reclaiming her home, she could not say. Regardless, the army behind her kept in step at much the same pace, footsteps thudding against the packed dirt in a discordant rhythm.

So focused on the village was she, and so deafened by the howling wind complementing the resounding footsteps, that she did not even register someone calling her name.

"Tez! Tez!" a voice called to her left.

Tez turned, not breaking her stride, to find Ket standing off to the side, not exactly keeping in step with the rest of the force, managing a half-smile. She stifled a chuckle before pointing her spear once again and shouting, "Keep on!"

The army did as they were told, Tawa catching wind of the goings-on and jumping to the front of the pack, leading the slow charge just as Tez did.

Tez slunk away from the group, placing her spear down on the ground beside Ket. The healer seemed somewhat out of breath, noticeably panting as beads of sweat trailed down their forehead. A leather jerkin was half-covered with a pelt overcoat, standing somewhere between the cold environs of the base of the Heart and the rigors of an exhaustive day of travel.

"It's funny, isn't it?" Ket said. "A few days ago, we were rolling our eyes at the unnecessary blood shed among my people."

"And now, here we are, about to do the same to mine?" Tez said with eyebrows raised.

Ket shook their head. "That's not what I mean. You're...standing for something. Putting your life on the line for something greater than yourself. You understand the consequences and yet you are willing to raise your spear against your own despite that. It's different among my people. The bloodshed is never so...selfless."

Tez chuckled. "I wouldn't quite call the possibility of taking another's life 'selfless,' but..."

"But you are willing to do it because you know what is about to come. You're doing it for your people, for mine...for all of us. Better than those two fools we call Chiefs willing to gore each other over stolen trinkets." Ket looked down to the ground, hands folded behind their back. "Had I the ability with the spear that you possess...I would follow you into battle any day." They looked up, a glimmer in their eyes and a warm smile upon their face.

"Is that a high compliment among your people?" Tez teased, returning a smile of her own.

"You jest, but...it's not far from the truth." They reached out and grabbed Tez's hand, lifting it with one hand and covering the top of the hand with the other. "Thank you, Tez. It's not often that my people can unite under a common cause, even if Tenazt and Yhaan's truce is only temporary."

"I just hope they don't resort to killing each other before they reach the Arrow Tribe."

Ket quickly shook their head. "I would like to hope not, but...that's beside the point. *You* made this happen, Tez. I just wanted to say that I'm grateful to you. I know your reasons for doing so were strictly for your own people, but you arrived in our village a vagabond and in just a few short days you became someone we would all follow into battle. We respect strength. But more than that, we respect dedication. It is something our Chiefs have lacked for a long time. But the stories of you will be passed down among our people for generations."

Tez placed her free hand atop Ket's top hand, her thumb caressing their fingers. "Then I'll be sure to survive the battles to come. So long as you're ready with a pen afterwards."

"A pen and more." Ket winked.

Warmth rose in Tez as she put a hand to the back of Ket's head and pulled them in, pressing her lips to theirs. She made it quick, only two or three seconds, but when she pulled herself away, she winked just the same. "And more to come," she responded.

A wide smile remained affixed to Ket's face. "I'll lead our non-combatants just as you commanded. We'll inform all that you've returned to reclaim your Tribe, to give all of the Tribes the best chance to stop the Invaders. And when it's all done…"

The words were better left unsaid. But Tez felt them just the same. She released herself from Ket's grasp and picked her spear back up, turning to the army as it proceeded through the village. "Until then," she said, and rushed off to the front of the procession, her braid thumping against the top of her back as she tried not to give the impression of a headlong charge with spear still in hand.

Her heart was fluttering for a multitude of reasons, but her mind still remained focused on the task ahead.

As she passed by the rows of warriors and hunters, she could hear the muttered whispers of villagers watching them pass by. Distinctly, Tez made out the utterances of her own name, most often spoken with kind regard and not at all with the malice and hatred that she so feared may have heralded her return. But instead, many merely address the subject of her return with curiosity and hope, though anger, annoyance, and fear were still prevalent amidst that din of whispers.

Many faces peered out from windows and doors, some immediately retreating back into the sanctity and safety of their homes, while others remained beneath their thresholds, some with arms folded across their bodies, others with hands masking their mouths to hide shock, others shaking fists to denounce the return of the former Chief's daughter and the host of outsiders at her heel, though mixed with those of their own kin.

Tez did not match gazes with any of them, regardless of perception of friend or foe. She was not going to give any of them the satisfaction of acknowledgment. She was not here to instill in them fear or anger. She could only wonder what they had felt at what had happened those nights ago. Tez had already felt like she had abandoned them to Koelhe's madness. But it was not too late to free them from it.

By the time Tez returned to the front of the army, to where Tawa continued leading the charge, the Chief's hut had come within view. Though it still remained standing, something about it was unsettling to Tez.

She couldn't see a plume of smoke wafting out from the roof as was the norm during daylight hours. It gave the hut a rather ominous air simply for that alone. But more than that, gradually, she could spy more curious faces filtering out from huts near to the Chief's, not with the expressions of those who looked upon Tez's host with interest, but rather with the expectant and malicious undertones of those awaiting a great foe to return. Smiles flashed, none of them welcoming.

Nor did the glint of waning sunlight upon cold steel offer any joy to Tez's solemn return.

Tez's chest thumped loudly in her ears as she drew in a sharp breath. Her eyes panned from one edge of the village square to the other, fingers tapping along her spear shaft. She grinded her teeth, snarling as she stopped to take in the scene. A host of warriors emerged from points unseen, from around corners, alleyways, doors.

The clearing in front of the Chief's hut glowed in orange sunlight in announcing the fires soon to come. Before long, the square was filled with numerous of Koelhe's supporters, all folks with whom Tez had been acquainted, none of whom she would ever have presumed would be on the wrong side of this coup.

Not that it seemed to matter to any of them. Tez peered along the rows of eyes that she could see, and none among them bore any semblance of shame or regret. If anything, they displayed only amusement for the rabble before them, and anticipation for the rout they hoped to bring.

"Brace," Tez said under her breath and over her shoulder. The rows of Stone and Lake fighters stood to attention, spears clacking into place in a thunderous clap.

A clap that almost equaled the echoing and sardonic applause by one snarling and sneering face emerging from the corner, though the act was awkward by virtue of the man's mismatched arms.

"Well, hello again, Tez," Fann said, voice rife with condescension. "How lovely it is to see you again."

He filed in at the front of the separatist forces, holding a spear up against his shoulder by the strength of his one good arm. His shirt was fashioned in a Sun Tribe style for some reason, with only one sleeve remaining, covering his maimed arm. Still noticeable was the arrow wound Sharrabha placed in his exposed shoulder, though it had seemed to have recovered somewhat in the past few days.

"How's that shoulder feeling?" Tez said with a grin, inclining her head toward him.

Fann winced as he rotated his shoulder. "Still hurts like a bitch. I'll be sure to give Sharrabha one to match through her stomach."

"She wouldn't give you the opportunity." She spun her spear into position. "Neither will I."

"How amusing!" Fann said with an exaggerated laugh, putting a hand to his chest. "I seem to remember besting you into a cowardly retreat."

"A *tactical* retreat. I've bested both Chiefs of the Lake Tribe in single combat. You wouldn't even have lasted a handful of seconds against them." It seemed unnecessary to confess that all she did to Tenazt was walk up and punch him in the face, but it seemed to bring the point across, nonetheless.

Fann craned his head to his left, pursing his lips and raising his brow and the host of Lake fighters intermingled with the Stone. "And does that mean you rule over them? Is *that* how their idiotic brand of governance functions, hmm? Is this meant to frighten me, Tez?"

"Spare us all the false bravado, Fann. Your cowardice is well-known." Tez turned to her forces with a grin, chuckling softly to herself. "But no, there are more important matters here. A larger common enemy approaching. The

Invaders *will* be at our door soon. Do we really want to spend those waning moments before their arrival trying to stick spears in one another?"

Pausing in momentary consideration, Fann barked a laugh. "And you needed a horde of Lake fighters still deep in the throes of their bloodlust to inform us of this?"

Tez scoffed. "No," she said, baring her teeth. "I'm merely showing that I have no qualms about spearing you through before I take on the Invaders."

"How rich, Tez. The only Invaders upon our land that I see are the beasts standing behind you!" He shot his spear out in accusation.

"The Invaders are laying waste to the Forest as we speak, Fann! They may even have breached it by now. This is just wasting time. Did you not receive a messenger from the Wood Tribe warning you of the Invaders' arrival?"

There was a slight hesitation in Fann's posture. The tip of his spear descended ever so slightly, a frown creasing his lips, his eyes narrowing. And just as quickly, he shook his head. "We were not warned, no."

"Then either they passed you by or you are a fool for not listening to them. My guess is it's the latter."

"And what would you wish to accomplish should you be correct, Tezal-hat?" A voice rang out. Slow, methodical footsteps emerged from north, accompanied by an ever-stoic face and a bow that had felled numerous of his kin just a few nights prior. "Fann speaks truly. It could be that the Invaders may come, but you yourself stand at the front of an army of Lake Tribe warriors. Should we not feel threatened?" Rantalha said.

The hair stood tall on the back of Tez's neck. Her nostrils flared, her lip quivered. The memory of Rantalha loosing arrows so effortlessly and remorselessly into the throats and chests of so many of her kin still filled her with rage and dread. That he would side with Koelhe, slaughter those perceived to be her enemies, and then have the gall to label it as "practical" was perplexing. But it instilled in Tez a greater realm of focus than had been present when she only faced Fann.

"Look behind me, Rantalha!" she said, gesturing over her shoulder. "Look upon these faces! That you are seeing members of both the eastern and western Lake Tribes together, fighting as one, is proof enough of the threat that looms. It is enough for them to recognize the importance of coming together—as a unified north!—and put aside their differences. We need one common cause in the battles to come."

Rantalha's face betrayed nothing, but his lip ever so slightly sneered upwards with a huffed scoff. "And so we return to the question at hand. Are you not better than the Invaders as you disrupt the peace and unity that Koelhe has given our Tribe? Would you dismantle that solely for the sake of power that you think is *yours*?" He shook his head. "Accept defeat, Tezalhat. We are moving forward as a Tribe; please try not to bury yourself amidst the dust."

Tez couldn't help but laugh. "*You'd* admonish *me* for disrupting a false peace and unity when Koelhe did that just a few nights ago?!" She spat on the ground and narrowed her eyes. "You used to be an honorable man, Rantalha. It sickens me to see you sink so low as to fall to these lies."

Rantalha said nothing, only sighed deeply as he flexed his bow arm, rotated his shoulders. His face remained the same, ever unchanging, ever disapproving.

As Tez snarled at him, though, something struck her as odd. All this talk of Koelhe, and yet she was nowhere to be seen. *She insisted on making a show of things with her presence the other night, even if she didn't even take part in the fighting.* "So where *is* our eminent new Chief, then?" she barked.

"Hah!" Fann snapped, his sinister smile returning in full force. "She takes her duties as Chief quite seriously, Tez. Something your parents were never quite mentally adept enough to do."

The mention of her parents sent a chill up her spine. "Where's my mother?" Tez growled.

"Alive, if that concerns you so dearly." Fann chuckled to himself, not once removing the grin from his face. "She said she has so much to teach my mother after all—she absolutely *insisted* that she be kept alive. Of course, my mother is ever merciful in that regard."

Tez gripped her spear tighter, her eyes panning to the Chief's hut—her *family's* hut—and let out a deep growl. "What have you done to her?" she snarled.

Putting a hand on his hip, Fann gave a noncommittal shrug. "Nothing forceful, I assure you. The last I heard, I believe my mother was pressing her for any information by which she could dispel the curse which still looms tall over our Tribe."

"Bastard!" Tez screamed, feeling a tug on her shoulder just as she took those initial steps forward. She didn't need to look behind her to know it was Tawa's hand holding her back. She pointed her spear at Fann. "My sister has always been a better person and better kin than you ever were! She endured far more than you ever would—much of it because of your 'merciful' mother! And all the while, all *you* ever did was hide behind your mother's legs like the coward you are, waiting for her to turn around and comfort you in her bosom!" Fann opened his mouth to interject, some of his men snickering around him, but Tez did not give him the opportunity. "The only 'curse' upon our Tribe is you! You and your mother and all you other godsdamned bastards who dared to cast her out for something beyond her control, something she did not choose!"

Fann put a hand to his stomach as he doubled over with laughter, un-controlled and unrestrained. He pointed at Tez as he reveled in amusement, urging those around him to join him in laughter, though they did so with less exuberance. The uproar quelled to a soft chuckle as he wiped tears away from his eyes, shaking his head with that amused, shit-eating smile still plastered across his face.

"Oh-ho-ho, I've not laughed that hard in ages, Tez. That's truly rich." Fann licked his chops, slamming the butt of his spear on the ground. "You know that I've taken up gardening, Tez? It's quite relaxing, I must say. But if there's anything that drives me crazy, it's weeds. Leave a weed for too long and it multiplies, and before you know it, your entire garden has been overtaken." He pointed an unbalanced finger at Tez. "You, your mother...your dead father, your weakling brother, your godsdamned *Curseborn* sister! All of you are weeds. When one is shown a weed, it is customary to pull it, and that is what my mother has done: pluck the weeds before it overtakes our Tribe and our village, and *that* is what she continues to do! More than your parents ever did while they allowed the village to become infested with that cursed weed you call a sister!"

Deep laughter echoed over the village square as a collective march of footsteps approached from parts unseen. Doors slammed shut, some accompanied by sharp yelps or frightened screams. A quick clang of steel ended unceremoniously with an audible gargle of blood. Though the approach was outside of Tez's purview, she could see Fann's expression completely change from unrestrained amusement to disbelieving shock, and likewise, Rantalha raised his eyebrows.

The tip of a spear, coated in blood, peaked out from a southern corner, slowly inching forward until the burly man who held the weapon came into view. Never had Tez seen the man brandish his weapon, rarer still to see his face deep-set in anger. But when the imposing form of the Sun Chief Han'e stepped into the square, his arm splashed in blood, a host of equally angered Sun Tribe spearmen and yeomen at his back, Tez couldn't help but feel a tinge of fear.

"Chief Han'e," Fann said, arm outstretched in a questioning manner. "Might I inquire as to why you've so indiscriminately butchered one of my good men? What did dear Dolevhe ever do to you, I wonder?"

He's speaking to a Chief as though he were a mischievous child, Tez thought with disgust.

"He got what he deserved, just as you will, you faithless worm!" snarled a bowman standing to Han'e's rear. His nose was bunched together, his teeth bared, his eyebrows angled downward as though to signal he must show a permanent frown.

Han'e held his arm out. "Silence, Tol'e," he commanded, a fire burgeoning from those softly spoken words, fury and anger rife upon his tongue. "The worm was speaking to me."

"I will not suffer being spoken to in such a way, Chief Han'e!" Fann said. "Rantalha, put an arrow through the eye of the next to call me a worm."

Rantalha eyed Fann but offered no indication of acknowledgment.

At least Rantalha sees what we all see in Fann.

"Chief Han'e, I must remind you that this is not the conduct befitting an ally," Fann chided.

"Ally?" Han'e growled. "You would dare still call me an ally? Alliances are two-way streets, *boy.* In exchange for my help in your blasted uprising, I was promised assistance in reclaiming my people's lands. But what have I received in the days since?" He hawked and spat on the ground. "Little more than that. Your mother has done nothing since claiming the leadership but imbibe and waste the days away. I would be shocked if she has spent a moment of it sober. The two of you betrayed us all by not only dismissing the messenger of the Wood Tribe warning us of the Invader advance, but *butchering* the boy for your own satisfaction!"

There were some gasps, some murmurs. Many looked at Fann, who maintained the same grin, though his eyes flickered and narrowed, his fingers twitching.

"And where is she now?" Han'e continued. "She continues to not show her face. Already she has reneged on the promise she made to stand with the Sun Tribe to reclaim our lands from the Invaders—a promise she made only for the sake of offering my help in the proceedings those nights ago. Had I known that was to be the case, I would not have raised a hand that night." He scowled deeply, his fingers balling into a fist. "It is as Tezalhat says: the Invaders march upon us as we speak, but Koelhe would rather spend her days drunk, no care in her head but holding on to the power she seized just in time for her world to burn."

"Shut your mouth, you madman!" Fann bellowed, his fingers curling in an attempt at a fist but managing only what resembled crooked talons. "You're a traitor to this Tribe just as much as she is!" He pointed an accusing finger at Tez. "Rantalha! You and your Wolfsigns, put arrows between the eyes of every member of the Sun Tribe, *NOW!*"

Rantalha crossed his arms and raised his eyebrows at Fann, showing great disinterest in obeying.

Tez felt a shove to her right as Sharrabha barreled through, bow and arrow in hand, aiming squarely at Fann before the bastard could raise further objections to Rantalha.

"This is what your family has come to, isn't it, Fann?" Sharrabha said with a snarl, her aim staying true. "So intent on asserting control that you're quick to find that you have none. Any one of the men and women behind you would spear you in the back and not even think twice on it. They followed you only for the convenient solution of the one thing they hated; you inspire no loyalty otherwise. None will miss you when you fall, and I'm going to enjoy watching it."

"Don't be so quick to judge!" Han'e said, changing the trajectory of his spear from Fann to Tez and her contingent.

"Chief Han'e!" Sharrabha said, lowering her aim. "What are you doing? We have a common enemy here and a common enemy approaching! We could—"

"Spare me, huntress!" Han'e closed his eyes, shaking his head vigorously. "Spare me your talk of loyalty and convenient solutions! Do you want to speak on loyalty? What about the loyalty your departed Chief requested of me in reward for lands that we could not survive upon? Was that 'convenient' for your people? Did the loyalty of the Stone Tribe only extend as far as the earshot of the Sun? No, we've always just been the weak and sallow that you think nothing of the moment we leave your sight. But no more! No faction of the Stone Tribe has ever stood with the Sun Tribe in earnest, and from this day, we will no longer stand for the Stone Tribe!"

Tez pushed her way forward before Sharrabha could say anything further, gesturing her arms to both parties. "Chief Han'e, please! We don't have any time for this! The only one you need point your spear at stands across from us! It's them who have kept us from readying ourselves for the Invaders!"

Furiously, Han'e shook his head, his eyes closed, perhaps a hint of remorse in his face. "You simply do not understand, Tezalhat. You'd still ask me to fight your battles with nothing in return. No longer. I would rather die a free man, fighting those who abandoned my people, than continue living under the grasp of the Invaders and everything they took from us."

Tez felt her heart sank, but her spear found its way to a readied position in her hand nonetheless.

From across the square, Fann began to laugh again. The Strength pendant glowed brightly beneath his shirt. "Then allow me to grant you your wish, Han'e!" He turned to the bowmen behind him. "NOCK AND LOOSE! FIRE ALL!"

In the following moments, everything fell to a blur around Tez. The world seemed to stop, and yet in that cessation, there became chaos.

Instinct told her to fall to her left. She listened, planted the butt of her spear in the ground and swung around it like a pole, facing the direction of a handful of arrows that landed just where she stood previously.

From behind her, the war cries of countless Stone and Lake warriors echoed in the air, the oncoming stampede of spears like quills promising death just passing her by. Volleys of arrows followed them, raining down upon the unforgiving earth below, meeting the ground in a resounding chorus of blood spatter and gurgled breaths. Sharrabha, still exposed at the front of the pack, eschewed her weapon of choice and drew the hunter's knife from her hip, falling back in with the charging Bearsign warriors, seemingly eager to sneak within the guard of an unsuspecting opponent. Tawa screamed loudest among them all as he remained at the head of the charge, a fire erupting from his throat that would have done Tez's father proud.

Across the square, Han'e gestured his arms out to both opposing forces, the rune of Courage flaring from beneath his overshirt. He did not scream, he did not challenge. He merely charged, spear targeted at nothing but the emptiness ahead, at the center point of the converging armies, as though to goad anyone feeling brave enough to take him at arms. The act was matched by his own Sun warriors, led by the bowman Tol'e, who bellowed loud enough for the entire Tribe, screaming expletives and threats to all who wished to hear, and plenty who wished not to.

Fann stood contently as a wave of arrows erupted from behind him, most aimed at the approaching Sun warriors. Though Strength shimmered within him, Fann did not move from his position, resting his spear on his shoulder, that ever-present grin still strewn about his face as he was flanked by spears, their wielders fierce, though clearly lacking in the virulent enthusiasm enunciated by the two sides converging upon them. Arrows rained without care, some falling harmlessly in the space between while others found home in a leg or shoulder, not enough to deter the rageful Sun warriors and their fearless leader.

Tez focused, drawing a deep breath. The cacophony of battle erupted as roars and clashes of spear blades rang in harmony with the setting sun. Narrowing her gaze, she set her sights on her target: the Chief's hut. Home.
If Mother's still alive...
She lifted her spear, pounding it on the ground, and yelled, "TO ME!"

Several Bearsign warriors heeded the call, jumping out from the charge to flank Tez, spears at the ready in a horseshoe of deadly quills. Men and women, Stone and Lake alike, stood about her, pendants of Strength and Endurance and Restoration shining beneath their shirts with the intensity of a thousand glowing stars.

"We're taking back my home!" Tez screamed, ensuring her voice carried over the song of battle. She pointed her spear at the wall of death, where blood shot outwards in crimson arcs and spears and hunting knives sang their mournful aria. "BREAK. THROUGH. THAT. WALL!" She charged, drawing in Endurance from her pendant, feeling a reinvigoration coursing through her aching muscles, ignoring every ache and pain she had earned herself over these last few days. The trailing spears jutted out from her periphery, the wall ahead about to find out if it could withstand the might of the intertribal charge. A volley of arrows landed in front of them from some unseen direction, a mere hurdle to the wall ahead.

Ahead to meet them was a small force of Fann's legion, standing at the ready. They were the preferable target; Tez did not want to fight any Sun forces if she could help it, but if it came down to it...

The gap closed. Twenty paces became fifteen became ten.

Tez tucked her spear inwards, the shaft propped between her forearm and side. She flared her nostrils, bared her teeth, and roared.

The challenge was met ahead, even as a volley from behind Tez's charge took one of Fann's men in the throat. Defiant even in the face of death, the warrior stood for as long as he could, even as blood spurted from his mouth unceremoniously, his unaccepting glare all he could offer before falling to the ground, his blood joining the puddles forming in the earth around him.

Tez snarled and lunged forward, leaving her feet as she brought her spear out, the steel finding the belly of the man at the front of the resistance before he even had the opportunity to raise his own weapon in defense. The spear tip took him all the way through, jutting out from his back. The forward momentum found Tez nearly off-center, landing awkwardly, compensating with a few extra steps forward. With all her momentum, she used those extra steps to push her first target backwards, the exposed spear finding the thigh of the man behind him, sending him to the ground. Finding her weapon too lodged within the bodies of two foes, Tez pried loose the spear of her initial target, the strength already leaving him, and swung the steel in an arc, catching one foe across the face and another across the throat.

Before any could react to Tez's vengeful charge, her accompanying force met them with spears raised, taking each of them in a mighty lunge, unable or even unwilling to meet the challenge. One of the Lake fighters took the extra step forward to drive her spear through the throat of the incapacitated challenger with the spear tip driven through his thigh.

Typical of Fann, Tez thought. *All the talk, none of the prowess.*

In her periphery, she could make out vague shapes and forms of the chaos of battle. She could see Han'e standing tall among all around him, his skin unmarred by the trials before him, the blood splatter on his clothes very evidently not his own. His eyes seemed to wander, scanning the battlefield even as hapless opponents tried with futile effort to introduce him to cold steel.

Some rows over, Sharrabha was very much up to the challenge of using only her hunting knife, ducking in and out of cover, her steel kissing exposed flesh and cutting through swaths of opponents, Sun and Stone alike, as though they were made of tissue paper.

Another volley of arrows redrew Tez's attention, the arrowheads finding their way into the brains and necks of several around her, including one of her own. She inclined her head toward the hut, finding it still standing tall beyond the rows upon rows of resistance ahead of her.

"Keep moving forward!" she shouted, urging her fighters onward.

Just as she took three steps forward, she felt a surge of movement to her right, countless combatants knocked aside, an intermingling of forces all sent to their feet indiscriminately. Finding the opportunity, Tez jabbed downwards in quick succession, finding the throats of several opponents.

For the briefest of moments, the call of steel silenced, if only to indulge the curiosity of what led to an entire column bowling over. A low growl permeated across the crowd, even as death groans punctuated each heavy step. It was as if a boulder rolled through, crushing everything in its path.

Han'e crashed through every fighter in his way as though they were made of glass. Many did not even seem able to raise a weapon in defense, even as his approach was well-telegraphed. With his girth and strength, the Sun Chief was able to plow through with ease. Tez could not initially determine the reasoning for Han'e's sudden charge.

Not until the Sun Chief bellowed for all to hear, "NO MORE HIDING, COWARD!"

Tez narrowed her gaze to find Fann still standing outside the reach of steel, his spear remaining atop his shoulder. *A worm, indeed.*

Fann gritted his teeth, and even from this distance, Tez could see the thinly veiled fear bleeding out from his eyes. All the same, though, the Strength rune shined with bright intensity beneath his shirt and, seeming to muster up what little courage he had, screamed in what was less of a battle cry and more of a shrill shriek, charging ahead just as Han'e broke the final plane of the battle wall, crashing into him, able to push the Chief back into the throng by virtue of the enhanced Strength coursing through him.

The chaos resumed, Tez taking a handful of inattentive Stone defectors in a smooth arc, blood spraying off to the left. Her contingent encircled her, creating a wall of spears from which she could emerge at any side, spear at the ready.

As her spear wall pushed forward, a circle opened up in the middle of the throng, Fann and Han'e at the center of it. Whether the circle opened voluntarily or if it was littered with the bodies of those the two combatants wanted out of their way, Tez could not determine. But immediately, the two disappeared below the sea of curious heads, each throwing the other to the ground. Only their growls and snarls were audible to Tez.

A swath of Fann's forces fell in front of her, the charge led by Tol'e and a contingent of Sun spearmen behind him. His face was drenched with blood, his hair entirely matted in it as though he impaled someone merely by the strength of his own skull.

From the manic look on his face, I wouldn't doubt it.

Even at this short distance, Tol'e kept his bow raised. With speed unparalleled by anyone Tez had seen, the Sun hunter nocked and loosed and took one of Tez's Lake fighters through the eye. Before Tez could blink, another found an arrow penetrating their throat.

Tez snarled and charged forward, sliding on her knees below the next shot, thrusting with her spear but missing as the attempt went wide, missing Tol'e by the length of a few hairs. Her momentum carried her through the mixture of mud and blood until her face was at knee height.

Tol'e seized the opportunity, bringing his knee to Tez's face.

Feeling a crunch, Tez's vision was immediately dazed. She could already feel the blood pouring out from the crack in the bridge of her nose. The world spun about her, her head in a heavy fog. She rolled to her knees, but the butt of a spear took her in the side of the head, knocking her over.

As steel scraped against steel in the skirmish around her, the rhythmic thudding of another arrow volley finding either its targets or the earth, Tez's vision cleared just enough to find Tol'e leaning over her, a sinister snarl adorning his bloodied face, fire and fury erupting in his eyes.

Just barely could she hear the scrape of steel exiting its sheath. The golden rays of the setting sun glinted off the hunter's knife.

Tol'e's head jerked to the side, something long protruding from the right side. Blood sprayed in the same direction as the Sun hunter fell, the knife leaving his loose fingers, the tip landing in dirt just beside Tez's leg.

Her head no longer swirling, Tez recovered her sight just in time to see Tol'e's accompaniment meet the same end, arrows burrowing into their skulls or throats, dropping to the ground just as unceremoniously.

Tez pushed herself up to her feet, the pain in her nose burning even as she drew in a wealth of Endurance to fight it off. She furiously scanned the battlefield, blood and sweat streaming down her face, trying to find the source of the strikes.

Off to the side, out of the reach of close quarters, stood Rantalha, off by his lonesome, an arrow nocked to his bow. He nodded to her, his gaze focused, his face betraying nothing as it always did.

Her breath catching in her chest, Tez felt relief swell within her.

Until Rantalha loosed his arrow, taking one of Tez's remaining contingent in the chest.

Tez followed the path of the arrow, her body freezing in place. Before she could even turn back to the stoic hunter, two more arrows felled the final ones still standing.

Slowly, she turned back to Rantalha, the battle still raging furiously behind her as screams met roars met clashes of steel.

The hunter tilted his head ever so slightly, as though to invoke Tez to a challenge. His bow arm fell to his side, a loose arrow dangling between the forefinger and middle finger of his other hand. He tossed the arrow aside, holding his hand out a few inches from his waist. Something resembling a smirk creased his lips.

If this was Rantalha's way of offering a challenge, then Tez was loath to refuse.

Pushing off of the unsteady mud, Tez sprinted forward, closing the gap between her and Rantalha, the traitor remaining just as still as he was moments prior. Ten paces away he stood, five paces.

At two paces, Tez lunged with her spear, aiming a forceful jab to Rantalha's chest.

The hunter sidestepped the blow with ease, permitting Tez to slide past him along the slick mud.

Drawing a sharp breath, Tez swung high behind her, spinning on her heel to face Rantalha, but the arc of her swing missed as he ducked his head backwards. In the same motion, Tez backed away a step, repositioning the spear above her head, and swung down, a blow that would have opened the hunter up from brain to balls, but he casually spun away from it. Spear tip still in the ground, Tez pushed forward, vaulting ahead inside Rantalha's guard, aiming a punch to his stomach, which she hoped she could have followed with a blow from her spear, but he caught her fist with little effort, pulling her into his shoulder just as he jutted it outward, Tez taking the full force of the blow, knocking her square on her back.

"Surely, you can do better than that, Tezalhat," Rantalha said mockingly. "I have fought snow leopards with nothing more than a stone and a knife. Is your spear meant to threaten me?"

Tez spun over on her backside, rolling herself to a kneeling position, holding her spear out to the side, the end of it tucked beneath her armpit. She flared her nostrils, a low grumble in her throat. "Why?" she asked. "You see what they have wrought already. Why do you still fight for them?"

Rantalha stared blankly at her, and though Tez searched furiously within his eyes for any pang of regret, sadness, or anger, she found nothing but the same stoicism inherent in everything the man displayed about himself. "It was my pledge. I do not break as easily as the Sun Tribe."

Tez held her hand out to the blood still being spilled, the spears and arrows still raining down upon a once-proud people. "Even seeing this, you do not break?"

He tossed his bow aside, drawing two hunting blades from the sheaths on the small of his back. "I believe I made my position clear."

Tez snarled. "As have I." Pushing herself up to both feet, she lunged again at Rantalha, feinting with a forward thrust before withdrawing it, spinning around, and aiming the butt of her spear at his head.

Rantalha rolled out of the arc's path, found his footing, and then pressed on Tez. He swung his right-hand knife in a reverse grip, just barely missing Tez's brow, though she knew that the miss was intentional. Stopping the momentum of his arm, Rantalha jerked his hand downward, aiming for the space between Tez's neck and shoulder.

In just enough time, Tez brought a hand up to catch him by the wrist, Endurance flaring in her veins as he pushed him off. To counter, she swung her spear, not necessarily to slash him, but to get him to a better distance. She knew she was at a disadvantage with her spear, but she had no other options. But it was a range she knew best.

As the spear tip passed Rantalha by, Tez flipped her grip, spinning the spear back in a jabbing position, and quickly sent a flurry of jabs in the way of her opponent. Though the hunter backed away from some jabs and turned away others with the hunting knives, Tez knew she had him on the defensive. She pressed him, pushing him back step by step, each successive jab met with a more exhaustive block or dodge.

The mud squished beneath her feet as she readied what she hoped would be a final blow. It was clear he was tiring. That was something over which she would always have the advantage. She planted her feet, drew in Endurance, and fired off a furious series of jabs.

Rantalha, for his part, stood firm in his spot, turning away one jab, two jabs, three...

And then he side-stepped the fourth, running alongside the shaft of the spear. With knives drawn, he slid over toward Tez, swinging his left-hand knife toward her throat.

Caught off-center, Tez slipped backwards, falling on her back with a hard thud. Her spear came loose, bouncing away from her for the force of the impact with the ground, rolling several feet away.

Seizing the opportunity, Rantalha jumped down, bringing his fists down toward Tez, knives out.

Tez's arms shot out, catching Rantalha by both wrists. Her arms wavered with the effort, but the Endurance kept the energy from depleting from her body. Despite the advantage Rantalha held, she held her own, keeping the knives at an arm's length, the hunter's own arms quivering. The stalemate carried on for a minute, Rantalha's face straining, sweat dripping off his face and onto Tez's, but Tez was unperturbed. The force of her arms began to prevail, the blades pushing back up toward Rantalha, and she aimed a forceful knee to the hunter's backside, flipping him over her entirely.

Springing back to her feet, Tez still found herself without a weapon. Rantalha had already rolled back to a standing position, shaking his arms to quell the exhaustion surely coursing through them. Tez knew she had no chance to run over to her spear.

She positioned her hands in a fighting pose, ready for Rantalha's impending strike. Her head roared in protest, the deep cut on the bridge of her nose stinging with the amount of mud and muck seeping into the wound. She wiped away a trail of blood from her nostrils and, with a slight stutter step, goaded an advance.

Rantalha jumped forward, aiming one knife to Tez's shoulder. Tez grinned, sidestepping the attempt, allowing the hunter's forward momentum to push him into the empty space, and she pried the attacking knife free from the man's tired hands.

Fury in her heart, Tez swung the hunting knife, skimming the skin of Rantalha's cheek before he could duck out of the way. Thin droplets of blood sprayed off of the swing and she pressed again, bringing her arm up to his throat and aiming a thrust for his chest. Rantalha brought his knee up and kicked Tez's leg out from under her, the aim of her thrust thrown asunder.

Her momentum carrying her forward, Tez rolled ahead, planting herself smoothly to her feet, and turned around just in time to block a flurry of quickly timed strikes.

Tez swung her knife and met Rantalha's thrust, turning it away. The blades met in rhythmic concert, steel screaming against each other in protest, sparks flying as one blade scraped against the other, all the anger held within Tez reflected in each swing, each strike.

The flurry ended, the skirmish pausing as each combatant caught their breath. Exhaustion settled upon Rantalha's face in a way that Tez had never seen from the man. His face glistened with sweat, intermingling with the cut on his cheek that was now dripping blood.

Tez drew in a well of Endurance, the aches in her muscles once again quelling.

The momentary pause stretched for what seemed like ages. Tez and Rantalha both hunched over themselves, trying to catch their breaths. Rantalha's hand was quivering, his eyes hungry but his body finding means to protest. Tez stood at the ready, her chest pounding and ears ringing.

As his hand ceased quivering, Rantalha jumped forward, reaching the blade behind his head for added momentum, and aimed a horizontal slice at Tez's throat.

Tez held out her blade, spinning around the origin of the strike, her steel scraping against his, and as the strike passed her by, she found herself within Rantalha's guard, her arm rising instinctively.

Her steel opened up his throat.

Rantalha fell to his knees, the blade tossed aside, his hands attempting futilely to cover the wound even as rivers of blood streamed through the slits of his fingers. Tez stared down at him, shaking her head as she dropped the blade to the ground beneath her. Wistfully, she walked over and picked up her spear, turning back to Rantalha with not even a sneer or an elated grin. Only disappointment.

"Remember, there's no betrayal at play here, nor is there taking a side," she said. "Only acting in the best interests of the Tribe."

And she drove the spear through Rantalha's chest.

Within moments, the stoic hunter collapsed dead upon the earth, his blood pooling upon the same ground where he spilled so much just a few nights ago.

Tez jerked the spear out from Rantalha's body, a stark emptiness filling her. She did not know what she would feel should she have gotten this opportunity. She just didn't expect that she would feel...nothing at all. Not even a pang of regret of having to fell someone that her father trusted so dearly, by her own hands.

"Damn it," she whispered, sparing one final glance at the departed hunter.

The roar of battle still raged, but most of it was centered upon two men. The circle around Han'e and Fann had grown larger and fiercer, the surrounding clamor becoming less of a battle between opposing forces and more of an intrigued audience watching these two fierce warriors duel to the death. Arrows had ceased raining, spears remained still.

Tez walked to the perimeter of the field, her own interest piqued by the proceedings. Han'e's weighty blows continually knocked Fann off-center, but the crafty Fann kept finding his way inside the Sun Chief's guard. Blood and muck adorned both of their bodies, hair shredded loosely from their Tribal adornments, clothing torn threadbare with noticeable rips and claw marks upon each combatant.

The two men had devolved from the need for words, finding greater solace in the ringing of steel as each spear strike grew louder, fiercer, more violent. With each strike, the men growled and grunted, both bearing greater resemblance to the Bear than the men in whom the Bear's power dwelled.

It was almost as though the combat was choreographed, each strike rhyming with the next, a poetry of violent battle and vicious anger. Their spears clanged together once, twice, thrice, roaring with the same intensity as the men wielding them. Each union of steel met with it a louder echo over the mountains, a shriek, a scream.

A thunderclap.

With the final clang, the gathering silenced, but Han'e and Fann continued, blind to their respective bloodlust for one another as they roared and screamed in conjunction with their strikes, neither man finding an advantage over the other.

Dread rose in Tez's heart as she looked past the crowd to the southern horizon, to where the attention of all others was drawn, no longer attentive to the virulent proceedings of the two men before them.

Han'e and Fann each aimed a vicious thrust at one another.

Han'e's found home in Fann's bad arm.

Fann planted his spear in Han'e's chest.

Han'e wavered on his feet, seemingly frozen, until Fann pushed the Sun Chief off of his spear, kicking him to the ground, meeting the earth with a thunderous thud.

With a cry of pain, Fann slowly pulled the spear out from his arm, throwing it to the ground and walking over to where Han'e's dying body lay.

"WHO'S THE WORM NOW, YOU BASTARD!" he screamed for all to hear, but none to pay attention to, as he brought his spear down again and again until someone grabbed his shoulder and diverted his focus to the southern horizon. Just barely, Tez could hear a strained gasp escape Fann's throat.

Tez shuddered as she caught sight of what seemed to be the full force of the Invaders' army, all standing at the southern entryway to the village.

At their head stood the man who killed her father.

CHAPTER FIFTEEN

POWDER AND STEEL

THE YEAR 1556 ANNO SALVATORIS
15 YEARS AFTER THE INVASION

The distant clamor had been silenced by a lone flintlock shot fired into the late afternoon sky. Sen could not be sure who had fired and for what reason, but she could see a plume of smoke dancing in the breeze some dozens of rows ahead.

It had taken her much of the day to catch up to the Acrarian march, longer still to situate herself amongst the throng rather than trailing at the back of the pack. She was unsure just how long she had been reviewing the remainder of Brin's stored Memories, but for however long it was, the Acrarians had long since breached the northern borders of the Forest and proceeded soundly into the as-yet unmolested north.

By the time Sen had returned, the peaks of the Heart had already stood tall against the horizon. Somewhere within that gathering of soldiers, within that nest of beasts readied to kill at a moment's notice, that madwoman waited. Kamataa had clearly *yearned* for what was soon to come.

Even as Sen pushed and shoved her way through the rows of Acrarians, much to the chagrin and confusion of those she shouldered past, she had no idea what she would do once she found the old Eclipseborn, or any of those she briefly considered her kin. She had seen none of them since yesterday's slaughter in the Forest, heard neither hide nor hair since her admonishment at Ziia's hands.

But along the marching wave of matching blue attire, Sen knew she had to find Kamataa. Find her and…then what?

Great plan as always, Sen, she had thought to herself. *Find her and gut her while a thousand Deatharms use your head as target practice. Stupid, stupid!*

Left to her thoughts for what seemed like hours as she pushed through the crowd, the one thing she knew for certain was that to demand of Kamataa that she cease this madness was futile; if not for the depraved state the Eclipseborn was in, then surely for the army in which Sen found herself, for reasons that she could no longer comprehend.

What would I even say to her? Stop? Why? How much is enough? None of it matters when I'm still standing on this side of it as well.

But by the time that lone shot fired into the air, and Sen had yet to find either Kamataa or any of the other Children of the Black Moon, she resigned herself to one task.

Find Tez and Mother. Explain it all later. Figure it out from there. She groaned under her breath. *Ugh, gods.*

When the procession stopped, Sen walked straight into the backside of some soldier she had no recollection of. Whoever it was, they paid her no mind whatsoever.

As the flintlock's echo faded into nothingness, so, too, did the uproar resounding across the unmarred plains of green before her. All Sen could hear was the distant clanging of steel, of spears meeting one another in a violent crescendo.

She peered her head around the shoulders and heads before her, standing on her toes as she tried to look ahead with morbid curiosity. She could see movement in the distance, but curiously…many who seemed not to be part of the Stone Tribe.

As she focused further on the scene, an immediately recognizable head floated by the front of the Acrarian pack. Seeming to glide along the gathering before Sen realized the man was riding atop a horse, she quickly felt a clammy chill run up her spine, palms damp, hands balling into fists. The image of her father falling to this man was permanently seared into her mind, like an old oaken tree crashing to the earth, blood raining in its wake.

She never thought she would be this close to General Aritz again, not since that night when she was forced into a game of cards with him, when she was later held back and forced to watch as this man upended everything she knew. Everything she had lost in the days since...it all went back to him.

I could end it all here, she thought. She felt for the flintlock still holstered along her thigh. *One shot is all it would take. If there was ever any good I could do for my people...*

But Aritz kept moving, the horse pacing back and forth along the front row, the general resting his own flintlock along his broad shoulders, his unkempt auburn hair bouncing with each subsequent trot. Sen flared her nostrils, her brow furrowing, knowing fully that between Aritz's constant pacing and the sea of heads separating him and her, not even all the Luck in the world would guide that shot through the man's brain. It still didn't make it easier to accept.

And besides that, a familiar voice roared in the distance, enough for Sen to redirect her attention back to the curious scene in her home village. The boorish bellow of *"WHO'S THE WORM NOW, YOU BASTARD!"* immediately recalled memories of Fann from their respective childhoods, and sure enough, as Sen craned her head around the sea of disinterested onlookers, she made out the image of Fann driving his spear up and down into the earth, an enormous gathering surrounding him but none paying him any mind whatsoever.

Sen furrowed her brow and quickly recognized, by virtue of customary attire, members of the Sun and Lake Tribes. *What...? What are they doing here? Wait...why...?*

Just as the confusion settled in regarding the presence of these two outland Tribes in such a number, Sen's eye caught the wealth of spears drawn, bows nocked, and, most importantly, blood that had been shed. She felt a tremor in her hand, a shaky breath escaping her agape mouth. *What's happened here? Why...what's going on?!*

Among the people of all present Tribes, some took tentative and hesitant steps forward, weapons drawn even as the expression of fear was visible even at this distance. Many were faces that Sen did not know, primarily those approaching who hailed from the Lake and Sun Tribes. Even a few survivors from the Wood Tribe stood shoulder to shoulder among this lot.

Whatever drew them here today, it was now irrelevant to them, apparently. With blood still staining their clothing, those cautious few became a fearful several became a courageous many.

Within those many, the faces of Sharrabha and Tawa stood out to Sen. Her heart leaped to see them still alive amidst all this, and just as quickly, it sank again.

Even Fann took those cautious steps forward, though it was clear he had taken some type of wound to the arm or shoulder; his bad arm dangled listlessly at his side, blood glistening along its length.

As her eyes fluttered across the approaching Tribal warriors, a panic set into her chest. A loud call in the Acrarian tongue roared in her ear, Aritz holding his flintlock high in the air. Her heart pounded as she looked from one end of the procession to the other, finding more faces she knew, but none among those were the ones she wanted to find.

Another shout. The flintlocks and rifles clicked into place.

Where's Tez? Where's Mother? Her breathing quickened, her chest catching fire, her head heavy. An enormous weight bore down upon her as she blinked away a well of panicked tears. She shoved her way forward, five rows from the front, four rows.

Aritz's hand remained raised, his horse trotting along the outer perimeter. Three rows now.

Aritz stood a dozen paces from the end of the row.

To the second row, where the initial wave of rifle fire was to originate before falling back a row.

Sen reached for her flintlock, her arm obstructed by the close quarters of the soldiers beside her, each of them looking upon her with a dirty look and some muttered foreign utterance that she assumed was equivalent to telling her to fuck off.

With a growl, Sen tried once more to force herself to the front.

Aritz reached the end of the row and shouted once more.

Sen could not sense anything beyond the plumes of smoke clouding her vision. The resultant thunderclaps deafened her to the point she could not hear her shrieks pleading for the wellbeing of her mother and sister.

The sound of the Deatharm volley was unlike anything Tez had ever heard. What felt like a thousand cracks of thunder sundering the earth immediately brought with it a heralding of instant death.

She put her hand to her mouth as many among the foolhardy charge fell to those monstrous weapons at the hands of those monstrous Invaders. Despite her protests, despite her desperate pleas to fall back and ready themselves properly, there was no getting through to those whose lives had been so drastically impacted and uprooted by the Invaders' arrival.

Even as their Chief Han'e lay dead upon the ground, the cause of his death debilitated by a wound suffered in the duel, the object of the Sun Tribe's rage now approached. Even depleted as they were from the previous fight, none were eager to back down as the Invaders aimed their deadly weapons.

For the handful of Wood fighters who accompanied Tez from the Lake village, it was a chance to avenge their people's near-extinction, the pain and insurmountable loss still a wound pulsating, the knife only just been withdrawn. Shadow stayed behind among the other yeomen of the various Tribes present, but those hapless few who stood to march clearly had but one goal in mind: for each Wood life lost, take from the Invaders ten more.

And though the Lake Tribe had yet to lose anything of substance to the Invaders, they were hard-pressed to refuse a fight, even in the face of insurmountable odds.

If anything, Tez wanted to run forward and hold Tawa and Sharrabha back. They were two she could not bear to lose, even after everything of the last week.

But though she screamed until her voice was hoarse, Tez could not hold them all back. She could not prevent their avoidable demises.

In an instant, a full row of Tribal warriors was hit. Many among the Sun Tribe appeared too stubborn to die and took the blows in stride, eager to plant their spears into the throats of the enemy. Some succeeded. Others left themselves open to the equestrian charge of Fannalhen's murderer, subjecting themselves either to trampling or a Deatharm blow to the skull.

Yet still, as plumes of smoke rose, the acrid smell mirroring the revolting sight, Tez found herself in awe of the persistence of her people. It took to the last moment, but before her, she saw a *union* of Tribes, fighting for one cause.

And when this ends, I'll look forward to putting Fann beneath the earth.

More and more people from the different Tribes rammed past Tez, discontent with allowing the action to unfold from afar and discontent with allowing the day to pass with a clean spear. It was enough for Tez to lose her balance, get knocked to the ground, kicked by charging passersby vengeful in the face of stupefying odds. Some feet found their way to her ribs, others to her face, still tender from the broken nose she received from Tol'e. Snarling, she raised an arm, knocking aside two people as she scrambled out of the way of the charging stampede.

She found her way over to a nearby hut, leaning against it as she sucked in a sharp breath, trying desperately to hiss away the pain in her side and face. She drew in her well of Endurance, and though the aches in her muscles quelled, the other aches remained. Endurance wasn't useful for mending broken bones; her nose still throbbed with pain, and she felt she had a cracked rib now, as well.

It gave her time to survey the field. It was immediately apparent that all semblance of order and tactics were thrown out the door. The spearmen, caught in what Tez assumed to be a cross between a mindless panic and a berserker rage, charged headlong at the Invaders, despite either falling in droves or ignoring the blows they had taken in order to take at least one Invader down with them. But to her shock, it seemed to be working to some degree.

The Invaders barely moved from their positions. They stood in long rows, too many for Tez to count all at once, but they worked in such a way that the pause between the thunderclaps from their Deatharms was but a few seconds. She remembered the time it took for the Invader to kill her father to reload the weapon, a multistep process that would take far too long when faced with a warrior skilled in the way of the spear, or even a competent yeoman.

But the way in which the Invaders managed this long process was…frightening. It was mercilessly efficient.

But her people were mercilessly resolute in defending what remained of their homes.

As volley after volley erupted from the field, Wolfsigns set their aims to a heavy arrow storm of their own. Though in poor position to efficiently loose a successful volley, hunters from all four Tribes present stood and knelt together, nocking their bows and launching their shots. On the receiving end of it all, Tez could see many Invaders take arrows to the face, the throat, the arm.

With the spear fighters acting as well enough a distraction, the Invaders had no opportunity to quell the Wolfsign yeomen with adequate attention.

Their lines were beginning to break ever so slightly, some breaking rank entirely to charge ahead.

Tez held out an arm, catching the Wolfsigns' attention. "They're out in the open!" she shouted. "Nock!"

Without sparing another second's glance, those hunters near her, some twenty or thirty yeomen, the Wood messenger Shadow among them, knelt and nocked their respective arrows.

"LOOSE!"

Another torrent of arrowheads descended from the skies, taking several hapless Invaders in stride, knocking them clumsily off their feet as they feebly attempted to remove the arrows from their bodies, some just meeting an end as a spearman happened to run by and finish the job with an unceremonious spear to the gut.

Tez's vision blurred, her head still a swirl from the pain. Part of her wanted desperately to charge among her brethren. But despite the numbers of Invaders falling, she was not blind to the rows upon rows following their departed comrades.

And despite that, there was still something she had to do.

"Shadow!" she shouted wearily, her voice a pained rasp.

The Wood hunter loosed another arrow before scampering over to Tez. "What is it?"

She clapped a hand on their shoulder. "Take charge here. I'll be back in a moment."

Shadow looked at her with suspicion, raising an eyebrow. "You're not deserting us, are you, Tezalhat?"

Her gait unsteady, Tez managed to shake her head, though it made her slightly more dizzy. "Not at all." She turned to the Chief's hut. "I'm just hoping there's a bear to set loose from her cage."

Spearheads jabbed past her as she desperately tried to force herself away from the front lines. Sen felt splashes of blood against her exposed skin as thrusts found home in the throats of those standing beside her. What once was a mild tingle coursing through her arms whenever her Luck triggered became a flaring sensation as arrows fell from the sky like hailstones, bludgeoning everything in their path, missing her entirely as though they redirected their own trajectory, instead finding a target in the ostensible comrades surrounding her.

Sen looked to every side around her. From behind, rows upon rows upon rows of Acrarians stood in wait, rifles and pistols at the ready, all still as stone as they each awaited their opportunity to join the fray. To her right and left, the Acrarian soldiers settled into their rhythm of loading, aiming, firing, reloading, the eruption of powder having deafened her so much that they had no more the auditory impact on her than a pebble falling to the ground.

And to her front, the wall of furious Bearsigns, spears thrusting and slashing, blood spilling upon the unforgiving earth, Acrarians and Tribespeople falling in death just as soon as they dealt death to one another.

And all the while, Aritz charged along on his horse, leading a cavalry of those he apparently trusted enough with steeds of their own, trampling those in their way. A sickening smile was visible upon the general's face in performing the act. At one point, Sen thought she could see him laughing.

She had to get away from all this. Against the spears and raining arrows, the Acrarians lacked the advantage they held in the confined quarters of the Forest. In the open air, they were more vulnerable to the incoming volleys—but by the same token, they held the same deadly hand. Their own volleys were unimpeded by obstructive trees, and here, they could deal death with the same reckless abandon that Sen had seen before.

In witnessing the falling bodies from so far away, it was as though she was experiencing Narva's death all over again.

Her hands shook, even as she continued to hold firmly to her flintlock, despite doing little else but just that. The intensity of the approaching Bear-signs was growing too much for the front lines. Their firing routine was more than adequate when faced with a foe from afar, but with no close-quarters weapons at their disposal, the soldiers were left with little else between volleys than to attempt to bludgeon the incoming Tribal warriors with the butt end of their rifles.

Seeing the futility of such a maneuver did push a slight smile to Sen's face. *Our greatest warriors have fought wild beasts with their bare hands,* she thought. *What hope do you all have against that?* But as the front lines broke and the spearmen entered the throng of soldiers, she immediately realized, *And what hope do I have right now?*

From the foreign commands to either side of her, it appeared the Acrarians had the same thought. Their lines broke, the steady and calculating slaughter at the hands of the Deatharms being reduced to an exposed, rampant, and frazzled display. As Sen pushed her way to the ranks further back, she saw some soldiers pulling out their flintlock pistols, perhaps hoping the smaller weapon would be at all an assistance in these tight quarters. The shots from the surrounding guns buzzed as a dull roar in Sen's ears. Acrarians and Tribal fighters collapsed together, the forward momentum of the latter carrying them into the former even as the fatal blows hit. Rows of Acrarians tumbled, a great wall crumbling to bits, a breach exposed in a great defensive position.

Out from that breach poured a stream of spearmen, bottlenecked into one position as many saw the same opportunity to reach the outer flanks of the Acrarian wall. Horseriders trotted along the perimeter, rifles pinning down the Bearsigns attempting to breach; with each shot, they cantered past and along to the front lines, trying to relieve the felled soldiers of the mass converging upon them, many either oblivious to or disinterested in the arrow volleys still peppering the battlefield, some themselves falling to the rain, others finding themselves thrown to the ground as their mount was speared from beneath them, leading either to their own trampling or instead a fatal spear blow as they lay broken in the mud.

Sen wedged herself between several Acrarians much taller and broader than herself, her own personal shield from the Tribal counterstrike. From this vantage point, she could see those who survived the breach defense running along the perimeter, spears drawing the trailing rows of riflemen out of position, goading them to abandon their posts and draw them out.

Whether it was due to a lust for battle or a sense of duty, the ploy worked. Sen could feel the rear rows shift position, a disjointed and chaotic formation where several rifles pointed off to the side, disrupting the standard flow. A separate bottleneck seemed to be forming from the rear, an onslaught of advancing soldiers attempting to funnel out into one section of the field.

What Sen assumed to be objecting screams fell on deaf ears (literally and figuratively) as the organized rows began to twist and knot amongst each other. The Bearsigns fought their way through the second breach created by the break in formation. Half the soldiers surrounding Sen about-faced, turning the rifles in the trailing direction, inadvertently aimed squarely at their own comrades while spearmen cut a swath through a disoriented cadre. The other half retained their attention dead ahead, maintaining a watchful eye on the continued influx of approaching Bearsigns. The cavalrymen continued to shout from atop horseback, even as arrows rained down upon them or their horses in their inattentiveness.

Before long, the organized and deliberate army devolved into a chaotic and freeform mob. Frustration was boiling within those around Sen, evident from the snarling aims and growled orders that broke the former wall of merciless and indiscriminate bloodlust that had adorned their faces while amongst the Wood Tribe.

Sen ducked under the barrels of the aimed rifles, feeling the sensation in her arms flare once again as another volley landed around her in the throng, taking many a confused soldier in the neck or head. Dipping and diving out of the way of gunfire and spear thrusts alike, Sen pushed her way toward the breach created by the Bearsign offensive, mud kicking up all over her trousers, blood spattering against her face.

The sensation in her arms would not quell. Angry hands would grasp at her shirtsleeves; whether they were Acrarian or Tribal hands, she could not be certain; but more often than not, those hands would quickly lose strength and grip just as soon as they touched her. At one point, she walked into the line of sight of a rifle about to fire, only for the weapon to backfire and disarm the attacking soldier instead. Arrows continued to pepper the field, soldiers falling in waves as the sharp rain spared nothing.

When Sen finally reached the breach, her legs nearly gave out, the open air refreshing and reinvigorating despite the stagnation and stench of death which pervaded it. She rolled to a clearing, the mud below covering her uniform top in a thick layer of muck. Sweat poured down her neck, her skin glistening with a thick sheen, the chain of the Illusion pendant providing a stark dissonance between the heat of her body and the divine chill that ran through the ornament. Her hands continued to tremor, her legs still weak, and despite the rain of arrows precipitating down toward her, she could not will herself to move. As the flare of Luck persisted in her arms, the volley landed about her in a perfect circle. Still disbelieving, she looked up to the sky, finding the Moon peering out from the horizon. All Sen could do was shake her head.

A faint snarl was audible enough to catch her attention. A Bearsign, Lake Tribe from the man's appearance, charged at her, seeing her open and unguarded. Sen holstered her pistol and rolled out of the way of the initial thrust. She ducked beneath a second swing designed to open her throat before grasping the shaft as it passed by her head in another attempted killing blow. Fighting for the spear was enough to distract the Bearsign from the bullet passing through his skull from behind, blood splashing on Sen's face and into her mouth.

In a panic, she spat out what she was sure was brain matter, nearly retching at the thought. Whoever helped her in her struggle had already returned to the throng by the time she was able to look up.

"You're not gonna let me go, are you?" she muttered, looking back to rising Moon. As she again found a steady footing, she held her trembling hand and slowly started walking toward the village. She paid no heed whatsoever to the battle around her, either side of it. Luck did not leave her, no matter how many steps toward the village she took. The Moon would allow her this much, it seemed.

She spared no glance to the throng of battle behind her. She had no interest in playing a part in the Acrarian offensive. She had not the willpower to stand and die among those who would long have celebrated her death.

But there was still one place she could go. One place that, despite it all, despite everything she had learned, she was still willing to die for.

As she eyed her destination, she was relieved to see that whatever prior conflict precipitated battle and death in the village square had dissipated.

But it had also cleared enough for her to see someone in a blue uniform on their way to the same place as she was.

When Tez burst through the door to the Chief's hut, she fully expected to find armed resistance within. Despite the jolt of pain in her rib as she barreled through, she stood with spear drawn, ready to meet the challenge of anyone who dared oppose her. She put the persistent din of battle behind her, the unceasing firing of Deatharms and the clash of steel nothing but a backdrop as she focused her attention on what awaited her inside.

But though she steeled herself to face an armed guard or two upon entry into the Chief's hut, into the hut she called home for twenty-six years...

She found it empty.

The central room stood whisper-quiet. The meeting pyre had been reduced to nothing, as though it hadn't been lit in some time. When Tez carefully walked up to examine it, she didn't even find any smoldering embers within. She narrowed her gaze, surveying every inch of the room for a trace of someone hiding in the shadows, but just as she thought, it was completely empty.

Perplexed, she walked back to the door to shut it, but as the wood met the frame, she heard a stifled gasp from one of the back rooms, from the direction of her parents' room. She drew her spear back to attention, not bothering to shut the door the rest of the way, knowing fully that whatever dwelt in that room was already made aware of her forced entry.

Slowly, Tez made her way to the back, her footsteps light and careful, her spear leading the way in front of her. As the tip broke the threshold and peered into her parents' room, the stifled murmurs became more frantic and panicked. Tez gritted her teeth and quickly sidled around the corner, immediately holding her spear in an offensive position, ready to strike at the first provocation.

She didn't expect to see her mother coddling a despondent Koelhe.

Tez's eyes widened, her spear lowering to the ground. She couldn't believe the sight. First of all, her mother. Regardless of the bandage wrapped tightly around her thigh where Ran had stuck Koelhe's knife, Dennalhir looked to be in great shape, unperturbed by these days in captivity, the cuts and bruises lining her face and arms likely more a product of the battle the night of Koelhe's coup.

But for Koelhe, it seemed the woman had lost herself entirely. Her gaze was unfocused, her eyes wide with terror. Her cheeks were marred with fresh claw marks, four to each side; her fingertips were stained red. Her long grey hair was undone entirely, thin wisps falling in front of her face like a poorly constructed mask. She rocked back and forth in a fetal position, leaning into Dennalhir's comforting embrace but still emitting a choked and stifled series of gasps.

Tez looked back and forth to each woman. Her mother looked up at her with a warm smile that didn't quite reach her eyes; between whatever *this* was and the proceedings outside, there was not much to smile about in earnest. "M...Mother?" Tez said with hesitation, loath to withdraw her spear.

Dennalhir stared at her for a few silent moments, the smile on her face slowly disappearing. "Tez, what happened to your face?" she asked.

Tez raised an unamused eyebrow but felt a throb of pain pulsating from the bridge of her nose in so doing. She put two fingers to the wound, the blood still slick upon her fingertips. "It's that bad, huh?"

"Only if whoever did it to you is still alive."

Tez offered a tentative chuckle. "No. He's not." *Nor is the man who killed him.* She wanted desperately to run to her mother, fall into her arms. She was beyond relieved that she still lived. Beyond relieved that she was unharmed. But as she looked about the room, her eyes always finding their way back to Koelhe, she could not bring herself to do so. "Mother, what is this?" She gestured toward Koelhe. "What...what's going on here?"

Dennalhir shut her eyes and sighed. "Did you know that it had been years, perhaps *decades*, since Koelhe made use of her Foresight?"

Tez propped her spear against the wall and sat cross-legged before her mother. She furrowed her brow. "No, I didn't. Why? Was it..."

Her mother offered a half-hearted nod. "When visions of your sister did not herald the destruction she so adamantly wished to see, she stopped using Foresight altogether, throwing away entirely the charge that the Owl had bestowed upon her. I don't know if her obsessive madness was a curse put upon her by the Owl. All I know for certain is that from that moment on, she became...well, the person you know now."

There was a pregnant pause. Tez looked at the Futureseer, realized that she was hardly cognizant of the words being spoken about her. *She's not said a word since I arrived*, she thought. She pointed a finger at Koelhe and then raised an eyebrow toward her mother. "Then, what's this? Did she tap into it again, or...?"

"At my urging, yes, but..." Dennalhir grimaced and bit her bottom lip. She tried to remove Koelhe from her comforting embrace, but the motion sent the other woman into a swirling panic, clawing absently for Dennalhir to hold her once more. "I didn't anticipate this to be the result."

"I don't understand. This shouldn't happen...right? The Deities wouldn't bestow their Boons upon us if they intended them to harm us...right?"

Again, her mother paused, taking an extended look at the sordid state Koelhe was in. "Remember, Futureseers are exceedingly rare. Perhaps the Owl only wants a select few to know what the future holds for us all. Perhaps there are some things we're not meant to see. We couldn't possibly understand the full depths of them. But, still...I urged Koelhe to look ahead, to be able to say with confidence that we need not worry about the Invaders' arrival. She was so quick to dismiss all of it. Little did I know what seeing all of this death and destruction would do to her. That she prepared for nothing, that she was so engrossed in pitting us all together that she cared nothing for what was next to come. And now the consequences have arrived. Seeing it all just seemed to...destroy her."

Tez leaned forward expectantly. "Is it...inevitable, then? What did she see? Can we...?" She trailed off, eyes drifting away. A deep pit began to form in her stomach.

Dennalhir shook her head. "I don't know. It was quick, her turning to this." She gestured toward Koelhe, a pang of regret and anger visible upon her face. "It's not for me to say what comes next, and it was apparently not for me to know. She could not even get a word of it out before she was reduced to incomprehensible wailing."

She withdrew her arms and pushed herself gingerly up to her feet, wincing as she put weight on her wounded leg. As she sucked in a sharp breath and walked a handful of steps away, Koelhe reached up and screamed, seemingly unaware of her surroundings, unaware of just what was supporting her but distraught nonetheless of her removal from it.

"I simply never thought I would see her reduced to this," Dennalhir said, her arms crossed.

Tez rose to her feet, looking down at the mindless shell that was once Koelhe. "Am I meant to feel sorrow for her, Mother?"

Dennalhir remained silent beyond the vocal winces resulting from the wound in her thigh. Tez could see both stained and fresh shades of red in the bandage.

"It's not up to me to tell you what to feel, Tez," she said. "But I would advise that you do not celebrate *this*, at the very least."

Tez narrowed her eyes at the still-screaming Koelhe, shaking her head at the woman. "I'll not celebrate this. But I won't mourn it, either. Maybe this is what remorse feels like for her. I'd be surprised if she's ever felt it before. But regardless, she at last has come to terms with the consequences of her actions. She has turned our Tribe against itself, and now we face what we have always feared to face." She turned away and walked over to her spear, glaring at the gleaming steel, seeing shades of her reflection past the stains of red. "I'll not celebrate this, but I also won't deny that this selfish and misguided idiot is finally suffering what she deserves to suffer."

A deep sigh escaped Dennalhir's lips. "Tez, I don't--"

Sharply, Tez turned around, gripping the shaft of her spear. "And what about you, Mother?"

Dennalhir raised an eyebrow.

"We don't know what's coming next. But you told me just a few nights ago that we stand as we stand, and if we fall, we will do so on our feet rather than our knees." She walked over and put a firm hand on her mother's shoulders, ignoring the pain shooting through her side. "Fuck Koelhe right now. Let her scream in horror until her voice is forever gone. If we survive this night, we will worry about her then. But for now, we have a battle to win and Invaders to kill. Nothing else matters."

Her mother chuckled despite Koelhe's desperate screams.

"What is it?" Tez asked pointedly.

Quickly, Dennalhir shook her head in dismissal. "It's nothing. You...for the briefest moment, you were the spitting image of your father. So ready to stand and fight—and if need be, die—for our people. I could hear the clamor outside, the war cries of the Lake Tribe. That you managed to bring them here is just..." She trailed off, choking back another chuckle, wiping away a single tear. "Your father would have been proud of you this day, Tez. As proud as I am of you. You're the leader our people will need one day when this all ends. However it ends."

Tez sucked in a sharp breath, damming up emotions of her own. "Then I guess I'll need to be sure to make it through all of this, won't I?"

Dennalhir smiled, turning back to grab one of Fannalhen's spears from along the wall, a noticeable limp in her stride. She held the weapon with both hands. "And still, your father will be fighting with us today."

Tez primed herself to respond, but Koelhe's shrieks reached a zenith as she desperately reached for someone, *anyone*, to take her hand. Instead, Tez rolled her eyes, walked up to the woman, and bashed the butt end of her spear into Koelhe's forehead.

The Futureseer was immediately silent.

Looking back to her mother, Tez gestured with her arms and said, "I trust you have no further objections?"

Dennalhir stifled a laugh and gently shook her head. With a deep breath, she steeled herself and walked over to Tez, clapping a hand on her shoulder. "So, what's the plan here?"

Tez shrugged. "Fight. Don't die."

"And now you're the spitting image of your sister."

"She and I always were cut from the same cloth. Now, let's go."

As they made their way back into the central meeting room, though, a woman sporting an Invader uniform sat beside the fire pit, a Deatharm drawn across her lap. She rose to her feet, holding the short weapon casually at her side, a sly smile creasing her lips. A spattering of blood stained the blue fabric of her uniform jacket as short curls of auburn hair descended down her cheek, loosely tied at her broad shoulders. She took a handful of steps forward, keeping a hand wrapped around her weapon, and stared expectantly at Tez and Dennalhir.

Tez held an arm out in front of her mother, barring her from moving forward, and held her spear out with the other arm, ready to strike at the right moment.

The Invader shook her head, her smile growing wider. "Now, now, there's no need for that," she said in a perfect Tribal accent and dialect.

Tez's eyebrows shot upwards, ignoring the sharp pain in her nose even as her eyes watered. "Who the hell are you?" she demanded.

The woman began pacing back and forth, her posture still as casual as ever. She shrugged. "You wouldn't believe me if I told you, but I suppose *seeing* is believing, after all."

She reached beneath her shirt and pulled out a pendant, a bright glimmer emanating from its center. Tez's eyes widened as she recognized just what it was. Not just any pendant.

A *Tribal* pendant.

The rune dimmed to nothing, and suddenly the Invader's appearance changed. No longer was she the spitting image of so many of those Invaders fighting and killing indiscriminately out in the field. No, now her appearance grew much older, her face sporting a canvas of deep-set wrinkles, her hair stark white, fastened at the neck in a long braid.

She was of the Tribes. And of the Stone Tribe, at that.

Tez readjusted the grip on her spear, adopting a position much more suited to an imminent battle. "What's a Tribeswoman doing carousing with the Invaders?"

The Stone woman chuckled to herself, walking about in place quite spryly for someone her age. To Tez's eyes, she was ancient.

"You'd be quite surprised, the number of us who stand among those you call the 'Invaders.' Alas, you narrow yourselves to your own limited purview."

Tez scoffed. "Why would one of our kin consign themselves to their own destruction?"

"Don't be so naïve. The Lake Tribe have reveled in their own self-destruction for centuries. And, if I am not mistaken, *your* Tribe had just found itself in the throes of battle against its own, did it not?"

"We fight amongst our own. That happens. Humans do that," Tez said bluntly. "What you're siding with, it's destroying our entire way of life. It's genocide!"

The woman stopped, flashed a furrowed brow toward Tez. "And the Tribes are not guilty of the same? Do the Tribes not cry havoc and wish death upon those among them? You're not so different from those you call the 'Invaders' as you may think."

"You talk of the Eclipseborn." Dennalhir stepped forward before Tez could interject.

The woman smiled. "And you must be the Chief of the Stone Tribe."

Tez narrowed her eyes. "Technically, the current 'Chief' is mindless and unconscious in the back room, but my mother is the rightful Chief, yes."

"Irrelevant," the woman said. She turned back to Tez's mother. "You must be Dennalhir, then."

"How do you know who I am?" Dennalhir asked, holding out her spear.

"When you've been around for as long as I, the names and titles grow meaningless, but you learn them all the same." The glint in her eyes grew malicious, her smile now more bared teeth than anything else. "And, of course, I've heard plenty of tales of you, Dennalhir, of you and your husband both. And especially of your husband's...'untimely' death. I've heard much of that recently."

Tez watched her mother's nostrils flare.

"Who are you?" Dennalhir demanded. "What is it you want?"

The woman began to laugh, doubling over at the bluntness of the question. "Well, *who* I am is surely of little consequence to you, I promise you. But *what*

I am, I'm sure you're wholly familiar with. After all, it was the very reason for your own demise, was it not, Dennalhir?"

Dennalhir grumbled beneath her breath. "You're Eclipseborn."

"I'm a Child of the Black Moon, yes. I believe you're altogether familiar with them. I've grown ever so acquainted with dear Sennalhat, after all."

Tez's ears perked at the mention of Sen's name. She leveled her spear. "What have you done with my sister? Where is she?!"

The woman waved a hand dismissively. "You see, I was born to this Tribe, long ago," she said, ignoring Tez's question entirely. "But much the same as Sennalhat, I was reviled, denounced, defiled, merely for the fact that my mother birthed me during the Eclipse. It was nothing I had control over, and I was labeled a curse just the same! Of course, I needn't inform you of that, no? I am certain you're both all too familiar with the concept."

"We treated my sister no differently than anyone else," Tez asserted.

"Oh, yes, I'm sure *you* did. But what of the rest of this sorry lot? Gussy it up all you like, but the very reason your Tribe took up arms against one another was *because* of your sister, no?"

"How would you know that?" Dennalhir said. "It happened mere days ago."

"The proceedings of Tribal society grow predictable after centuries of observation," the woman said. "One foot follows the other. Panic begets violence. The Eclipseborn is blamed for it without reason. And so it goes, on and on."

"It was *not* by our choice that Sen was treated that way," Tez said. She shook her head. "And we fight to unite our people again, and that is *including* the Eclipseborn. Don't lump us in with the same hateful lot you love to blame for the pain you've been forced to endure."

The words didn't seem to reach the woman. She feigned a brief smile before settling into a frown. "And...what of the banished folk? The ones who did not complete their Trials? What of them? Have you forgotten them?"

Tez and Dennalhir both flashed confused looks, their brows furrowing.

"Hmm, yes, I thought as much. Unfortunately, I must inform you that 'all' means 'all,' not just those you deem convenient. I wonder, Dennalhir. If you had a child who failed their Trial, would you have given them the same preferential treatment as you did Sennalhat? They are meant to be discarded from the Tribe, never to be seen again. Would you break customs just the same as you did with your Eclipseborn daughter, simply because it is within your power to do so as Chief?"

Dennalhir hesitated with her answer, and before she could say anything, the woman laughed again.

"And *there* you have it," she said. "Hypocrisy. Were it any other child, you would dispose of them just the same. How convenient. Do not deny yourselves how alike you are to the 'Invaders.' You commit much the same crimes; you only do not view them as crimes because you yourselves are not the victims."

"You know nothing about us," Dennalhir asserted.

"Oh, I know *plenty*. I know that I have longed for the destruction of the Stone Tribe for centuries. I know that I have bided my time, waiting for the right moment and the right method to do so. I know that the Acrarians offered the greatest opportunity for me to walk about the ashen remains that you will leave when you are gone. I know that I am happy to see this day finally come, to play a personal part in this final act of a sinful people." She held out her Deatharm, clicking back the clip at her thumb. "And I know that I'm going to *enjoy* this. Very...very...much."

A second click echoed behind the woman, followed by quiet footsteps.

"And *I* know that you are taking a step too far, Ziia." A second Invader entered the hut, circling around the woman called Ziia, dressed in much the same regalia but absolutely covered in mud, blood, and filth. None of the blood or filth seemed to be her own.

Tez's ears perked at the voice.

Ziia tsked her lips, not even averting her gaze from Tez and Dennalhir, but still leveling her Deatharm at them, regardless. "And so, the mask is removed for all to see. How disappointing."

The second woman settled in beside Ziia, her own Deatharm aimed squarely at Ziia's head. "This mask was a poor fit. I'm much more content with the face the world already reviles." She reached beneath her shirt, revealing another glimmering pendant, the rune's glow dimming to a dull flicker before at last extinguishing. With a sharp yank, the chain broke loose, bits of it clattering unceremoniously upon the ground. As the image of the battle-weary Invader vanished, the pendant was tossed aside, meeting the floor with a resounding thud.

Tez felt her breath catching when the face re-formed into that of one she had known her entire life.

"Sen?"

If Ziia were to have pressed her attack then, Tez would have been entirely defenseless. She stood with mouth agape, eyes fixed on her sister with complete and utter shock. *Why...is she with the Invaders?*

Beside Tez, their mother was utterly speechless. Dennalhir covered her mouth with a shaking hand, eyes quivering as though fighting back tears, though if they were of relief or anger, Tez could not say with any confidence.

Ziia looked at Sen from the corner of her eye, an expression of complete bemusement stretching across her face. "I must admit, Sennalhat, I am surprised you decided to join us today. A shame that you could not let go of it all as we hoped. Now you'll just have to perish alongside the rest of your people."

Sen shook her head, though it did not particularly invoke any confidence in Tez as she did so. Her eyes were wide and unfocused, her arm unsteady as she held out the Deatharm. But she snarled with the same intensity she would display whenever faced with one of Fann's outbursts. "I'm not laying down my life for the madness you've sided with, Ziia. I've lost enough because of you, because of Aritz, because of the Invaders. If I lose my life standing against you all, then that will be enough. At least I would die with a cleaner conscience."

Ziia dropped her arm, turning toward Sen. "Oh, the moral high road, is it?" She glanced at Dennalhir, gesturing a thumb at Sen. "I must congratulate you for raising such a morally upstanding daughter, Dennalhir. Aren't you proud that she can now die with a clean conscience?"

Dennalhir said nothing, her hands grinding against the shaft of her spear. Tez could feel the anger radiating off of her.

"Look around you, Sennalhat. What you thought was home is soon to be reduced to nothing. Aritz's army will crush your Tribe until it's naught but mere pebbles. You were witness to our great victory against that savage Wood Tribe. You saw it all unfold."

"I saw," Sen said, her hand still wavering. "But I did not participate."

"Didn't you?" Ziia raised an eyebrow, walking toward Sen until she was standing right against the barrel of her Deatharm.

Sen didn't answer. What appeared to be shame colored her face.

"Sen?" Tez said hesitantly, inclining her head toward her sister. "What did you...?"

"Oh-ho!" Ziia exclaimed, turning swiftly to Tez and Dennalhir with arms outstretched, almost dancing in the motion. "Would you like to know? How easily Sennalhat fell into our lap? How easily swayed she was to commit to the destruction of the Tribes? Toss a couple deaths at her feet, add in a touch of personal betrayal, and how quickly she was to jump at the chance for a new family, new kin, a new *Tribe*! Oh, Sennalhat, how eager you were to find a new home with your fellow Eclipseborn! It was what you were meant to be part of! We knew it, you knew it, *she* knew it. But alas, you saw fit to toss it aside, and for what? A quick death because you feel it makes you morally superior? Absurd."

Tez didn't know what to say. She dropped her hands, the spear falling out of an attacking position, and she stood in silence, waiting expectantly for her sister to decry it as a falsehood.

Sen narrowed her eyes. "'She.' I presume you mean Kamataa. Where is she?"

Ziia laughed giddily, turning her attention back to Sen. "Oh, how it will shatter Kama's heart to see you abandon us all. She truly wished the best for you, you know."

"Where. Is. She?" Sen repeated, steadying her arm, her weapon no longer wavering.

Putting her hands back on her hips, Ziia craned her head and hummed with consideration. "Hmm, perhaps it's not some loose concept of morality you're trying to preach, is it? You had another reason for staying along with us. You want to kill her, don't you?" A sinister smile stretched across her lips.

Snarling, Sen stepped closer to Ziia. "Answer me, Ziia."

"But first, tell me, Sennalhat. What do you believe will happen should you manage to kill her? Does all of this suddenly...stop? Do you think Aritz will stop because just one of his soldiers was killed? I'm sure you've realized by now that he does not care for the lives of those beneath him."

A subtle, shaking breath escaped Sen's lips, her whole body tremoring. "I don't care," she said, her voice soft, yet sharp. "I don't care that it will change nothing. She...tricked me. She...she..." Sen trailed off, wiping away tears with the back of her wrist. From the expression on her face, Tez could not discern if they were sad or angry tears. "She took Narva from me." Her voice broke.

Tez's breath caught in her throat. *Narva? Oh, gods, no.*

Sen's face contorted, displaying a full array of emotions. Her eyes flared, her mouth a quivering frown. "She took Brin from me."

The words almost sounded muted to Tez. She leaned forward, hoping that what she thought she heard was untrue. Beside her, their mother choked back a sob, her hand covering her mouth as she dropped the spear to the ground. In a panic, Tez did just the same, allowing her weapon to clack against the floor as she put a comforting hand on Dennalhir's shoulder, her eyes wide with shock, words unable to come to her mouth.

Sen continued to stare at Ziia, and their expressions could not be more opposite. For Sen, it was a clear onslaught of emotions, trying to maintain an air of strength despite the words clearly tearing at her to say in front of her remaining family. But for Ziia, she delighted in the sight, a gleeful smile strewn across her face as though deriving great enjoyment from Sen's distress and despair.

"You think...that I would stand by that monster?" Sen growled. "After what she took from me? After what she did to the people of the Wood Tribe. No." Furiously, she shook her head. "She will die by my hand if it's the last thing I do. Answer me, Ziia. Where is she?" A moment of silence stretched on. "WHERE IS SHE?"

The anger in Sen's tone took Tez entirely by surprise. Her heart nearly jumped out of her chest.

All Ziia did was laugh and gesture nondescriptly to the door. "She's somewhere out there, of course, fighting with everybody else. If you want to go and find her, then be my guest, Sennalhat. But once you fail in that, she will move along with the rest of Aritz's army deep into the Heart, all the way into the True Heart, and she'll strike down the gods where they stand. In the end, it won't matter where *you* stand, for everyone around you shall fall! Have you ever wondered what will happen in those critical moments when one of the gods breathes its last? Oh-ho, it will be such a sight to behold."

Sen clicked her Deatharm once more, holding it steady toward Ziia's face. "I won't allow that to happen."

Ziia scoffed, flashing a bemused smile and unearthing a hearty smile. "Sennalhat, I don't give a fuck what you allow." Her arm shot out, and she aimed her Deatharm back at Tez and Dennalhir, not breaking her line of sight with Sen.

A loud bang echoed in Tez's ears, her eyes clamping shut. She could hear a body falling to the ground, something clattering along the floor.

When she opened her eyes again, Ziia lay dead on the ground, the walls backsplashed with blood and viscera. A trail of smoke wafted from Sen's weapon as she continued to hold it out, her face seemingly in shock at what she just did. For a long series of moments, Sen just stood there in sullen silence, her arm eventually falling to the side, the weapon hanging listlessly in her hand.

Tez shook her mother to attention, and they both rose back to their feet, staring at Sen with hesitation after what they had just seen, what they had just heard. As she approached her sister with caution, Tez reached out and put her hand on Sen's shoulder, keeping her at an arm's length. "Sen?" she said softly. She inclined her head toward her sister, raising an eyebrow. "Are you okay?"

Sen broke from her trance, depositing the Deatharm to its holster, and slowly made eye contact with Tez. She didn't say anything, but she absently nodded her head.

Tez stared at Ziia's lifeless body, a puddle of blood pooling from beneath her withered head. "Was she...the first for you?" She looked at her sister expectantly. "Your first...you know."

Grimacing, Sen closed her eyes, drawing a deep breath. "The first who deserved it."

Dennalhir filed in beside them, though it was clear that she knew not what to say.

"What really happened, Sen?" Tez asked, still holding tightly to her sister's shoulder. "Was she telling the truth?"

Sen looked at Tez for a long moment before nudging her hand away from her shoulder, gently pushing past her and their mother. She walked toward their bedroom, to the three beds that seemed to have not permitted anyone to sleep in ages. She fell to her knees at the threshold of the room, leaning against the frame.

"Does it matter right now?" she said in a whisper, barely audible. "I...I couldn't save him. I couldn't do it. I tried, and I...I failed. I..."

Tez looked to her mother and nodded, and they both walked beside Sen, holding her in a soft embrace. Each of them sobbed softly as they found a warmth in each other's arms, staring intermittently between themselves and the empty bedroom.

"I'm sorry," Sen said meekly, her voice breaking. "I wish I could bring him back, but I failed. It was my fault, and now he's gone forever, and now everything is—"

Dennalhir hushed her, taking her head in her hands and caressing the long braided locks like she used to do to both of her daughters when they were young. "You're still here, Sen," she said. "The three of us are all who remain. And if these are our final moments, then we'll share them together as a family."

Tez watched Sen look back up, her eyes red and puffy with tears, and took hold of her trembling hands. The battle continued to rage outside, the resounding echo of Deatharms still pounding the horizon. She had no idea of which side held the advantage. But for now, she was content to share this final serene scene between the three of them. Once they stepped out that door and back onto the field of battle, she knew that everything would change.

She looked to the door with hesitation. "Are you all ready?" she asked.

They each rose to their feet. Sen wiped away the streams from her eyes, then took hold of the muddied uniform jacket and tore it off, the threads coming completely undone with ease. She threw it aside, leaving her with little else but a thin shirt and trousers covered in muck, reached down and pulled the Deatharm from the holster on her thigh, gulping down what may have been her final shred of apprehension, and looked to the door.

There were no words necessary. Tez and Dennalhir retrieved their spears from where they dropped them, and they walked as a family to the fading light outside. Past that threshold, the sun was waning, the golden hues of the battlefield disappearing for another evening, as if this village and this Tribe could even look forward to another golden hour. Tez broke the plane first, stepping into the stagnant air, rife with the stench of blood and death, and looked to the fields to the south where the chaos of battle still raged.

Sen and Dennalhir settled in beside her, and as they shared one final glance at one another, they raised their weapons high, bellowing with all their might, and took off running toward the fight. Tez damned the pain that pulsed from her side with each heavy step, regardless of how much Endurance she drew in. She didn't care. There would be plenty of time not to worry about pain in the Otherworld. This, this shared moment of steel, would be a worthwhile final memory to share with Father and Brin when they saw them shortly.

Arrows rained down over the throng of battle as it had since the Invaders arrived. But something prompted Tez to stop, the volley seeming unnatural to her. At her slowing, her mother and sister followed suit, staring at her with curiosity.

"What, Tez?" her mother said, still holding her spear out toward the crowd some two hundred paces away.

Tez closed her eyes and listened. For the first minute, it was hard for anything to drown out the persistent thunderclap of the Deatharms, even as the volleys became more sporadic and desperate. But as Tez held out a hand and put a finger to her lips, she couldn't help but feel a smile oncoming. "Listen," she said.

Faintly, a rhythmic, unified voice echoed over the western horizon. Tez inclined her head in that direction, and out from the backdrop of the setting sun, there emerged another hail of arrows, dense and powerful enough to cast the entire world in shadow.

Tez whooped and jumped in place as the approaching force came into greater view, their voices within clearer earshot. An undulating, persistent chant sundered the fields, the voices announcing the arrival of reinforcements with such pomp and circumstance that even those among the fighting throng in the mud and muck could be heard cheering.

Running up to the nearest grassy dune, Tez planted her spear in the ground and hollered to the approaching force, finding familiar faces at the head of the pack.

Even silhouetted, it was hard to mistake the tall form of Yhaan for anyone else, and it was equally difficult to identify the person beside him as anyone other than Tenazt. Behind the two Lake Chiefs, the Arrow Tribe spread out, bows drawn, and out from the setting sun erupted yet another volley, their accuracy unmatched as it seemed only the Invaders were the ones on the receiving end of the strikes, even as Tribal warriors remained entangled in the throng.

Within a handful of volleys, the Invaders turned tail and departed to the south, leaving behind all their dead as though they mattered not at all.

The Tribes did not give chase, instead opting to raise their spears and bows and triumph and howl and roar to the skies, invoking the gods from which they drew their power. The air came alive with the feeling of hope, and despite the Arrow Tribe's late arrival, they celebrated just the same.

Tez sat herself down upon the hills overlooking the battlefield and stared in silence for a length of time she could not be sure of. The sun had long since set, the warriors returned to the Stone village with raucous voices proclaiming a tremendous victory, and stories were already being shared with the fellow survivors of the great travails of the day.

But despite it all, Tez did not find herself in a mood to celebrate, even with the opportunity to fight another day. She did not expect company, but she was pleased to see Sen had found her way to her, sitting beside her.

Tez knew not how to address the matter of her sister arriving alongside the Invaders. For her part, Sen seemed in no rush to divulge.

Instead, they shared a companionable silence for some time until Tez finally asked, "Do you think she was telling the truth?"

Sen plucked at a few blades of grass, flicking them back and forth. "You mean Ziia about the gods?" She scoffed. "Oh yes, I do."

Tez's eyes widened at the bluntness of the answer. She didn't turn to face her sister. "I'll expect a full explanation for everything later. But for now...this isn't a time to celebrate."

"I agree," Sen said, her voice rasping. "I've seen too many lives lost for this. I don't want to see any more. We can't sit on our hands here. The Deities need to be protected."

Tez closed her eyes, trying not to think about the implications. But behind her eyelids, she could not help but see an impending firestorm.

"It's time to go and pay the Keepers a visit."

CHAPTER SIXTEEN

The Savior's Sword

The Year 1556 Anno Salvatoris
15 Years After the Settling

"Sir."

A sallow breeze fluttered in through the tent as Aritz faced the back wall, depositing his muddied and bloodied field jacket atop a nearby chair. As he wiped away sweat from his still-glistening brow, the back of his hand showed a smear of blood, still fresh upon him, though the wound was not his own. He massaged his hands, coercing a stubborn knot to leave his presence, paying little heed to the splashes of mud and muck littering his skin.

Soon, a bath to be drawn, and we start anew on the morrow, he thought.

"Sir," the voice behind him repeated.

Aritz clucked his tongue and turned to find one of his soldiers, Lieutenant Dark-Hair—whatever his true name may have been—at the entryway to his tent, the man's posture prim and proper, back straightened, arms clasped behind his back. Aritz wanted little for company at the moment and ensured Dark-Hair was aware of it as he flashed a disapproving glare toward the man.

Dark-Hair was wholly unperturbed by it.

"I believe I requested no disturbances, son," Aritz said in an admonishing tone. He turned toward the table to his right, toward the flagon of wine he ensured was brought with him on the march north. Wars did make for thirsty work.

Dark-Hair held out a slip of paper from his rear pocket. "I come with the battle dead, sir," he said, disregarding Aritz's displeasure at his presence.

Aritz scoffed and poured his drink almost to the brim of the glass, the aroma enchanting as it wafted up through his nostrils. He didn't even spare a glance toward Dark-Hair. "It matters not," he said. "So long as we have enough to win the morrow."

There was silence on the receiving end.

Rolling his eyes, Aritz said over his shoulder, "Do we have enough to win the morrow?"

Dark-Hair took it upon himself to fully enter the tent, seating himself at the war table. Behind him trailed Pock-Face, whose hands twitched at his side, his gaze sunken against the pock scars littering his face. The second lieutenant sat beside Dark-Hair, both waiting expectantly for Aritz's full attention.

Aritz flashed them both a disapproving look, hands still occupied with his wine. "Why, yes. Please, enter." He rolled his eyes once again, a heavy sigh escaping his lips. With a frown on his lips, he slowly walked to his seat at the table, the backrest of his ornate chair towering high above him, gilded his silver carvings. Placing his wineglass atop the table, its contents splashing over the oaken surface beneath, he crossed his legs and held his arms out, elbows propped on the armrests. His eyes narrowed at his two present lieutenants and then to the two empty seats across from them.

"Where are the other two, then?" he said.

A silent moment stretched on as Pock-Face forced an awkward cough. "Um, sir. Ludovico fell to an arrow during our march through the forest. Baltasar was...last seen with several spears running through him."

Aritz grunted in acknowledgment. "A shame, that." *I've no idea who is who,* he thought. He gestured his hands toward the two present, inviting them both to speak further. "I believe I inquired as to our readiness for the morrow, gentlemen."

Dark-Hair crossed his arms, his eyes not fully meeting Aritz's. "Aye, we will be readied at first light." He hummed something to himself under his breath, not unheard to Aritz.

"It seems you've further to say, son?"

Tapping his fingers along his broad forearms, Dark-Hair's expression was…almost annoyed. Frustrated, even. "Scouts have caught sight of a mass exodus to the north. It seems they're retreating into the mountains."

That caught Aritz's full attention. He uncrossed his legs and leaned forward, crossing his hands in front of his face in a thinking gesture. "Into the mountains, you say. Then their village is abandoned."

"Or soon to be, at any rate." The lieutenant shrugged.

"And what know we of the traverses of the mountains?"

Dark-Hair remained silent, closing his eyes as he let out a long sigh, shaking his head with once more that visible frustration.

Pock-Face inclined his head toward his compatriot, brow raised, before finally turning back to Aritz to say, "Little at all, sir. Likely less than little. If they deem it advantageous to abandon themselves to the mountains, then surely, they must have some reason to."

"A reason, you say?" Aritz raised his brow, chuckling deeply to himself. "Do you think they are capable of reason? Or strategy?"

Stammering to find the necessary words, Pock-Face merely chewed at his lower lip and threw his hands up. "It…would be wise to at least presume they may? Sir?"

"You give them far too much credit, son. Would you assume them capable of rational thought? Or would you see them for the beasts they are, clawing at the auspices granted by the Savior though they would defile them just the same?"

"I…am merely ensuring we are adequately prepared, sir."

"And for that, you have my gratitude." *Naïve as you are. I am sure the savages will feast on your bones first.* "But among us, we carry the banner of the Savior. What further preparation need we have?"

"The cowardly one does offer a valid point. I'd be loath to underestimate the savages, myself."

Aritz did not even notice the soldier standing casually by the entryway to the tent. Blood and dirt spattered her face and uniform, complementing the flowing red hair she allowed to fall past her shoulders. She caught Dark-Hair's attention, slight as it was.

Pock-Face huffed and puffed. "*Cowardly*?" he said, his face darkening to an embarrassed shade of red. "How dare—how—who the hell are you, soldier? Show proper respect to your superiors!"

"At ease, son," Aritz said, brushing his sputtering aside with a wave of his hand. "I would hear what she has to say."

The red-haired soldier flashed a smile and bowed her head. As she did so, Aritz noticed a tear in the shoulder of her uniform jacket, probably from an errant spear. She seemed none the worse off for it, not even displaying a wound from the tear.

"Might I request an audience in private, General?" she asked.

Pock-Face shot to his feet, knocking his chair over. "Perish the thought, soldier! Any intelligence you have for the General may also be shared in front of us."

Despite the protests, the woman paid Pock-Face little heed, focusing squarely on Aritz, instead.

"Answer me, soldier!" Pock-Face bellowed, his face beet-red. "To whose unit do you belong? Who is your commanding officer? We will not suffer this insubord—"

"Permit her to speak in private," Dark-Hair said, his arms still crossed. He looked to the red-haired soldier and nodded, ignoring his fellow lieutenant entirely. Bypassing Pock-Face, he glanced back to Aritz. "By your leave, of course, sir."

Aritz considered it a moment, flashing a smirk at the still-fuming Pock-Face, and waved his hand in acquiescence. "Very well. Both of you, leave us. I would speak to her alone, per request."

Pock-Face glared irately at Aritz until the General's imposing and threatening glare instantly deterred him from saying anything further.

Please, cry foul further about "insubordination." I would gladly show you what happens to insubordinates.

Instead, the "cowardly" lieutenant shoved past Dark-Hair and rammed his shoulder into the red-haired soldier on his way out, his angry mutterings echoing as he disappeared into the camp.

Dark-Hair shook his head and slowly rose to his feet, pushing in his chair as he left the war table. Bowing graciously to Aritz, he turned and left, but not before exchanging a slow nod with the new arrival.

"My thanks...Lieutenant," the woman said, a slight smile on her lips. She inched past him as he left, standing at the front of the table, her arms folded behind her back.

Raising his brow, Aritz considered the woman silently, twiddling his thumbs as he leaned back in his chair. *Chummy with the lieutenant, is she? Curious.* Dismissing the thought, he raised what remained of the decanter of wine to her, gesturing to an empty glass at the adjacent table. "A drink, then?"

She stood firm, posture remaining stoic, though a shadow of a smile inched across her mud-spackled face. "I must decline, sir, but thank you."

Aritz scoffed and shrugged, taking a large sip of his glass. He nodded his head toward an empty chair, belonging to one of his departed lieutenants, though to which one, he could not say. "Sit."

The woman bowed her head and sat herself in the chair opposite from where Dark-Hair sat. As she settled in, she displayed none of the formal body language expected of a soldier of her rank. Instead, she relaxed much in the way Aritz did, hands folded in her lap, one leg crossed over the other, nearly reclining if only the chair had allowed for it.

Patiently, Aritz awaited the purpose for her arrival and (welcomed) interruption of the brief war meeting, still sipping at his wine. He tapped his dirtied fingernails along the body of the glass rhythmically, clucking his tongue, staring at her expectantly. "I'm waiting," he said with a hint of annoyance in his voice. *I could be enjoying a long moment of solitude.*

The smile growing more pronounced on the woman's face as she leaned forward, long tufts of red hair falling past her shoulders. Propping her elbows on the table, she hummed to herself, visibly suppressing a chuckle—much to Aritz's curiosity, that—and narrowed her eyes toward him. "Tell me, Aritz a Mata," she said, her voice all command, lacking any misgivings or apprehensions. "What drives you to come this far north?"

Aritz considered the question in silence for a long stretch of seconds before finally placing his wine glass down, now half emptied, and said plainly, "It's proper etiquette to refer to me by 'General' or 'sir.'"

"I did not think you so adherent to matters of ceremony," she said in response. "You must know that the savages will not stop to call you 'General' were they to drive a spear through you. Nor would you, were you to put your flintlock to the head of a Chief and pull the trigger. Though, of course, I am to understand you have done that already."

"And who are you," Aritz asked, "to ask these things of me? To demand your own discourse with me? Of what matter is it to you the reasons for my goals here to the north?"

Slowly, the woman rose back to her feet, pacing along the rim of the table where the empty wine glasses still stood, tracing her finger along the edge, tapping a fingertip once she reached the pointed corner. "After all these years, who I am has grown irrelevant. To you, I could be called Kama. Your soldiers, they saw my hair and took to calling me Red so much that it became a name all its own. To this land upon which I was born, I should be considered equal to those standing on the other side of our guns, but I am instead regarded as its blight. But to be called that for so long, seeing such a blight ravage this savage land is...calming. Cathartic, I suppose you could say."

Aritz crossed his arms and regarded the woman, this woman called "Kama." He watched her stand in silent introspection, a vibrant smile adorning her lips as she closed her eyes tightly, drawing in deep, comforted breaths. Much more than the concerned nature of his lieutenants, much more than the desire for solitude instilled within him, for her, she seemed utterly content. She beamed as though all of this reinvigorated her, as though born anew from the blood she played a part in shedding.

It was something that Aritz could not help but respect in one of his soldiers, to be so committed to this task that she would be drawn to the battle with rife eagerness. And yet, something irked him just the same. "Hold a moment," he said, rising cautiously to his feet, his hand hanging loosely at his waist. "You claim to have been borne of this land. We have only been here for fifteen years. Conscription is not permitted, by law of Their Majesties, until the age of eighteen. So, explain to me how you—"

Kama cut him off with a sly chuckle. "I do not recall saying I was Acrarian...Aritz." She turned to him with a grin, fully facing him but making no erratic movements otherwise. "I was here long before the Acrarians, and I am sure I will remain long after they have departed. It was to the west of here that I grew up, and to the west of here I was born again under a new banner of my own creation. One that I hope to still see flutter in the calming breeze when at last this has ended."

Aritz approached her, and before she could greet him with so much as a blink, he drew his pistol and held it squarely to her forehead, clicking the hammer in place. "And so it is you expect me to carouse with a savage such as yourself." His hand held steady, his finger on the trigger, readied to respond to the slightest of provocations.

Calmly, Kama pushed the barrel aside with a finger, repositioning Aritz's aim off to her left. "You have been carousing with more 'savages' than you know, Aritz, but that is beyond the point. I am not of these Tribes, if such is your concern."

"And I am to take you at your word, then?"

"Yes," Kama said, nodding her head with an exuberant jolt. "Would you think me so mindless as to prostrate myself before you, begging you to take my life, or rather, would I be so poor at my role if I were to announce that I was of the Tribes ahead of my intent to claim *your* life?"

Aritz did not lower his pistol. "I have seen these savages. It is not something I would put past—"

"Yes, yes, you deem them all mindless and brainless, bereft of any inclination toward rational thought. Justify that to yourself all you would like, but they are of greater intelligence than you give them credit for. In some respects, of the same level as an Acrarian, just in their own way."

"And is this meant to dissuade me from considering you agent among them, if you are so quick to defend them?"

"I defend only their acumen and propensity toward their own survival. For you, I advise only to listen to your cowardly lieutenant, just this once." Kama maintained eye contact with Aritz, not even offering a passing glance to the barrel of the pistol still held just outside her periphery.

Aritz's arm was starting to waver from the weight of his weapon. "Explain to me why I should trust you, then."

Kama scoffed, raising her brow, gesturing to the blood on her uniform, the tears in her coat. "This blood is not my own, nor is it of the Acrarians. These mars to my uniform are not the make of my comrades-in-arms. I have been among your people for the last ten years, waiting for this day to arrive. My commitment to you and your charge is an earnest one—of this, I can assure you."

"And you would be content to see the ruination of your people? To stamp into the earth by your own boot a horrid legacy?"

"I must reiterate," Kama said, the grin on her face growing slighter. "It is not *my* people whose blood I have spilled."

If anything, Aritz still felt a slight reluctance to lower his weapon. But strangely, he could also feel an earnestness to her words, an admittance that fell beyond the pale of committing to the act as an agent for these savages. He looked again at the tear in her jacket, the slice of the blade of a spear cutting it clean. From the angle, it could not have been self-inflicted. And the contentment she displayed at these admissions, too—surely, there would have been some tell, some break in the role, that would have been an indication of any falsehood in her words.

Sensing a strange feeling that some might have said bordered on "trust," Aritz lowered his weapon and returned it to the leather holster strapped to his thigh, though he did not offer her so much as a smile beyond that. He looked her up and down, homing in on her face and the fire that dwelt within her eyes. "I would be loath not to ask how you came to look like one of our own."

Kama laughed dismissively, tucking a tuft of hair behind her ear. "Were I to tell you, you may be quick to put me to the stake as a witch. You need not fear my presence, regardless, even if you were inclined to decry me as some sort of...spellbinder." She leaned back, propping herself atop the wine table. "My reasons for being here are my own. Just as yours are yours."

Aritz grunted, turning to his half-empty glass of wine. He reached for the decanter, depositing its remaining contents into his glass despite the slight overfill, and walked toward the opening to the tent with wine in hand, looking out to the camp, the imposing peaks of the mountains taunting him in the background. *Somewhere within those ranges, the savages have fled,* he thought. *One last trumpet to sound from the Savior's troubadour.*

"Kingdom and glory," Aritz said softly.

"I beg pardon?" Kama asked. Her footsteps tapped behind him against the hard and uneven surface of the grass and stones underfoot.

Taking a long gulp, Aritz turned over his shoulder, a trail of liquid trickling out from the corner of his mouth. "You asked what it was that drove me here, to this foul land. It is what all Acrarians desire—or, what those of ambition seek, at the least. To have the scribes mark a great man's accomplishments is an honor of the highest degree. To extend the will and testament of the Acrarian Kingdom to all the lands it can reach is of greater import still. It is...paramount to instill the authority of Their Majesties that much further, such that the sun may never set upon their mighty holdings, that there shan't be a waking eye that does not pay tribute to the names Ferrand and Catelina."

A silence dragged on, save for the whistles of the wind, a silence broken by a suppressed snort and laugh. Aritz turned sharply to see Kama holding her hand to her mouth, amusement visible in her eyes. "Are my words risible?"

"Risible? Yes," Kama said without any hesitation. "Dispassionate, uninspired, and generic? Also yes." She crossed her arms, flashing an accusatory glance at him. "Come now, Aritz. Of what value does this small island truly hold to Acraria? There are natural resources in the mountains, true, but you have not set foot within their reaches in your fifteen years here, and to the south, there is very little of worth to pilfer."

Aritz could not help but grin at the comment. "My father...he was a man of means and ambition. As a boy, I never wanted for anything. I suppose you could surmise that it was, in a sense, to follow in my father's footsteps by being a man of means and ambition, myself. It has been fifteen years since we settled this land, and fifteen years since I settled myself along those southern shores, stepping naught but a foot inside that woodland labeled as inescapably dangerous. But in that time, I have already established the most efficient trading route the Kingdom has ever known, the most prosperous trading route the Kingdom has ever known, by linking this land to the wild frontier far across the western seas. Without my planning and knowledge, this all would have been for naught."

"So, all of this is to impress your father, then," Kama said plainly, her arms still crossed.

"*Heh*, no," Aritz said dismissively. "My father passed some time before my departure for this land." *And if not for his stubbornness and short-sightedness, he could be here by my side today.*

It was clear that Kama was growing disinterested. She trailed her gaze elsewhere, almost through Aritz. Were it not for his blocking the exit, she probably would have departed right then and there.

Aritz frowned and closed his eyes, drawing a deep breath. *All fancy words. Hardly true words, though.* In his mind's eye, the memories flashed of sharing a horrid, spoiled slop with a host of seafarers; of crushing a haunting mask underfoot as a heap of bodies began to pile by the southern shores; of arrows raining down from an unforgiving tree, only for the rain to cease at the pull of a trigger; and, of animalistic carvings being worshipped like scripture, an unintelligible prayer being uttered to an inattentive north.

All the memories coalesced into one. And they made him shudder.

"They disgust me, all of them," he admitted.

Kama raised an eyebrow, regarding him once more with curiosity, folding her hands behind her back as a sly smile returned.

"These 'Tribes,' they live in ignorance of everything the Savior has provided for them, and in defiance of all He asks of them." Aritz turned his head and spat on the earth outside his tent. "From the moment I set foot on this land, their wicked ways ran afoul of the Savior's teachings. They tried converting me with their wicked sorcery, learning my tongue simply by touching my forehead. How freely they admitted their blasphemy to me then, confessing their reverence of beasts as gods, of nature as a spirit. Those seafaring savages were unworthy of the beautiful land they defiled; someone needed to remove them from it. By the Savior's blessing, it had to be me. For the good of everything the Savior provides us, I would gladly act as His sword, and so I act. Until such time as this sickness is washed away from this verdant earth, I will be an agent of the Savior, a Savior in my own right for this land and the people who would rightfully inhabit it."

Kama took a handful of steps forward until her lips were just beside Aritz's ear, close enough for only him to hear. "I would wager that there is still glory in this for you, then."

"Aye," Aritz said. "There is."

"What better glory would there be, then, to be known as a god-slayer? To prove that their gods are false by felling them by your own hand?" She clapped a firm hand on Aritz's shoulder. "What better use for the Savior's sword?"

Aritz turned his head toward her, nearly meeting nose-to-nose. "Perhaps this *is* the destiny the Savior has laid bare for me. Some nights ago, one of His Envoys came to me in my sleep, informing me of the existence of their gods on our earth, but little more besides. Do you mean to tell me you know of a way to slay them?"

Kama backed up two steps, reaching behind her back. Her response was tepid, to say the least, as though unsurprised by Aritz's vision. But she smiled nonetheless, drawing a sheathed blade, no longer than a hunter's knife, out from behind her, holding out with both hands. "May this offering be my humble pledge to you, Aritz a Mata. The Tribes may have departed through the mountains, but my eyes travel with them. They shall not be able to hide from us. There can be only one place where they mean to flee, a place most holy to them all." She drew the blade from its sheath, and Aritz quickly caught sight of an elaborate carving embedded in the steel that almost seemed to glow. "Do not disparage all the Tribes stand for, for their tools have their uses. There exists within their blood some manner of wicked spellbinding, and with that magic comes boons beyond your ken."

Aritz's breath caught in his chest at the mention of "magic," but Kama was quick to hold out her hand. He presumed it to be a means to calm him.

"Do not despair, Aritz. It will not harm you. This, I promise you. Look upon this rune." She gestured to the glowing mark carved into the blade. "By this mark, this blade is imbued with strength. And you may need that strength sooner than you think."

Aritz's eyes widened, his body freezing.

Kama held the steel out further, nearly close enough to cut were one of them to avoid caution. "Will you take up this steel, Sword of the Savior?" Her smile was almost sinister, her eyes a well of fire.

Hesitation held Aritz in its firm grip.

But then he reached for the hilt.

MEMORY

Enemy of My Enemy

The settlement stood in wait, faint billows of smoke dissipating against a horizon adamantly holding on to its remaining gold and glimmer.

It had been five years since Kamataa and Ziia had ventured south of the Forest. Five years they had decided to dwell within the Heart, pilfering what forbidden knowledge they could from the Keepers, perusing records they were surprised still existed after all these centuries. Five years since they heard tell of this mysterious foe that many had taken to calling the "Invaders." At the first word of them, Kamataa was eager to hear more of the people who beguiled Han'e and the Sun Tribe into wandering into wanton slaughter by the hand of the Wood Tribe, who stripped the Arrow Tribe of their horses and livelihood, and who decimated the Dusk Tribe to the point of near extinction.

But as she crested the cliff face overlooking the inlet to the northeast of the "Invader" settlement, Kamataa felt her breath catch. It was unlike anything she had ever seen before.

What she remembered of the Dusk Tribe settlements was gone, and in their place stood a dense mass of buildings comprised of sturdier materials than anything the Tribes ever used, tall constructs of steel breaking the horizon's plane, filling the surrounding air with dark smoke. It was something so much larger and more expansive than any sight Kamataa had set her eyes on. She had taken in many gorgeous scenes in her four hundred years—perhaps the view of the Forest from deep within the mountains was the greatest—but this? It was…

Breathtaking.

She felt Ziia clap a hand atop her shoulder as she stood beside her companion. It had been a long journey these past couple weeks. Not for the distance, as the typical journey from their position in the Heart to where they stood now would ordinarily take no more than three to five days, but for the sheer amount of changes in what they had known their world to be. The north was much more crowded than it used to be, with Stone territory acting as a refuge for all of the displaced peoples of the south.

They could not help but sate their curiosity at the sordid state of the Sun and Arrow Tribes, so despondent and downcast at their sudden upheaval and exile. From what Kamataa could tell, the Sun Tribe was especially miserable at their new home, despite the generous plot of land given to them by the Stone Tribe's Chief, and they were not particularly making any concerted effort at adapting to their new home even five years on. And for the Arrow Tribe, she had heard rumors that their few remaining horses were rapidly dying out, though for what reason was beyond Kamataa's knowledge.

But here in the south…there was nothing. None of the sparse liveliness that she had known these last few centuries. In this very spot, on this cliff with the grassy steppes beside, she remembered seeing wild horses roaming, the Arrow Tribe coexisting with them not as master and animal, but as equals in nature. But as she stood atop this withering height, the rolling hills of green began to lose their green hue, the livelihood of the earth just barely holding on to what life remained in it, and she took in the sight of the fruits of Tribal culture expelled from its home, smoke and metal against tall wood beginning to impede the view of the shimmering water beyond. In that moment, the excitement returned. But with it also came jealousy.

"Remarkable, is it not?" Ziia said softly, dropping to a knee as she blocked the golden sun rays from her eyes.

Kamataa crossed her arms as a sharp seaside breeze rolled through. "It's almost as though the Dusk Tribe never existed at all. What do folks call them these days, again?"

Ziia scoffed. "The Haunted, I believe? Who's to say whether they've taken to calling themselves that at this point?"

"Who's to say whether they've the people remaining to call themselves anything? The ghosts beneath their feet are merely compatriots now."

"Save for those who still have their lives but are too occupied to heed the words of the dead."

"Eh?" Kamataa questioned with a raised brow. "What do you mean?"

"That boy who sought us out some years ago. Do you remember him?"

Kamataa shrugged. "Not by name, but...the Eclipseborn boy?"

Ziia nodded. "And left just as quickly, pestered by the voices of the lost, by his own admission. Truly haunted, one could say." She flashed a smile. "At the time, it all seemed a ramble, but seeing this, it all makes sense now."

"What does?"

"Slave labor."

Kamataa raised an eyebrow. "Huh." She stroked her chin and looked at the tall constructs within the foreign settlement. "Here I thought these 'Invaders' were merely efficient in crafting something so elaborate in such a short length of time, but..."

Slowly, Ziia offered an acknowledging nod. "It would seem they had some help." She winked. "Voluntary or otherwise."

Taking a seat and taking in the sight, Kamataa wrapped her arms around her knees and sighed. "And perhaps at long last, recompense for the Pale Night. All of the fellow Eclipseborn we could have met...the Moon may have served the Dusk Tribe Her own justice, but these 'Invaders' have granted them the justice they have always deserved."

"However long they'll bide their time, they'll see to it that the rest of the Tribes receive theirs, as well."

Kamataa chuckled. "'However long?' Why don't you just look ahead with that?" She tapped at the Foresight pendant dangling out from Ziia's shirt. Her companion was always averse to glimpsing too far ahead into the future for fear of witnessing and experiencing her own demise, tempting though the knowledge of what was yet to come may be.

"They'll make their mark. That, I'll promise you," Ziia said. "We've waited centuries for this moment. A few more years is nothing."

It was a promise that Kamataa was more than satisfied with, but all the same, she couldn't help but feel a pang of jealousy at the thought. "Do you look at this," she said, gesturing toward the Invader settlement, "and feel even the slightest of envy?"

Ziia inclined her head curiously. "What do you mean?"

A grimace settled upon Kamataa's face. "Look at everything they've done in five years. The whole of the Land's south is theirs. Glimpse here for as far as your eyes allow, and you will see not see a single soul belonging to the Tribes." She bit her lower lip, grumbling wordless nothings to herself. "But what do *we* have to show for over three centuries of effort? A hundred-year war that resulted in nothing? Some stolen knowledge from the Keepers? Was anything we did worth it?" A heavy sigh rumbled in her throat.

A kind hand grasped hers. Ziia nudged her and indulged Kamataa to look at her. "Everything has its purpose. The Moon has ensured that we are still here for a reason. What we learned of the Deities these last five years *will* be useful. The Lake Tribe may never trust one another again, despite the peace we drafted. And a new generation of Eclipseborn will come of age soon. We've already met one of them, and I'm sure we will encounter him again one day soon."

A tentative smile creased Kamataa's lips. "A new generation," she repeated. "Children of the Black Moon we shall be once again."

"Yes," Ziia said, her voice rife with reassurance. "Somewhere above, Ruhr and all the rest of them will be smiling down on us. Their dream still lives with us. A dream we'll share with the new Children as their time comes." She tugged at the chain around her neck, jingling the Foresight pendant in place. "For some, it may not be long before they're welcomed into their new family."

Kamataa leaned back, propping herself on her elbows as the western waters glimmered against the sun's wondrous glow. She stared at the settlement, a reluctant excitement finding its way into her heart. "A new family to bear witness to our dream. And perhaps all our dream needed was the introduction of a nightmare."

Ziia leaned beside her, rolling onto her side. "You find it worth the envy, then?"

"If they can achieve what we ourselves cannot...then perhaps it's wiser not to get in their way, wouldn't you think?" Kamataa bared her teeth; she knew it did not so much constitute a smile as it did more a hunter preparing its prey for the inevitable.

Ziia bared her own teeth in response, a promise of the reckoning to come by the will of the Moon. "The enemy of my enemy is my friend, is that it?"

"How lucky we are to find such a useful and powerful friend. And after all..." Kamataa rose to her feet, dusting off the dirt and grass from her rear. "Friends help one another, do they not? Whatever these 'Invaders' need, they still find themselves in a strange land. I'd be a poor host not to offer my assistance."

"I'm sure the Children will feel much the same." Ziia chuckled.

To the east, the sun's light began to vanish. The Moon was due to be at Her fullest this night. Kamataa felt a renewed vigor within her.

By Your blessing, my Lady, she thought. *We are once again returning to You. And soon, this Land will belong to You. Your Children will see to it.*

CHAPTER SEVENTEEN

Before the Storm

The uneven ground below grew slick with freshly fallen snow and compacted ice as the Heart's winding trails led further than Sen had ever deigned to venture.

Since her reunion with her mother and Tez, she had said hardly a word to anyone. Nor did any seek her out, save for the glares shot her way, laden with suspicion. She could not fault them for that. *I remain suspicious of myself, as well,* she had thought.

The mass exile to the depths of the Heart, to the True Heart, as the Keepers were fond of calling it, was expedient and without protest. Those whom Sen had just seen fighting tooth and nail against one another, wounds still fresh from the spears of their brethren, now walked together as though nothing had occurred between them. There had not yet been time for her to inquire about the reasoning behind the conflict, but she had her assumptions all the same as to the root of it all.

Myself. Flames fanned by Koelhe. What other reasoning is there?

From the sordid state she found Koelhe in as she changed out of her Invader clothing and back into comfortable attire, Sen had to wonder whether the woman thought it was all worth it. Not that she would be in any rush to come to her aid, at any rate.

Sen watched as the motley crew of Tribal warriors—this strange combination of Stone, Sun, Lake, Arrow, and Wood fighters—funneled out from the village's northern exit, up through the winding inclining trail leading to the Trial Precipice in the Heart. At the head of the pack, Sen had noticed Sharrabha. Unsurprising, given the huntress's warm familiarity with the Keepers from all her years traversing the mountains. From what she heard, Sharrabha had sent a missive ahead of time, informing the Keepers, and the great Owlsign Ko Endra specifically, of the inbound army, not so much as requesting their aid as emphasizing the importance of their support. For them, and for the Deities for whom they acted as stewards.

Much like her days amongst the Invader forces, Sen felt much more inclined to relegate herself to the rear guard. This time, not for avoidance of battle nor the fear of taking from one of her own their spark of life.

Rather, it was for avoidance of her people altogether. Despite reuniting with what remained of her family, she was in no dire straits to commune further with them, at least not yet. There was much more to build to. She needed to steel herself for that conversation. But then she had dreaded an unwelcomed spat with Fann, and all the vitriol that was sure to leave his lips. *Those who were always quick to jump to Koelhe's side must have delighted in hearing of my return amongst the Invaders,* she had thought.

But worse than that, she couldn't fathom her reunion with Tawa. She had seen him bloodied but otherwise unharmed shortly after the battle's end, flanked by Arrow Tribe yeomen with whom he was evidently acquainted, judging by the grin strewn upon his face and the laughter shaking his belly. But for all the joy in his eyes, Sen knew it was only a shallow pool of happiness. She knew he yearned for news of Narva. The memory of that night still shattered her. The nightmare that followed that evening ground the shards of her into dust.

The rage that filled Tawa's face, the fire in his eyes, the demands for Tawa to return to him.

WHAT HAVE YOU DONE TO MY BOY? rang the memory in her ears.

A pang of guilt ran the length of Sen's body at first sight of Tawa, and it had yet to dissipate for the entire walk through the trails of the Heart, up past the Trial Precipice and beyond the Keeper dwellings. The self-imposed solitude certainly did not remedy matters, but she remained ill-inclined to seek accompaniment along this snowbound walk, her only companions the spear she was barely adequate enough to use and the flintlock pistol she kept hidden beneath her undercoat, for what good she hoped it may do.

However long the trek took—she could not say for certain—Sen felt a wave of relief when the steady incline leveled off and the trailhead widened. Collective gasps passed through the menagerie of Tribal warriors in waves until they finally reached her, and she turned her gaze to the source of the disbelief.

The valley gave way to a wide clearing compacted with well-trodden snow, flanked on all sides by impossibly tall oaken trees, branches waylaid with fluffy snow glimmering and basking in the bountiful glow of the autumn sunlight. Light and wispy mists danced along the snowy surface like ghosts of a time long past, stubborn still to leave this plane of existence for one final waltz among a like kind. It was almost ethereal in nature, a natural beauty that Sen could scarcely believe, even as the wisps continued to twirl about her.

But as the crowd dispersed into the clearing, a wealth of Keepers of all disciplines awaiting them with solemn eagerness, Sen stood at the final precipice, alone save for her companionable weapons, at felt her jaw drop.

For it was in that moment, her vision unobstructed by the passing crowds behind whom she chose to remain, that she bore witness to something unimaginable, something that, despite her and her people's ardent beliefs, still seemed impossible.

Beyond the clearing, upon a series of altars perhaps larger than several of the huts in the Stone village, laid in peaceful respite three beasts of enormous stature.

One, a mass of dark fur, all bulk and girth, surely the height of five men were it to stand on its four burly legs, the soft rumble of its snores threatening to sunder the earth.

Beside it, a tall and spindly frame of grey and black fur, sitting in silent watch, its assuming eyes glinting sharply in the sunlight even at this distance.

And perched on a thick branch at the end sat a calm avian form, feathers appearing sharp as ice, wings spread in a wide stretch spanning enough distance to cover half the length of a street in the village.

Sen's breath caught as she stared wide-eyed at the Bear, the Wolf, and the Owl. The gods taken flesh.

A flare of anger pulsed within her as she looked over her shoulder, back toward the base of the mountains, where the looming threat approached.

Gripping her spear tightly and adjusting the holster at her waist, she drew a deep breath and walked forth to join the rest of the Tribespeople, regardless of what they may have chosen to say in her presence.

"Kama. I've found her."

The tone of Hollow's voice did not instill in her any vote of confidence.

Kamataa stood at the center of the Stone Tribe village, hands folded behind her back as she took in the looming heights of the Heart's peaks. The southerly winds from the mountain's valleys whipped her red hair about her shoulders, her eyes wincing and watering for their sharp and cold bite.

Concern had run rampant when Ziia did not report back after the withdrawal induced by the arrival of the Arrow Tribe. Once she had convinced Aritz of the Tribes' retreat into the mountains, it became all the easier to search the village alongside the rest of the Acrarians.

She had personally requested Hollow and Vanta to comb the village for any trace of her while she ostensibly volunteered to keep an eye to the north for any returning Tribespeople. In truth, she needed the time to herself to seethe.

But as Hollow led her around the backside of what she assumed was the Chief's hut, the gaze of her burly companion downcast and unwilling to meet hers, Kamataa knew precisely what to expect.

Regardless, it still pained her to see Ziia dumped on the ground so unceremoniously, tossed aside like a piece of garbage. Vanta was already knelt beside the departed woman, her hand pressed to Ziia's forehead as she muttered the Departed Rites as a solemn hymn to the Moon, fresh blood still seeping out from gaping wounds on either side of Ziia's temple.

Kamataa flared her nostrils and scrunched her nose as she felt a wave of tears flooding her eyes. She nudged Vanta aside with a sharp force from her hip and knelt over her lost companion. She closed her eyes, trying to center herself against the wave of nausea she felt rising within her. She gripped at the fabric of Ziia's uniform top, clutching it tightly in her shaking fist. As she drew a heavy breath, she pictured the perpetrator of the act. It was hardly difficult to deduce, judging from the entry and exit points of a bullet traveling through her head.

"Sennalhat would trade an eye for an eye," Kamataa said softly, her voice an angry rasp as she opened her eyes to look down once again at Ziia's motionless form. "She would *dare* to say that the eye of her brother was of greater value than the value of Ziia's. She knows nothing of such things. She knows nothing of what it means to cherish a companion for nearly four centuries. She is a rat too weak of courage to perform that which is necessary…but she slays Ziia in cold blood without hesitation." Kamataa broke her gaze away from Ziia, exchanging sharp glances with Vanta and Hollow both. "I would gladly blind the world whole if it meant taking all away from Sennalhat that she treasures dearly."

Hollow grunted, crossing his arms. "Her death will not go unpaid," he said grimly.

Vanta flexed her hands, cracking her knuckles. "We'll all see to that, Kama," she promised, holding her hand out, but clearly cautious not to graze either of her companions with the Touch. She balled one hand into a sinister fist. "I'll be sure of it."

Kamataa frowned and rose back to her feet. Sharply, she shook her head. "She knew she would meet her end before our time arrived. She knew she would not live long enough to see our sun rise just as the Tribes' sun fell." She looked to her neck, the chain of a pendant escaping the confines of her uniform pocket. Kamataa dug through and pulled out the ornament, examining the carved rune of the Futureseer no longer glowing. "Yet still, she welcomed death as an old companion—a companion that she and I have known just as well as one another. This, today—" She gestured to the hollowed shell of the Stone Tribe village, the sound of Acrarian rummaging echoing in the distance. "—it was her dream as much as it was mine. We shan't waste it."

"And the others?" Hollow questioned, his head inclining toward her. "Do you trust them not to waste it?"

Kamataa was quick to narrow her eyes, unable to break free from the sight of Ziia's motionless body. "Sha'a, Zara, and Cin know what is to be done. As do the others already among them. All among them know the stakes. I trust them not to fail in their tasks."

"And us?" Vanta said, hands on her hips. "Are we given the same margin of trust?"

Exchanging a knowing look with Vanta, Kamataa forced an untruthful smile. *The only one among us in whom I place my undying trust is dead at my feet,* she thought. *But the Moon will see Her Children through should She deem them necessary. It is not for me to decide.*

"Yes," she said instead.

An echo of hollers rang out over the emptied village. Hollow shuffled in place, grumbling something imperceptible beneath his breath, and turned toward the source of the sound. "Any indication when we leave?" he said gruffly.

Kamataa shook her head, offering a hasty glance toward the noise before returning her gaze to Ziia as though her friend would disappear if not paid the requisite solemn attention. "Aritz intends to raid the village dry for supplies and food. Let him. He'll find the food repulsive and supplies useless, but it will please him nonetheless."

"However long that takes."

"The more the Tribes have to plan, the greater the advantage for us." Kamataa flashed a quick grin, but this one was at least genuine. "For the rest, it's in his hands now. Pray the Sword of the Savior cuts deep enough."

The three Eclipseborn nodded to one another, silent against the sharp howls of the mountain winds. As though on cue to cease the silence, they looked to Ziia's body, the stench of her corpse becoming overbearing.

Kamataa knelt beside her dear companion and placed her hand atop Ziia's cold forehead. She closed her eyes, allowing nothing beside her but the sound of her own breaths. "O Blessed Moon," she whispered, "carry again into Your warm arms Your humble servant Ziialhan. Bless upon her in death the light of Your radiance so bestowed upon her in life, and lead her again into the eternal flow of Your embrace. In death, she is again Yours as she was Yours in life. Watch over her...and care for her as I did."

Leaning over Ziia's corpse, Kamataa removed her hand from her friend's forehead and pressed her lips against it. "Goodbye, dear friend. May we meet again in the Moon's embrace." She turned to Hollow, nudging him toward the corpse. "Take her inside. The only one among this Stone Tribe worthy of sitting the Chief's hut is her."

Hollow nodded and hefted Ziia's limp form in his arms, her limbs falling slack, her head lolling listlessly to the side as blood continued to drip out from the bullet wound. Kamataa followed solemnly, Vanta in tow behind her, and she battled once again the tears for her lost friend.

Placing her beside the fire pit inside the hut, Hollow bowed his head toward Ziia, a frown on his face but no words escaping his lips. He only clapped Kamataa softly on the shoulder before returning to the open air.

Feeling Vanta's presence still looming over her, Kamataa sat beside Ziia one last time before turning to the young Eclipseborn and saying, "Would you give us a moment, Vanta?" *You would not mourn her as I do.*

Vanta nodded in acquiescence, quickly following after Hollow.

As the raucous commotion of the Acrarian plundering continued outside, Kamataa held Ziia's cold hand, smiling softly to herself, breathing slowly in an attempt to quell her racing heartbeat. The sound outside dulled as she closed her eyes, focusing intently.

The tears flowed freely as the memories of nearly four hundred years of companionship flashed in an instant in her mind's eye. But no matter how much Life she Drew into herself, none of it flowed back into Ziia.

The air was tense as Sen filed in at the rear of the gathered crowd, all among them grouped in front of the daises housing the three Animal Deities.

Atop the dais stood Ko Zaran, his long flowing locks of silvery white glistening with the freshly fallen snow of similar complexion. On either side of him stood An Rhan, the great Bearsign who had conducted Tez's Trial, and Ne Shanne, the revered Wolfsign who presided over Sen's own failed Trial. Sen couldn't find it within herself to look upon the hunter, nor could she in the brief moments she was present for Brin's Trial.

The steely Owlsign Ko Zaran raised his arm skyward to quell the din of the assembly, ruminations of stark panic and distress still murmuring through the surviving members of the previous day's fracas.

"Peace, all!" Ko Zaran shouted, his voice carrying over the crowd by virtue of the cavernous valley in which they stood. "Peace!"

"You declare peace?!" a voice cried from in front. Sen couldn't be certain of its source. "South of the mountains has not known peace for fifteen years, yet you would speak so softly in declaration for it?!"

Muttered agreements passed through the crowd, the protestation echoing over the valley in like measure as Ko Zaran once again raised his arm for silence. "Do not think us ill-prepared or uncaring for these days," he remarked to the belligerent voices. "We have all of us been secured within these mountains for an age, but do not think we have rested on our laurels with no anticipation of inbound horrors." He gestured his arm toward the Deities, all three of them restful, perhaps inattentive to the faces of terror before them or the nightmares that soon approached. "Our gods have demanded of us preparation as they have patience."

Sen crossed her arms, feeling a frown crease her lips. Kicking at a mound of snow before her, she hardly felt at ease by that promise. *You could scarcely prepare yourself for what is coming. The Wood Tribe should have been prepared, yet they were nearly extinguished just the same.*

As vocalized disagreements and disparaging remarks were roared, Ne Shanne waved her arms for silence, the effort nearly futile if not for the sudden bellow for quiet from somewhere within the crowd. It seemed a wave of dread overwhelmed the gathering, and judging from the person towering over all in their midst and the attention being directed there, Sen had to assume it was the western Lake Chief Yhaan, whom she had heard some descriptions of on the march northward.

Ne Shanne cleared her throat with some embellishment, narrowing her eyes at the crowd. She seemed to be wordlessly conversing with someone at the front. "We have been well informed of the proceedings south of the Heart. Trust us that we do not take the Invaders' approach lightly. Thanks to the Stone Tribe's Sharrabha, we are well aware of the dangers the Invaders pose, of the tactics that they will surely employ, and the ferocity with which they will fight."

Sen felt an itch at her waist where the flintlock pistol was still nestled in its holster. *I don't think you can be aware well enough,* she thought. As Ne Shanne continued to plod on about the Keepers' confidence in making this final stand, Sen allowed herself to turn in place, taking in the scenery about her. An overwhelming well of dread bore down upon her as she glanced at the pristine surroundings, unmarred by outside wars and conflicts. The True Heart was perhaps the last remaining pure surface upon this Land, one to which the Keepers were often loath to permit the admittance of outlanders. *It must have been a convincing letter that Sharrabha sent. "Let us in or we're all fucked," I'm sure was the tone.*

"We Keepers have stood for this bastion from the time we first stood upright," Ne Shanne continued, seeming to be building to something. "It has not been breached before, and it shall not be breached now. On this, we Keepers stake our lives."

"But what threat have the Keepers ever faced?" called the belligerent voice from the front again. "Your years of peace in the snow have made you greener than the grass in the steppes!"

Ne Shanne sneered at the words. "Fen-Osenta, have you words to say? Let's hear them, then!" She raised her arms in challenge.

A man jumped up to the dais in a single bound, his black hair draped over his shoulders with twin ornate braids. Fen-Osenta was a lanky and spindly man, adorned in heavy brown leathers with a thick fur scarf flanked atop his shoulders. He and his younger brothers, Fen-Detu and Fen-Poven, were considered living legends among the Arrow Tribe, heroes for their actions in the Steppe Conflict of four decades previous when they repelled and a rogue splinter of the Tribe intent on sacrificing their horses—the Tribe's livelihood—in hopes of dispelling a years-long drought. The title of "Fen" was bestowed upon each of them, though there was no linguistic equivalent to the title in either the Stone language or the common Tribal Words; Sen assumed it to mean something akin to a "Chief," though the Arrow Tribe had no need or want for such ranks.

It was the first Sen had ever seen the man in the flesh, though she was sure he led the entourage of remaining Arrow hunters to battle in the Stone village alongside his brothers. He looked every bit the intense warrior that Sen expected of him, having heard the tales from her father and Tawa both. The man's reputation preceded him.

An Rhan was quick to jump forward at Fen-Osenta's approach and the Arrow Tribesman did not hesitate to hold out a commanding hand, which almost instantly beckoned the Bearsign to stop.

Fen-Osenta was near enough to Ne Shanne to whisper in private conference, but instead, he visibly sucked in a breath to enunciate loud enough for all to hear. "And when was the last you took up arms, Ne Shanne?" he said. "When was the last the True Heart faced the danger of an outlander threat, ah?"

Ne Shanne crossed her arms and stood her ground, matching her gaze with that of the Arrow Wolfsign. "Wild beasts try to claim this valley for their own use all the—"

"I am not speaking of *hunting trips*, Ne Shanne. And looking upon our gods, I hardly think we need worry about a snow leopard fouling in front of the Bear." A smattering of laughter murmured throughout the crowd at the remark. "I mean, when was the last an outlander, with intent to kill, found their way to this sacred ground, and you needed to take up your bow against them, ah?"

The Keeper Packmind briefly opened her mouth to retort, but the words did not come to her.

Fen-Osenta put his hands on his hips and shook his head.

"I…" Ne Shanne said. "I've been through the lands beyond the Heart. I have seen the horrors to the south. Just as Sharrabha informed us, I am well aware of—"

"That does not address my concerns." Fen-Osenta inclined his head to the watchful gaze of the Wolf. "Does it address yours, my friend?"

The Wolf, naturally, said nothing, save for a deep snort that could be heard even where Sen stood. But though remaining silent, it maintained its watchful gaze on the proceedings as though in complete comprehension.

"You may be willing to lay down your lives, and that is admirable," Fen-Osenta continued. "But peace among the gods has left you careless."

"I assure you, Fen-Osenta," An Rhan said, stepping forward, a spear drawn at her side. "We do not rest peacefully without a care in the world. We ensure our spearmen and yeomen have trained every day for any and all incoming threats. We have the utmost confidence in our abilities to hold off these Invaders."

"What have you lost to the Invaders, ah?"

The question hung in the air for a long time with no answer. Fen-Osenta looked to each of the Keeper leaders expectantly, turning to them all before turning to the gathered crowd.

Sen crossed her arms, huddling herself together tightly against a sudden chill in the air followed by a gust of snowfall. Her chest felt heavy as she considered the question herself, chewing at her bottom lip. She eyed the crowd, finding in the eyes of those she could see an air of despondency and doubt. This degree of collective retreat was unprecedented in the annals of Tribal history. All of them knew it. And the unheeded question only reminded them of that fact all the more.

Fen-Osenta clucked his lips, a heavy sigh seeming to pass through his lips. He turned back toward An Rhan. "You have much to protect here. All of us do. But you will not fight with the same and necessary ferocity if you do not fight as though you have already in honor of something you have already lost, ah? While the Keepers have enjoyed the sanctity and peace of the mountains, the rest of us have lost friends, family, some of us our *homes*." He pointed a sharp finger at the three Keepers. "We will not win this fight if we rest on our laurels in the guise of 'confidence.' We need to be angry, fearful, vengeful.

Roar with the voices of the thousands we have already lost. Elsewise, what ferocity can we even claim to have?"

A loud din of approval hummed in the air, the ground beneath shaking rhythmically against the impact of countless clapping spears.

"But to win this fight," Fen-Osenta said, "we *need* the Keepers. This is the one place the Invaders have not set foot in. We need your expertise on how best to hold them off, where we can ambush them." He looked once more to the Deities, all three of them restful, attentive, at peace. "Fight as though in honor of something you have already lost."

The Keepers fell to a hush as though in deep thought. Ko Zaran had a hand to his chin, stroking it thoughtfully. His eyes trailed upward, and Sen followed the track of his gaze to the parallel ridges overhanging the valley before it opened up to the clearing. Sen frowned and furrowed her brow, wondering just what was up there that caught the Owlsign's eye.

"It is said," Ko Zaran began, "that the valley used to expand much further. That the narrow pass carried almost to where this dais is now, and it was chiseled away and eroded over time until it became the formation we see now."

"What are you saying, then?" Fen-Osenta said, his interest piqued, judging from the tone of his voice.

Ko Zaran pointed to the ridge, where several misshapen rock formations sat. "We get to work on separating the rock formations from the ridge, loosening them. And when the time comes…"

Fen-Osenta pointed his finger again, but this time in an acknowledging, approving manner. "…we can drop the boulders on them and take out the rest."

"Precisely," Ko Zaran said with a nod.

"And then, we can station Wolfsign hunters along the ridge to lie in wait. When the rocks drop, we can take advantage of their disorganization to pick off the rest. Naturally, my hunters can handle that much. Brothers, come up here, ah? Right, so at the front of the dais, we should put the majority of the Bearsign warriors to protect the gods. Where are the Lake Chiefs? Could you both come up here? What I think we should do is…"

Sen tuned out the rest. Despite Fen-Osenta's insistence against resting on the Keepers' confidence…it would certainly still be nice to feel some modicum of confidence.

They could have the most coordinated defense plan in the history of the Tribes, she thought. *But what happens when the worst comes in the blink of an eye? How quickly it can all change.* She still felt heavy, her chest tight, a pit forming in her stomach. With uneasy eyes, she looked to the Deities, all three of them exuding an air of peace as the proceedings continued, their interest in the discussions unknown, but the fate that awaited them was all too stressful for Sen to continue dwelling on.

She needed a walk to separate herself from all of this. As the defense discussions pressed on, Sen turned tail and sauntered away aimlessly, Fen-Osenta's rapid speech barely another voice on the wind fading away in the distance.

Raucous cheer and pronounced elation rang in the air as Aritz's army raided the abandoned village, finding nary a soul remaining but a wealth of food and supplies within the waylaid huts.

Such activities were beneath Aritz, though. The air was stagnant with the stench of death, the food tasted like piss, and the supplies were of heathen make. It almost appalled him to be setting foot in this village again, such that he could nearly feel the bestial essence still permeating every surface around him.

He scrunched his nose, holding a handkerchief to his face to mask the stench. *How these beasts live in such squalor is beyond my ken,* he thought.

Still, as the mountain ranges loomed tall in the distance, his ultimate prize awaiting him there, he felt drawn to a particular place. It called to him in whatever horrid tongue these tribal folk deigned to use. The building stood firm and wide, the lingering smell of stale and poor alcohol wafting out from the doors as they opened and closed with each drove of Acrarians entering and exiting.

He had no interest in a drink—not of this detestable make, at any rate—but of particular interest to him was a table. A small and familiar table, one that he had sat at quite recently. He felt inclined to sit at it again.

Fluffing his coattails out from beneath him, he sat by his lonesome, expecting none to join him and pleased to see that none did. A presence in his inner coat pocket lured him, the memory of that night stirring once again within him. He reached inside, withdrawing the marred card that he had taken with him on that night when he played that card game with the savage girl, the girl who had cheated him out of a deserved victory. It had been a game he had taken pleasure in, learning it from some of his men who apparently dallied with the slaves in the pit. Never had he lost; he would not tolerate defeat in any regard.

And yet, as he stared at this damaged card of eight, he couldn't feel any pang of anger at the defeat. He couldn't say what precisely compelled him to take the card with him. *A memento?* he thought. *No, the promise of another challenge. A reminder of the few to best me.* He pointed his gaze to the mountains, narrowing his eyes at their tall peaks. *I'm sure I'll find you there, girl.*

A cleared throat drew his attention, divided though it was sure to remain. Aritz looked over his shoulder to see Pock-Face standing at attention, maintaining a salute.

Aritz brushed him off with a dismissive hand. "At ease, Lieutenant."

"Sir." Pock-Face nodded, resuming a casual posture. "We have obtained eight barrels of ale, ten pallets of—"

"Yes, yes," Aritz said, still not giving the Lieutenant his full attention. "Inform the men to double their pace. The less time I need to spend in this piss-pocket, the happier I shall be."

"Very good, sir," Pock-Face said, shuffling his feet as he nodded thrice for reasons Aritz could only speculate.

"And tell...what's-his-face, Dark-Hair to meet me here posthaste."

Pock-Face raised an eyebrow. "Dark...hair?"

Aritz rolled his eyes. "Your fellow Lieutenant, son."

The lad made a wordless "O" shape with his mouth. "Gaona, sir? I've not seen him since we last sat in your tent. I'll inquire around, though." He nodded again. "Is there anything for which I might be of service, General?"

"No," Aritz said bluntly, turning back around to flick the marred card against on the table.

There was only silence behind him—not even a shuffling of feet to indicate a hasty withdrawal after a hasty dismissal. Aritz looked up, not bothering to turn around, and shook his head, rolling his eyes once again. "What else, Lieutenant?"

A startled gasp broke the plane behind him; Pock-Face was apparently surprised that Aritz was still aware of his presence. "N-nothing, sir. I was just...curious of the card you have there. I...didn't know you played."

"I don't. Direct your curiosities elsewhere, son."

"I...apologize, sir. It was just an...interesting thing to keep with you, is all."

"When at last you emerge from the shadows of greater men, Lieutenant, you may carry with you whatever memento you desire. Until then, leave the greater men to their solitude and follow your orders as given."

The resultant silence prolonged for a greater time than even Aritz was comfortable with, but Pock-Face eventually acquiesced and left in a hurry, his footsteps disappearing into the throng of raucous noise and hearty laughter.

Aritz returned to his solitary view, spinning the card on the table, not breaking his gaze from the snowcapped peaks of this mountain range he heard called "the Heart of the Land." He knew that if he played his cards right, it could very well become the Heart of the Kingdom. The thought soothed and relaxed him.

He held on to that goal, doing his utmost to ignore the excitement over fouled meat and threadbare fabrics made from inferior materials.

The defense discussions continued on and on, and all Sen could think about was having a drink.

It hadn't been much more than a week since she made her promise to Brin to give up drinking. It had felt like an eternity since then. So much had happened.

At one point, she had eyed Ko Seln, the tavern owner who owned the hole that Sen had crawled into near the Trial Precipice, but for whatever mad reason, the man did not pack up shop and bring it all with him to this holy site.

Sen sat by her lonesome, well out of reach of the still convening crowd, sweat dripping from her forehead and underarms. A wave of nausea began rising from her stomach, her hands shaking as she gripped tightly to her forearms, curling herself into a ball as she sat atop a shallow ledge away from everyone. She clenched her eyes shut, her heart pounding in her chest as she tried to steady herself. *Deep breaths, Sen,* she thought. *Deep breaths. In. Out. In. Out.*

When she opened her eyes, though, her chest still thumped heavily. "*Fuck,* I need a drink," she growled under her breath. It wasn't a want. It was a severe *need.* The Invaders were coming, and she was party to them for a time; the gods were in danger; the only surviving Eclipseborn in the Land apart from her were genocidal maniacs who wanted to destroy her people; she feared the due label of "traitor" being affixed to her alongside everything else that had been levied upon her; and those closest to her were dying one by one before her very eyes.

So, hell yes, she needed a godsdamned drink. Several, even.

Gods, where to find one, though, she thought, craning her head backward, allowing her face to be pelted with the falling snow. "Father...Narva...Brin..." she whispered. "Would it be repentance enough for me to end everything now? Would I see you again in the Otherworld? Or do the gods not take kindly to the traitorous Curseborns who almost blight the Land with their own hands?"

"I can't speak for the gods, but I'm sure most of us normal folk won't."

Sen shuddered at the sound of the familiar voice, and not due to the severe need for a drink. She groaned as she dropped her head, only looking at Fann from the corner of her eye. He evidently was not part of the defense planning, having arrived from the direction of a hut tucked away along the tree line, a cozy edifice comprised of wood and stone, propped up with a small staircase leading upward.

Fann looked a bit worse for wear since the last time Sen had seen him. His bad arm was hanging more limply than it normally did; she remembered him looking like that when she first arrived with the Invaders. His shirt was slightly opened, enough for Sen to see the white bandages wrapped heavily around his left shoulder, a prominent dark red stain spreading out from underneath his shirt. His eyes looked sunken, heavy, exhaustion clear and evident on his face, giving him a starkly morose appearance that was uncharacteristic of the haughty and arrogant air he usually carried around him.

Sen could barely focus on him. It was taking all the effort she had to quell her tremors. A chill ran through her, independent of the frigid temperature and snowfall.

Fann grimaced. "Nothing to say to me, traitor? Huh?" He took a predatory step forward as though ready to pounce.

Clenching her eyes shut as another wave of nausea rushed through her, Sen waved the back of her hand at him dismissively, shaking her head with a long exhale as it felt like she was about to vomit. "Just say what you came to say, Fann. I don't have the patience to deal with you right now."

Biting back a laugh, Fann snarled at her. "So, you don't deny it, then? That you sided with the Invaders? Probably slaughtered half the island along the way for your trouble, right?" He spread his arms wide, pushing through the apparent pain as he lifted his left arm past his pain threshold, the bandage coming loose with fresh blood streaming down his chest. "Where are they now, huh? Hiding in the trees? You're only here as another trick, aren't you? You led them right to us, didn't you, bitch? We're going to blink, and suddenly the Invaders are going to spring up out of nowhere and kill us all, aren't they? All thanks to your efforts, right, Curseborn?"

He was just about frothing at the mouth when he was done. Sen had to assume that only part of it was due to the pain in his shoulder. He already had a bloodstain trailing down to his waist, the blood pooling at the end of his tucked-in shirt seeping through the fabric.

Sen rolled her eyes, suppressing a chuckle, if only because of the impending danger of vomit. "The Invaders haven't—*nnghhh*—needed to spring up out of nowhere to...kill indiscriminately." She had difficulty getting the words out. Sweat was pouring down her face. "Just look south of the Forest."

"They probably had help from filth like you," Fann snarled, paying no heed to his reopened wound. "You made it easy for them."

"You really think someone like...*nnngh, shit*...like Han'e would not find dissent in his ranks? That he would just...allow the Invaders to take everything from him?"

Fann spat on the ground, right in front of Sen's feet. "Ugh, Han'e," he said. "Traitor's blood, just like yourself, Curseborn."

"And I bet you feel like a real big man for slaying the 'traitor,' aren't you? If only..." Sen grimaced through another wave of nausea. *Shit, I was really about the slam him, too.* She drew in another deep breath, trying to center herself. When she was ready, she looked to Fann from the corner of her eye and said, "If only the whole situation wasn't your fault."

"Hah! Mine?" Fann knelt beside her, his arm hanging slack at his side. "Hardly. He backed out of an alliance that *we* promised in blood, and he paid for his transgressions in blood. May he *rot*." He stood back up, towering high above Sen, the sun peeking out from behind the clouds beyond his head. "You want to speak of sins? Don't look at mine; all I've done has been for the good of the Tribe. Look to your own sins before you cast your stones."

Sen closed her eyes, wrapping herself up tightly. "What does it matter what I have or haven't done? I'm here now, aren't I?"

"So, in view of the gods, you would say that your sins don't matter? Even after you used the pendant of another, robbing a deserving Tribesperson of their Boon? Even after you killed your own?" He took another step closer, narrowing his gaze at her as he dwarfed her, standing as a mountain over her. "Even after you failed to save your worthless brother?"

The tremors returned in full force. Sen wanted to stand, punch him squarely in his open wound. Her lip quivered as she bit back her tongue. As much as she desired to rise to her feet, she felt herself frozen in place, unable to move. *I'll suffer the gods' punishments for breaking the taboo, or for taking the Chieftain's life, mercy though it was. But I will not suffer you speaking of my brother any longer.*

"Aww, not going to talk back because you know I speak truly?" Fann laughed in that sneering, nasally way he always did. "How many of our people *died* because of *your* actions, Curseborn?!"

"And how many lost their lives for your mother to stage her coup, Fann?"

Fann sharply turned on his heel just as Sen craned her head around his legs. She was happy to hear Tawa's voice again after all this time, after everything that happened, but her heart still sank just the same. She had been dreading this reunion.

Tawa looked no worse for wear, save for some freshly healed cuts and bruises along his face. He approached wearing a long overcoat of snow leopard fur, likely loaned from one of the Keepers, and held a large cup of some type of liquid in one hand.

"Hold your tongue, Tawa," Fann said. "I ought to gut you where you stand for everything you've done."

"Everything I have done?" Tawa said, raising his brow. "Do you mean, after all the care I have given your mother since we arrived here, despite her not deserving it? Do you mean, trying to ensure that our people—not just the Stone Tribe, but *all* of our people—were adequately prepared for the arrival of the Invaders, which you and your mother so horridly neglected?" He took a few steps forward until he was face to face with Fann, near enough to kiss him if he had lost enough of his mind to do so. "Know this, Fann: the only reason you still draw breath is that we need every fighting body we can get right now. And you still have *one* arm you can use, which makes you more useful than a dead man."

Sen stifled a chuckle. *When did Tawa get such a sharp tongue?*

Fann sputtered something inaudible, instead putting a hand to his open wound, his fingers coming back red with fresh blood.

Tawa scoffed. "Go back to the medical tent. Get that shoulder fixed up again. And then see to your mother; I believe she soiled herself as I was leaving. I left it for you to deal with."

With a growl, Fann spat in Tawa's face and scurried off, muttering something under his breath as he left, back toward the raised hut, or the "medical tent," as Tawa called it.

A sullen silence passed between her and Tawa as he sat beside her, unperturbed by the cold ground underneath. After a moment, he passed the cup of liquid over to her.

Looking at it with suspicion, Sen sniffed the top of the cup. "What is it?" she asked.

Tawa laughed. "Water, Sen. Did you think someone would not notice?"

Sen was able to force a laugh as she grabbed the water, downing the contents of the cup in an instant. It didn't do much to quell the tremor or nausea, but she supposed she did feel marginally better.

The defense briefing finally ended, the gathering dispersing into all directions, some headed up to the ridge to work on those ambush points she heard about, each of the present Tribes participating, many of them faces Sen did not recognize. In an instant, the once-open clearing became quite crowded.

Tawa suddenly clapped a hand on her shoulder, startling her to attention. "Ah, sorry, Sen," he said sheepishly. "Just...it is good to see you again."

A genuine smile creaked across Sen's lips. "It's good to see you, too, Tawa. I...I..." She knew what she had to say, but the words did not find their way past her tongue. "It's good to see you," she repeated, instead.

Tawa's gentle hand left her shoulder, and he began twiddling his thumbs, looking off into the distance, not seeming to be focusing on anything in particular. "You know what I want to ask, do you not?"

The tremors returned in full force as Sen closed her eyes. The image of Narva spurting out blood, his expression speaking nothing but pain though his words try to say otherwise, was seared into her memory. "Yes," she managed to squeak out.

Tawa drew a deep breath, a tear already trailing down his cheek. "Narvarho...is he...?" He trailed off, turning to Sen for the answer, his expression already despondent, fearful of the inevitable, and perhaps expectant and accepting of it.

All Sen could do was shake her head, and a river of tears flowed from her eyes.

Immediately, Tawa's face scrunched, and he buried himself in his hands, his body convulsing with tears as he sobbed into his palms. "Oh...my boy," he said, his voice muffled in his hands. "My boy..."

"Tawa, I'm so sorry," Sen said, unable to face the man so near to being her uncle, burying her face in her own hands instead. "It's all my fault. I shouldn't have let him come with me. If it wasn't for me, he'd still be...he'd still be..." She couldn't keep herself from sobbing.

But once again, that gentle hand found itself on her shoulder.

Sen looked up, her face slick with tears, to see Tawa reaching out to her, holding her tightly, even if he wasn't quite able to look at her yet. "It was not your fault, Sen. I...I fully expected it once word of the Invaders' northward march reached us. I..." He trailed off, drawing a deep breath, then another, and another. "The Invaders killed my boy. There is no one to blame but them." He looked at Sen, eyes red, lip quivering. "And when they arrive here, I will not let a single one of them draw another breath."

Sen felt a modicum of relief at that, to know that Tawa's desire for revenge extended only to the Invaders. But all the same, it did not stop the tears from flowing, nor the nausea from pulsating in her stomach.

Tawa's hand left Sen's shoulder and found her hand instead, holding it tightly. "He loved you, you know," he said softly, a slight smile finding its way to his lips. "There were days where...you were all he wanted to speak of. I...looked forward to the day I could call you a daughter."

Some combination of laugh and sob burst out from Sen. She covered her mouth with her free hand, the rivers still flowing from her eyes. Everything she could have had with Narva, she wished for it so dearly, but instead, everything that they could have been was distilled only in one tender moment together, a moment that lasted forever yet fell altogether too short.

"I loved him, too, Tawa," she said, unable to look at him. "Dearly. I...I wish he was...I wish we had more time. It wasn't enough. We deserved more together." She realized the futility of saying that to Narva's father, of all people, but she still felt it deeply, regardless. "You raised a wonderful man, Tawa. I know you must be proud of him. He protected me, he stood up for me, he was one of the few in the village who ever extended to me any show of genuine dignity and respect, and I...I..."

"Is that why you were keen to throw it all away and stand instead with the Invaders?"

The sudden question shook Sen as she looked to her right, and saw both her mother and Tez maintaining a pronounced distance away from her.

Dennalhir looked at her daughter expectantly, clearly waiting for an answer to the question.

Tawa's hand slipped away from hers, slick with tears though it still was. "I will leave you three to yourselves, then. I...I need to..." He looked off to some nondescript place off in the distance, bereft of any further words to say. He made to stand, but Sen immediately grabbed his hand one more time.

"Tawa..." She said, looking up at him as best as she could. "You've always been as near to being family as possible for me and mine. My father always said you were as a brother to him. And I...I would have loved to call you a father, as well."

Flashing a smile, Tawa choked back a sob and stood up, walking away with his hands in his pockets. After a handful of steps, he was burying his face in his hands again, paying little heed to those passing him by.

Despite some of her anxieties being unfounded, the reunion with Tawa still pained her terribly. And now Sen had to confront the other anxiety.

Dennalhir and Tez sat on either side of her, both hesitant to lay a finger on her, and so they each remained at an awkward distance from one another. Close enough to embrace but not brave enough to do so.

"You must think me a monster, don't you?" Sen said, after a prolonged silence, huddling herself into a ball once again.

Her mother and sister both gasped at the question and were quick to shake their heads.

"Sen...never," Tez affirmed, hesitantly putting a hand on her shoulder.

"Then why is it that all I feel is...shame?" Sen wiped a new stream of tears with her forearm. "I finally found...other Eclipseborn. And...after everything, everything that's happened to me, to us, to our family and Tribe...it was the first time I felt I belonged anywhere. But I blinded myself for too long to the reality of what they wanted to do...what they already did."

"Sen..." Dennalhir said, inching closer to hold her daughter, rummaging her fingers through Sen's knotted hair. "My dear child. None of this...none of what's happened is your fault. I do hope you know that."

She wanted to believe that but shook her head into her mother's shoulder, regardless. "I was a fool. So easily swayed. Everything that's happened…it made me feel like it made more sense to embrace the Eclipseborn. I was finally experiencing everything they had, and it seemed like…if I didn't belong with them, then where? And when I finally saw the reality of what I was doing, it just seemed like…a punishment. For being unable to feel anything but jealousy toward Brin after he completed his Trial. For causing Father's and Brin's and Narva's deaths. At that point, it seemed right to have been tricked into parsing through Brin's Memories just to see him and Father denounce me as a curse. So, I—"

"Stop right there, Sen," Dennalhir said, putting a finger to Sen's mouth. "No, absolutely not. You are not a curse. We have told you that from the beginning. The only ones who curse our Tribe, who curse our people, we all know them for what they are, and one of them is completely catatonic right now. *You*, my sweet—" Dennalhir gently grabbed Sen by the back of the head, forcing her to look into her mother's eyes. "—are perfect as you are."

But Sen was quick to shake her head and dismiss that. "I saw…the Memory, though. After Brin completed his Trial. And everything he said after that, and Father didn't disagree. And even when he was brought to the slave pit in the City, he even…called me a Curseborn."

"It's nonsense, Sen," her mother assured. "Yes, your brother was angry when you were not there for his Trial. We *all* were. But you did your best to make amends. And Brin never thought of you as anything less than a wonderful, loving sister. Don't pay any heed to what he said in the slave pits. We all say our worst when at our lowest depths of despair. You still tried to rescue him, didn't you?"

"And failed at it," Sen quickly added. She shook her head again. Tears began to flow once more. "I lost my way. So easily. I proved so many assumptions and accusations about myself to be true. If I could take all of it back, everything that I've done…then Father would still be alive. And Brin, and Narva. But, I…I can't do anything more than what I'm doing right now."

Dennalhir nodded, a tear in her eye. "That's good. Very good." She pressed her forehead to Sen's, still holding softly to her head. "Sen, I blame you for nothing. Just as I know Tawa blames you for nothing. None of this was caused by you. You are my daughter; my fierce, driven, fiery, and caring daughter, and I love you."

Sen choked back a sobbed laugh and buried herself in her mother's chest, wrapping her arms around her. "I love you too, Mother," she said, muffled by Dennalhir's shirt.

A voice shouted Denna's name from afar, to which she audibly groaned. She gently pushed Sen off of her and said, "I'll be right back. The Fens apparently cannot do anything without a Chief's input." She chuckled and kissed Sen atop the forehead. "See you soon."

As their mother walked off to join the Arrow Fens, Sen and Tez regarded each other in silence. The tremors did not leave Sen, and she still needed that drink now more than ever, though the water that Tawa gave her was helping a little bit in that respect.

"So, are you ready?" Tez said hesitantly.

Sen scoffed. "Hell no. Are you?"

Tez shook her head profusely. "Absolutely not. But we're going to fight anyway."

Sen felt for the flintlock at her hip, relieved to still find it there. She drew it to show Tez, much to her sister's shock. "I know it's just one, but...it's more than we have."

"Gods, Sen, do you know how to use that thing?"

With a shrug, Sen merely said, "Aim it, picture I'm shooting someone I want to kill, and pull the trigger. I haven't put the theory into practice yet, though."

Tez pushed the weapon downward. "And we probably don't need to put it into practice just yet, either."

Sen chuckled and holstered the pistol. "There's...another thing. That I think should belong to you." She reached slowly into her pocket, feeling for the familiar chain and ornament. The pendant that had caused her so much grief and pain. But it was still a memento that needed to be saved and cherished. Pulling Brin's Memory pendant out from her pocket, she wrapped the chain around the ornament and pressed it into Tez's open hand.

Tez looked at the pendant with shock, averse to touching it more than she already was. "Sen, I can't. It's...you know it's taboo. I know you've already broken it, but I..."

Quickly, Sen shook her head. "Tez...I know. Trust me when I say it's okay. But the reality is, Brin is buried somewhere near the City, far from here, far from home where he should be buried. And...it's better kept in the hands of someone better than that fate. So, please...take it?"

Tez's hand shook, but after a moment of solemn consideration, she nodded and stowed Brin's pendant in her pocket; once securely inside, she tapped the outside of her overcoat for good measure.. And just as she did so, she reached out and grabbed Sen's hand, holding it tightly, an effort that seemed to quell the tremors a bit.

"Are you anxious?" she asked.

"Well, yes, dear sister," Sen said. "I also *really* need a godsdamned drink."

Tez chuckled. "Given everything...I think all of us could right now."

Sen loosed a shaky breath as she held on to her sister's hand, sitting on the ridge as snow daintily drifted down to the earth, basking the clearing in a pristine glow, unmarred by the taint of the world beyond, but hesitantly awaiting the coming day when the immaculate white canvas would be painted in smears of violent red.

CHAPTER EIGHTEEN

CRY HAVOC

At dawn two days later, the sun shone in a blood-red glow. Sen awoke still feeling the aches and tremors resultant from her need for a drink, but the lack of any drink thereof was enough to stop her from imbibing herself into a stupor. For that, she supposed she had to be thankful.

It did not, however, prevent the nightmares from arriving on consecutive nights. An army of Kamataas and Aritzes staring her down, all by her lonesome, abandoned by all she once thought stood by her, knowing full well she deserved it for betraying her Tribes to the Invaders, and then deserting the Invaders for the Tribes.

When the volley roared for her, she would open her eyes, finding herself in the same frigid tent nestled in the pristine woodlands of the True Heart as she drifted off in. But as soon as she shut her eyes, the nightmare would resume.

So it went. And so, she barely slept at all since then.

Despite the exhaustion, the anxiety of the morning was enough to keep her alert and focused. She donned a heavy winter pelt of Keeper make, the elongated scruff of the neck hiding her Stone braid underneath as it protected the nape of her neck from the force of the elements. Her boots were water-stained but otherwise kept her feet warm. Propping herself up by the sturdy weight of her spear, she fastened the holster for her flintlock around her waist and deposited the weapon into its home for safekeeping. She was wanting for bullets, so she knew she had to make every shot count; she trusted herself more with that weapon than a bow and arrow.

Emerging from the snowcapped trees, she surveyed the clearing, making note of the panicked hustle and bustle of Tribespeople readying themselves. The Packmind scouts had reported an hour ago that the Invaders' arrival was soon to come, and not a soul tarried for long after receiving word of that. Sen had intended to situate herself along one of the upper ridges to provide supporting fire for those engaging the ambush boulders. She thought herself more inclined to join the ranged fighters, especially given she once believed herself to have been born a Wolfsign. Despite donning the spear, it seemed more appropriate to her talents, particularly with the Deatharm at her side.

The snow crunched beneath her feet as she walked across the clearing to the opposite ridge, weaving in and out of the way of numerous warriors walking in the direction counter to her own. Several cursed mutterings were uttered by either party, Sen's typically in response to those levied at herself.

To the rear, as they always were, the Deities sat prominently atop their pedestals, a host of Keepers standing guard over them. Sen noticed Ko Endra, the steward to Ko Zaran, standing at the center, an ornate spear stuck in the snow beside him. She was curious just how much use the weapon ever received, judging by its shimmering sheen.

The Wolf and Owl both seemed as content as they had been the entire time the Tribal forces had been here. The Bear, however, appeared a bit more agitated, sniffing at the Keepers standing guard before it. *Been sleeping the entire time we've been here,* Sen thought. *I'd be agitated, as well, if I were woken up before I was ready to wake.*

The opposing crowds passed her by as she took in the sight of the displeased Bear until, finally, none surrounded her. Sen grimaced as a momentary chill ran up her arms, but it was quick to dispel. The nausea still persisted, but she assumed it was more due to the anxiety of the day.

Brushing away a few beads of sweat, she continued on her way, but off to the corner, at a small ridge off the beaten path, hidden from view from the main clearing, she caught sight of Tez. Initially thinking nothing of it, Sen continued on her way, but as she roamed closer to her destination, she noticed another person with Tez. She had seen this person before: Lake Tribe, from the look of them.

They and Tez were locked in a tender embrace, lips locking in intermittent intervals, but nothing so scandalous beyond that. Were she in her sister's position, Sen would have wanted for privacy and solitude in sharing that moment with someone—the one time she ever received the opportunity.

But, given the circumstances, Sen could not help but have her curiosity piqued by the sight. She planted her spear in the snow and watched from afar as Tez continued to hold her companion tightly until, after a handful of minutes, she finally looked up and flashed a sneer at Sen's grinning face.

From afar, it was clear Tez had an expression of embarrassment upon her face and was quick to brusquely brush her shirt to clear the accumulated snow, offering a hand to her companion as she jumped to her feet. To the other person's credit, they couldn't help but laugh when they noticed Sen staring at them.

Both of them walked up to Sen, Tez a bit more sheepishly. Though Tez looked primed and ready to slap her sister across the face, her companion was much more welcoming upon reaching Sen. They held out their hand, taking hold of Sen's hand. "Somehow, I assumed we may have met this way, Sen," they said, suppressing a laugh.

Sen stifled a chuckle, mainly for Tez's benefit. As she held the person's hand, she took in their features, noting the gentle warmth of their face, the inviting blues of their eyes, and the softness of their skin. Light snow flurries glistened on the thick dark blue coat they wore, the hood drawn up to cover the shorn hair atop their head. "It's quite rare I catch my sister in the act," Sen said teasingly. "It's an honor to be a part of this."

The companion laughed and winked at Tez, planting a kiss on her cheek before they nodded and turned away. "If this was our final night," they said, smirking at Tez as they continued to walk, "then I am glad we made it memorable, Tez of the Stone Tribe."

Sen watched Tez's nocturnal visitor walk toward the clearing in the direction of the Deities in silence. When she opened her mouth, Tez was quick to place her hand over it. "Not a word, Sen."

Prying her sister's hand from her mouth, Sen flashed a wide grin, chuckling to herself. "For all the times you teased me with Narva, can I not have just this one? I thought I heard the wind carrying some interesting noises last night..."

Tez closed her eyes, apparently trying to deliver herself to somewhere else entirely. "Consider yourself lucky, dear sister, that we need every abled body ready today." Despite the threat, she still smiled.

On this day of judgment, it was all they could do but find the humor and laughter in what they could. There was no telling if it would be their last opportunity.

Knowing this, Sen extended an arm and wrapped it around her sister's shoulder. She barely knew what to say. Pre-battle speeches were hardly her forte. Speeches when death itself knocked at their door? Where would she even begin?

Sen swallowed, taking a deep breath, breathing in the crisp air. "I look forward to seeing you when this has all ended," she said.

Tez closed her eyes, and it appeared a lone tear threatened to shed. She reached up and grabbed Sen's hand, gripping it tightly. "Get up there, dear sister," she said, nudging her head toward the ridge, her voice shaking. "Don't think I won't be protecting you."

Sen laughed. "One of these days, it'll be my turn to protect you, just you wait."

They embraced, holding each other as though it was the last time they would ever get to do so. Sen couldn't say for how long they held each other, but after a time, it felt right to let go. They looked at each other for one more moment, and then turned toward their respective positions. Tez went to the front lines, where all the Bearsigns gathered in front of the gods, where their mother stood at attention, positioning warriors alongside the other surviving Chiefs. In between orders, Dennalhir seemed to have caught sight of the approaching Tez, and Sen beyond her, waving an arm to them both in simultaneous greeting and well wishes on the battlefield before returning to her post. Sen sheepishly waved in return but felt out of place among the powerful lot and did not approach.

Sen, meanwhile, turned to the ridge, climbing atop it, using her spear as a walking stick, and found herself a position at the end, still some distance to fill between her and the Wolfsigns grouped with her. Looking down the line, she noticed a sterling combination of Arrow, Sun, Stone, and Lake yeomen along the ridge, readying their arrows and ensuring they were up to snuff. The only face she recognized was that of Daralhat, a lanky Stone Listener with whom she was familiar in passing, being around the same age as her, but she had not said more than two words to him in the last few years. He was never much of a talker, regardless.

Nodding to her comrades, some of whom nodded in return, she sat atop the ridge, legs dangling over the precipice, and she pulled the flintlock pistol from its holster, keeping a weathered eye on the southern horizon. Looking at the Deatharm, she knew not the efficacy with which she would handle the weapon.

All she knew was she would feel no guilt at pulling the trigger when the time came.

The caravan had been a bitch to navigate through these mountain passes, but Aritz would suffer no insufficiencies on the final leg of this journey.

He sat atop his steed, paying little heed to the cursed utterances echoing behind him, the rickety cracks of the caravan drawing him to attention intermittently. There was bickering behind him, calls to pull when others were pushing, horses whinnying in protest, men and women braying in protest just the same.

Aritz felt as though he was presiding over schoolchildren instead trained soldiers. But he would not permit them to ruin this moment for him. The trek through these mountains may have taken substantially longer than he anticipated due to the ineptitude of those drawing the caravan, but the moment had come at last, the moment promised to him all those years ago, the moment he promised to himself as he set out from the Acraria and off to this new world.

The day of glory was at hand.

The morning sun glowed beyond the snowcapped peaks, shimmering just into view and shining over this narrow valley, just wide enough through which to navigate the caravan and the men pushing and pulling it alongside. To the north, snow clouds were forming, the ground underneath growing slicker against the packed ice. Aritz's steed suffered a handful of missteps but nothing that warranted him being thrown aside.

He took a glance over his shoulder, making note of the fabric awning overhanging the caravan, which had soaked through with the previous day's snowfall, as well as the tears and tatters resulting from the bumps against the narrow valley walls. At the front of the caravan, which had carried all of the plunder they had taken from that tribal village, Aritz saw Pock-Face, all wily-eyed and smug, deserving of neither for his overt cowardice in all other situations. He still did not see Dark-Hair and had not seen him in the days since he championed for Kama to consult with him. He found it odd but would not stress over it. Lieutenants came and went. He could always replace them. *And if desertion is the case, then I am the more entertained.*

He did see Kama, however, to the immediate rear left of the caravan, her fiery red locks bouncing freely atop her shoulders. He had not said a word to her since that day, and yet, despite her background as one of the savages, he could not help but feel intrigued by her and why precisely she found her way among his people. *A question for another day.*

The hunter's knife she had bequeathed to him still felt strange to him, both in its idle capacity and in use. Aritz was not one for blades; he found them to be too cumbersome to carry about, and more so when battle called more for the precision of a rifle. He kept it sheathed at the small of his back, the scabbard bouncing rhythmically against his tailbone to the point that it had started to become sore. But stranger still was the sensation he felt when Kama handed it to him. As though there was some innate power housed within the blade's foundation. He hardly wanted to believe in the sorcery that Kama had explained to him; it was all hogwash to him, fairy tales told to entrance children. He was not the audience for such fables of power. Rather, he was the storyteller, or the story-crafter, at that. And whether he had to draw that blade again—which he hadn't since receiving it from Kama—was irrelevant to the next chapter of his tale that was yet to be written.

As his horse continued to canter along the uneven, rocky walkways of the mountain path, he closed his eyes, envisioning that fateful day when he took up his father's place, to embark upon the journey that Lord Nofre a Mata was so keen on setting out upon. This journey to a new world, a land of wealth and riches and glory.

The journey that was always meant for Aritz himself.

The necessity of his father's passing aside, Aritz still felt grief for his father's death. He had always envisioned taking this journey with him. He decried it as a shame that it could not become a reality.

But as the mountain path crested before him, he took a deep, assured breath, feeling nothing but the satisfaction of the victory to come. He opened his eyes, pulling his horse to a stop, and took in the sight, a pristine and beauteous landscape marred by the presence of the horrid savages standing in wait for him.

Despite it all, he could not help but chuckle to himself. *If this is the calling upon which the Savior beckons me, then gladly I will take up as his sword. I will cut through each and every one of them if that is required of me.*

Bowing his head, he offered a prayer of safety to the Savior, for his own triumph in this battle to come, and for the glory of the Mata name, on this day, and all the days to follow.

Motioning his steed to turn, he faced his soldiers and raised his arms out to them. They all looked upon him with great interest, but on the faces of some, there was visible exhaustion from the continuous trudge through these mountains with minimal time afforded for rest. *Victory awaits no man*, he had often thought to himself.

"We are at the precipice of a glorious day!" he bellowed to his soldiers. "The history books shall speak fondly on this day. The day when at last, an abomination was purged from this earth, and the light of the Savior shone brightly, unimpeded! Steel yourselves, soldiers; the brightest day in the history of our Kingdom awaits us!"

The soldiers roared in response, perhaps not with the same ferocity of the great lions from the sandsteppes to the east of Acraria, but enough still.

Aritz chuckled to himself as he turned his steed back toward the clearing ahead. *And to my own history, may this be the finest chapter the scribes shall write. The day Aritz a Mata fulfilled his destiny as the Sword of the Savior!*

Kamataa had never been one for wanton celebration, but even she could not help but join in on the declarations for victory alongside her fellow soldiers.

Seeing Aritz atop that horse, expounding rhetoric that he very clearly did not believe in, it put quite a smile on her face. She had seen many a man like Aritz a Mata in her days, hiding the truth behind hollow platitudes and proclamations that were simply easy for the audience to digest and celebrate. Some of them died by her own hand.

But none quite had the same ambition that Aritz displayed. And none quite had the same unbridled hatred for the Tribes to see that ambition come to light.

It was enough to make her laugh.

The air was rife with anticipation as she rested her hand atop her flintlock, her fingers tapping eagerly against the holster at her thigh. Hollow and Vanta stood at either side of her, themselves sandwiched between the carts of the caravan. It was quite humorous watching these sad sods force the coaches up through these mountain ranges and impressive that none of the cargo was lost along the way. Aritz was rather insistent that every cart was brought along.

Whether that was part of standard Acrarian military practice, Kamataa could hardly care enough to know. All that mattered to her was the outcome of this day. The culmination of centuries of waiting. All the friends and comrades lost along the way. Everything she had done to ensure this day came to pass.

The loss of Ziia was still fresh on her mind. She felt numb to all her emotions, save for the anger that propelled her forward, and the excitement at this day finally arriving.

"May the Moon bless us all on this day," she said to Hollow and Vanta. She was licking her lips with anticipation. She felt like a dog being presented with a thick slab of meat, though not yet permitted to go about consuming it. She wanted nothing more than to run past the lines ahead of her, breaking the ranks so inadequately set, bolting past Aritz himself, and leading the charge on the battlefield. She feared nothing that awaited them. They held no surprises for her.

Everything in its place, she reminded herself. *And for what we must wait, we shall wait.*

Vanta kept her hands behind her back, keeping certain not to touch anyone around her. "By the Moon's grace, may we claim victory in Her name," she said.

"A victory we claim, guided by Her light," Hollow finished.

"And for Ziia," Kamataa said, her teeth gritting. "All that is to come, I shall do in honor of her memory." Sennalhat's face flashed in her mind; the very idea of that turncoat betraying Ziia to the Tribes, to the very people who stripped her of everything, only fueled her eagerness and anger. *Do not think I have forgotten you, Sennalhat. I will rob you of everything you believe you have remaining.*

The entourage seemed to be moving again as Aritz finished with whatever rousing speech he pulled out from his ass. The snow clouds were forming a dense barrier overhead, the gentle white flakes falling delicately upon Kamataa's nose as she looked up. *Enjoy this last peaceful snow while it lasts, you monsters.*

As she marched in step with the rest of the army, Kamataa flashed a smile to her two Eclipseborn companions. "Are you both ready to play?"

They nodded without hesitation.

Kamataa flicked the hammer of her flintlock. "Then let the games begin."

The roar of the Invaders carried over from the southern horizon, their echo akin to the beckoning of hellhounds. Almost immediately, the Tribes stood to attention, the Bearsigns on the ground preparing their spears, the glimmers of the Bear's Boons acting as a beacon against the thickening snow squalls, as though to warn against the forces of nature themselves that the Tribes would not be deterred, would not be quelled, and would not be afraid.

Atop the ridge, Sen slid away from the edge, laying prone against the ground, feeling the snow piling atop the back of her thick coat. She tightened the scarf around her neck, drew the flintlock pistol from its holster, checked her pocket for her supply of bullets, and placed the weapon in front of her. Her hands shook as she examined the gun, this tool of death that had so easily felled countless of her people, that had felled her father and her brother and Narva. It almost felt wrong to wield it.

But it also feels right to turn it against these bastards, she thought.

She held her quivering hand in place, grasping the weapon, resting it atop the cold stone beneath her, and laid in wait. To her left, she could see the row of Wolfsigns doing much the same, some more attentive than others, all the way to the carved boulders where Daralhat knelt alongside others, all ready to loose the ambush. All it would take would be a collective shove, the formation chiseled down to its final threads, for the boulders to fall down the ridge and hopefully crush a significant number of the Invaders along with it, both on the initial impact and on the subsequent slide down the slope back south.

Sen closed her eyes, the pounding of her chest echoing in her ears. The waiting was the hardest part. She remembered her father telling her much the same from his tales of ambushes and combat, long ago though they were. *Surely, a trap was never such a matter of life and death for you, was it, Father?* She felt a chill run through her that was independent on the snow piling atop her. All she could do was look to her comrades to her left, and then to the opposite ridge, where the equivalent ambush was being led by the Arrow Fens, and then to the clearing, where she could just barely see her mother's face illuminated by the glow of her pendant, Tez not far from her.

The pit in her stomach felt cavernous. Drawing deep breath after deep breath, Sen kept a watch on the Wolfsigns to her left to see how they were managing. Some twiddled their thumbs along the frame of their bows, others seemed to be offering prayers to the gods, others stared straight ahead with no anxiety on their faces at all as though they had done this sort of thing before. She envied them for their calm dispositions.

The commotion of the Invaders grew louder. They cared little about masking their arrival; they knew the Tribes were aware of their coming. There was no point in hiding it. The clacking of horseshoes on the icy rocks echoed through the valley, along with the creaking and cracking of something large that they were towing along with them. Sen couldn't say for certain, but she was at the very least impressed at their dedication to bringing it this far into the Heart with them.

Sen got in position, still lying prone but positioning her foot in a way that would allow her to pounce quickly once the boulders dropped. She gripped her pistol in one hand, her thumb hovering over the hammer, and reached for the shaft of her spear, readied for whatever surprises may come up the ridge.

The horses clacked ever closer, the arrival of the Invaders imminent. Sen's breathing quickened, every part of her body quivering. She gritted her teeth, clenching her eyes shut, waiting for that heavy impact to accompany panicked screams and death cries. It was soon. It had to be soon.

Closer and closer came the Invaders, the sound of their approach growing so loud that it almost felt as though they were right on top of her. The snorts and whinnies of the horses were almost...too close.

When she opened her eyes, she shimmied along the ridge, careful not to drop any accumulated snow over the side. She peeked her eyes over the edge, all the clever sneaking she had attempted to do as a young child all coming back to her in the attempt.

Her eyes widened when she saw the Acrarian host all but clearing the opening to the clearing, Aritz sitting tall atop his horse, all the satisfaction in the world strewn atop his face as though nothing was amiss.

Immediately, Sen shot a glance to her side, shuffling back to her prior position, ignoring the bite of cold as snow slid underneath her coat. The boulders were still in place, with barely any movement at all among those at the ambush point save for Daralhat, who was trying with little success to drop the boulders on the Invaders. Across the ridge, she could see some animated gesturing from one of the Fens, wondering much the same.

"What the hell is going on?" Sen whispered harshly to the Wolfsign beside her.

The yeoman, a Lake Wolfsign with wild and bright eyes, shrugged with much the same confusion.

It was only when Sen rose slowly to a knee that she realized the true state of what was happening.

Almost as one, several of the Wolfsigns along the ridge rose and nocked their arrows, opening fire...but not at the Invaders. Sen dove out of the way, feeling the Luck surge through her arms as all the plumes passed her by. She regained her footing and realized the Lake Wolfsign beside her had been run through with several from the small volley; one was jutting out from his skull. He barely had a chance.

All along the ridge, it seemed every other Wolfsign had lost their mind. Arrows zipped by Sen, all the while some drew their hunting knives or even loose arrows and forced them down into the throats of their brothers- and sisters-in-arms.

Sen's eyes widened, her arms shaking. She dove for her spear, Luck flaring in her limbs, and almost instinctively swung the weapon in a wide arc, opening up the stomach of a charging traitor, the ground steaming underneath as the woman, someone who Sen assumed was of the Arrow Tribe, stained the vibrant white snow in a pool of red.

On the opposite ridge, it was much the same. Several seemed to be pushing toward the ambush point, meeting heavy resistance from more traitors.

Staring down at the dying woman before her, Sen felt a sickening sensation rising through her. Another Tribal life, taken by her own hand, even if only in self-defense. But then a nagging voice irked at her, a memory from what seemed like ages ago.

It is all of those who were rejected from the Tribes for not "proving their worth" in their Trial...They're among us, too, patrolling this city, roaming the Land, standing among what remains of the Tribes.

The reality of Kamataa's words had never sunk in for her. Sen had only assumed the Children of the Black Moon to be those borne of the Eclipse. *Just how deep do Kamataa's claws dig?* she wondered.

The thunderclap of Deatharms roared over the valley. Sen ducked away from the precipice, feeling simultaneously the surge of Luck and chills of fear overcome her. Enough commotion had been drawn atop the ridge for the Invaders to take notice. True Wolfsigns and traitors alike felt the impact of the Invader assault, blood-red snow falling unceremoniously to the earth.

With a deep breath, Sen faced the road ahead, witnessing the confusion and paranoia over who was truly of the Tribes and who was planted among them.

And as Sen eyed the sight beyond, where Daralhat still tried with all his might to engage the trap, a feeling of dread overcame her. A figure, unseen to her from behind Daralhat, walked away from the boulder, staring at the skirmish ahead.

It took barely a second for Sen to recognize the other immediate threat among them.

She clicked the hammer of her pistol back and aimed.

As arrows rained down without discrimination or recourse, Daralhat knew his time was running short.

"Are you going to help me or not?" he growled to the woman beside her, a Lake woman with hair falling well past her shoulders, scars running along the length of her fingers. Daralhat had been pushing at the boulder for some time now, ever since he heard the approach of the Invaders' horses. He was eager to send it over the ridge. He had always wanted to prove himself to his Tribe ever since his father was killed unceremoniously in a hunting accident and his mother died due to his sickness. But no matter how hard he pushed, the boulder would not budge.

He was meant to be teamed with three others; it was determined that the strength of four was more than enough to set this trap in motion. But when the traitors revealed their hand, the two to Daralhat's immediate right were stuck in with a volley of arrows, one of them only barely skimming his shoulder. Though he could feel his shoulder slickening with blood, the wound was superficial at best, no more than a sharp sting.

The Lake woman was hardly any help at all. Though she shoved at the boulder, it seemed she was putting none of her strength into the effort, doing little more than just placing her hands on the stone and spreading her legs wide.

"Come on, now, push!" Daralhat said with more venom to his tone, spittle flying from the force of his words.

"I'm trying, I'm trying!" the woman said. Nothing on her face said she was trying at all.

Blood splashed on Daralhat's boots as an arrow protruded from the hunter beside him. He eyed the man, someone from the Arrow Tribe, as he continued to shove at the boulder, amazed that the Wolfsign was still standing, the shot having taken him through the chest, probably missing his heart by mere inches.

The Arrow fighter flashed a glance at him and nodded as though to promise he would protect him. He drew the hunter's knife from the small of his back and charged forward, taking two of the traitors in one fell swoop before meeting a match with another's blade. The steel rang together in a raucous chorus, echoing over the hills, sure to draw the attention of the Invaders if they had not already.

As his protector fought on, Daralhat looked to the Lake woman beside him, her effort still barely matching that of his own. Her pushes seemed to grow more exaggerated as she bent her body at a strange angle not at all conducive or safe to this degree of physical strain, the chain of her pendant nearly falling out from underneath her shirt.

He slapped her on the back, trying to urge her forward. "Come on, we're running out of time here!" His plea fell on deaf ears as nothing happened beyond the woman's pendant escaping from beneath her shirt, hanging slack around her neck as she continued to place her hands firmly on the stone.

Daralhat drew in a deep breath and nearly tried to run through the boulder, his feet finding no purchase in the unpacked snow beneath him. He slipped and slid as he turned around and propped his shoulders against the boulder, trying and failing to use the strength of his legs to engage the trap. But still, it would not budge.

You should have been there with your father. It should have been you!

His mother's dying words still rang in his head to this day, five years on though it had been. His father's ill-fated hunting trip was one that Daralhat was meant to join, but he fell to a minor sickness and opted instead to stay home. His mother, always resentful of him for reasons beyond his understanding, never forgave him for leaving his father to be slain. He never forgave himself, either.

I'll show you, Mother, he thought. *This time, I will protect everyone!*

He strained and strained, his skull aching as the heat rose through him. If this Lake woman was not going to help him, then he would have to do it all himself.

The Invaders' Deatharms roared from below in the valley, his fellows on the ridge falling indiscriminately to their strikes just as the arrows continued to rain down.

"Shit, shit, come on, come on!" Daralhat growled.

He looked once more at the woman beside him, staring at her dangling pendant as he continued to strain against the weight of the boulder. Something about the glow of the rune on the ornament struck him. There was little need for a Wolfsign to draw in their Boon in this situation. *Is she of a different Sign?*

And then the rune became clearer to his eyes. *Illusion? Why does she need Illusion up here? She's among her fellow Tribespeople.*

When the woman caught his glare, she looked down to her pendant and grinned, motioning her head and raising an eyebrow. Almost instantly, the rune dimmed, and her Illusion dispelled, revealing a young adult probably more or less the same age as him, the contours of her face growing more defined and harsh, her hair nearly disappearing to a more traditional Lake Tribe length, her eyes equal parts intense and wild.

Daralhat was befuddled by the sight and the need for her Illusion.

He only grew more befuddled as she stopped pretending to shove at the boulder and began to walk away.

"W-wait!" he said. "Where the hell are you going? We—"

The young woman reached out and touched a hand to his shoulder, tapping him lightly. "I have other matters I must see to," she said, flashing a smile.

As she walked away, Daralhat looked at her with indignant confusion. She was so nonchalant about her desertion, so noncommittal to her own survival. It perplexed him to no end.

Torn between engaging the trap, for what little good it would do at this juncture, and chasing after the woman, Daralhat chose to remain where he was. *Someone else will take care of her*, he thought to himself. *I need to...I need...protect...pro...what?*

His vision grew spotty, his head heavy with dizziness. He shook his head back and forth, trying to regain some visual clarity, but it only made everything worse. He clenched his eyes, but the light began to tunnel before him, and before he knew it, all of his strength was sapped. As he pressed up against the boulder with one final push, he felt the warm splash of blood on his face as his Arrow protector fell next to him, a long gash adorning his throat.

Daralhat slid down against the boulder, feeling none of the cold of the ground below him, and as the blackness surrounded him, the last thing he saw was that Lake woman flashing a sinister grin at him.

Mother... he thought. *It seems you finally have your wish.*

Zara stared at the Stone man pitiably, chuckling to herself. It had been a long while since she willfully used the Touch. Or perhaps to say it had originally been "willfully" was a bit of a stretch.

But regardless, when she felt her power surge through the man as he futilely attempted to push over a rock...it felt invigorating. Incredible, even. Looking ahead along the ridge, there were plenty of others with whom she could feel that sensation again.

She stretched her head in one direction and then the next, feeling her neck crack in the motion. "Time to get to work," she said, a smirk upon her face.

The Acrarian rifles continued to roar down in the valley, met in response by the roar of the Tribes charging headlong into the fray. *How delightful*, she thought, seeing the two forces meet in a crash of bodies. *I think I'll make my way there.*

As the volley of rifle fire continued, Zara suddenly felt a sharp bite in the meat of her shoulder, knocking her completely off-balance. She dropped to a knee, pressing a hand to the wound. It seemed the bullet went clean through, her flesh searing from inside. She sucked in a breath, almost relishing the pain. "Now that's a lucky shot," she muttered, but as she surveyed the valley below, she raised a brow at how that shot made it her way...until she saw the plume of smoke from further along the ridge.

Zara smiled, wincing as she stretched out her arm through the pain, blood still seeping out from the wound, and kept her eyes peeled to the source of the smoke. "Well, hello, Sennalhat," she said softly. "Let's see how far your Luck takes you, shall we?"

A wall of Wolfsigns stood behind her and Sennalhat. As she cracked her knuckles, she cared little to distinguish who among them pledged themselves to the Children. She was only here to follow Kamataa's orders, and that extended to punishing deserters.

She shot forward and shoved a yeoman aside, feeling the rush of the Touch surge from her to him, and watched his confusion as he lay on the ground, unaware of precisely why his life was leaving him. Licking her lips, Zara wove in and out of the paths of arrows and gunfire alike, pressing her hands to everyone she passed through, the energy flowing through her electrifying, addictive. In droves, these warriors fell about her, all drawing a collective last breath.

It amused Zara greatly to see Sennalhat struggling on her own at the edge of the ridge, her Luck hardly a useful tool for the throes of battle.

Those remaining atop the ridge stopped in visible horror at the sight of Zara, seeing the host of dead bodies behind her, all felled with hardly an effort at all. *Why...why did I hide this?* she thought. *This is exhilarating!*

She outstretched her arms, beckoning for more to challenge her. *Ah, I can only hope Sha'a is having just as much fun on the other ridge as I am!*

Several stepped forth, ridding themselves of their cumbersome bows and charging at her with their hunting knives. Zara welcomed the challengers, ducking in and out of blows, feeling the surge run through her with just the slightest of Touches as she gripped a wrist to turn away a blade, shoved a man aside, or tackled another to the ground. It was so...easy. She had barely a scratch on her.

The next wave of challengers approached her, steel glistening with snowfall and blood both. This intermingling of Tribes and backgrounds, of outcasts and warriors, none of it mattered to her. Not on this day.

Two Wolfsigns, one from the Lake Tribe and one from the Sun Tribe, charged her at once, while another fired a twin shot of arrows above them. Zara rolled to the side, tarrying along the ridge, and punched at the two knife-wielders. One strike connected, but the other was turned aside with the blade, the edge cutting a swath through Zara's hand, blood pouring out from where one of her fingers had once been.

She sucked in a breath, welcoming the pain again, when another gunshot caught her in the arm, the plume of smoke again indicating Sennalhat had found a moment to line up a shot. The impact pushed Zara back, and suddenly, her leg dangled over the edge of the ridge, her weight supported by her arms and opposite leg. She snarled in Sennalhat's direction as she pushed herself back up, in search of solid footing. "You won't get Lucky a third time, Sennalhat!" she screamed as the pain surged through her, the energy she had exerted finally catching up to her.

The yeomen and warriors approached her with caution as she tried to get her footing stable once again. Even in a weakened state, she was happy to see them so fearful of her. *As you all should. With each one of you that falls to me, it's like claiming my bastard uncle's life all over again!*

She was just about to place her left leg back atop the ridge when the strength of her right leg left her entirely. Blood erupted from her thigh, bursting forward in a rush, and as the searing pain coursed through her, her foot slipped. And she fell backward.

Reaching up with nothing to grab, Zara could only wait for the earth below to rush up to meet her. The last thing she felt before it all went black was a sickening crunch.

Porico was never one of the best shots in his class, but he was quite proud of the target he had hit. That savage was knocked clean off the ridge. He was happier, though, that he didn't hear the impact when she hit the ground.

It was the first shot he had made all day. That was hardly anything new for him. When he was merely a cadet, he would go days in between hitting his targets properly. The only reason he was ever admitted into the army was that his parents were once a family closely tied to the Matas. Not that that accounted for much these days. General Aritz probably didn't even know his name.

He couldn't see any more of the savages atop the ridge where he hit his shot, but he could still see their arrows flying in wide arcs. He had to wonder why they were firing at each other, but he was not going to look a gift horse in the mouth when he did not have to duck out of the way of them. He had enough of that in that forest with all the tree-dwellers about. No one needed to know the number of shields he had made out of his comrades, alive or otherwise.

The smartest are the ones who survive. That was what his father always told him. And right now, Porico felt pretty damn smart.

He found himself in something of an advantageous position. He was far from the frontline fray, and therefore did not need to meet the spears head-on, even if he was being gradually pushed in the direction by the forward march. It was only a matter of time before the rear guard he found himself in would reach that clearing ahead, then he could find a place to breathe and recuperate.

It was also advantageous that the savages atop the ridge were more set on fighting amongst each other than launching their arrows at him. Not many around him seemed to relish being placed in the rear guard, but he was all the happier for it.

And when this is all over, I can return home to my family and retire a hero to the Kingdom. A commendation for my services from General Aritz, too, maybe?

Slowly, Porico reloaded his rifle, taking his time since there was no rush to defend against either side of the ridge. The clearing was approaching ever closer, the savages apparently being pushed further and further back against the Acrarian might, as was to be expected. The Acrarian army was unrivaled, as far as Porico was concerned. They never retreated, they only rested. And he had gotten plenty of rest after the battle a few days ago outside that village.

The caravan carts pushed past the clearing, some twenty or thirty rows ahead of him. Anxious to see that open air for himself, and eager to remove himself from the horrid stench of death permeating through this valley, Porico pushed himself through the rows ahead, much to the chagrin of his fellow soldiers. Many cursed at him as he shoved them aside, some of them lining up shots of their own, readying themselves for the returning fire from the high ground, whenever it was due to arrive.

For his part, Porico moved the rifle barrels out of his way when necessary. One soldier spat in his face as he did so. "Come now, my friend," Porico said to the spitter. "They're a bit preoccupied with themselves up there. There's no need to worry so."

He barely felt the arrow run through the side of his neck and couldn't comprehend why blood spurted from his mouth until it was far too late.

With a fire in her heart and lightning at her fingers, Rek'na fired a furious volley down toward the amassed Invaders, hitting several in non-extremity locations but one through the throat.

For fifteen years, she had vociferously voiced the necessity of taking the fight to the Invaders with her brother Tol'e. She was forever irate that Chief Han'e was far too much a coward to take a stand for the Sun Tribe, to take back what was theirs.

Now, Tol'e and Han'e were both dead, and all Rek'na had was this. This bow, this fire, and this fight.

She had to hand it to the Arrow Fens. They were quick to make note of the traitorous uprising among those situated among the ridge, quicker still to note that Eclipseborn who ran off to who knows where. Now she had all the time in the world to line up her shots and take down the Invaders, one by one, until they were all bleeding and screaming.

The valley was just about cleared. A small host of Invaders were dead upon the ground, intermixed with several of the Tribal fighters who had fallen from either ridge. But otherwise, the rear guard of the Invaders was making its way toward the clearing, and from there, it would be up to the Bearsigns to bear the brunt of that assault.

Rek'na drew a handful of arrows from her quiver, planting each one in the ground in front of her, and took a knee. The Invaders were no longer paying any mind to her. One by one, she drew, nocked, and loosed her arrows, the harsh winds of snowfall no longer the only danger to the Invader army. She felt a flare run through her with each subsequent arrow, the fury in her growing ever fiercer.

"How do you like *that*, you foreign bastards!" she bellowed, laughing uncontrollably as she watched her arrows rain down on them. "Give us back our home! Give it back!"

When one quiver emptied, she reached for another, performing the same ritual as before, placing each arrow before her, ready for the next strike. She only wished she could hear the death cries of each Invader she stuck, to see the look in their eyes when they realized the futility of facing one of the greatest hunters the Sun Tribe has ever known. But the air was too dense with the snow and sound of Deatharms. With her Boon of Movement, she could *feel* the tremors in the earth as the Invaders fell to her arrows, but their dying breaths were beyond her. She would only have to imagine them. The gurgling of blood and prayers to return home to their mothers was an image of the Invaders that truly helped Rek'na sleep at night sometimes.

A Stone hunter set up beside her, seeing the open and unperturbed setting as one worth camping at. Rek'na eyed her carefully, recognizing her as the huntress Sharrabha. It was only a few days prior that she had crossed paths with Rek'na, their blades and arrows both meeting, and yet, in this moment, it was water under the bridge. Anyone who shared the same proclivity for felling Invader bastards was more than okay to her.

Sharrabha smirked at Rek'na and nocked not one but *two* arrows to her bowstring. She fired them simultaneously, the wind taking them to separate locations but finding two separate successful targets just the same.

Rek'na sneered. "Won't do you good to show me up, now, will it? You're just wastin' arrows!"

"No, I'm just *efficient!*" Sharrabha replied, performing the same act once again.

Rek'na shook her head, content enough to proceed through her line of arrows, nock them individually, and watch her target fall unceremoniously. To her, it was a much more personal approach. She felt a greater connection to her prey that way. Elsewise, it was little more than just showing off.

As more and more Invaders fell to Rek'na and Sharrabha's volleys, a sudden wave of Tribal Bearsigns seemed to collectively collapse. It was hard to tell from this distance just how it happened; many of them fell forward. *More dissent in the ranks?* Rek'na wondered.

She shook her head, and packed up her remaining arrows, depositing them back into her quiver. "Come on," she said to Sharrabha. "How the wind's pickin' up, we're just about useless back here."

Sharrabha quickly shook her head. "Go ahead, I'll cover!" And then she aimed squarely across the valley, taking one of the traitors on the other side clean in the throat. "Just shoot with the wind!"

Rek'na stormed off, feeling the snow kick up underfoot, nearly slipping for the effort. *Damn this fuckin' cold,* she thought. *Sooner we can get our home back, the better.* The final row of Invaders had cleared the valley, standing squarely in the clearing, no longer impeded by the narrow confines of the high rock walls, leaving the massive carts they had dragged in at the valley's mouth. She saw the Fens holding several of the Invaders down alongside other Wolfsigns, not allowing any of them to ascend the ridge. That was where Rek'na wanted to be.

She took off in a sprint, nocking an arrow as she slid down the snow-covered hill, and loosed a quick volley, one arrow after the other, finding several Invaders either between the eyes or through the skull. Deatharms deafened the air as she drew closer to the action, such to the point that the shouts of her comrades surrounding her were little more than vague murmurings from far away.

Someone was shouting for her. Distantly, she could hear someone calling her name. It mattered little. While she presided over the precipice, lining up her next shot, something caught her on the heel. Nothing more than a little bite from something. But whatever it was, it kicked up the ground behind her foot, and she lurched forward, her balance leaving her. All her momentum carried her on, and, unable to grasp on to anything for purchase, she tumbled over the ridge, landing with a heavy impact in the snow below, the soft piles breaking her fall. Her bow slid past a line of Invaders upon meeting the ground.

Her sudden arrival was not lost on the Invaders. Several in the rear guard turned to attention. Rek'na welcomed the challenge.

Rolling to her feet, ignoring the pain shooting up her back, she dashed toward the Invaders, ducking under the path of their long Deatharms, drawing her hunter's knife in one hand and a stray arrow in the other. Sliding beneath their weapons, she slashed at the leg of one with her knife and stuck the arrow through another's groin, but that was all she managed.

As the ankle-deep snow slowed her forward momentum, her face met the butt end of one of the Deatharms, knocking her flat on her back, a surge of pain flaring through her nose. Something had to have been broken. Her vision clouded, the world a blur. Something billowed stagnant smoke before her face, and then there was a flash.

Borredan ignored the pained groans of his two fellow soldiers. However much they were bleeding mattered little to him. Everyone bled on this battlefield. If you were not bleeding, you were not trying.

That tribal girl's knife must have cut an artery on one of them, though. The blood was gushing forward in a crimson eruption. The soldier was reaching out to Borredan with one hand while trying, without success, to put pressure on his leg to slow the bleeding.

Borredan smacked the hand away and then shoved the soldier to the ground, joining him with the other who had the arrow stuck through his groin. "Sorry, boys. I'm no medic. They'll sing songs of your exploits of this day: 'The Soldiers Who Were Also There' seems a good title for you."

"F-f-fuck you, Borredan!" cried the soldier with the sliced artery, his voice a shrill shriek. "They'll...they'll...they..."

Whatever "they" would do to him would never be known. The lad bled out rather quickly.

Despite the chaos that surrounded him, Borredan was content to take his time reloading his rifle. The inevitability of death in battle was a welcomed certainty. In his early years, fighting alongside the King's Own, he supposed he feared death. But nowadays, after three decades on the battlefield, serving one upstart lord or another, the only thing he feared was being forced to survive.

Slowly, he aimed his rifle, pulled the trigger, and came up empty, feeling no disappointment at missing his target. As the fracas pushed onward, Borredan wondered what the future had in store for this General Aritz. He was only assigned to him within the last two years after his prior liege lord had taken an unfortunate fall from a horse and found himself on the wrong end of a gorge in the Acrarian Mountains. The bottom end of the gorge.

The lord previous to that fell in an unwarranted battle with some tax collectors, who had come to collect the taxes he had opted not to pay for many years. The prior lord to that simply blew his own brains out on a whim.

After a while, the only death that Borredan had never bore witness to was his own.

He aimed his rifle again, finding a head peeking out from atop the ridge. But when he pulled the trigger, something bit sharply into his arm, sending his shot far wide and into the snowcapped forest beyond.

He looked with disinterest at his left arm, finding the quill of an arrow lodged directly into the meat of his bicep. "Huh," he grunted. "That's unfortunate."

With some degree of pain, he set about the process of reloading his rifle, unsure of the number who waited for his counterstrike atop that ridge. But at this point in his life, he was fully accepting of the result.

He grunted as another arrow took him in his shoulder blade, turning him on his heel. Another to the chest spun him around in the other direction. He could only laugh.

Borredan tossed his rifle aside, feeling blood trickle down the corner of his mouth and into the stubble of his graying beard, catching sight of the sharp arc of a final arrow launched from over the ridge.

With a smile, he looked forward to finally introducing himself personally to the cold hands of death.

"Poven! Two approaching from the left!"

Fen-Detu slid in and out of cover, taking aim from behind a natural rock formation at the tree line of the sacred forest. The way the Invaders broke free of the valley walls, one would think that they would not be so welcoming to a quick death. Regardless, Fen-Detu was more than willing to offer that to them.

With a smile on his face, Fen-Detu timed his slide to when Fen-Poven loosed his next volley, using the covering fire to take down two additional Invaders, his brother felling his own targets with ease. Meanwhile, off to the right, Fen-Osenta, weaving in and out of the range of the Invader weaponry as though it was a dance, cut a swath through the enemy ranks, blood falling to the earth in a waltz of red.

The Fen brothers had faced worse during the Steppe Conflict. The Arrow Tribe prided itself upon its unpredictability in the throes of battle, maintaining unconventional battle lines, spreading out only to link back up again, raining down volleys of arrows from every which direction.

The Invaders, though? They made it all too easy. They assembled in orderly lines, hardly deviated from that tactic, and their weaponry took far too long to reload. There was precious little to fear.

"Osenta!" Fen-Detu bellowed, his dark hair coming undone from its long braids from the force at which he slid from one point of cover to the next. "Point of weakness at the front line! Seven from the left!"

The elder Fen nodded, flipping over a nearby rock, catching his breath to draw an arrow. Only just barely turning his head over his shoulder, Fen-Osenta quickly aimed and fired; the weak point marked by Fen-Detu crumbled in an instant. For his part, Fen-Detu spotted another weak point in the second row, some thirty soldiers to the right, barely taking the time to aim before launching and felling that foundation as well.

Just as those two soldiers fell, the Bearsigns pressed their advantage, taking the opportunity to catch the Invaders while they were in between reloading.

"Brothers!" Fen-Osenta shouted, the other Wolfsigns joining rank to meet them. He put two fingers to his eyes and then pointed them at another weak flank at the rear.

Fen-Detu nodded, tucking his braids behind his back so as to not impede his vision. Drawing one arrow to the bow and holding another in his mouth, he aimed in a wide arc and loosed. The bolt cascaded down through the heavy squalls, and just as it was about to hit, he quickly took the arrow from his mouth and immediately fired, the process easily taking two unsuspecting Invader soldiers before either had any idea of what happened.

The scrape of steel rasped in Fen-Detu's ear as Fen-Poven drew his hunter's knife beside him. "Low and silent," the youngest brother said. "We can cut a swath through that rear guard."

Fen-Detu narrowed his eyes, taking a good strong look at that gathering. With the two he just felled, it was clear that that section of Invaders was reserved for the unskilled and infirmed, many of them displaying clear signs of exhaustion or sickness; perhaps it was they who were fool enough to drag those carts into the mountains. Many of them held on to their Deatharms unconventionally, or barely held them properly at all. Despite never having wielded such a weapon, the practical means of wielding it was not lost on Fen-Detu.

If there was one thing that the Arrow Tribe had learned since its defeat at the hands of these Invaders all those years ago, it was to learn from past mistakes, study the enemy. They had plenty of time to do so in the years since.

Looking to his brother, Fen-Detu joyfully slid his knife out from his sheath, twirling it around in his fingers until he nestled it in a reverse grip. Nodding to Fen-Osenta from across the path, he pointed at the Wolfsigns from the other Tribes, instructing them with hand gestures to offer covering fire from behind these rock formations.

Sliding out into the clearing, the three Fens nearly ran on their knees for how low they kept to the ground, their blades ready to strike at the first opportunity presented to them. Snow kicked up in white tufts as the first blade was brought down into an Invader's back, his heart an easy target ripe for the taking. Fen-Detu quickly withdrew his knife and moved along the line, hamstringing a quick succession of soldiers before just as quickly drawing his steel across their throats. Off to the side, a collective gurgle of blood squelched onto the glistening snow, red spray splashing against the backsides of those in front of them.

Just as soon as the Invaders were aware of the bloodletting behind them, they were greeted by the vengeful arrows of the Wolfsigns remaining on the ridge, taken down before they even had a chance to recognize what was happening. Fen-Detu could not help but grin at the ease at which they fell, nodding with appreciation to his brothers and the Wolfsigns covering him.

"Detu!" shouted Fen-Poven, pointing to something behind his brother.

Fen-Detu felt his breath catch in his throat. He knew his brother would never willingly give away a location like that. But it was not anywhere near enough time to stop the heavy impact at the back of his neck.

As he brought down the butt of his rifle again and again on the savage's head, Bernaldino laughed through his hacked coughs. Tears streamed down his cheeks as he clicked his rifle into place and fired, missing widely at the two blade-wielders as they scurried into the throng, blood spraying every which direction from the path they carved.

Bernaldino quelled his cough and looked down at his dead brother, Bitores. Blood pooled in the snow underneath while his brother's lifeless eyes stared out into the voidless nothing. Wiping away the tears from his eyes, smearing blood across his face, Bernaldino closed his Bitores's eyes and could not help himself from laughing.

Laughing at how preposterous it was that it was he who still lived while Bitores was gone.

Laughing at how unheroically Bitores fell at the end of the day.

Laughing at how the dream the two of them held together, of one day exploring the world beyond this island, was nothing more than pointless faff now.

All Bernaldino could do was kneel in the snow, soaking up blood through his blue uniform trousers. *I never wanted any of this*, he thought. *I never wanted to be a soldier. But* you *had to promise riches if we did so, didn't you, Brother? Well, look around you. There's nothing here but blood and death; the sickness will take me anyway if the savages don't first. We could have stolen away the wealth from the General's manor. Why would you think there was anything for us out here?*

Shaking his head, Bernaldino spat on his brother's corpse. "Fuck you, Brother. I'll find my own riches."

As he turned on his heel and walked away from the battlefield, his lungs still burning from the force of his coughs, a steel kiss greeted him, as did the cold and unforgiving earth below, where there were no riches or promises of heroic tales to be found.

Dispelling their Illusion, Shadow shook their head at the deserter. As they stood at the rear of the Acrarian guard, they could not help but feel pity for the sickly lad. Still, at the same time, Shadow could never suffer a deserter, regardless of the side.

A figure filed in behind them, paying no heed to the Acrarians behind them. "I did not picture you as an executioner, Shadow," the woman's voice said.

"As I've told Kama, I am whatever I wish to be, Sha'a," Shadow said, looking to the Eclipseborn beside them, disguised as just another Acrarian soldier, as she was wont to do. "I am self-made, and I don't need the Children or the Tribes to recognize that."

Sha'a chuckled. "All we need from you is what we've asked. And there's another deserter to whom you may be interested in meting out your 'justice.'"

Two arrows passed by either side of Sen's head as Luck surged through her once again. Spinning out of the way of the twin volley, she slid to a knee, cocked back the hammer of her pistol, and fired, the surge in her arm guiding the bullet to its intended target, the traitor's blood spurting onto the red snow below, the body falling unceremoniously over the edge and onto the ground below.

The second traitor closed in on Sen, drawing his hunter's knife to get inside Sen's guard, inside where she could reasonably swing her spear. A thrust aimed for her gut, then another, Sen dodging the first with a backstep and then rolling out of the way of the second, dropping her spear in the act. As she holstered her flintlock, she slid back toward her spear, narrowly avoiding the downward thrust of the knife. Swiftly, she grabbed the turncoat's arm, pulling him down and releasing the blade from his grip as he was thrown to the snow. On instinct, Sen picked up the knife before her foe could and, planting her knee on the middle of his back so he could not return to his feet, drove the steel through the back of his neck. The man responded only with a meek gurgle as the life poured out of him. Sen ripped the scabbard from the traitor's back and wrapped it around her own waist, sheathing the blade for her own safekeeping.

She was short of breath. Her hands stopped shaking long ago, the adrenaline coursing through her keeping her mind occupied from the reality she faced. As another Wolfsign approached her, she was quick to draw her flintlock, cocking the hammer back even though she had not reloaded it, but the yeoman was quick to raise her hands in a "we're on the same side" gesture; Sen gritted her teeth and holstered the weapon. It seemed the traitors—the "outcasts" who had joined with the Children—had been defeated well enough on this ridge. But the cost at which they were defeated was haunting. By Sen's estimate, roughly a quarter of the Wolfsigns here—the *true* Wolfsigns—had fallen either to the turncoats or to Zara. She could only imagine what it may have been like on the opposite end, but she saw no further movement on that side. Evidently, the Fens' side had moved along toward the main fray, taking rank with the ferocious Bearsigns, the whole force of them encircling the tight formations of the Invader forces.

Sen's nearby comrades passed her by, seeing no further need to stay along this ridge when the fighting was almost entirely in the clearing now. They each exchanged with her a glance, all with bows at the ready, setting up camp at the bottom of the ridge, aiming straight into the fray.

It allowed Sen to survey the damage they left behind, that *she* left behind.

So much death. So much wanton loss of life. In her fight-or-flight instinct, she barely kept count of how many fell by her own hand. The more she thought on it, the more it sickened her to her core. She took a knee, letting loose a shaking breath, the clatter of steel and the thunderclap of the Deatharms barely registering with her. It was like everything around her was underwater.

Sen looked down at her hands, her skin coated with blood both dried and fresh, none of it her own. The nausea rose in her stomach, and she could not prevent herself from vomiting. The acrid taste upon her tongue burned at the back of her throat, the bile steaming amidst the combination of snow and blood. Her body began to quiver as another wave rose within her, and she vomited again. The stench of it all—the blood, the death, her own vomit—was repulsive.

She pushed herself to her knees, her arms and legs feeling altogether weak. Slowly, she rose back to her feet, trying not to think on the host of death piling up behind her as she turned toward the battlefield.

It amazed her, the sheer prowess of the Lake warriors. She had never seen a Lake Bearsign in action before, but their reputation truly preceded them. They met the Invaders with a ferocity she had never seen before. In a sense, it could only have been called bloodlust for the absolute inclination by which they welcomed death. But the Invaders before them fell in droves, all led by a fiery old man who Sen could only assume was Chief Tenazt, with the giant Chief Yhaan standing by him. Yhaan's fighting style particularly impressed Sen, given that it was rather unrefined, and yet the Invaders still seemed to fall in droves, unable or even unwilling to block his wide sweeps and hasty thrusts.

Despite that, though, the Invaders kept pressing forward, no matter how many they lost. There was only so much the Tribes could do to quell that forward march. The Tribes could encircle them, cut off their escape…but the might of the Deatharms was still enough to rain death even from the middle of the pack. There was a reason why the Invaders were able to kill with such merciless efficiency. They were not suited for close-ranged combat…but they didn't need to be with those weapons. And with each step the Tribes had to take backward, it only pressed the Invaders that much closer to the gods.

Even though her legs remained unsteady, Sen pushed herself forward, keeping herself upright by the length of her spear. She couldn't see her mother or Tez in that throng, but she needed to be down there. She needed to help them. She needed to fight.

Luck surged through her once again as a plumed arrow zipped past her head from behind, nestling into the neck of one of the Wolfsigns at the base of the ridge. As quickly as her legs would allow, Sen turned on her heel, finding a Wood Tribe hunter aiming another arrow at her, their matted hair sporting a few remnants of twigs and leaves, their eyes sunken with dark, heavy bags underneath.

Sen groaned beneath her breath, drawing the flintlock from her waist and cocking the hammer. "I'm tired of this shit," she said.

The Wood hunter did not flinch at all from the sight of Sen's pistol. Sen had hoped her bluff would not be called since it was still not loaded, but it seemed such was the case.

A crunch of snow from behind caught her attention, and she spun again on her heel, swinging her spear in a wide arc. The hunter's arrow fired and scraped the pelt of Sen's coat but missed her otherwise, passing by her new assailant, who ducked below the path of Sen's spear.

Instinctively, Sen bailed on her feet, throwing herself to the ground as an empty hand reached out for her, the snow erupting upwards as she flattened herself against it. The hand struck down, and Sen moved her head out of the way just in time, rolling toward the edge of the ridge, reaching behind her back to draw her new hunter's knife.

She supposed she wasn't altogether surprised to see Sha'a so soon after Zara's demise, but she still had to let loose a deep sigh regardless. "You all really need to learn to let someone go, you know," she quipped through heavy breaths.

Sha'a shook her head, crossing her arms. "It's not up to me, Sennalhat. You only brought this upon yourself."

Sen scoffed. "Horseshit," she said, and she charged forward, keeping her spear in one hand and the hunter's knife in the other. She thrust the blade with a quick jab, missing Sha'a's throat by inches and then her chest by just a hair.

Sha'a reached out, grabbing only the steel of Sen's knife, drawing blood as Sen pulled it back with a quick withdrawal. Luck flared again in Sen's limbs as she ducked beneath the next volley from her Wood assailant, and she redirected her focus to the yeoman instead. Charging with her spear at the ready, she offered a furious thrust, only to be turned away and nearly thrown off the ridge. She danced around the assailant, using her spear as leverage to maintain her balance, and then wrapped the knife around them with a backhanded grip, aiming to slit the yeoman's throat. She misjudged the distance and only cut at the air behind the hunter's head.

The momentum caught Sen off-balance, and she fell to the ground, rolling in the blood and departed bodies as the hunter pressed forward, Sha'a not far behind. Sen tried and failed to find even footing but instead kept catching her foot on a dead body, her mind otherwise deterred from that fact sheerly by the pure adrenaline coursing through her. She held both her spear and knife out, threatening to keep her assailants at an arm's length, but she could only back up so much further, either to the edge of the ridge to throw herself down to the valley, or to the rock wall where the boulder traps were never engaged. Neither Sha'a nor the Wood hunter seemed at all deterred by Sen's prowess.

As she drew a deep breath, Sen feinted a step forward, but it elicited no reaction from her opponents. She offered a quick jab with her spear, but her arms were still weak and growing weaker, her heart pounding. She did not know just how much longer she could keep this up.

Quick footsteps crunched from behind the assailants, and Sen saw nothing but the glint of steel rushing down in a downward thrust when Sha'a quickly sidestepped clear of its path. Sen's eyes widened when she saw Tez on the other end of the spear, bloodied from the day's travails but otherwise in good health. Offering no words other than a quick nod, the sisters settled into formation, Sen pressing her advantage against Sha'a while Tez focused on the Wood hunter; her sister apparently had an inclination to face them. Sen pushed against Sha'a, using what strength she had remaining in her legs to press her backward toward the contingent of Wolfsigns, whose attention had been placed on the main fracas. Despite the dwindling strength in her arms, Sen alternated between wide horizontal slashes, quick jabs, and elongated vertical strikes to keep Sha'a at a distance, loath to allow her to get inside her guard. With each thrust, Sha'a jumped backward, unable to find a hole in Sen's defense to exploit. That her fellow Eclipseborn had come this far without a weapon was rather foolhardy, but Sen supposed she could not fault Sha'a for that when her own hands were a weapon unto themselves.

Sen grunted and snarled as her arms ached with exhaustion, crying out for a reprieve. Still, she pushed onward, offering slash after strike after jab, disallowing Sha'a the opportunity to breathe. Sen knew full well that her attacks were only barely coming close to hitting Sha'a, but it didn't matter. All that mattered was getting her away, cornering her, maintaining strength in numbers, because Sen knew she could not keep this up for much longer. The ridge trended downward, the packed snow growing slick, and Sha'a misjudged her footing on a backstep, sliding and tumbling down the slope into the group of Wolfsign yeomen, bowling through them but apparently not touching them in a way that would engage her power of Death. She disappeared into the throng and did not re-emerge. Sen sighed with great relief. *Gods, what a stroke of luck.*

Falling to her knees, Sen felt all the strength leave her as the adrenaline wore off. Weakly, she turned her head over her shoulders, and caught sight of Tez driving her spear through the chest of the Wood hunter, who already had an arrow jutting out from their arm for some reason. Tez planted a foot on the hunter's chest and kicked furiously, knocking them clean off her spear and down into the valley below.

Sen smirked as she watched her sister trudge on over to her, exhaustion plain on her face, though certainly of more a mental variety, given how brightly her Endurance pendant was flaring. Tez knelt beside Sen, wrapping an arm around her shoulder, and let out a heavy breath.

"What are you doing here, Tez?" Sen asked, trying desperately to catch her breath.

"Isn't it obvious, dear sister?" Tez said with a smile. "I'm saving your ass."

Sen wearily waved a hand. "I had it covered." They chuckled together, sweat pouring down their faces, their faces and clothing absolutely drenched in blood. "I take it you knew them. That Wood hunter."

Tez shook her head in disbelief, raising her brow. "Not well enough, apparently. What's been going on up here?"

Still panting heavily, Sen stared blankly ahead, still scarcely believing it herself. "Later. It's too long to get into. All you have to know is *she* is the ringleader of it all."

Sen pointed a weary finger to the middle of the throng, to where a red-headed woman in Acrarian regalia wove in and out of the Invader lines, finding her spots and pulling the trigger without hesitation; even from this distance, Sen could see the exuberant smile plastered along Kamataa's face. Somewhere in that throng, she knew Aritz was still standing, too. He was too much of a bloodthirsty madman to fall here.

"Have you seen Mother?" Sen asked, her voice tinged with hope.

Tez was quick to nod. "The last I saw her, she was barreling through a whole host of Invaders while they collectively shit their pants. I've seen her at worse odds recently. She'll be fine."

It was enough to draw a smile to Sen's face. "That's good."

Knowing she had to sit out for some time, Sen took this moment to survey the battlefield. She was still amazed by the Lake Bearsign prowess and the cohesiveness of the Tribal defense, given the overlapping strategies among the different Tribes...but something still struck her as odd.

"What's wrong with the Bear?" she asked pointedly. The ursine Deity was still visibly agitated, in stark contrast to the Wolf and the Owl, who only continued to observe the proceedings with a more dignified silence.

Tez shook her head, raising her brow. "What do you mean? It's been like that all morning."

"*That's* what I mean. It wasn't this agitated when we arrived—shouldn't the other two be noticing something?" Unsteadily, she rose to her feet, maintaining her balance against her spear. She took a close look at the Bear, and all three gods as a whole. The Bear seemed to be sniffing at something...or someone?

It was then that Sen realized. The Wolf and the Owl were not watching the proceedings; they were watching their attendants. Just as the Bear was. Something was wrong.

All the agents of the Children of the Black Moon who have been here today. And all the Eclipseborn proper, too. I've seen Zara and Sha'a. Kamataa is down there. I'm certain I saw Hollow and Vanta alongside her. But that just leaves...

She took a step forward, her heart catching in her chest. "Where's Cin?" she wondered aloud. And wondered perhaps too late.

As the Invaders drew ever closer to the dais, Ko Endra could not help but notice the more ferocious the Bear's growls had become.

Turning to the god, he prostrated himself, head to the floor of the dais, his skin protesting from the frigid impact of the earth, and called, "Almighty Bear, please, tell me what troubles you. What may I do to quell your anger?"

The Bear did not answer. It only continued to growl as it sniffed and snarled at each of the Keeper attendants present.

Ko Endra took a panicked step backward, holding his hands out in an attempt to placate the angry god. He turned to his right and said, "An Nara, is there anything you can do? You share a greater affinity with the Bear than I."

An Nara walked over and shook her head, a frown deep-set on her face. She planted her spear and crossed her arms, staring into the jaws of the beast but finding no answers in her god's eyes. "I'm sorry, Ko Endra. It's beyond my understanding, as well."

"I was certain your understanding extended only so far as the tavern," Ko Endra muttered under his breath.

"I'm sorry, do you wish to repeat that?"

"No, I do not. Now, please, quell the Bear. It is far too agitated for it to be comfortable to be around right now."

"Oh, beg pardon, Ko Endra," An Nara said, her voice tinged with anger. "Do you wish to be *comfortable* guarding our gods while an army of Invaders is intent on killing them?! Or have you grown too comfortable parsing through Ko Zaran's books to care for anything else?"

"Now, listen here! I—"

The Bear roared, the earth sundering for the forceful echoes. It snorted fiercely at all of those present but did little to deter the battle as it progressed. Its large snout sniffed at each of them with curiosity and suspicion, its eyes flaring with indignant agitation.

"You're arguing over nothing," said another Keeper, though one unknown to Ko Endra. He walked over with his arms folded behind his back, his long hair wild and unkempt, tossed about by the snow squalls and high winds. His face was mostly hidden by his thick locks. "The Bear knows your defense is futile. As do the other two. All there is to do now is just...accept it."

Ko Endra's nostrils flared, and he shot an accusatory finger at the man. "Accept it? Who the hell are you to say we should accept it?!"

The man offered no answer other than to draw a knife from within his sleeve. "I am the Tribe's eclipse." And he jumped forward, burying the knife deep in Ko Endra's chest.

With a vicious snarl, the Bear bit down at the assailant, but the man just avoided the god's mighty jaws, and then the Wolf's own jaws before evading the Owl's talons. The Bear let loose another mighty roar and swatted its front paw in a wide arc, knocking all of the Keeper attendants out of place, the assailant included, who went soaring into the forest.

Ko Endra bore the brunt of the impact, crashing into an adjacent column. The force drove the steel of the knife deeper into his chest. His vision grew cloudy, his breath short. He didn't know who was stopping the gods from departing, but he personally could not do anything as the Owl flew away from its perch. The Wolf followed suit and immediately began to prowl through the woods beyond the altar. Ko Endra coughed up blood in violent spurts, his mouth impossibly warm against the snow squalls. With the last of his strength, he reached toward the Bear, and in those final moments, he knew there was nothing that could quell the beast's rage.

When the Bear bellowed its fury, Yhaan knew it was the perfect time to use his Boon. Fear emanated from him in a manner he had never used before, the air around him his weapon as the lingering echoes of the Bear still resounded across the battlefield.

Beside him, his rival—his sworn enemy, and now his ally—Tenazt nodded his approval. The two roared together as one, thrusting their spears into the oncoming throng.

Yhaan took one step toward the oncoming Invader threat, then another, and another. With each long step he took toward them, the Invaders took two fearful steps back. What he looked like in their eyes was beyond him, nor did he care much to know. Whatever he was to them, it was the last thing they saw before he brought his spear down with a mighty swing. Skulls caved in and abdomens opened wide without struggle or resistance. Fear was his ally, one that he intended to grip more forcefully ever since his defeat at the hands of Tez of the Stone Tribe.

He barely had to lift a finger as his Fear pendant glowed like a bright beacon through this storm. His presence was met only with violent screams, some so distraught that they immediately put their Deatharms to their foreheads and pulled the trigger.

The Bear's anger only added to it all. He was the harbinger of their destruction. The very embodiment of the Tribes' rage and anger. He was the gods' judgment. A title he enforced with each mighty swing, each explosion of blood and viscera that he meted out.

Beside him, Tenazt fought with greater acumen with the spear, greater fluidity, able to link together one strike to the next with hardly a pause. Between the two of them, none stood in their way. Yhaan felt so close to being a god himself. This sensation was exhilarating as he expunged his foes' greatest fears and used them to his advantage.

The essence of Fear was permeating through the Invader contingent so far that it only seemed inevitable that a retreat was imminent. Yhaan needed only to force it just a little while longer. His head strained with the effort, blood rushing to his head, the force of a thousand hammers crashing at his skull. He growled and roared just as the Bear did, channeling his own silent fury into something of use. He had never been one to tap into his temper for the purposes of his Boon of Fear; simply his own imposing figure was enough for that. But on this occasion, with all the rage buried inside him, there was no better opportunity...

"Yhaanlookout!"

Tenazt's voice was a sharp and shrill mash of words, but no matter how quickly the warning came, it was not enough to block the hunter's knife from coming hurtling towards him.

His focus dropped as the blade stuck into him just below his clavicle bone. Yhaan dropped to a knee, the aura of Fear quelling, his pendant flickering. He looked around in a panic, trying to find the source of the knife, when a burly man came bursting out from the front line, barreling over the soldiers still recovering from the Fear. More beast than man, the soldier leaped the distance between them, dropping his knees against Yhaan's shoulders, and pinned him to the ground. In one fell swoop, he drew his Deatharm and immediately fired to his left, taking Tenazt in the throat without a second glance.

Yhaan had no chance to protest before the beast of a man brought his immense fists down upon his face again and again and again.

Hollow's fists felt raw as he bore down upon the giant's skull. When he was done, the man's face was nothing more than pulp.

He was not going to be beholden to the whims of a Frightener. Judging by the aversion of those surrounding him, he had all the power of Fear that he needed.

Ripping the spear from the dead man's hand, he ran through the first three warriors he could find, all from the Lake Tribe from the look of them. They barely had a chance to react. The spear stayed lodged within the ribcage of one of those he slayed, and thus he charged off, hardly finding the need for a weapon. He was all the weapon he needed.

Drawing Strength from one of his pilfered weapons, he aimed a punch at a Stone fighter's chest, nearly crushing every bone in the warrior's abdomen in the effort. He felt the pain of spears jabbing him and arrows puncturing him, but with the power of the Draw, the wounds closed up, pushing the arrowheads out of him entirely.

"DOES ANYONE DARE TO CHALLENGE?" Hollow bellowed, extending his arms at his side. Some hapless Lake and Sun fighters stepped forward, leveling spears at him, but Hollow snapped the spear shafts with ease just by the Strength coursing through his hands. With a wide grin at the sight of stunned warriors, he reached out to the fighters themselves, gripping them by the throats, and crushed their windpipes.

The Acrarians had finally recovered after the Frightener's blast of Fear, gradually rising back to their feet, no longer befuddled or encumbered by the giant's wicked aura. Hollow continued to plow through the crowd of Bearsigns, Strength still surging through him, more than he had ever drawn, and the more he drew, the more the Bear roared in the distance. *That's right, come for me. I'm waiting, beast.*

He was ready to force a path through the throng until he reached the Bear's dais, some twenty or thirty rows of fighters back. His fists still felt raw, but he had no qualms about Drawing in Life to mend the split skin and repair the cracked bones. But a stern hand gripped him by the shoulders, pulling him back behind the front rows of Acrarian soldiers, the frontline riflemen ready to lock and load, the roar of their weapons sounding just as soon as he was thrown to the bloody snow underneath.

Hollow snarled, ready to force himself back into the fray, but two soldiers barred his entry with the barrels of their rifles. Despite his initial instinct to throw them aside, Hollow was forcibly turned about-face, and he was surprised to see the glare staring furiously at him.

Clearing his throat, Hollow bowed his head and said, "General Aritz," remembering to adopt the Acrarian tongue, shedding the berserker rage as quickly as he could.

Aritz blinked at him, disapproval glowering in his eyes. There was a slight twitch in the man's lips, his face a smattering of mud and blood against his auburn stubble, his curly locks matted down with muck. "There is no room for beasts in my army," he said matter-of-factly.

Before Hollow could voice an objection, the General's flintlock stared him down, and all went dark in a flash.

There was a certain dignity that Aritz expected of his army. What he had seen of this man was something beyond explanation. Something more akin to the animals kept in public captivity back in the homeland, not for a man fighting for his liege lord. He held no sympathy for such acts.

That thunderous roar continued to echo beyond the wall of savages. It was loud enough to entice him to wince initially, but at this juncture, it was merely an empty threat. He could see some tuft of fur peeking out from behind the savages' defense line but nothing more.

Pushing his way several rows back, he gave the order to continue the assault while he went about reloading his pistol after being forced to waste a shot on that bestial soldier. *A poor use of resources and supplies, that,* he thought.

Suddenly, the beast's roars ceased, and there was a dull quiet over the battlefield. His soldiers stopped firing their weapons; the savages stopped thrusting their spears and loosing their arrows. Aritz turned around with curiosity and heard a loud, slow thumping, like the footsteps of the giants from children's stories back home.

But the pace of the footsteps quickened, turning from less of a warning to more of an immediate threat. And just as that tuft of fur seemed so unimposing, it finally gave way to the sight of the largest bear that Aritz had ever laid eyes on.

His breath caught in his throat, but he continued reloading his flintlocks regardless. *If this is one of the gods that the Envoy informed me of, then it is my charge to fell it. Enjoy your final breath, beast.*

The savages parted, paying no heed to the soldiers before them, clearing a lane for the beast to charge through. For the soldiers at the front line, it seemed their first instinct was to run, but just as they turned around, Aritz aimed his flintlock pistol and rifle at them. "Do not think of running, cowards! Any deserter will be executed on sight! NOW TAKE DOWN THAT BEAST!"

With reluctance, his men turned around, many quivering in their boots, but Aritz drew a deep breath, holstered his pistol, and aimed his rifle, trying but failing to maintain a steady line of sight as the earth quaked underneath the giant bear's mighty footsteps.

It roared a challenge as it drew closer, the very air around it quivering as though able to create a sonic shockwave with just its voice. The force of the roar knocked Aritz back a step, but he maintained his footing and gritted his teeth. He matched the beast's snarl with his own.

"READY!" he bellowed, ordering his men to stand to attention. Vocal protests from all sides sounded around him, some audibly sobbing as they felt their way to a quick and dusty death approaching.

"AIM!" His arms continued to shake, but he was not going to back down from this challenge. This was his destiny, his calling, what the Savior mandated was his charge. To fail in this would be to fail in his duty and devotion to his God, the true God.

Aritz sucked in a breath to command his soldiers to fire, but his vision was immediately obscured by a hail of arrows, the squalls of snow obfuscated by the presence of a deadly wind. The front lines of soldiers fell unceremoniously, and perhaps to them, that was some relief. They were too cowardly to face their destiny like this.

Channeling a scream to challenge the beast all his own, Aritz took aim as the bear drew ten paces closer, twenty paces, thirty, until it was finally within spitting distance.

The bear lowered its head and flung itself forward, knocking Aritz some twenty or thirty feet back, knocking loose the grip he held on his rifle and sending his flintlock pistol skirting away. Aritz hit the ground with a mighty thud, the fresh snow lessening the impact ever so slightly, but a surge of pain still coursed through him.

His vision blurred as he propped himself back upright, but it was just enough for him to see the beast tearing through his soldiers, its vicious maw dripping with dark crimson blood, his men tossed aside like rag dolls, clamped in half in its mighty jaws, sliced open with its tremendous claws. It was a savagery unlike anything Aritz had seen. *No wonder they worship this beast. It is their highest ideal!*

Reaching blindly for his flintlock, Aritz maintained a line of sight on the beast just as it locked eyes with him. He felt his heart quickening as he started to reach for the weapon in a panic, the bear snorting out steam from its snout, its eyes all malice and fury and evil. It dug a path underneath its giant paws, readying itself for a headlong charge, paying no heed to the soldiers around it as though it *knew* Aritz was at the head of them all. So disinterested in the other soldiers was it that it would swat away any approaching challenger, a hidden strength in the act such that it sent his men flying back further than he was, some meeting their end against the valley walls. It was treating his men like nothing more than gadflies.

Aritz found the grip of his pistol and quickly aimed and fired, hoping to plant a bullet square in the beast's skull, but not only did the shot find its way to the bear's shoulder, it merely *bounced off*, as though Aritz threw no more than a small pebble at it.

The bear seemed to look at the point of impact with disdain. A puff of steam erupted from its angry snout, and it roared its final challenge. Finding purchase in the snowy landscape underfoot, it shot forward, the stones in the chasm walls knocking loose with the resounding thud of each subsequent thud.

Aritz needed to reload. But he knew he had no time. He was out of time. Out of chances. Out of—

Wait.

He reached behind him to the small of his back, finding the hilt of the knife that Kama had given him. Drawing it, he felt a surge of...something coursing through his arm, a foreign feeling unlike anything he had experienced before. He remained on his backside, the bear bounding towards him, just a handful of paces away. It drew closer, closer, closer, opened its jaws wide, lunged for Aritz—

And Aritz a Mata drove his hand up underneath the beast's jaw, diving out of the way of its massive maw, the blade finding a home in the beast's throat. A warm gush of viscous blood streamed out over Aritz's arm, and he pulled the steel free before the beast could crush his limb beneath its weight. The maneuver cut a further swath into its flesh.

Standing in shock, Aritz watched as the bear wavered on its feet, its eyes still filled with indignation toward him. But notable exhaustion also began to set in. It offered what Aritz could only assume was another challenging roar, but it came out instead as a meek gurgle, and the body of the beast collapsed in a resounding thud, the impact so massive that stones from the chasm walls came entirely dislodged.

Disbelieving what had happened, Aritz's hand trembled. He looked at the blade, the carved rune still glimmering just as it had been when Kama first gifted it to him, but the glow was flickering. He looked at the beast, wondering if the two were connected. He needed to be sure.

Standing tall above the dying bear, this apparent bestial god, Aritz held the blade high and drove it through the beast's skull.

The battlefield was starkly quiet.

Sen stood in shock with her mouth agape. She could scarcely believe what had just happened.

He did it. Aritz really did it. The Bear was dead. The Bear was *dead*.

How is this even possible? she thought. Tears streamed down her face.

But before the dread of the Bear's death could even sink in, her gaze was drawn to the north of the battlefield, back in the clearing near the dais, where one by one...the Bearsigns started to fall.

When one is exposed to the Boon granted to them by their respective Deity, they grow...inseparable from it. It only grows worse the longer they are exposed to it.

Sen's hands shook as Kamataa's words rang in her head. Their link to the Bear...it was gone. Because the Bear was gone.

As Sen surveyed the battlefield, she saw familiar faces that had once stood tall suddenly collapse. The great Keeper guardian An Rhan. Fann, wavering in his convictions but always resolute with his spear.

Her mother. Dennalhir...collapsed into nothing.

"S...Sen?"

Sen shot her gaze to Tez, her sister wobbling on her feet, her eyes growing unfocused. Sen reached out quickly, holding tightly to her sister.

"Se...Sen?" Tez said wearily. "Wh-what's happ...ha..." Her eyes closed.

"Shit shit shit, Tez, stay with me!" Sen looked at her sister's pendant in a panic, ripping the chain clear of her neck, removing the ornament entirely. "Shit, no, that's not gonna work, it still cut the link. Shit shit shit shit, what to do, what to do, what to do!"

With a gasp, Sen immediately rummaged through her sister's pockets, first through her jacket, then through her trousers. "Come on come on come on, please be in here, please be in here!"

A cold metal greeted Sen's hand, and she ripped it free, relieved that Tez kept Brin's pendant with her throughout the day's battles. Immediately, she wrapped the chain around Tez's neck, pressing the ornament to her chest.

"Please work, please work, please work," Sen said almost in prayer.

Tez's eyes flared back open, her breath panicked and ragged.

"Oh gods, Tez, Tez, Tez!" Sen wrapped her arms around her sister, holding her tight. She muffled a brief sob against Tez's shoulder.

Tez groaned and put a hand to her head, her eyes clenching open and shut. She seemed too groggy to form words.

Sen forced a smile and steadied her sister and then rose to her feet to survey the field. Though for a brief moment, she felt relief at saving her sister...her heart sank to the pit of her stomach when she took in the sight before her.

It was so quiet that ghosts may have wandered the battlefield. All of the Tribes' mightiest warriors had collapsed or were in the process of. The Wolfsigns and Owlsigns looked to one another in silent horror. The Invaders unsteadily rose as one back to their feet, calmly drawing their weapons, engaging the slow process of reloading their rifles.

And the Bear, the symbol of strength and courage among the Tribes, was dead.

A shaking breath escaped Sen's lips as she stifled a sob into the palm of her hand.

"Oh *gods*."

MEMORY

FREEDOM

The hapless eyes stared at Kamataa as she went about her patrol. Her hand rested atop the grip of her flintlock pistol, and she whistled a tuneless melody, flashing glances of all varieties toward those she passed by.

The faces were growing boring. They were the same, day in and day out. Each passing day differed little from the one that preceded it.

Either there would be work for these slaves—building new constructs along the exterior or interior of the factory, laying the foundation for new homes, paving the earth with the intention of well-crafted roadways—or they would sit here in their own filth and squalor, the odor rank and nauseating.

But such were the whims of the General Aritz. Such was the routine these last ten years.

She supposed some entertainment may come from that "institution of higher learning" for which the foundation was soon to be broken. A "university," others called it. Kamataa had hardly an inkling as to what it meant, but there was apparently a wealth of them across the sea in the Acrarian homeland.

Each day seemed to wear the same face, but at last, today would be different.

Walking along the perimeter of the pit, Kamataa reached the entryway and saw a fellow soldier standing beneath the threshold. Her light brown hair was tied neatly in a tight bun, the jacket of her blue uniform unbuttoned to allow for a cooling breeze on this warm day. She placed her hands on her hips as though in a stance to reprimand, but the look in her eyes told a different story. "It's time," she whispered as Kamataa sauntered by. "Be quick about it." Though her face betrayed nothing, her eyes smiled just the same.

"Sterling work as always, Sha'a," Kamataa said softly, offering a discrete wink.

Sha'a disappeared along the outer wall as Kamataa continued her patrol, placing a watchful eye on those she walked by. Most of them stared blankly at the ground, their minds already long since destroyed, barely a shred of willpower still remaining within them. Others exuded fear as Kamataa glanced at them, shying away from whatever demon they thought they saw within her.

Not a demon, she thought with a smile. *Just a trickster and a fiend.*

Those still defiant enough to scowl at her hardly bothered her at all. They were the ones who had never known the throes of power granted to them by their gods. The unruly boys and girls yet to truly become men and women of the Tribes, never having been given the fortune of completing or failing their Trials while their chains kept them here. They were the rebellious sort, eager to flee at a moment's notice, but those who took the opportunity no longer remained on this plane, and those who did not were merely searching for their chance.

They won't do.

At the back of the fourth row to the left, Kamataa found her mark. They were what she assumed to be a mother and son, huddled closely. Judging from the darker tone of their skin, she had to guess they were once of the Haunted Tribe. *The name still feels odd to me.*

Something struck her about them. They lacked the mindless gaze of those stripped of their link to the gods. Their eyes showed no fear, as though they still felt they had something to lose. No rebellion in their hearts, as though they still had something to gain.

Instead, the woman and her son—the former still gripping her pendant tightly, apparently having been able to keep it; and the latter appearing too young to have gone through a Trial in the first place—seemed to be utterly accepting of their lot in life, knowing full well that what the world held for them extended only as far as the hand that fed them in this room.

And Kamataa was about to offer them a large meal.

She knelt beside them, paying no heed to any eyes drawn to her curious interaction. The Haunted woman flinched, perhaps fearing some manner of retribution or recourse she felt she may have deserved. The boy held tighter to the woman's waist, his hands trembling but his eyes still exuding enough false bravado to keep Kamataa interested.

"What are your names?" Kamataa asked.

The woman's eyes widened. The Haunted Tribe were a hidden bunch even before they were nearly rendered extinct. They were not privy to the tongue of the Tribe's Words, content to use instead their own language. That an outsider was knowledgeable of their vocabulary, and with a natural accent at that, was surely a surprise.

Such as Kamataa surmised, given the woman's stammering response.

"Your names," Kamataa repeated, a bit more tersely than the first time.

The woman nodded brusquely, putting a hand to her chest. "Sh…Shara. My name is Shara." She looked to the boy, wrapping an arm around his shoulder. "He is called Ran."

Kamataa grunted with a smile. "Very good," she said, and then set about releasing the clamps fastened around their ankles.

Shara gasped, taken aback. "Wh…what are you doing?"

Spreading her hands out placatingly, Kamataa flashed a kind grin. "What does it look like? I'm freeing you."

Looking so surprised that she may have started to cry, Shara put a hand to her chest, gripping the tattered collar of her shirt. "But why? Who are you?"

Kamataa shook her head. "Do you need a cause for your freedom? Go now. We run on precious time."

The ankle clamps came free, and Shara and Ran were both untethered. It was clear upon their faces that they were hesitant, the boy especially—Kamataa wouldn't have been surprised if he was born in this pit, never knowing a life outside of it. She couldn't blame them for believing it to be a trap.

But as it became evident they sensed the genuineness of the gesture, Shara and Ran slowly rose to their feet, taking a handful of crouched steps forward.

When they looked back to Kamataa, they were greeted with a nod and a wave of the hand.

It was all the motivation they needed to sprint toward the open gates and never look back.

Kamataa grinned, rising back to her feet, flashing glares at those who gestured to their own chains, questioning when it would be their turn. With an amused shake of the head, Kamataa drew her flintlock, resting it atop her shoulder as she walked by, the silent threat immediately understood by all as they resumed their wordless groveling.

When Kamataa exited the slave camp, locking the series of gates tightly, she found Ziia awaiting her in the middle of the paved pathway, her uniform jacket discarded and her disguised hair flowing past her shoulders, fluttering along with the coastal breeze.

"It's done, then," Ziia said, flashing a grin. She looked toward the entrance to the settlement, the two Haunted slaves shrinking to mere dots on the northern horizon.

"And the bodies are taken care of?" Kamataa asked, glancing around the streets as though continuing her patrol, listening to the words of a concerned colleague.

"Sha'a is seeing to it as we speak."

Kamataa grunted with approval. "And so the wheels are set in motion." She glanced over her shoulder, to the tall manor looming high above her. "I'm sure this will quell Aritz's boredom."

Ziia reached beneath her shirt and pulled out her Foresight pendant, the chain hanging slack in her grip. "I'd say this is just the hunt he's looking for." With a sly smile, she dropped it back beneath her top. "And so it begins."

Kamataa returned the smile. "And so it begins."

EPILOGUE

His Hour Upon the Stage

At one point, Aritz a Mata would have laughed. He would have brushed aside the empty threats inherent in false words.

But the mystery deterred him from his natural inclinations.

"So, you want me to speak on the Harvests, do you?" he said, narrowing his gaze, digging his nails into the rich leather of his chair, the odorous smell of low tide wafting in from the open southbound window.

The woman, this woman who looked so much like the memory of Kama, nodded slowly, her grip on the flintlock unwavering in her hand. The smile upon her face disappeared, but the malice in her eyes still remained.

Aritz readjusted his posture and took a breath, folding his hands in his lap, attempting to reclaim some semblance of his dignity while he still was faced with the barrel of a gun.

"You enter my estate, slaughter my family and attendants, label me a war criminal while breaking into my private quarters, and now you want me to speak of myths and slander?"

The impostor looked down at her fingernails with demonstrated disinterest, flexing her joints and brushing off some dirt or residue along her shirt. "You're most of the way correct, Aritz," she said, stifling a chuckle. "Though I would be loath to call the Harvest a 'myth.' Many were slaughtered in the pursuit of your 'myth.'"

"Many were slaughtered—and justifiably so—to ensure the betterment and safety of my people," Aritz said, his voice tinged with anger. Were he a younger man, he would have shot to his feet and shown this murderer just what "slaughter" was. Age had slowed him, though. He was wise enough to know it. "But if this blasted 'Harvest' were to have happened, it seems absurd for there to have been no demonstrable result."

The sneer on the woman's face was unsettling as the orange light of the late afternoon sun illuminated her, darkening her face in shadow. "But you *are* aware of the nature of these 'myths,' what rumors they whisper among those willing to listen. The macabre details, they simply sound far too perverse to have appeared out of nowhere."

Aritz leaned back, flaring his nostrils with frustration, the wooden floorboards creaking beneath his weight in protest. "And yet, you yourself have proven the lengths one will go to sully the good name of one whom many declare a hero. You savages are so reprehensible; you will stop at nothing to drag through the mud the reputation of your betters, just to satisfy your own bruised egos."

The woman scoffed, feigning some manner of shock. "Such bold claims. But *we* were not the ones who attempted to harvest the essence of an entire people solely in the name of technological advancement. Such a strange and oddly specific 'myth' to create, wouldn't you say, Aritz?"

Undeterred, Aritz remained as he was, leaned back with as much control as he could muster, given the circumstances. He shook his head derisively, tutting his lips. "I do not rank myself among those adept at spinning such lies."

"No, you don't," the woman acquiesced. "You needn't anyone to spin these lies for you. You craft the lies all your own. It's only a shame the Harvest is not among your lies."

"One you seem so adamant at proving, is it not?"

"But of course," she said, rocking the pistol back and forth in her hand. "As I said before, I was not there."

"You did say that," Aritz said. "Which means you're not Kama, are you?"

Aritz was expecting the woman to step back, panic that her cover was blown, perhaps force her hand and act without thinking. But no, her smile only grew wider and more sinister, her eyes only more haunting. What he had assumed to be a piece to unravel the puzzle was only one ill-fitting for the missing space.

"No," she said, amusement in her tone. "I did watch her die, after all." She hummed, shuffling in place, a stark air of calmness surrounding her. "I only hoped her image may have helped loosen your tongue." She leaned in closely, harshness in her voice, the wood of the armrests cracking as she held them in a tight grip, towering tall over him.

"I had nothing to say to her phantom," Aritz declared. "What makes you think I will have anything to say to you?"

Slow breath after slow breath wafted through Aritz's hair. With deliberate motion, the woman backed away by five paces, and cocked back the flint-lock's hammer once again.

"Because you should fear what I shall do, should you say nothing. I am one who *escaped* your Harvests. I didn't suffer their atrocities.

"I suppose you could say I was one of the lucky ones."

End of Book Two of
The Spellbinders and the Gunslingers

GLOSSARY

The Stone Tribe: Occupants and landholders of much of the territories bordering the southern ridge of the Heart of the Land, the Stone Tribe has been considered the gatekeepers to the Heart. The most populous Tribe of the Land, they are a melting pot of multicultural roots due to the large number of adept warriors, hunters, and scholars who dwell within the Tribe's borders. Since the Invasion of the Acrarians, the Stone Tribe has offered land to the displaced peoples south of the Forest, most prominently the Sun and Arrow Tribes. Physically, they are easily identifiable by the braids they fashion at the nape of their necks and the face paint they adorn in adulthood in correlation to the Sign under which they were born: red for the Bear, blue for the Wolf, and yellow for the Owl. An adult bearing no face paint is considered an outcast not to be interacted with.

- **Sennalhat:** Also known as Sen. Second daughter of the Stone Chief Fannalhen and Dennalhir. An Eclipseborn allowed to stay within her village, but still branded an outcast. Currently held within the City.

- **Tezalhat:** Also known as Tez. Firstborn daughter of the Stone Chief Fannalhen and Dennalhir, eldest sister to Sennalhat and Brinnolhat. An adept warrior Bearsign who was granted the Boon of Endurance. In exile after surviving an insurrection waged by Koelhe.

- *[Brinnolhat]:* Also known as Brin. Youngest child of the Stone Chief

Fannalhen and Dennalhir, younger brother of Tezalhat and Sennalhat. A bookish and shy young man who recently completed his Trial as an Owlsign and was granted the Boon of Memory. Executed by a firing squad in the City.

- *[Fannalhen]:* Also known as Fanna. Former Chief of the Stone Tribe, husband of Dennalhir, and father of Tezalhat, Sennalhat, and Brinnolhat. A revered Bearsign granted with the Boon of Courage. Killed by Aritz a Mata during a standoff in the Stone village.

- **Dennalhir:** Also known as Denna. Wife of the late Stone Chief Fannalhen, mother of Tezalhat, Sennalhat, and Brinnolhat. As equally revered a Bearsign warrior as her husband, her talent with the spear is unparalleled. Held captive after Koelhe's insurrection.

- **Tawandhar:** Also known as Tawa. A member of the Tribal council, a close friend to Fannalhen's family, and the father of Narvarho. An Owlsign of the highest order and a master of Knowledge. In exile alongside Tez after surviving Koelhe's insurrection.

- *[Narvarho]:* Also known as Narva. Sen's closest friend. A Wolfsign imbued with the Boon of Sound. Killed by Acrarians after attempting to rescue Brin.

- **Rantalha:** A member of the Tribal council and one of the Tribe's most accomplished hunters. A Wolfsign granted the Boon of Stealth. Took part in Koelhe's insurrection.

- **Sharrabha:** A member of the Tribal council. An accomplished Wolfsign imbued with Packmind who makes frequent trips through the Heart on behalf of the Tribe. In exile alongside Tez after surviving Koelhe's insurrection.

- **Koelhe:** Current Chief of the Stone Tribe after waging an insurrection. Mother of Fannadhan. An Owlsign bearing the rare Boon of Foresight.

- **Fannadhan:** Also known as Fann. Once a close friend of Sen, now a bitter rival. A Bearsign granted the Boon of Strength. Took part in his mother's insurrection.

- **Grafhar:** A mute Owlsign granted the Boon of Language.

The Lake Tribe: Settled upon the Big Lake north of the Forest, the Lake Tribe is a warlike group often more at odds with each other than with the matters of the outside world. There is wide infighting amongst the Tribe, specifically on opposite ends of the Big Lake. They are skilled naval fighters if only because they've constantly warred with each other on boats along the Big Lake, leading to the body of water to be nicknamed the Lake of Bones by other Tribes.

- **Tenazt:** Chief of the eastern Lake Tribe. A Bearsign endowed with the Boon of Courage.

- **Ket:** A healer of the eastern Tribe. An Owlsign with the Boon of Knowledge.

- **Barrha:** Once a trusted Wolfsign with the Boon of Stealth from the eastern Tribe. Now rendered mindless for reasons unknown.

- **Yhaan:** Chief of the western Lake Tribe. A Bearsign with the Boon of Fear

The Keepers: Dwelling within the mountainous ranges of the Heart of the Land, the Keepers are the conductors of the Trial and the guardians of the Bear, the Wolf, and Owl. They are the only Tribe not to be displaced by the Acrarians nor have their territory occupied by displaced Tribespeople. The Keepers are the most prolific of the Owlsigns, with many of the Land's greatest scholars being born a member of this Tribe. They are bestowed an honorific dependent upon which Sign they were born under after they complete their Trial: Ko for the Owl; Ne for the Wolf; and An for the Bear.

The Tribe is home primarily to Owlsigns and Wolfsigns, with very few
Bearsigns.

- **Ko Zaran:** An Owlsign with the Boon of Knowledge who conducts
  Brin's Trial. One of the most learned scholars in the Land with an
  enormous collection of tomes in his personal library.

- **Ko Endra:** An Owlsign with the Boon of Memory. Ko Zaran's direct
  steward.

- **An Rhan:** A Bearsign with the Boon of Strength. One of the most
  adept fighters in the Heart by virtue of being one of the only ones.
  Tasked with guarding the True Heart where the Animal Deities
  sleep.

- **Ne Shanne:** A well-respected Wolfsign bearing the Boon of Packmind. One of the few Keepers who has ventured beyond the Heart.

- **Ko Seln:** An Owlsign granted the Boon of Language. Runs a tavern
  that can be found on the ascent through the mountain ranges of the
  Heart.

- **Ne Arsah:** An embittered Wolfsign with a Boon of Stealth. Spends
  much of his time at Ko Seln's tavern.

- **An Nara:** A Bearsign with the Boon of Restoration who spends much
  of her time at Ko Seln's tavern.

The Sun Tribe: One of the Tribes displaced by the Invasion of the Acrarians,
the Sun Tribe once dwelt along the southeastern coast of the Land, making
a living off of fishing and other seafaring activities. They were the first to be
displaced by the Acrarians after their arrival. At first resettling in the Forest,
they were then further attacked by the zealously territorial Wood Tribe,
leading to lingering animosity between the two Tribes. They have since
settled in the Stone Tribe's territory at Stone Chief Fannalhen's offering, but
many in the Sun Tribe are eager to retake their homeland. Members of the

Sun Tribe are distinguishable by their hide garb bearing only one shirtsleeve, their long hair tied in two vertical buns at the back, and their tribal paint of two red lines crossing vertically over the eyes.

- **Han'e:** Chief of the Sun Tribe. A Bearsign with the Boon of Courage. Formerly party to an uneasy alliance with the Stone Chief Fannalhen, now a supporter of Koelhe after taking part in her insurrection.

- **Tol'e:** A Wolfsign bearing the Boon of Movement. One of Han'e's most trusted hunters.

The Wood Tribe: The de facto guardians—or rulers—of the Forest, the Wood Tribe is fiercely defensive and territorial, such to the point that they attacked the displaced Sun Tribe merely for trying to settle within their lands. Many Tribesfolk from the south who were merely passing through to the Heart to complete their Trials considered passing through the Forest a trial unto itself. The Wood Tribe makes its home high in the trees of the Forests in order to hold a strategic position against any would-be infringers of their territory. Leadership of the Wood Tribe is denoted by their makeshift crowns crafted from tree leaves and branches. Rarely is their skin kept bare; normally, it is painted in greens and browns to camouflage themselves amongst the trees.

- **The Elder:** A fierce old Bearsign with the Boon of Fear. In critical condition after a battle with the Acrarians.

- **The Matron:** An Owlsign healer bearing the Boon of Knowledge.

- **The Chieftain:** A Wolfsign often accompanied by a contingent of yeomen with Boons of Packmind. Recently led a counteroffensive against the Acrarians.

The Arrow Tribe: Hailing originally from the Plains encompassing the southwestern regions of the Land, the Arrow Tribe were a once-proud group of nomadic wayfaring horselords until the Acrarians displaced them and stripped them of their horses. Comprised almost entirely of Wolfsigns, they have since been allowed resettlement in the north within the Stone Tribe's territories.

- **Fen-Osenta, Fen-Detu, and Fen-Poven:** A triumvirate of Arrow heroes and brothers once responsible for quelling the Steppe Conflict.

The Haunted: Perhaps the most mysterious Tribe of the Land, the Haunted Tribe bore the worst of the Acrarians' assault, and the few who remain have been forced into servitude by the Invaders. "Haunted" is not the true name of the Tribe, but rather a somewhat derisive term used to address the Tribe's fascination with the plane of existence after death, particularly believing they could commune with the souls of the dead.

- *[Shara]:* An escaped slave from the Acrarian City. Killed during Koelhe's insurrection.

- *[Ran]:* An escaped slave from the Acrarian City. Had never known freedom due to the Acrarian Invasion happening when he was only a year old. Killed during Koelhe's insurrection.

The Acrarian Kingdom: Labeled merely as the "Invaders" by the Tribes, the Acrarians hail from a continent far to the east. They laid claim to the Land after mistaking it for the mythical Great West before deciding to formally settle the island while displacing the native population. The Acrarians are subject to an industrial age with steam power driving innovation and exploration forward. To an extent, Acrarians are also religious zealots who follow the teachings of an unnamed Savior figure in whose name they have claimed the Land with the idea of spreading his will unto the world.

- **Aritz a Mata:** Leader of the invading Acrarian forces. The son of a lord in tremendous favor with the royal family.

- **"Red"**: A soldier in the Acrarian army. See: Kamataa

- **Master Hernan:** A sycophantic Scholar.

The Children of the Black Moon: A collective of Eclipseborn from all throughout the Land, the Children of the Black Moon offer home and hearth not only for those born during an Eclipse, but also for those who were cast out from their Tribes. They currently live in the City amongst the Acrarians, serving in their army.

- **Kamataa:** Also known as Kama, Red. Leader of the Children of the Black Moon alongside Ziia. Formerly of the Lake Tribe. Due to choosing the power of the Draw, she has lived for over four hundred years.

- **Ziiahlan:** Also known as Ziia. Leader of the Children of the Black Moon alongside Kamataa. Formerly of the Stone Tribe. Due to choosing the power of the Draw, she has lived for over four hundred years.

- **Zara:** Formerly of the Lake Tribe. Chose the power of the Touch.

- **Hollow:** Formerly of the Wood Tribe. Chose the power of the Draw.

- **Sha'a:** Formerly of the Sun Tribe. Chose the power of the Touch.

- **Vanta:** Formerly of the Arrow Tribe. Chose the power of the Touch.

- **Cin:** Formerly of the Haunted. Chose the power of Luck.

<u>RELIGION AND BOONS</u>

The Tribes revere the will of nature, and more specifically, the three Animal Deities: the **Bear**, the **Wolf**, and the **Owl**. Each Deity is represented in the fields of strength, community, and wisdom, respectively.

When a Tribesperson is born, they are born under a celestial "Sign" that correlates to one of the three Deities. When a Tribesperson comes of age at eighteen, they go on a pilgrimage through the mountain ranges of the Heart to receive a Trial from the Keepers, which tests their acumen in the fields relevant to their Sign. If a Tribesperson fails their Trial, they are exiled from their respective Tribe and considered an outcast. If they succeed, however, they are granted a specific Boon which enhances certain physical or mental capabilities. This Boon is later carved as a rune into a pendant or a weapon, such as a spear. Once inscribed, this object will hold the power of that specific Boon. In theory, this means that any who holds the object will be subject to those abilities, but this is a strict taboo, and those who break it are immediately banished.

Each Animal Deity offers five possible Boons.

Boons of the Sign of the Bear:

- *Strength*: amplifying power and force

- *Endurance*: increased stamina

- *Fear*: masters of intimidation

- *Restoration*: quicker recovery from injuries

- *Courage*: heightened bravery

Boons of the Sign of the Wolf:

- *Stealth*: muted footsteps

- *Packmind*: thought sharing within a group

- *Scent*: heightened sense of smell

- *Sound*: heightened sense of hearing

- *Movement*: can more easily detect movement in the earth

Boons of the Sign of the Owl:

- *Knowledge*: high intelligence

- *Memory*: storage of the history of the world

- *Illusion*: masters of disguise

- *Language*: quick to learn any foreign tongue

- *Foresight*: can observe glimpses of what is yet to come

THE ECLIPSE

Those born during an Eclipse are known as "Eclipseborn" and are looked upon with distrust and fear. Unlike those born under one of the Signs corresponding to one of the three Animal Deities, the Eclipseborn are granted abilities by the Moon that are deemed unnatural by the Tribes. If a person is discovered to have been an Eclipseborn, they are to be banished from the Tribe without question, though some take more violent approaches to addressing an Eclipseborn in their midst. There are three known abilities associated with the Eclipseborn:

- *The "Draw"*: The drawing in of life energy. Allows a recipient to extend their lifespan beyond natural means as well as heal from wounds that would otherwise be fatal.

- *The "Touch"*: The employ of death energy. Allows a recipient to kill another living being with just a touch.

- *Luck*: Manipulation of chance. Allows a recipient success more than is natural.

It is unknown if there are other abilities associated with Eclipseborn at this time.

A MESSAGE TO THE READER

If you've made it this far: you have my heartfelt thanks for reading THE CHILDREN OF THE BLACK MOON

If it's not too much to ask, I would very much appreciate you giving a quick review of THE CHILDREN OF THE BLACK MOON on Amazon and/or Goodreads. Reviews are incredibly important for authors (and indie authors especially!) as they enable us to expand our reach and let more and more potential readers know that our books exist! On top of that, I would love to hear your thoughts on this book, regardless of whether they are good or bad, and I hope to see you again for the next book.

Thank you,
Joe

ACKNOWLEDGMENTS

This was a wild one. I had been looking forward to writing some of these scenes for years, and to see them finally put to paper is incredible.

And, of course, I happily do it for you, the reader. Thank you for continuing on with this series. It's because of you that I continue to write, and it makes it all the easier for me knowing that there is a captive audience eager to turn the page. You will always have my gratitude.

As will the excellent people with whom I worked to help bring this book to life. To my editor, Michele Perry, thank you for helping make this book everything that it could be. Your guidance is incredibly invaluable. And to the dream team of Felix Ortiz and Shawn King, you guys knocked it out of the park yet again on the cover art. Drinks are on me once we drag Shawn up north.

To my dear friends Adam Maguire and Samantha Smith, there are only so many things I can say before I just wind up repeating myself. It's thanks to you both that I found the confidence to pursue this creative path. You have always been the first eyes and ears, my first audience, the first to tell me when something isn't working, and the first to tell me when something is great. All these stories would not exist without you both.

To everyone in the Indie Accords Discord server: you're all amazing. Navigating the indie publishing world is so much less scary when I have you all as a resource. I offer a bowl of raisins in your honor (especially you, Thiago).

And to my beloved Annie. You enrich my life every single day. Thank you for supporting me every step of the way. Your excitement for and championing of my stories help me move forward.

Finally, I would like to give a special shout-out to these wonderful people who helped back my successful Kickstarter to fund an audiobook for The Bleeding Stone: My parents, Pat and Andrea (and to my dad, especially, for his tremendous help in getting to the goal amount) | My sister, Maureen | Brandon Robertson | Russ Reed | Michael H. Sugarman | Meredith Carstens | Robert K. Barbour | Jord – Middle of Nowhere | Mihir W. | L.L. MacRae | Johannes Tuchscherer | Gage oSpaceGhoat Troy | Joshua Scott Edwards | Brian Sweeney | Rex Regun | Jon Auerbach | Astridd

Joseph John Lee is the author of The Spellbinders and the Gunslingers trilogy. A true product of New England, he prefers Dunkin' over Starbucks, sometimes speaks with a Boston accent, and does not say the word "wicked" in casual conversation as much as one may think. He currently lives in Boston with his fiancé, Annie, and their robot vacuum named Crumb.